CROSSED WIRES

CROSSED WIRES

Rosy Thornton

headline
review

First published in 2008 by Headline Review
An imprint of HEADLINE PUBLISHING GROUP

1

Cataloguing in Publication Data is available from the British Library

Hardback ISBN 978 0 7553 4554 0

Typeset in AGaramond by Palimpsest Book Production Limited,
Grangemouth, Stirlingshire

Printed and bound in Great Britain by
CPI Mackays, Chatham ME5 8TD

Headline's policy is to use papers that are natural, renewable
and recyclable products and made from wood grown in sustainable
forests. The logging and manufacturing processes are expected
to conform to the environmental regulations of the country of origin.

HEADLINE PUBLISHING GROUP
An Hachette Livre UK Company
338 Euston Road
London NW1 3BH

www.headline.co.uk
www.hachettelivre.co.uk

For Fadela and Natalie – hoping that you will never be too old for fairy tales.

ACKNOWLEDGEMENTS

As usual, I owe much and to many. To my editor, Clare Foss, whose confidence is unwavering, even when undeserved. To Leah Woodburn and the rest of the Headline staff, for their efficiency. To Louise Fryer, who wielded her literary toothpick to great effect again. To the members of the WriteWords WF group (especially Julia, Irene, Sam, Charlotte, Sharon, Katerina, Geri and Rosy B) for their help with the early chapters, and to everyone in the C19 Writers' Workshop for their support and encouragement. To Phillipa Ashley for always being there to listen. To my agent, Robert Dudley, a good friend and a much too forgiving man. To Mum and Dad, as ever. And above all to my family – Mike, Fadela and Nats – who had to put up with me writing another flipping book.

Chapter 1

'Autocare Direct Motor Insurance. My name is Mina, how may I help you?'

It was the forty-eighth time she had said it today, according to the computer log. Nearly fifty policy-holders – anxious, irritable, impatient or merely bored – and it wasn't even eleven a.m. Number forty-eight was a man, and appeared to be none of those things; if she'd had to plump for a description, it would probably have been . . . hesitant.

'I'd like to make a claim, please. That is, I've had a bit of an accident. Nothing too bad, but you know how it is with any bodywork, it's never cheap. So I thought I'd better put in a claim, if that's OK.'

Embarrassed. That's how he sounded: embarrassed. As she could not recollect any previous caller in her three and a half years at Autocare's Sheffield call centre showing the slightest compunction about getting something back in return for the annual premiums, Mina found herself taking his details with more than her usual professionally pretended interest.

'What's your policy number, please?'

'Is that this long one beginning JDN/00 something?'

'That's the one.'

They went through the ritual soft-shoe shuffle of verifying that he was indeed Dr Peter William Kendrick of 9, Flattery Fen, Allington, Cambs. His mother's maiden name was Midwinter – rather pretty, Mina thought – and his date of birth was 9 April 1968. A spring birthday was always nice, even if it did make him all but forty. Maybe it was the sheepishness that made him sound younger.

'And could you confirm the make and registration of the vehicle, please, Dr Kendrick?'

'Land Rover Discovery, K643TDR. It's a kind of dark bluey-grey, if you need to know that. At least, I expect it probably still is, underneath all the grime.'

A joke. Not a very good one – the embarrassment again – but the way he knocked himself like that touched a chord with her. Mina could talk herself down with the best of them.

'Thank you. Now, I need to take some details about the accident, if that's all right. Where did it take place, exactly?'

'Just past the Dorlinsons' gateway. That's where the cat was from. It's a black one, you see, that's why—'

'What street, I mean. What was the name of the road you were in?'

'Oh, sorry.' If possible, the awkwardness in his voice upped a further notch; she could almost hear him wince. 'Stupid of me. I was just coming home. It was at home in the lane.'

Forefinger on mouse, she scrolled back up the on-line form on the screen in front of her. 'That would be in Flattery Fen, Allington, then?'

'That's right, yes.'

'And were there any other vehicles involved?'

'No. No such excuse.'

Beating himself up again – making her grin.

'No, there are hardly ever any other vehicles in our lane, not past the Dorlinsons', except the bin men coming on a Tuesday or people turning round because they're lost.' A laugh, unexpected and vivid though still self-mocking, as he added, 'Flattery will get you nowhere.'

For a moment Mina floundered. 'Flattery . . .?'

'Will get you nowhere. The lane, Flattery Fen, it's a dead end. My daughters' idea of a joke, sorry.'

Married then. Well, he would be, wouldn't he, by almost forty and with that startling laugh? No other named driver on the policy, but probably the wife had her car insured in her own name. Muddy old Land Rover for him, with his doctor's bag thrown on the back seat; what would she have, the GP's wife? Smart little runabout, handy for parking in town: Renault Clio, or maybe a Peugeot 207.

'. . . really derived from its contours,' she heard him continuing. 'Or rather, lack of. Being flat, you know – at least I've always supposed that's it – and it reminds me of being blattery, too, which is how it is for nine months a year. Blattery, you know: muddy. Except I'm not sure that's a word, is it? Just a thing my grandmother used to say.'

Mina's nan had said it, too, though she imagined there was rather less blatter to be met with living in a high-rise on the Manor estate than down south in the country; Nana had much more often had call to complain of its being parky, up there on the deck access. But there were three insistently repeating flashes now on the 'call waiting' light; Mina determined to focus.

'No other vehicle involved, you say.'

'No.'

'So could you describe to me, please, exactly how the accident occurred?'

Peter William Kendrick coughed. 'Well, it was the cat, you see. The Dorlinsons' cat. I can never remember what they call it, one of those girls' names like Tabitha or Topsy. But anyway it's a black one, as I said, all except for a little patch on its tummy, and it was getting on for five o'clock and pretty well dark. I just didn't see it.'

Now it was Mina's turn to wince. She closed her eyes and tried not to hear the outcry of brakes, the judder of radials failing to grip on mud, the sickening crunch of impact. Maybe he caught her intake of breath.

'Oh no, it's OK, Tibby was fine. Shot straight across and dived under the hedge. Missed her by a couple of feet at least. But unfortunately I didn't miss the hazel stump. Mr Dorlinson took the tree down in September after those high winds we had or I guess it could have been worse. As it is, it's just all the underside of the front wing.'

'Passenger's side?' she asked, visualising the scene with a practised mind's eye, while she pondered the miles between their lives. Not just geographical ones: this man could identify a stump of wood by the kind of tree it used to be.

'That's right.' Then came the sudden laugh again, like a flash of sunlight off glass. 'My daughters think I should have a sticker in the back window. You know, like those ones that say "I slow down for horses"?'

She didn't know, not really. There wasn't a lot of call for that particular form of consideration in Sheffield 12. But she had sent herself up often enough to see the punchline coming in his case.

'Don't tell me – "I swerve for cats"!'

Meena, thought Peter as he replaced the receiver. Just Meena: working in a call centre meant never being graced with a surname. Maybe he should have asked her. Must be hard to remain human in a mind-numbing job like that, but she had been really . . . well, very decidedly herself. Great South Yorkshire accent – he loved the living multi-culturalism that breathed through those second-generation voices, their vowels rooted in regional Britain and their ancestry in the sub-continent or the Caribbean. Third generation, even, perhaps: she sounded young, though you could never really tell on the phone.

Anyway, now he just had to complete the rest of the form when she sent it out to him, including a sketch of the position of the vehicle at the time of impact ('but not necessarily', she had added dryly, 'that of the cat'). And get a second estimate for the repairs. That was a pain because he had never entrusted the car to any but the nurturing hands of the Land Rover dealership in Cambridge and really did not fancy doing so now. He could ask Dan in the village, of course, who as well as supplying fuel ran a small side-line in repairs, but he hated to put him out when he knew he wouldn't be giving him the work. The lawnmower was one thing – though even that had been stuttering a bit when idling ever since Dan serviced it last spring.

No time to worry about it just now, in any case. Cassie and Kim had toothache and he had made a dental appointment for them at twelve. He would already have to sweat and drive right up to the speed limit – more radical or illegal measures being beyond the range of his contemplation – if he was to get to school in time to pick them up and drive them round to the surgery.

Packing into his rucksack the work he should have been doing if he hadn't been on the phone to the Land Rover garage and the insurance company half the morning, he grabbed his coat from where it hung on the back of his study door and headed out towards the college car park. RR:31 proclaimed the digital display on the dashboard as he pulled himself up into the driver's seat. The clock had ceased to register the hour some years ago, but it was rare even for Peter not to have a reasonable apprehension of what the number to the left of the double dots should be. The minutes worked perfectly – and right now they were against him.

There was an additional problem at the moment, too: Allington Road was on the left. Not only that, but the turning where it split from the main Histon Road was a tight one; not far from a right angle, in point of fact. Even allowing for swinging out, should a gap in the oncoming traffic permit, he would never make it. 'Is the vehicle currently roadworthy?' Meena had asked and he had replied that it was. Not a lie exactly, because there was no problem whatever in driving it, provided one wished to proceed forwards or turn to the right. However, on tight left-hand corners, he had discovered, the compressed and mangled lower portion of the near-side wing came into squealing contact with the front passenger tyre to the accompanying smell of scorched rubber, and it was not an effect he was anxious to repeat. It was surprising how, with careful route planning, it was possible to get from A to B without ever turning left, circling in towards one's target in a clockwise direction. From home to college this morning it had been child's play; from college to home now it was trickier – doable, but it would add a good five minutes to his journey time.

As luck would have it, his lectures this term all fell between Wednesday and Friday, so clearing the middle of the day to get to school, dentist, school and back had not been prohibitively difficult. But Wednesday always seemed comfortably distant from the vantage point of the weekend and resolutions to prepare his notes on Sunday afternoon always crumbled with very little resistance in the face of demands for a bike ride or a game of Cluedo. Monday had gone by, as Mondays do, with too many unexpected demands upon his time and not enough achieved, and that just left today to update four sets of lecture notes on top of three hours of supervisions this afternoon. He might just about have got through it – insurance claims and right-only turns notwithstanding – had the twins not suddenly developed toothache at breakfast time. Now he faced the certain prospect of another Tuesday night sitting up working until the small hours. He said 'the twins' had toothache, and indeed that is the phrase he had used to Mrs Moore when he called her from work to warn her of the time of the appointment. It entered neither of their heads that just because, strictly speaking, it was only Kim whose tooth was actually giving her pain, he would do other than pick up both girls from the classroom and ferry them to the dentist's and back. They would be less than pleased to see him – not because either of them feared the dentist's chair but because Tuesdays before lunch it was spelling test and they had last night cracked not only 'receive' and 'belief' but the fiendishly vowel-littered 'conscientious'.

Approaching the school car park from a side road on the left with the clock standing at RR:52, Peter pulled in, stopped and jumped out, flicking the central locking over his shoulder as he sprinted towards the double front doors. Joy on reception, watching his agitated progress with an ironic eye, had the signing-out book open with the time and the twins' names and form all filled in ready for his signature and his visitor's sticker peeled and waiting on her thumb. Her name suited her, he always thought; she never evinced any, but still managed to spread quite a lot.

'Thanks. It's their teeth,' was all he took time to say before she buzzed him through and he loped down the corridor in the direction of 5M. They were at opposite sides of the room as he entered, Kim at her desk and Cassie over by the wastepaper bin sharpening her pencil, but the turn of their heads was equal and opposite, the mutinous jut of their chins perfectly synchronised.

'Oh, Dad, not now!'

'What about spellings?'

He exchanged apologetic smiles with Mrs Moore, both of them taking responsibility for this small show of dissent: her classroom, his daughters. They were by his side, anyway, with only a token dragging of scuffed toes on linoleum. He passed an arm round each.

'Sorry, no choice. I'm teaching this afternoon, and this was the only appointment Dr Szymański had before lunchtime.' Then, turning to their teacher, 'Won't be long, I hope. They'll be back in time for their lunch, anyway. Very sorry to disturb your lesson.'

Not that his appearance and extraction of the twins had caused more than a momentary ripple of interest before the room returned to its habitual state of chaotic activity, which he liked to assume was more purposeful than it looked. But apologising was a core component of Peter's nature; in his experience it never did any harm to say sorry, just in case. Mrs Moore smiled and wafted a don't-mention-it arm in his direction but her attention had already been reclaimed by two boys, one of whom Peter was fairly certain was called Max, in jostling dispute over the possession of a white-board marker pen. God knows how they do it, he thought, picturing his own peaceful study as he ushered the girls out towards the cloakroom to pick up their fleeces.

'It's cold out, you'll need them.'

They hadn't said anything, but when time was short it made sense to head off protest before it began. It was when he started the engine, as always, that they began to talk.

'Mr Elsworth took assembly –'

'– but it was hymnbook assembly today –'

'– and he can't sing.'

Kim began a low, grumbling warble at the back of her throat, joined by Cassie who squawked up into falsetto as they both carolled tunelessly, *'And I'll lead you all, wherever you may be...'*

Peter winced, though not at their singing. They had both inherited not only Bev's ear but also her easy mockery of the tone deaf; like her, they sometimes forgot that this included himself.

'Leonie's back. Still got spots, though.'

'She reckons the doctor says they aren't catching any more once they stop itching.'

'But I saw her scratching in literacy this morning. Those ones on her arm. I could see because I was right next to her on the carpet.'

'You'll probably get it, then.'

'You will, you mean.'

'No, you.'

'Was it impetigo, you said?' intervened Peter smoothly. 'I'm sure the doctor wouldn't allow Leonie back to school if she was still contagious. Probably it's just a few scabs she's got left, that's all. And it isn't very nice to be talking about the poor girl that way.'

'Leonie's OK,' said Cassie defenisively, as if somehow it were he who had called into question her health or habits of personal hygiene. He gave up and just drove.

'What's in our sandwiches, Dad?' asked Kim.

'Cheese and cucumber.'

'Dairylea or real cheese?'

'Farmhouse cheddar. Grated not sliced.'

More work to make, but they claimed it made all the difference.

'I'm hungry.' This was Cassie. When was she not hungry?

'Are you sure we'll be back by lunchtime?'

'Maybe we should have brought our packed lunches with us, just in case we have to queue?'

'Of course we shan't have to queue.'

He spoke shortly, sincerely hoping it was true, and trying not to think about the essay and a half he still had to mark before his two o'clock supervision. But he was right, and the receptionist asked them to go straight through.

'Hello, girls,' said Dr Szymański in purest RP; only her paternal grandfather was Polish, she had once explained in response to Peter's inquiry. 'Hop up.'

And they did: both of them in the chair together, as they had sat every six months like clockwork since their first teeth came through. Right-handed Cassie on the left, left-handed Kim on the right. That's the way round they sat in the car, too, and at the kitchen table; quite possibly it was the way they had lain in the womb. When they were small it had been a way to help them remember which was left and which was right. Now it was simply the way things were.

'Which of you has the poorly tooth, then?' asked Dr Szymański cheerily and both twins pointed dumbly at Kim.

'Open wide.'

Kim obliged, while Cassie assumed an air of quizzical sympathy. The two pairs of slim nine-year-old hips fitted side by side in the grey leatherette chair with room to spare and Peter found himself easily able to push back into the future the question of when they might be too big to sit this way.

'Ah yes, this one here at the back, is it? Well, it looks like the adult molar is trying to come up and hasn't quite room at the moment. I think it's just butting on to a nerve down there. But this one above should start to wobble soon enough, and then the thing should resolve itself.'

'Ii aa-e-y ii o-ii,' said Kim.

The dentist nodded sagely and prodded the tooth in question

with a gloved fingertip. 'Already is wobbling, is it? Oh yes, I think I do feel just a little give in it. You're right.'

'Mine, too,' chipped in Cassie, fingering a back tooth on the other side.

Peeling off her gloves, Dr Szymański turned to Peter with a clinically regular smile. 'Keep an eye on it. If the milk tooth comes out and it's still bothering her then it may mean we don't have room in there, and you'll need to bring her back. But it doesn't look too crowded to me.' She cast an approving eye back at the girls as if assessing horseflesh. 'Lovely broad jaws, the pair of them.'

Suppressing an urge to laugh, he thanked her gravely as the girls slid from the chair.

'Can we get back to school now, Dad?'

'They might still be doing the spelling test.'

It was when he had dropped them off and was halfway back to college, with theories of urban poverty concentration occupying the forefront of his mind, that an image intruded that made laughter rise in his chest even while it disconcerted him. If Cassie and Kim were separated, he speculated, would each of them be condemned to turn endlessly in circles like a winged Land Rover?

Chapter 2

It was ironic, really. There she was, spending her days logging the details of every variety of car – she could have recited seating and engine capacity and replacement value as new for most popular models, for goodness' sake – but she had never learned to drive. Not that she needed to, even if she could have afforded to run a car, because the number 27 bus ran from straight opposite Autocare Direct to within fifty metres of her front door.

There was a pretty regular service, and Mina could read the buses the way a mariner read the seas. It wasn't just the timetable; in busy periods that told you nothing, but the true salt could sniff the air and tell which way the tide was running. Dry weather or drizzle, the length of the queue and the speed of the traffic shuffling down towards the traffic lights: she always seemed to know exactly how long it would be before a number 27 swung round the corner.

This afternoon, though, she had to go round by Mum's first to pick up Sal, which meant getting off two stops earlier than usual and then either waiting for the next bus or, if it was fine and they felt like it, walking the fifteen minutes home. If Sal generally didn't feel like it, it wasn't that she had an aversion to fresh air and exercise like many of the girls in her class, prematurely hobbled by high heels and recognising no outdoor recreation but shopping. It was simply that for Sal the bus meant five more minutes to sit with her nose in a book, something she found more difficult (though not impossible) when walking.

Actually, although she thought of it by now as 'Mum's', it was really Dave's house. He was at home, too; when Mina turned the corner of the cul-de-sac she caught sight of his substantial lower portions, the rest of him being hidden beneath the bonnet of his car. Dave had bought the house a dozen years ago, though Mina found it difficult to imagine how he had managed to talk his way into obtaining mortgage finance on the basis of the earnings from his minicab business. It was in a small 1970s development and boasted a front garden and a drive, the latter an essential since Dave seemed to spend most of his time on it, carrying out vehicle repairs. Which was in itself another source of mystery: how he made any money when the car was more frequently off the road than on it.

'Hi, Dave.'

'Hello, sweetheart,' came the voice from the muffled depths of the Mondeo's engine. 'They're in the kitchen.'

'Thanks.'

In fact, in Mum's case the information was unnecessary; she was already tapping at the window with rubber-gloved fingers, a gobbet of suds sliding from her wrist to miss the sink and flop down on to the tiled sill. She always used too much detergent and never rinsed, comfortable in the belief that soap was clean and that swallowing quantities of it could therefore not be bad for you. The convictions of her generation came from before they'd invented the environment and if Sal's earnest badgering could not shake her from them, then there didn't seem much point in Mina's starting.

'Door's open,' she lip-read, and stepped round the side and into the overheated fug.

'Jeez, Mum, it's like the planet flipping Mercury in here. You know it's only September, don't you? Do you really need the radiators turned up to maximum?'

'I thought it was chilly out, and Sal might get cold sat there.'

Mina turned to where her daughter was coiled round a paperback in the corner farthest from the radiator, on the floor with two pilfered settee cushions. Stepping towards her, Mina grazed a greeting hand along her shoulder and arm.

'Venus, you mean, Mum.'

Sal's eyes left the page and locked on her mother's through a rick of straw-yellow fringe. Mina returned her gaze with the all too familiar feeling of being slightly at a loss.

'Venus is the one where it's baking hot. Mercury's nearer the sun, but there's no gases and stuff so it gets really cold there at night.'

Squatting down on the floor beside her, Mina tried for more orthodox ground. 'Good day at school, love?'

''S all right.' But the book had already reabsorbed Sal's attention, leaving Mina adrift.

'What are you reading?' This could generally be relied upon for a result of sorts and, indeed, Sal tilted the paperback so that its cover came into view.

'Jacqueline Wilson.' Her voice was heavy with patience. 'You know, as in *Tracy Beaker*. 'Cept this is for older kids.'

Love Lessons, read Mina, the bold white letters on the crimson heart squaring up to her challengingly. Maybe she should be the one reading this.

'Why don't you both stay here for your tea?' said her mum from the sink, peeling off the rubber gloves and reaching for the first wet saucepan on the draining board, tea towel in hand. 'Dave will be in in a bit, and we could all eat together for a change. I've done a macaroni cheese – it's in the oven, won't be very long. There's plenty.'

'You know why not.'

Mina said it quietly but Mum had heard OK, for all that she ignored it and sought instead an ally in Sal.

'You like macaroni cheese, don't you, honey? It was always your favourite when you were a tot.'

When this received not even a 'Hmm? Yeah', Mina seized her moment. 'We need to go home in case Jess comes in. She'd hardly eat otherwise – you know she never fixes anything hot for herself.'

Mum went back to drying her saucepans with rather more than necessary vigour. Sensing that she had managed to strike beneath the armour, Mina pressed her point home.

'I've bought chops – three of them. They're in my bag.'

The tea towel paused. 'Pork?'

'Lamb. Thought I'd do two veg as well as potatoes.'

'Well, mind she does eat. That's if she turns up. I'll bet she's just had chips already and gone out with one of those boys of hers.'

Mina sighed. There was a particular rising note that appeared in her mother's voice when she was working herself up into having a go about Jess. As always, Mina tried placation.

'There's just one at the moment, actually. He's called Danny and he's working, got a job in TV repairs. Does day release at college and everything.'

She might as well have been addressing the fridge. Mum's rigid rear view clearly indicated that she knew better. Mina took a step forward, even though she knew she would be wiser to let it drop.

'He's not like some of the others – really. She's been in at quite reasonable hours lately. And she hasn't had to ask me for money this week at all.'

The saucepans, clean and dried, hit the back of the cupboard with an emphatically unpersuaded clang. Standing watching her mother's bending back and wrestling down the urge to say more, Mina almost jumped to find Sal alongside her, book closed over her thumb.

'Can we have mash, Mum?'

'Sorry?'

'Can we have the potatoes mashed? With the lamb chops? I like the way the juice from the pan runs down into the mash, if you put them on top, you know.'

Mina smiled, grateful for the more comfortable territory. 'Yes, love, good idea. And what about I fry an onion and stir that in, too, the way I do it sometimes?'

'Yeah, OK.'

Sal slid free of Mina's sideways half-hug and back to her corner to gather up her coat and school bag.

'Please can it not be cauliflower? And it's Dari.'

'It's what?'

'Dari. Jess's latest one. His name is Dari, not Danny. Like Darius Danesh, Jess says.'

Darius . . .? Mina was floundering again, but the scorn in her daughter's voice as she pronounced the name told her that her ignorance might, in this case, be pardonable.

'Anyway, I think we'll be off, Mum. Thanks for having her, you know how it saves my life.'

But the tendered olive branch was left to dangle.

'Any time.' Her mum smiled tautly, lips still pinched from the fight that was not with Mina. 'Tell Dave his tea will be half an hour, could you, love – and to mind he leaves time to get himself cleaned up and changed. I'm not having those oily jeans sitting down in my kitchen.'

An hour and a half later, Sal was fed, bathed, dressing-gowned and slippered, and back inside her book. Eight o'clock. Half an hour before it was time for Sal to go up, leaving Mina to her evening alone but for the cast of *The Bill* for company, followed later on by *ER.* Unless she fancied watching Jeremy Paxman torturing some know-it-all college students on BBC2. Funny how, when Mum first left to move in with Dave, she had often longed for Sal to be in bed. Not to be free of her daughter's presence, exactly, but just for the novelty of walking around a silent and empty house: *her* house now. Jess was out most nights, even then.

Mina glanced at the TV listings and then at her daughter, balled up on the settee like wool in her fleecy pink robe, sleeves pushed back and elbows out at angles like speared knitting needles.

'Give you a game of rummy?'

No response.

'Uno? Triominoes?'

'No thanks, Mum.'

Sal's glance did not stray from the page. *We never play games any more*, Mina was tempted to whine. Then heard herself and grimaced inwardly. *Can't you find something to amuse yourself?* Mum had said it to her often enough, but she could not recall ever needing to say it to Sal, even when she was smaller. She reached for the remote.

'Will it disturb you if I have the telly on?'

Not a flicker – which was answer enough, really, even if the question had been more than mere politeness. Sal could have read through earthquake, terrorist attack and alien invasion.

'Did you know there are three dinosaurs in the street? Cloned from those old bones they found in Endcliffe Park, I dare say. There's a velociraptor having a go at the stone mushrooms by June's front path.'

'Shut up, Mum.' Eyes still on Jacqueline Wilson, after a short pause she added, 'And velociraptors were carnivores, anyway. They're the ones a bit like running kangaroos with teeth and claws. They'd never have touched mushrooms. Don't you know anything?'

'June had better call Sooty in, then.'

Satisfied with having at least procured a smile, Mina switched on the television and repaired to Sun Hill. Before Reg Hollis was on to his second mug of tea, however, she felt Sal stretch and uncurl beside her, and then a warm, Radox-scented arm appeared across her lap, followed by a damp tumble of hair drying back to blonde. Mina smoothed a hand down over the tangle, coming to rest on a bony shoulder that scarcely filled her palm.

'Better give it a brush before bed, sweetie. It will be a nightmare to get straight in the morning, otherwise.'

'Straight?' Sal's head rolled back so that her eyes looked up into Mina's, round with mock delight. 'D'you promise? And will it be black, too?'

Mina laughed. Her daughter's thick mass of hair with its stubborn kink cost Sal great penance with the hairbrush, and its striking egg-yolk colour attracted unwelcome notice from strangers – thankfully still elderly ladies, for the most part.

They settled back to book and screen, still loosely entwined, and presently there came the sound of a key in the lock and then the front door opening and closing with a casually brutal crash, rattling the metal window frames.

'Jess?' called Mina, sitting up a little straighter, while Sal jerked back to her own end of the settee like a guilty lover.

There was muffled giggling from the hall, masculine discernible below the feminine.

'Dari?' she wondered aloud, mainly to prove to Sal that she did listen. But when the door flung open and Jess appeared, the shadow hanging back behind her in the hallway was not Dari or Danny but an unknown boy, too skinny for his jeans and with a face that glowed pale even in the half-light of the doorway.

'Just going up to my room, OK,' said Jess, with no attempt to pretend this was a question. She didn't sound as if she'd been drinking, at least. Most of the pubs asked for ID these days, as well as Morrisons and the Co-op, and this one she was with appeared no older than seventeen-year-old Jess – in fact if anything he looked even younger, as boys do.

'There's a chop in the oven with some mash and veg. I kept it warm in case you came. If you want to share it with . . . with your friend, you could have some bread and butter, too, to fill up. There's a loaf in the bread bin, barely started.'

She might as well have been speaking German, by the way Jess stared at her. God, she hoped that glazed look wasn't drugs. Then, a grudging concession, 'Sean.'

'Hello, Sean.' Mina smiled round the edge of Jess's hip, wishing she didn't feel so much like a mum – filled, in fact, with the sudden nasty conviction that the skinny youth mistook her for such. 'Are you hungry?' Might as well satisfy expectations.

A brief resumption of the giggling, rapidly stifled.

''S OK, we had chips.'

And with that the pair disappeared again, leaving the door to swing shut as they headed for the stairs.

*   *   *

17

Much later again, when Mina had been asleep for maybe an hour or two – though she did not open her eyes to peer at the digital alarm clock – she dimly heard the soft click of her bedroom door. Barely bothering to groan, she rolled over towards the middle of the bed, vacating the warm patch at the side nearest to the door, and flipped back the duvet to let Sal slide in.

'Bad dream?' she mumbled, voice gummy with sleep.

'Tummy ache.'

Tummy ache, burglars at the window, feet too cold, sheets too hot. Sal might go up like a lamb at eight-thirty and be very soon asleep, but there was always some reason for her to come creeping into Mina's bed long before dawn.

You're ten; you're a big girl. Go back to bed. The words sounded wholly unlikely when she tried them out in her head, like a snatch of a bad play on TV.

'Is it the kind of tummy ache that gets better with a cuddle?'

No reply, just a quiet rumble of satisfaction and her daughter's slight form nestled close against her belly, one arm pillowed on her own.

'Thought it might be, somehow.'

Sal's skin was hot to the touch beneath her rucked pyjamas. Not feverish hot, just hot in the way that children feel when they've been in bed for a while. Which was odd, really, because they were meant to be thirty-seven degrees when you took their temperature, the same as adults, weren't they? So why did men always feel colder in bed than Sal did – especially their legs and feet?

Awake now, her mind frustratingly active, Mina asked, 'What time is it, anyway?'

'Dunno. About half-past four, I think.'

Her eyes, losing their reluctance, had found their way open and were adjusting to the darkness, no longer even prickling. Two and a half hours until the alarm; still a nice long stretch of sleep if she could recapture it. She forced her eyes to shut again and tried to empty her brain.

'I don't have to go back to my room, then?' said the small, hopeful voice.

'OK, but turn round, keep still and shut up.'

Obediently, Sal turned so that Mina was nursing the curve of her back, the way they always settled; curls that smelt of kids' strawberry shampoo cluttered the pillow in front of her. It was a wonder she could even remember what cold male feet under the duvet felt like, it had been so long. But how was she supposed to get a man back in her bed if Sal was always there – even if she got the chance to meet any, which was pretty flipping unlikely? Measured, shallow breathing told her Sal was already back to sleep but her own eyes, stubbornly, had opened again and were staring at the repeated vine-leaf pattern on the wallpaper.

Chapter 3

'But is it normal, do you think?'

For once he didn't mean normal in terms of standard deviation. What did he care about other kids, elsewhere on the curve? Peter just meant, well, *normal.* Though quite why he was asking a childless widower of sixty-five for advice about the expected parameters of child behaviour, he was not sure.

'Is it every night?' asked his friend Jeremy, putting down his mug of Earl Grey. Peter watched him stir in another quarter-spoon of honey. A gay childless widower, to be exact about it.

'Without fail. Since they were babies. They've had separate rooms from the age of five, and they do keep their things separate, most of the time – clothes and stuff, you know. If I put Cassie's socks on Kim's pile or Kim's T-shirt in with Cassie's, they are on to me like a shot. It's just the sleeping thing.'

'But they start off in their own rooms, you say?'

Peter nodded. 'It's never an issue. They wanted rooms of their own. They both hop into bed, and I sit on the landing by the two open doors and read the story there – or sometimes Kim and I sit on Cassie's bed, or Cassie and I on Kim's. Then I tuck them both up, give them a kiss, lights out, good as gold. It's not about getting off to sleep: if I check when I come up, they are asleep in their own rooms, as often as not. But by morning when it comes to getting them up for school, they are invariably cuddled up in the same bed. Clinging together like the Babes in the bloody Wood.'

He glanced up at Jeremy, catching the lift of an arch eyebrow. 'No slight intended.'

Jeremy had worked for forty years as an illustrator of children's books and his tastes had been known to run to mock Victorian pastoral kitsch.

'None dreamt of for a second, I'm sure. And is it always the same bed?'

Peter nodded again. 'Like I said.'

'No,' said Jeremy patiently, 'I know you said you find them together in the one bed. But I mean, is it always the same one: Cassie's or Kim's?'

'Oh, I see what you mean. Well, no, it varies. Sometimes Kim has gone in with Cassie, sometimes the other way round.'

They drank their tea in silence for a short while. Jeremy leaned his long spine into the spindle back of Peter's kitchen chair until the junk-shop pine gave a premonitory creak, making Peter wince. He really ought to stop the twins from swinging on those chairs – or else have a session with the Evo-Stik. Just as his ears began to tingle with the imagined sound of splintering wood, his friend sat forward again.

'Well, I suppose there's no real harm in it, is there?'

'Um, not as such, perhaps; not at the moment.'

But later on, what then? They couldn't sleep like that all their lives, could they?

'I honestly don't see that you have much to worry about, Peter. That is, unless you think . . . You're not concerned that they might be, shall we say, experimenting, are you?'

The tea in Peter's mug slopped in alarm as he stared at Jeremy. Surely he didn't imagine that was why . . . Both eyebrows were eloquently high. Damn the man – he was being teased.

'Because you know, it's not as if you have a girl and a boy,' his guest went on serenely. 'I mean to say, what could two little girls possibly get up to together?'

'Oh, shut up, you old queen,' said Peter.

Anxiety thus somewhat dispelled, he topped up both their mugs from the old Denby teapot. 'Want some more hot water in that or is it all right?'

Jeremy raised a don't-bother-yourself hand and rose to fetch the kettle. Peter took a sip of his own over-strength brew.

'Leaving aside for a moment my homophobic fears about my daughters' incipient lesbian tendencies' – the tannin furred his teeth and turned his grin into a grimace – 'there is also the question of separation.'

He had been reading the chapters on it last night in every twin book on the shelf, and there were a lot of them. Probably every one published in the UK in the last thirty years; almost certainly, in fact, since he had been through the University Library catalogue when Bev's obstetrician first told them the news. A fair number from the States, too, although American twins sounded to Peter as though they came from quite another planet.

'At some point they are going to have to cope with being apart, living more independent lives. Going places alone, making their own friends, having separate jobs, separate homes, separate relationships. Yes, I can buy them different clothes. I can encourage their individuality all day long.' Cassie's unique talent for owl noises, Kim's singular dislike of poached egg. 'But it's just rearranging the deckchairs, isn't it, if they're glued together every night?'

Reseated with mug and kettle, Jeremy suggested the obvious dispensation. 'They are only nine.'

'That's what I told myself when they were seven – that they were only seven, I mean. What when they are only eleven, or only fourteen?'

What about boyfriends? He saw them again as they'd been in the morning when he looked in to wake them at seven. Not hugged together front to back like spoons in a drawer – somehow that would have been less disconcerting – but face to face in each other's arms, foreheads touching and knees locked. The closest image was those conkers you find with two together in the shell, each one a normal shape apart from the side that faces its twin, smooth and shiny and completely flat. What boy would have a chance, coming into the middle of that?

'Well, what is there you can do, even if you think it is a problem? Act the patriarch and lock them in their rooms?'

Lock up your daughters. Wasn't that supposed to be for the opposite thing – to stop them having boyfriends?

Even topped up from the kettle, Peter's tea could have halted rust. He pushed his mug away. 'I guess you have a point. I don't imagine forbidding it is going to help, really, is it? It won't alter what they appear to want – need, even, perhaps – just make for a lot of conflict and unhappiness.'

Steadfastly he blocked the persistently lurking thought: Bev would know what to do. Jeremy commanded his eye. 'So do the sensible thing.'

Peter matched his friend's grin. 'Ignore it and hope it will go away?'

Through their comfortable laughter, Jeremy summoned his book-learning on nine-year-old lifestyles. 'How about sleepovers? Start small: the odd night over at a schoolmate's without the sister?'

'No good.' Peter pulled a face. 'Same friends. They always get invited as a pair.'

'Well, couldn't you suggest to one of the other mums that she invite just Cassie or just Kim? Easy enough to make up some story about there only being one camp bed. Not enough cushions for two, that kind of thing.'

Choosing not to rise to 'the other mums', Peter shook his head with a smile of resignation. 'But that's the whole point, isn't it? Only one camp bed would be just plenty.'

This produced a rich, throaty laugh; but still Jeremy waggled a finger, warning him against over-concern. 'Don't forget that we are, after all, social animals. Creatures of the pack: by nature we flock together. We are none of us made to sleep alone.'

It was Jeremy, soon afterwards, who glanced at his watch and made Peter realise it was almost half past four. He groaned; twelve essays he had brought home to mark that afternoon and he had read through barely three.

'Oh God, I really ought to get down to a bit more work before it's time to pick them up.'

Rising in stage affront, Jeremy contented himself with a 'Well, then' and stalked to the sink with his mug. Peter ignored him. Two pounds seventy per hour per twin he'd been paying for them to be at Afterschool Club since three o'clock – approximately the time that Jeremy had dropped round for a chat – though it wasn't wasting the money that was making him feel suddenly guilty.

'Haven't you got some fairy toadstools to be drawing at home?' he asked.

'Cockroaches, as a matter of fact.'

'Sorry?'

'Rodney the Roach and his carapaced chums. They befriend a small boy whose parents, if any, appear never to be around to tackle the housework. Shockingly low standards of hygiene.' He spread his hands in a despairing gesture, milking Peter's laughter. 'It seems our five to eight year olds wish to consume only books that pertain to the slum or the sewer. Fairy toadstools are completely out.'

'Well, I suppose there was always the grinding poverty of the woodcutter's hut, wasn't there? Cinderella probably had a few cockroach buddies in her scullery. And broken families and abusive step-parents are nothing new.'

'Perhaps so,' conceded Jeremy. 'But at least in the old stories there was a little more romance about it.'

With that he swept out, Peter following him distractedly to the door before returning to the kitchen table and the neglected pile of essays. 'How does the concept of "home" relate to marginalisation and alienation in the urban environment?' The title was not his own but one of Ian Stanbury's, lifted from last summer's Urban Communities exam paper. Despite having co-marked the ninety-odd scripts with Ian in June, he was still unsure whether he knew what the answer was supposed to be, or even whether the question had any real meaning.

He picked up the top essay from the heap. Maybe this one would provide enlightenment – or maybe not. Nor the next one after that, either, it appeared. *This is a complicated question,* the young author opened charily, *because the concept of 'home' is somewhat fluid . . .* Well, yes: 'dur' as his daughters and their classmates might say. But you could hardly blame the poor student for prevaricating, when the title seemed specifically to invite such empty nothings. Sometimes he was tempted to agree with Kim and Cassie about his field of specialism. In their view, the urban geography of the UK was not 'real' geography at all, involving as it did no volcanic mountain ranges, river deltas or nomadic tribespeople dressed in stripy blankets.

Speaking of the twins, it was now five to five and he must go and fetch them. Pocketing his keys he flipped his outdoor jacket off the back of his chair. He would take the car but there was a late-October chill in the air and coats were like cycle helmets: difficult to insist the kids put them on when you neglected to wear one yourself.

Afterschool Club took place in the village hall. The bedlam within was such that a ring of the doorbell could never be heard; the door being half glazed, however, the attention of a member of staff or one of the older children could normally be attracted by means of animated gesticulation outside the glass. Today it was Kim who spotted him and hurtled towards the door, slamming so hard up against it that the imagined impact blocked his own breath.

'Dad!'

By the time she had finished struggling with the latch, Cassie was by her side, and as soon as he was over the threshold they were sandwiching him, talking in eager stereo.

'I got two brick points in numeracy –'

'It rained, so we had indoor PE –'

'– it was percentages; I got them all right. I was the only one who did.'

'– and Abby Fox's trainers were muddy so she had to do it in

25

bare feet and then she got a splinter and had to go and see Eve and she got it out with a needle and Abby said it bled a lot and really, really hurt.'

One arm round each daughter, Peter merely smiled and was grateful for the bombardment. There was no saying how long it would last, after all; some of the Year 6s, in particular – girls as well as boys – were already coolly distant when their parents arrived to collect them.

As he scrawled on the signing-out sheet and ushered them out towards the Land Rover, the competing monologues gradually resolved themselves into a single, trackable narrative, like a radio homing in on a signal from the background chatter.

'There's a new girl in our class –'

'– Shannon, she's called –'

'– Shannon Mahoney, except she says it more like "Marney" –'

'– and Mrs Moore made her sit next to Christopher Bradwell –'

'– but we talked to her at playtime, and she's really nice –'

'– her hair is so long she can tie it in one of those French knot things without a hairband or clips or anything –'

'– she lives on the traveller site and she says she's allowed to ride the ponies whenever she likes, and she said we might be able to go and ride them one day – can we?'

'Please, Dad, can we?'

'Please?'

He started the ignition, glancing back over his shoulder.

'All strapped in? Yes, of course you can go round and play. Do you think Shannon would have a hard hat you could borrow, if you were going to ride?'

He edged forward in a slow, wide circuit of the car park. The Land Rover was finally going into the garage tomorrow, now he'd had the estimate approved; it would be strange to be able to drive normally again. Would their bike helmets do, he wondered, or did you have to have a different kind of crash hat for horse-riding? A head hitting the ground was surely much the same whatever you had fallen from. But perhaps it was something to do with the hooves. He tried not to picture iron-rimmed feet making contact with tender flesh and bone.

'These ponies, are they well trained, do you suppose? How big . . .?'

But Cassie and Kim had moved on and were now relating from opposite sides of the back seat a story about slippers.

'We can bring our own in, so that we can look at how they're made, Mrs Moore says.' This came from the right: Kim.

'We're going to make our own. Out of felt. We're going to sew them.' From the left: Cassie.

'We've got to draw round our foot on a piece of paper first, to work out the size.'

'Or we can do someone else's foot, if the slipper is for them. Abby says she is going to make hers for Alex Popovic.'

Both girls sniggered knowingly.

'Why doesn't one of you make a pair for Shannon, then, if she's new?' suggested Peter. 'That might be a nice way of making her feel welcome.'

'One each you mean,' said Cassie. 'Mrs Moore says we can only make one. It'll take too long, otherwise. And I don't think there's enough felt.'

'Anyway, we're making ours for us.'

Kim said it as if stating the obvious and, really, he had to concede the logic of it. Quite what all the other children, who did not have a twin at home, would do with one carefully fitted slipper was not immediately evident. But these things no longer surprised him; even allowing for the distorting filter of the nine-year-old mind, much of what seemed to go on at Allington Community Primary made very little sense at all.

'Oh, and have we got any old shoeboxes lying around?' Cassie asked him.

'Probably, in the garage somewhere. Are you going to make them into something?'

'Ye-es, Dad,' came the reply in unison.

'What, then?' Had they told him and he'd forgotten?

'A box for the slippers, of course.'

Bouncing down the lane and pulling up in the drive, he bundled them out and into the kitchen in a trail of bags and scarves and pac-a-macs. Shoes were flung off, to be retrieved and wiped free of mud later – he only bothered to polish them on Sundays – and plastic lunchboxes were dumped unceremoniously in the full washing-up bowl, where balled-up cling film and browning apple cores would float up through the bubbles later when he peeled off the lids.

'Can we watch telly?' called Kim and they were gone, leaving the kitchen to slop gently back to stillness in their wake.

Turning his back on the sink, Peter moved to the drawer where the tin-opener was kept; almost before it was in his hand, he heard the swish and clunk of the pet door and Ollie appeared, tongue lolling, at his side.

'Oh, now you bother to come home, do you?' he demanded, rumpling one of the spaniel's unfeasibly long ears. 'Where have you been all afternoon, anyway?'

Out ratting in the field at the end of the lane, probably. Well, they called it 'ratting', although Ollie had never been known to catch anything; she just liked to patrol the hedgerow and stare at holes, dreaming her self-important doggy daydreams. Just like they always called the cat flap a 'pet door' in deference to her feelings. It pre-dated Ollie and indeed Peter, no doubt a relic of some previous, feline occupant of the cottage; but she could just manage to squeeze through, attracting frequent jibes about Winnie the Pooh and Rabbit's front door.

Opening the cupboard, Peter reached for a tin of baked beans. The Pavlovian business with the tin-opener went back years, to when Bev had occasionally brought home tins of meaty chunks in jelly as a treat to spice up Ollie's regular diet of dried dog food. Personally, he couldn't stand the smell of the stuff and never bought it, but evidently hope still lodged somewhere in that obstinate, woolly head. Tonight the tin-opener spelled a gourmet meal for nobody. He tipped the beans into a saucepan and arranged four slices of deep-frozen bread in the toaster, twisting the setting round to 6 and depressing the knob. Tomorrow he would shop and cook a proper meal; tomorrow he would mark the essays – or, better still, tonight, when the girls were in bed.

As it transpired, this last resolution was quickly to evaporate. Kim and Cassie had only lately been dispatched, each to her own room, when the telephone rang.

'Hi, Peter. Look, sorry to disturb you and all that, but can I ask you something?'

Trish. Peter walked to the kitchen table, pulled out a chair and sat down: usually a necessary precaution when Trish was on the phone.

'About my bibliography. Do I need to include everything that I've read – as general background, I mean – or only the things I've actually referred to in the text?'

'Well, strictly speaking, only the latter,' he replied cautiously. 'Some authors like to have a separate listing headed "Further Reading" to give a sense of the wider literature, but the PhD regulations don't make it a requirement.' Then, trying not to let his sinking feeling colour his voice, 'Why do you ask?'

The line crackled with hesitation.

'Well, you see, there are a few things I've read as background – really only as background – for which I seem to have mislaid the full reference.'

Peter put a hand over the receiver to cover his sigh. He had only seen inside Trish's college room once – it was not part of the PhD supervisor's remit to make house calls – but he had received an indelible impression of chaos. Piles of paper everywhere: on the desk, on the floor, on the bed, even (unless memory was tweaking his fears) stacked in the hand-basin. Not a card index in sight.

29

'It's just a few page numbers, you know, for journal articles, and the odd date or place of publication for monographs. Of course I could go back and check it all up. A lot of the information would be in the University Library catalogue or on the Net, or else I can dig out the materials again. Except . . .'

'Except?' he prompted grimly.

'Except maybe one or two that I had on inter-library loan – or on microfiche. They might be more tricky. I'd have to order them again, I suppose.'

Of course he could – probably should – go into his supervisorly speech about the importance of organised habits of scholarship: careful note-taking and the rigorous referencing of all sources, not only to avoid such unnecessary labour as Trish was about to be obliged to undertake, but also to avoid accidental failure to attribute an idea to its originator. The danger of plagiarism should be the researcher's constant guard. But she had heard it all before – and in this case it was probably two or three years since the horse had bolted.

'But anything I don't refer to in the text, you say I needn't include in the bibliography?' Trish sounded more hopeful.

'That's right.'

'If they were just background reading?'

'Yes. But . . .' A suspicion was forming in his mind. 'You know, Trish, you can't just remove references from the text at random and relegate them to being "background", not if you are relying on them as part of your argument. I mean, you can't just delete all mention of something just because you've lost the page number and can't be bothered to go and look for it.'

Maybe he'd gone a bit far, because there was a pause that, even through the medium of the telephone wire, had a decidedly crest-fallen ring. But then she laughed. That was the great thing about Trish – one of the great things: even when she got herself in a hopeless muddle, laughter was never far from the surface.

'You're right. I can go and look them all up again. It won't take that long. Couple of days in the library will be fun – make a change from staring at a computer screen all day.'

'Writing up is deadly,' Peter sympathised. 'Look, why don't you come over for supper tomorrow? Come early, the girls always love to see you.'

Now he would definitely have to shop and cook, he thought as she thanked him and rang off. It was good, it would force him to make the effort; he'd been very lax about meals recently. And he had to admit he got pretty fed up with baked beans and frozen pizza himself, too; with just the three of them it made sense to share the children's tea, but the diet was a depressing one for anyone over the age of eleven. With Trish coming he might do pasta with a proper sauce: fresh aubergine and tomatoes or perhaps even some Florence fennel. And a dressed salad. It wasn't that the kids didn't like more demanding fare; they could normally be relied upon to devour his cooking with curiosity and, in Cassie's case at least, some relish. Trish could play Monopoly with them while he cooked, or let them be hairdressers and put her hair in tiny plaits like last time. Yes, inviting her had certainly been a good plan all round. But however much he might rationalise it, he knew that the invitation was really motivated by pure foolishness on his part. She had been his research student for three years and now, with her studentship at an end, she was entering her fourth year and attempting to finish her thesis with no visible means of support. He knew perfectly well, though, that it was not his job as her supervisor to twist the Bursar's arm to let her keep her college room, nor was it incumbent upon him to farm bits and pieces of research assistance her way, or pay her to do his photocopying. And he certainly had no duty to provide her with meals. But she was almost as skinny as Cassie and Kim – and, well, she was Trish. He couldn't help it: he always felt compelled to feed the girl.

His shelved marking held his attention for the length of only two essays before the ten o'clock news exerted its lure. There was something so refreshingly adult and external and big-picture about

31

the news, lifting his mind away from the minutiae of either family life or academic geography. And then over to BBC2 for *Newsnight*, a little dose of Kirsty Wark was so soothing to the mind before bed – as good as a finger of fine single malt.

When he had switched off the television and taken Ollie out into the lane to contemplate the stars for a moment before he locked up, he headed upstairs, pausing en route to the bathroom to look in on the twins. The bedclothes in both rooms were reassuringly humped. And, well, if they did move later, who could really blame them? Not, surely, the man who was about to be grateful to share his bed with a slightly smelly spaniel named Olivia.

Chapter 4

What with Sal and Jess between them making her chances of getting out and meeting a man outside work pretty slim, Mina had finally bowed to the inevitable and accepted a date with someone from the call centre. His name was Murray, and while he was not exactly Richard Armitage, he had the advantages of being youngish, available and persistent. It was quite a while since she'd been out with anyone at all, and she found that she warmed to keenness that she would once have dismissed as desperate or merely sad. If he still lived with his mum, well, he couldn't be thirty yet, and she knew as well as anyone what they paid at the call centre. And a single bloke was hardly going to walk into a council place, was he?

A drink in a city centre bar at eight was what they had arranged. Eight o'clock was early enough for there to be the prospect of a film afterwards or maybe an Indian, if Murray hadn't already eaten, but late enough to give Mina a chance to feed Sal first and see her up to wash her hair, so Jess would have nothing to do except be here. The question was whether to have tea with Sal now, just in case food was not on the menu later; she didn't want to sit in a pub all night with her tummy rumbling like Nana's old twin-tub. On the other hand, if he did suggest eating out it wouldn't exactly lend an air of sophistication to admit she had shared sausage and egg with her kiddy at half past five.

'Sal, tea's ready,' she called, turning round from the frying pan to find her daughter at her elbow, book in hand. At least this was one Mina had read. One of her old ones, in fact: Laura Ingalls Wilder.

'Sausages,' said Sal absently. The lack of enthusiasm was

33

unusual; Mina suspected she was still seeing squash and corn-meal pancakes.

Mina shuffled up the sausages and tomato halves to make room for an egg. 'Wash your hands, then.'

There were only two left in the box and it didn't seem worth putting one back in the fridge. As the edges of the first egg began to bubble and turn opaque she squashed up the white with her spatula and cracked the other one into the pan next to it. She'd just have a bit now; that way she'd have room for a proper meal later if it was offered but not be too hungry if not. And if all the evening produced was a couple of awkward drinks, she could always console herself with bread and jam when she got home, couldn't she?

'If you want ketchup, could you get it out please, love?'

Sal struggled back reluctantly from the western frontier. 'Um, can I have brown sauce, actually?'

Mina laid down the plates as her daughter drifted back from the cupboard with both bottles.

'You remember I'm going out tonight, don't you? Jess is going to babysit.'

It surprised Mina how little, at ten, Sal yet took exception to the word. Carrying on criss-crossing her egg with sauce, she asked only, 'Where is she?'

Not knowing the answer, Mina sidestepped the question. 'Still out, but it's not even six yet. She promised to be back by half past seven, don't worry.'

Which of course made her begin at once to worry herself, taking all the enjoyment out of her single Lincolnshire pork chipolata. Change the subject, she thought. 'How was school today?'

''S OK.'

That was it. Always ''s OK' or ''s all right'.

'I could have gone to Grandma's. Tonight, I mean, so you could go out.'

'She'll be back all right.'

But by seven forty-five, with tea eaten and washed up and

Mina changed into clean jeans and her best boots – real leather with the pointed toes that rubbed at the side – there was still no sign of Jess. Sal wandered back down to the kitchen with her hair twisted up in a pink towel to match her dressing gown and a preoccupied expression that suggested she was still out at the prairie homestead with Pa and Ma Ingalls and Mary and Carrie and the rest. One day she would drop her book right in, propping it on the taps like that; the pages were beginning to crinkle as it was. But the fidgeting of Mina's shiny, cramped toes and her frequent glances at her watch soon dragged her daughter back to the present.

'I could still go to Grandma's if you like.'

'You've had your bath. You've got your pyjamas on.'

'I can get dressed again.'

Mina sighed. 'I'm sure she'll be here any minute,' she lied.

When the digital display of her watch reached 20:06, she went over to the phone and winkled from the tight confines of her back pocket the Post-it on which Murray had scribbled his mobile number. Smoothing it out flat, she hesitated, then picked up and dialled. *You have reached the voicemail* . . . Abruptly she replaced the receiver, not ready to speak into the void. How the heck was it going to sound, anyway? I'm not there because my useless kid sister hasn't turned up to babysit. Not exactly cool, was it? She wasn't even sure that Murray knew about Sal yet; she hardly wanted to load Jess on to him as well. How to explain? She's a lot younger than me. (Ten years, in fact, but that was another thing she wasn't sure she wanted to admit to yet, having a grown sister of seventeen.) My mum handed her over to me along with the rent book when she left to move in with her boyfriend three years ago. That's how other people saw it, for sure – people who didn't know. God knows what Murray would think.

20:25. It would be Sal's bedtime soon.

'Really, I could go to Grandma's.'

She eyed her daughter uncertainly. There would still be time:

35

they could be there by quarter to, Sal back in her pyjamas and tucked up before nine. And she could get the bus and be sipping Stella with Murray by not long after. If he waited that long.

'I like it there.'

'I know you do, love.'

And Mum liked having her; Dave too. As he always said, she's no trouble, such a quiet little squirrel, after all. It would be perfectly easy. Sal was past being carried home to bed half asleep later as they used to when she was smaller – though Dave would certainly have driven them back if she'd asked – but Mina could have the other spare room, or crash on the settee, and be there to get Sal up for school tomorrow.

'Please?'

She made a decision. 'No. Come on, off to bed.'

It wasn't Sal's style to pout or 'oh, Mum' her but there was a certain look that she got in her eyes sometimes, and she had it now. Mina knew the next move, though.

'You can read for an extra half-hour if you want, if go straight up now.'

Her daughter tucked in comfortably with the Ingalls family, Mina came back downstairs and lifted the phone. No doubt it would still be his voicemail, but this time she'd bite the bullet. I'm sorry I'm so late, my babysitter hasn't turned up yet; I hope I'll be along soon . . . A click, and the mechanical voice interrupted the ring tone. *Please leave a message.*

'Look, I'm really sorry, Murray. I'm not going to be able to make it. I'll explain at work.'

Not much chance of that, though, was there? It would almost certainly make no sense to anyone but herself – certainly not to Mum, quite obviously not to Murray. How could she possibly explain that she wanted to be in for Jess, even though Jess was out?

She switched on the television and sank into the settee, unzip-ping her boots to give her feet sweet relief. Murray might be single and not too much of a fright to look at, but he never seemed all that interesting, anyway.

Peter, meanwhile, did not lack for a babysitter.

'They've had their tea,' he told Trish for the third time. 'I've left some cold chicken and salad in the fridge for you; there's red wine open on the side there, and a fresh loaf in the crock. Unsliced. One of those ones with the budgie seed in, sesame and sunflower and quite possibly millet for all I know. So anyway, don't let Cassie inveigle you into giving her some because they've eaten already.'

'Got it.' She grinned. 'They've had theirs. Do not feed the animals.'

He knew she was laughing at him but couldn't help himself; it was the thought of all those little seeds. 'You see, they've cleaned their teeth, so—'

'Why do they put all that stuff in, anyway?' she wondered. 'They do rolls in the faculty buttery with flax and linseed and even hemp, for heaven's sake. Only good for tablecloths and oil painting, in my opinion, and, well, you know, spliffs.'

They both laughed now, but nervously, wishing she hadn't made this last remark, reminding them uncomfortably for a moment of being teacher and student.

'Where are you off out to, anyway? College meeting?'

'Pub,' he said shortly. 'I'd better be getting off; let's go through and I'll say goodbye.'

In the living room, Cassie and Kim were kneeling side by side on the floor, bottoms in the air as if praying towards Mecca. Each had her own packet of coloured pencils on the carpet beside her; between their lowered shoulders sat Ollie, eyes contentedly vacant, and between their heads lay a colouring book. They had chosen an intricate mosaic pattern and were filling the geometric grid with painstaking method, Cassie from the left and Kim from the right. Kim glanced up as he and Trish appeared; Cassie went on colouring, tongue tip trapped between seed-free teeth.

'Now, you two be good for Trish, won't you? Same rule as always: in bed by eight, lights out by half past.'

'Yes, Dad.'

Kim was crayoning again, too.

'So that means you've got ten minutes left down here, no more.'

'Yeah, Dad, we know.'

Trish nodded silently to him across their tilted backs, tapping her watch and smiling. The twins did not need to raise their heads for him to receive a strong impression, outsider in this female alliance, of being strung along.

'Trish, can you help us, please?' begged Kim.

'Well, I'm not sure there's room for three of us, is there? Maybe I could just sharpen the crayons or something?'

'Course there's room. You can go over there, facing us, and start on the top bit.'

'This bit here?' Trish was already down on the floor, dark head bent close to the two smaller, fairer ones and the grey-and-white topknot in between them. 'These small triangles have to be dark green, is that right?'

'Well, I'll get off, then, and leave you to it.' A pause, before he reminded the backs of three heads, 'Ten minutes, don't forget.'

Only Ollie's eyes followed him to the living-room door where he hesitated and turned. 'Oh, and nice pattern, by the way.'

It was a bit of a hike to the Drayman's Arms, which was at the other end of the village near the church, but Peter was in no hurry. Not that he could have a drink, or no more than one, because he'd still have to drive Trish back into town later on. He wrapped on jacket and scarf and set off up the lane towards the High Street. Jeremy's windows were unlit as he passed, as were Martin's in the adjoining semi; they must be out, and at this early hour he had little hope that their destination was the Drayman's. There was rarely anybody much in before nine, apart from those few with digestions stern enough to tackle one of Linda's steaks.

A swift visual reconnoitre as he entered the pub confirmed his fears. One table in the far corner – it looked as though they had dared the demons of dyspepsia and ordered the mixed grill – and Rex behind the bar polishing, either for show or from force of habit, glasses that already gleamed.

'Pint of bitter, please, Rex,' said Peter, pulling a bar stool towards his hip with one foot and leaning against it.

'IPA?'

The question was apparently pure form; the stream of lightly foamed copper was already eddying halfway up the glass. The Drayman's Arms was nominally a free house, but Rex's purchasing habits, like the drinking habits of his customers, were unadventurous: one barrel of winter ale at Christmas, perhaps, but the guest pump generally stood idle for the other fifty-one weeks.

'Cold out, tonight?'

It was a stock question of Rex's but Peter, nodding the affirmative, wondered whether any of the answers he received meant much to him. The landlord had seldom been sighted out of doors.

'I'll have a bag of cheese and onion, too, please.'

Pocketing his change, he reviewed his options. It was either the bar stool and an in-depth discussion of the weather with an un-initiate, or a table by himself near the fire. He chose the latter.

Pulling a beer mat towards him and setting down his beer, he stared at it until the narrow swirl of creamy bubbles that clung around its edges had given way to smooth mahogany before lifting the glass and breaking the surface to drink. It wasn't a bad pint. Peter liked his bitter flat, and the slow turnover at the Drayman's usually ensured that in this his wish was gratified; if only there hadn't been that slight aftertaste. Splitting open the bag, he crunched a handful of crisps, took another sip. Certainly it was not hops, nor even iron filings; disquietingly reminiscent, in fact, of detergent.

However, it was still only ten past eight by the brass ship's clock over the fireplace. If he was to avoid the queasy stomach that always followed more than two Britvics, he had better make this pint last.

39

He removed his jacket and hung it over the back of his chair, extracting from the inside pocket the furl of essays he had concealed there earlier, together with a green ballpoint pen. An hour and forty minutes before the earliest time at which he could reasonably contemplate heading for home. Ought to get seven or eight marked at least.

Really, he much preferred red wine. Not the kind that Rex would sell him from a five-litre Spanish wine box supplied by the brewery at rock bottom cost, but a nice Côte de Beaune like the one he'd started last night. The one Trish might be helping herself to a glass of right now, feet tucked up beneath her on his sofa, watching his television. The one he could have been sharing with her if he wasn't such an idiot. It did not take the half-empty pub and his lonely, soapy beer to ram the point home. Attractive she might be, indigent she most certainly was. But what kind of deranged lunatic would pretend to need a babysitter and sit on his own in the pub for two hours, just for the opportunity of slipping twenty pounds to one of his research students?

On her settee the same night – her watch by the flickering light of the late movie told her it was almost two a.m. – Mina awoke to disorientation, unsure whether what had roused her had been a click of the front door. She would have called out but her tongue was fat and uncooperative with sleep, her throat as dry as if she had had those lagers with Murray and a jalfrezi as well, instead of her solitary mug of tea and two cold sausages on a saucer.

If it was Jess, then she was unusually quiet and – even rarer – almost certainly alone. No smothered laughter or talking; no clump of trainers cast off in the hallway, or bag slapped down. Not for the first time in the small hours, Mina wished she had the courage to bolt and chain the door when Jess was out late, rather than just leave it on the Yale; in the daylight, though, intruders always seemed less daunting than having the argument.

Straightening cramped legs, she rose and moved across to the

TV, killing first sound and then picture, ears buzzing with the silence that followed. Maybe it had been something in the film which had woken her: a shout, a gunshot. But the idea of gunfire, somehow, did not offer comfort. The picture of Sal as she had left her – hair thatching the pillow and just a swatch of forehead visible above duvet and splay-cornered paperback covers – flooded into her head. Her feet told her to make for the stairs before her head had a chance to tell her not to be crazy.

Opening the door into the hallway, she ran straight up against the motionless figure of her sister. The first odd thing was that Jess was standing in the dark. Mina found her voice.

'What are you doing? Are you OK? Why don't you put the light on?'

It was surely not to avoid waking the house; Jess had never been known to think of such a thing, and a light downstairs wouldn't be a problem, anyhow. There was no reply. Mina reached for the switch, jarring them both into focus like a flashbulb.

Jess still stood rooted, swaying just a little, but Mina felt as if she were also swaying herself – something about her tiredness and the bright hall – and with Jess it didn't seem like alcohol, either.

'Are you OK?' she repeated more specifically, although carefully pressing her voice flat of any anxiety.

Jess's eyes were glassy; Mina was praying again that their un-natural shimmer did not mean drugs, when it blurred and blotched itself into the beginning of tears.

'No Sean tonight?' inquired Mina as gently as she could.

This produced movement, at least: a jerk of the head and a snort. ''S not him.'

What then? Tell me, she wanted to say, but they had never had the habit of confidence, not about this sort of thing. Instead she said the worst possible thing – the thing Mum would have said. 'Where have you been?'

The tears froze, the lids shuttered down. Mina attempted to backtrack. 'I don't mean . . . I just meant, it's very late, nowhere is still open, so I wondered if you were all right.' Which she had asked twice already.

'I'm fine,' muttered Jess thickly, sounding anything but. Then, eyes suddenly open and seeking rare contact, making Mina's throat tighten, she repeated, 'Really, thanks, I'm fine.'

There was no gratitude there, swimming in the speckled blue, only a mixture of warning and pleading. The message was loud and clear: *Back off.*

'OK. Night, then.'

Jess nodded and set off up the stairs while Mina went back into the sitting room to unplug the TV and turn out the light. Her mug was still on the floor by the end of the settee where her head had lain; an inch of tea was greying in the bottom, milk filming the surface with static whorls. Carrying it through to the kitchen, she put it in the sink next to the empty saucer which still bore, traced in white pork fat, the outline of two chipolatas. It was only then, directing a gush of water towards the mug to swill out the cold tea, that it occurred to Mina that she hadn't thought to mention the ruins of her night out.

Chapter 5

Guy Fawkes Night fell on a Monday and, as usual, Peter had been unable to withstand the dual assault on the subject of fireworks. Only sparklers on the actual day, though, he had insisted, with it being school in the morning; for the proper stuff they would have to wait until the weekend.

'But can we have whizzers and bangers and not just boring old Roman candles?'

'And a Catherine wheel on the apple tree like last time?'

'And rockets? Please, Dad!'

'Well, we'll see. There's not much point in rockets, is there? Last year they disappeared straight off over the house and only the Dorlinsons and people in the High Street got to see them.'

One thing about bangers, though: at least they didn't have the pet problem. Children's BBC had been warning people to keep their dogs and cats indoors all week, but Ollie didn't need the radio on loud and an extra old blanket for comfort. It was in her blood: the first sound of a firecracker and she was up and out through the pet door, scanning the skyline for plummeting pheasants.

'What about a bonfire?' he suggested. 'There are all those prunings, still, from when I did the hedge last month, and you two could rake up some leaves for me on Saturday morning. They're always good for getting it going.'

Nine was evidently still young enough to embrace with noisy delight a gardening chore thinly disguised as recreation.

'We'll go and buy them after school, shall we?' he said when the squeals had subsided. 'They have them at the hardware shop in Histon.'

'Can we choose?' pleaded Kim. 'Pick them out ourselves, I mean, not just have one of those mixed boxes?'

'Well, we'll have to see what they've got. And what they cost.'

Hence he was at the village hall an hour earlier than usual, and both twins thudded against the door to clamour at the glass. Coats, bags, gloves and scarves all present and correct and their collection signed for, he loaded them into the Land Rover.

'Shannon says they don't do Guy Fawkes,' Kim announced as they set off.

'Who's "they"?' asked her conscientious father. 'Travellers, do you mean?'

'Yes.'

'No-o.' Cassie strutted her superior knowledge. 'It's because they're Irish.'

It made sense. Roman Catholics, he supposed, were unlikely to take much pleasure in celebrating the torture, dismemberment and death of one of Catesby's conspirators against the hated Protestant oppressor.

'Must be sad not to have fireworks, though.'

'Except in the summer.' This time it was Kim's chance to correct her sister. 'They have them in June; Shannon said so. Something Eve – St John's, I think it was. They have a bonfire then, same as we do, and fireworks, too. And the kids all get to pull a stick out of the fire, still burning, and see how high they can throw it. I think it's a competition or something.'

'Oh, can we do that on Saturday, Dad?'

'Oh yes, please!'

Yeah, right, as they themselves would say. But the lecture on fire safety which was forming itself upon his lips suddenly struck him as invidious. Recklessly hazardous or not, this was their friend's cultural heritage. 'Um, no. No, I don't think we'll do that.' An idea struck him. 'It wouldn't be right. After all, we're not Irish, are we?' Out loud, however, this sounded worse, if anything. 'What I mean is, it's part of Shannon's family's tradition, isn't it, hers and the

44

other Irish families down on the traveller site? But it isn't ours. It's probably special to them and we shouldn't just copy it for fun as if it's nothing.'

'Well, it's not religious or anything, though, is it?' reasoned Kim. 'It's not like that time you got cross when Cassie felt-penned a red spot on her forehead and pretended to be an Indian lady.'

Reflected in the driving mirror, he caught the face Cassie pulled at her sister.

'It's just a thing they do,' Kim insisted, 'like some people have a tradition of always having toasted marshmallows at their bonfire. Or Adri Van Keuren's mum making those treacly chocolate cookies because they're Dutch.'

'Mmm, those cookies are the best ever,' said Cassie. 'You never said we couldn't have them 'cos we're not from Holland.'

'And what about hymns in assembly? We're not Christians, but you let us sing those. Even at home and in the bath and stuff.'

Feeling the argument beginning to run away from him, Peter thought it best to shift the ground. 'How about a game of I spy?'

'Charades!' came back the response in unison.

'I'll start,' said Kim. 'It's a film.'

They were out of the village now, on to the open road between fields of ridged black earth sown to winter wheat, heading towards Histon. This made watching in the mirror more feasible – or even the occasional glance back over his shoulder – but, in all honesty, the thing was still hopeless.

A burst of giggling, a quick flourish of Kim's black Start-rites, and – '*Happy Feet*,' proclaimed Cassie.

Well, maybe that one was rather obvious, but next it was Cassie's turn. 'It's a book and a film.'

All that Peter glimpsed was the reflection of surreptitiously darting eyes and a forefinger pressed to laughing lips before Kim was crowing in triumph. '*Harry Potter and the Chamber of Secrets*!'

House rules dictated that turns were taken in strict rotation, rather than going to the person who guessed correctly. It was the only way Peter would ever have got a go.

'This one's a book,' he said, eyes on the dusk of the road ahead, empty but for the tail lights of a dark red saloon thirty metres in front of them. *The Tiger Who Came To Tea* had been a huge favourite with both girls five years ago; how quickly would they remember now? He took his left hand off the wheel and held aloft all five digits, at the same time raising his right thumb as far as he could without compromising the steering.

'Six words,' they chorused obediently, playing this one by the book.

He brandished his left thumb and forefinger.

'Second word.'

Now then . . . really the only thing was to mime the creature's roar and pounce, with both hands raised and fingers splayed like outstretched claws. The road was straight and flat; it would only be for a second. Swiftly he let go and swivelled in his seat, launching over his left shoulder the pantomime of ferocious feline attack. A highly satisfying squeal arose from both sides of the back seat. The controls were back in his hands almost at once; there was still only the red saloon, a little nearer now, and a small blue van coming the other way.

'Lion?' Cassie hazarded.

'*The Lion, the Witch and the Wardrobe!*' cried Kim.

Cassie totted up on her fingers. 'Can't be. That's seven words. And it's a film as well.'

'Was it a cat?'

'*The Cat in the Hat?*'

'That's only five.'

The red car braked; Peter slowed behind it. 'It was a sort of a cat. But let me do some more.'

This time he held up all six fingers again, keeping the wheel as steady as he could.

'Sixth word,' they chanted.

The car in front pulled away again. Left hand held flat, palm upwards to serve for a saucer, Peter withdrew his right from the wheel for a moment and, his little finger elegantly crooked, parodied the drinking of afternoon tea.

'The Queen!'

'Is it Alice's tea party?'

'That's Alice in Wonderland, and it's only three words, stupid.'

'Don't say stupid! Dad, she called me stupid.'

'Nobody's stupid,' said Peter soothingly. 'But remember, this is the last word you're guessing now. Do you want the mime again?'

They were approaching the outskirts of Histon, already inside the thirty limit and following quite close behind the red saloon now; in front of that had appeared another four by four, something black and Japanese. He repeated his tea-drinking act more cautiously, with one hand only and eyes straight ahead.

'Tea. Is it tea?'

'*The Tiger Who Came to Tea*!'

'Yes! Well done, Cassie.'

Cassie's cry of triumph blended into one of joyful recollection, in which she was joined by Kim. '"And he drank *all* the water in the tap,"' they recited in glee.

And then, of course, he couldn't help it; he had to turn round, grinning, and share it with them, just for a second. A second during which the dark red car applied its brakes rather more sharply than expected, because its driver was retuning the radio to 5 Live to catch the result of the 4.05 at Newbury and failed to notice that the black Mitsubishi, indicating very late, had slowed to turn into a driveway on the left. Peter saw the road again just a fraction too late. Both feet jerked left and slammed down. The four-channel ABS braking system kicked into operation, but the momentum of the Land Rover's heavy steel chassis propelled it just far enough to shunt it into shuddering, shattering contact with the back of the red saloon.

*   *   *

Aside from one broken indicator light, there was very little damage to the Land Rover. However, its fortified front bumper had made embarrassingly major inroads into the red saloon's rear panelling. Peter was only thankful that he didn't have bull bars fitted. By the time he had helped the racing fan to prise loose what remained of his plastic rear trim and stow it on his back seat, and the two of them had exchanged names, addresses and insurance details, it was half past four; once the fireworks had been selected and paid for and the journey home negotiated in safety, it was not far short of five o'clock.

'Go and watch TV for a bit, could you, do you think? I need to call the insurance company before I put the tea on.'

He keyed in the telephone number and waited while he was placed in the inevitable queue. A member of staff would be with him shortly. Was it having kids, he wondered? Or being a single parent, anyway. Strains of a Bach piano prelude sounded with maddening tranquillity in his ear: the one in C major; Bev had the CD somewhere. He hadn't had an accident in fifteen years, and now two in a matter of weeks. Today's piece of buffoonery could certainly be attributed to the soft-headedness of fatherhood, but that was hardly true of the Dorlinsons' cat. God, this was going to be excruciating: charades, for pity's sake!

'Autocare Direct, my name is Debbie. How may I help you?'

The live human voice wrong-footed him for an instant. Maybe it was this that made him say what he did.

'Oh, hello. Do you think I could speak to Meena, please?'

There was a pause while Debbie – or more likely it was Debi, with one of those squiggled circles instead of a dot over the terminal i – summoned her most patient manner. 'Perhaps I can help you? Everything is logged centrally on to the computer, so it really doesn't matter who's been dealing with your claim up till now.'

It had only been a whim, but now he found that Debi's irritable patience made him wish for the nice Indian woman all the more. She had understood, last time; they had been able to laugh.

More doggedly, he pursued his point. 'All the same, I'd like to speak to Meena, if it's no trouble.'

Evidently it was; clearly his request was liable to send the entire Autocare call queuing system into immediate meltdown. Dark reference was even made to security issues. He stood his ground, however, and the well-tempered clavier clicked back to cover, no doubt, Debi's stream of invective.

'There's someone on line three wants to speak to you.'

Mina cringed, hoping Debbie wouldn't say anything to Mrs Gordon. She had told Jess over and over how absolutely forbidden it was to take personal calls at work. They could ring out on their mobiles from the coffee room during their breaks and if anyone needed them urgently – the bank or the doctor or the kids' school – they could leave a message on a mobile and be phoned back. But never were mobiles to be left switched on at the desk and never, never, never must family or friends use the main call-centre number, blocking out a line for all-important minutes. What havoc would this play with Mrs Gordon's call throughput statistics?

'Oh, God, it'll be my sister. She's not been having an easy time, and—'

'It's not her, it's a client.' Debbie was never exactly chatty, and her eye would be on clock and call sheet, too. 'Insists on having you deal with it. I tried to tell him, but you know some of them.'

Mina's 'tell me about it' died on her lips as the click told her the caller was through.

'Autocare Direct Motor Insurance. My name is Mina, how may I help you?'

'I'd like to make a claim, please, if that's OK.'

Funny, really: all those hundreds of callers every week, but there was something about his voice that made her remember at once. The man who didn't run over the cat.

'Shall I give you my policy number? It's JDN/0064298F. I'm Peter William Kendrick of 9, Flattery Fen, Allington, Cambridgeshire.'

Peter. That was it. The village GP.

'Please could I ask you to confirm your mother's maiden name?'

Which he did, along with the make and registration of his vehicle: the venerable Land Rover in the hard-to-describe bluey-grey colour.

'Thank you. Now I need to take the details of the accident, please.'

She heard him take a deep breath and wanted to tell him, it's all right, I remember you – if it wouldn't have sounded so silly.

'It was just now – well, about an hour ago or a bit less – in Allington Road, Histon. I'm afraid I ran into the back of another car. It was a dark red Vauxhall Vectra saloon.'

As she tapped in the particulars, he seemed to relax a little, until they came to the point. 'Now, please could you tell me how the collision occurred, exactly?'

'Well, as I say, I didn't manage to stop in time and ran into the back of the car in front. I had the kids in the back, you see. My two girls, they're nine. I may have been distracted.'

He wouldn't be able to hear her smiling, of course. He stumbled on.

'We had been playing a, er, guessing game. It might have broken my concentration for a moment.'

Finally taking pity on him, she grinned. 'No cat this time, then?'

The laugh – how had she forgotten about the laugh?

'Actually, don't tell anyone, but we were playing charades. *The Tiger Who Came to Tea.*'

'So, is it just the three of you, then?' Mina really had no idea what made her suddenly go off-script. Put it down to impulse, she supposed.

'In the car? Yes, like I said, it was just me and Cassie and Kim. My daughters, you know.'

'No. I meant, um, in the household.'

She was never impulsive – especially not at work.

'Oh, I see.' Though he didn't sound at all certain that he did. 'Well, yes, it's just us. And Olivia.'

Oh yes, the posh wife with the Renault Clio. Italian shoes, probably, and little drifty silk suits. Nothing from Top Shop or River Island.

'Mostly she gets called Ollie. Just as well, in a way; in fact, I suppose really it ought to be Oliver.'

What?

'It was when she went in for her operation. To be sterilised – a hysterectomy, you know. They found there wasn't a womb to remove; what they'd thought were ovaries were really undescended testicles.'

Mina's mind cartwheeled.

'A friend of mine wanted to write it up. An article all about her – in the *Cambridge Journal of Veterinary Medicine.*'

Veterinary? *Ah.* Light dawned, and with it some relief.

'He says I'm the only person on record with a hermaphrodite spaniel. Always asking "How's Tootsie?" at college dinners. Finds it hilarious.'

She was tempted to agree with his vet friend but the call-waiting light was winking madly already. Back to business.

'That's fine then, about today's accident. If you can just complete and return the paper form when it arrives with you.'

'Another artist's impression?'

'That's right. And two estimates for the cost of repair, as before, if that's OK.'

'Will do.'

Scrolling up and down the form to check that she had everything she needed, she reached the section on past claims. The computer threw up a tag to show that he had a protected no claims bonus, so there would normally have been no need to go into his history beyond the immediate two-year period displayed automatically on screen. But this was his second claim in as many months. It obliged her to dig a little further.

'Because there have been these two incidents so close together,

I'm afraid I'm going to have to ask you a few more questions, if you don't mind. About any previous claims. Everything in the last five years.'

Was that a momentary hesitation at the other end? Then he asked, 'Why?'

'Purely routine. It relates to your no claims bonus. You see—'

'But I thought I had a protected bonus? Don't I?'

'Yes, but when there is more than one claim on the policy within a six-month period—'

'Look, it's OK.'

'No more claims in the five-year period, you mean?'

'No, I mean it's OK. Don't bother.'

This bemused her completely. 'Don't bother with what?'

'About the bonus. I don't mind losing it, honestly. I'll just pay the higher premium. Forget it.'

She was still wondering quite how to respond when he seemed to remember himself, added, 'Thanks, anyway,' and was gone.

There were a number of reasons why, at the end of her shift when Mina completed and logged her 186th call, she did not immediately shut down her terminal in accordance with her usual habit. For a start, Sal was at Mum's again and had been promised toad in the hole for tea; it was also the day they changed their library books at school, so she would frankly hardly notice whether her mother appeared or not much before six o'clock. The second thing was that Peter had bothered to ask for her when he rang in; more remarkably, this meant he must have remembered her name. It was the novelty more than anything: anonymity was a fact of call-centre life. The least she could do in return was to save him a few quid on his next premium, if she possibly could. And also, if she was honest with herself, there was more than a small dollop of curiosity in there, too. There he had been one minute, chatting away about charades and transsexual dogs, and the next he was cutting her off in mid-sentence. Not that there was anything unusual in itself about abruptness from clients – though she had never come across one before who was so cavalier about forfeiting his no claims bonus – but it just seemed strange coming from him. Not his style, somehow. All wrong.

Mind you, she had no reason to imagine she knew what his style really was, she reminded herself as she selected 'search database'. Two five-minute telephone conversations hardly made her the expert on this man's moods. There was nothing to find, anyway. Here was his complete insurance record, since he first took out his policy with Autocare Direct in 1992. No record of any claim at all before the one she had logged herself in October this year. Not so much as a cracked windscreen. Which meant, of course, that his bonus would be fine after all; she could put a note on the form when she sent it out and save him the money. But it did make his rapid change of manner all the more inexplicable. If there was nothing he didn't want raked up, then why had he come over so uncomfortable all of a sudden, eager for nothing but to get off the phone as quickly as he could? It didn't make sense.

She had dragged her mouse down to 'log off' and was about to release the button when something made her change her mind. Going back to the database menu where the search box still contained Peter's name, she deselected 'policy holder' and clicked instead on 'named driver', then pressed 'enter'. The search took a little time, the thin blue oblong extending slowly from left to right along its track in edgy jerks. Then the box popped up. *One entry matches your search.*

The policy holder was Beverley Ann Kendrick of 9, Flattery Fen, Allington, Cambs; Peter appeared as the only other named driver. It wasn't a Clio nor a Peugeot 207 but something rather bigger and scruffier: an L reg Ford Sierra estate. The policy had come to an end more than three years ago, terminated following an accident on 18 January 2004. The Sierra had been in head-on collision with a Nissan Micra; both vehicles were written off. A note had been appended to the bottom of the file at the time of the settlement of the claim. Just three little words.

Policy holder deceased.

Chapter 6

'Good day at work, dear?'

That it wasn't a question to which Mina's mum was really expecting an answer was underlined by the clattering whizz of the hand-held electric beater that followed immediately upon her words, making conversation impossible. And in fact what was there to distinguish a good day from a bad one, generally speaking, beyond a full call sheet to please Mrs Gordon and, with luck, the absence of a headache? Break-time conversation in the coffee room was normally the only thing which varied, and that not very much.

When the Yorkshire batter was whipped free of lumps to her mother's satisfaction, the din ceased. There wasn't exactly much to tell, anyway.

'There was this caller today. A fatal accident.'

She'd handled fatals before. Usually it wasn't the spouse or parents who made the call but some other relative – son-in-law, uncle – or perhaps a stalwart friend and neighbour. Sometimes they dealt directly with the police. Still, it wasn't the first time she had spoken to a grieving partner. Not that he was exactly grieving – the accident wasn't even fresh. Three years; four, soon. Ancient history, in insurance terms at least.

'That can't be nice.'

Hands swathed in oven mitts, her mum lifted out the old Pyrex dish – larger partner of the one she'd left with Mina when she packed up to move to Dave's – and laid it on the work top, sizzling with browning sausages. She prodded them appraisingly with a fork, ensuring even spacing, before reaching for the basin of batter.

'What on earth do you say to the poor people?'

Mina shrugged, inhaling a scent of her own childhood as the slick stream of batter hit the bubbling fat. It was true: what was there you could say? And this time, in any event, she'd had no chance to say anything at all. She hadn't even known, had she, when he rang off so suddenly?

'Ready in ten minutes, then,' said her mother, hooking open the oven door with an expert foot and sliding the dish back on to the wire shelf with both hands. 'You are going to have some with us tonight, aren't you?'

'Go on, then. Thanks.'

If Sal was eating here, then she might as well, too, and Mum's toad in the hole was difficult to argue with. It's not as if she had much in the fridge at home, and Jess had not been in before nine any day this week.

'What veg shall we have with it? I've got carrots, or there's peas in the freezer.'

'Sal likes carrots. Shall I do them for you?'

'No, don't worry, love. You go and tell her it's nearly teatime.'

Only on a library day could Sal have resisted being drawn to the smell of sausages and roasting Yorkshire pud like the cartoon Bisto kid. Mina tracked her down on the landing, sitting lotus-legged on the floor with a cushion on her lap and her open book on top of it. She looked up at the sound of Mina's approach. How was it that kids' eyes actually looked bigger when they were scared or upset?

'What's the book?' She kept her voice light, upbeat.

'*Jane Eyre.*'

Probably not scared, then. 'Is it a sad bit?'

She had a vague recollection, from when she had read it at school, of a friend who died near the beginning of the book. Some palely virtuous child carried off by the fever, as generally seemed to happen to the pale and virtuous in those days. Like Beth in *Little Women*. You got so you could see it coming – but maybe Sal was too young to be that cynical yet.

'It's so *unfair!*'

Mina hunkered down next to her daughter on the landing carpet. 'What is, love?'

'Mr Brocklehurst. He makes Jane stand on a stool in front of everyone in the school and tells them she's a liar. And she has to stand there all through lessons, and nobody can talk to her for the rest of the day.' The cushion was hugged tightly to her now, her knees raised.

'Well, I guess they were much stricter in those days.'

'But all she did was drop her slate, and it was an accident, and anyway, she's not a liar, she really isn't. That's just what Mrs Reed told them, but *she's* the liar. And she wouldn't even have got any supper if Helen Burns hadn't brought her some bread.'

That was it, Helen: the saintly one, due for an early grave.

'And I bet it was her own bread and she'll go hungry – or else I bet they'll find out and she'll get in trouble for giving it to Jane.'

'Well, you'll have to wait till after tea, because Grandma says it's almost ready.'

Taking the book from her daughter's hands, she flicked through the pages before closing it. It was senior school where they'd done it. Miss Whelan's class: she must have been fourteen. Wasn't ten a bit young for some of what, as far as she could recall, came later on?

'How was school today, anyway?'

'All right.'

Events at Lowood Institution were apparently of far more pressing concern – or at least, easier to talk about.

'Come on, then.' She held out her hands and pulled Sal up by both of hers into a brief hug, though with the cushion still wedged between them. 'Go and wash your hands.'

Back in the kitchen, Mina helped her mother lay out the knives and forks. Three sets only, she noticed.

'Dave still out?'

'Yes, he's had an airport run.'

Mina nodded. The traffic was often bad at that time of day coming back from Finningley. Nobody was complaining, though; the development of Robin Hood airport had given Dave a useful occasional bonus, from holidaymakers too smart for public transport. Taking from the rich to give to the poor, he would always say, pocketing another fold of twenties.

When Sal emerged from the bathroom with dutifully clean hands she sat down next to her mother while her grandmother carried to the table the Pyrex dish, its sides now dwarfed by mountains of batter which rose in golden undulations between valleys of sausages.

'Sal? How hungry are you?'

Mum took a cooking knife and sliced into the nearest slope, releasing a soft belch of steam. Like one of those hot geysers you get where there are volcanoes, it struck Mina; but maybe that was hot water or bubbling mud, not steam, now she came to think about it. She had never paid much attention in Miss Manning's geography lessons. Sal would probably know, but she was far too busy giving her full attention to the broad wedge of toad in the hole which had just been laid before her.

'It's OK, don't wait, will you?' said Mina, leaning across to dish up the carrots and receiving only a full-cheeked grin from Sal in acknowledgement of the lapse in table manners.

'That's right, dear, you eat it while it's hot,' agreed her mum, indulgently oblivious of the crossfire.

All three ate in silence for a short while. Then Sal's grandma put down her fork, sipped her tea and announced, 'Jess was here this afternoon.'

Her voice might be neutral but Mina's stomach still plummeted, the batter she had swallowed suddenly greasily tenacious like a wet wash leather.

'Oh, yes?'

'Yes. And she had some lad with her, too, though he didn't come in. Sat outside on his motorbike, revving the engine, making the neighbours all take notice, I dare say.'

'Ed,' said Sal, spearing a carrot slice with her fork.

Both women looked at her.

'The one with the bike. He's Ed.'

'She came to try and get money off Dave, that's what I think. He says he doesn't give her any but I'm sure he does. Luckily he'd already set off for the airport.' Grimly she hewed into a sausage. 'And she knows better than to ask me.'

Mina had heard it many times before. *What has she got to spend it on, anyway? No responsibilities, no bus fares to work, she doesn't even have to feed herself.* Why did she always feel the need to defend her sister?

'Listen, Mum—'

But the older woman spoke at the same time, cutting through her words. 'I wish she wouldn't come here.'

It was more than an expression of opinion; not really a plea, even. It sounded, if anything, like an instruction.

'Dave doesn't like it,' she added, although they both knew that it wasn't really Dave at all. Mina felt helplessness overtake her.

'Look, I don't see how I can stop her, really.' I'm out at work all day. She's a grown woman. *She isn't my daughter.*

'I know,' said her mother, 'but—'

Picking up her teacup again she took a mouthful and eyed Mina over the rim. Her tone was more conciliatory but her expression was unwavering – not a look with which Mina had ever been able to argue.

'– if you could just have a word with her, that's all I'm asking.'

It was a dry night, chilly but clear, so Mina and Sal walked home after tea rather than wait for the number 27, which ran with less frequency after seven o'clock anyway. *Jane Eyre* would have to wait until bedtime. Where they left the pavements for a short way to cut up the gennel beside the newsagent's and then past the swings on the triangle of untidy grass (you really couldn't call it a park) at the back of their own street, the chemical glow from the street-lights thinned sufficiently to allow an impression of stars. It had been milder in the morning, overcast and drizzly, and neither of them had thought to bring gloves.

'Your fingers cold?' Mina asked Sal, feeling for her hand in the darkness.

'Ouch, gerroff! Not half as cold as yours, Mum. They're freezing!'

Despite her protest, Sal allowed her hand to be pulled inside her mother's coat pocket, and her fingertips gently chafed. Mina plunged her other hand deep in the opposite pocket. There, underneath her tissue and comb and the stub of this morning's bus ticket, she encountered something else. Her fingers closed around it, hugging it as if in concealment. It was the folded piece of paper on which, in breach of every rule in the Autocare Direct handbook and very likely the Data Protection Act as well, she had copied down Peter Kendrick's home telephone number.

Jeremy Fisher proclaimed the copperplate lettering on the gatepost mailbox, the ample dimensions of which allowed for returned proofs and other items which could not be accommodated by the narrow, Edwardian ironwork of the letterbox in the front door. It was not a name Jeremy had ever used professionally, of course – perhaps especially now that his output consisted largely of cockroaches. If he had ever found the jokes about his name and métier amusing, he had certainly ceased to do so long before Peter met him, nearly ten years ago now.

Peter opened the wrought-iron gate and was up the raked gravel path in two strides. It was two days since the lodging of his second insurance claim and three days until Saturday and the bonfire; it was to this that he had come to invite Jeremy and his partner, Martin. 'Partner' was Jeremy's own word; when in company, he liked to follow it with the explanatory gloss 'partners in crime' and a lascivious leer.

There was no response to Peter's knock but that was not unusual when his friend was working. For just this reason, the door was always kept with the Yale on its snib when the proprietor was at home.

'Jeremy?' called Peter, pushing open the door with its stained glass fanlight and stepping into the tall, narrow hallway.

The room at the back, which might have served others as a dining room, was where Jeremy worked, taking advantage of the unlikely amenity of north-facing French windows. Perhaps that was the reason, indeed, why he and Ruby had originally bought the house thirty years ago. For almost as long, no doubt, he had enjoyed referring to it as 'the drawing room'.

'In here,' he supplied unnecessarily as Peter entered. It was a testament to the length of their friendship, Peter chose to believe, that he did not look up from his drawing board.

'Rodney the Roach again?'

Peter moved behind Jeremy, careful not to obstruct his soft northerly light, and watched the bold, black strokes appearing. He himself would have hated to be watched – even playing Pictionary gave him stage fright – but Jeremy never seemed to mind. He drew directly in Indian ink, the image emerging from his head straight on to the cartridge paper in brisk, fluid lines.

'As you see.'

Already on the page, centre left, was a stack of filthy plates, balanced precariously on the first traces of a draining board. An apple core and an empty baked bean can topped the pile, the jagged edges of the can lid welling with wet ink like blood. To Peter's disappointment, Rodney himself was not yet in evidence. Perhaps he would be stage right, in the sink.

'You'd think a sociable cockroach could at least help out with the washing up, wouldn't you?' he observed. 'Three pairs of hands: plenty of scrubbing power.'

'He needs one pair to stand on. Besides – no opposable thumbs.'

'How does he zip up his little hoodie, then?'

It was just a stab, but he knew he had hit his mark when Jeremy finally sighed and put down his pen. 'Tea?'

There was a mug of Earl Grey cooling already, inches from his elbow. In fact, Peter had never seen him working without one; he wondered how many drawings had been lost that way over the years. Jeremy followed his gaze and raised an eyebrow. 'It's important to keep well lubricated, I always say.'

Laughing, Peter shook his head and tried to look scandalised. This man had been making Graham Norton look clean since decades before the star was even thought of.

'Come on through, I'll make a fresh pot.'

'If you're sure. I shouldn't want to interrupt.'

Actually, this was largely Peter's own guilt speaking. His afternoon working at home had been cleared with a view to making progress on his article, which had been sandbanked at the fifth paragraph more or less since the beginning of term.

'What nonsense. I can leave these dirty dishes for later, can't I?'

The irony was eloquent; Jeremy's kitchen, into which he now led Peter, was almost pathologically spotless. Even the stainless steel kettle that he filled at the tap was quite literally so. Who else in England polished their kettle?

'Actually, I came to see if you'd like to come round on Saturday? You and Martin. I'm having a bonfire and a few fireworks for Cassie and Kim, and I thought I'd do supper. Nothing fancy.'

'Ah, yes. *Al fresco* eating in November is so terribly British, isn't it?'

'Well, of course, if it's cold, we can—'

'No, no, I mean it. The mingled scents of woodsmoke, cordite and charred potato skin. Nothing like it.'

He emptied and meticulously rinsed his teapot, spooning in another measured dose of fragrant black leaves from the caddy. 'Just as long as I am not called upon to consume hamburgers.'

How much of it was an act Peter could not tell; in fact, he doubted very much whether Jeremy was quite sure himself any more. But you certainly could not picture him dining at McDonald's.

'What about Martin?' Martin was an equities analyst in the City and probably ate burgers all the time, when out from under Jeremy's maternal eye. 'Will he be able to come, too?'

61

'Why don't we pop round and ask him while the tea brews?' said Jeremy unexpectedly.

'Is he at home, then?'

Commuting by train to London meant Martin was not usually back before eight or nine, and Jeremy had barely trained him to recognise the concept of a day off.

'Laryngitis. Or a sore throat, at any rate. I rubbed him with some Vicks and wrapped him up in blankets on the sofa. Left him at three o'clock listening to *Moneybox Live*.'

Peter followed Jeremy back through the hall and out of his front door, where he stepped smartly over the low box hedge and unlocked its counterpart on the other side. Martin was not one for leaving things on the snib but Jeremy, of course, had had his own key for years. Exactly how long, even their close friends would not have cared to ask. Just as they would not ask why the two of them still chose to live next door to each other in the pair of semi-detached turn-of-the-last-century villas at the point where Flattery Fen met the High Street, five years after Ruby's death. Jeremy liked people to suppose that living in separate houses was 'cover' in rather the same way as his long, platonic marriage to Ruby had been; Peter strongly suspected that it went deeper than that, however – much like the marriage. For all his theories about creatures of the pack, it seemed that Jeremy's preference was for sleeping alone.

Perhaps it was odd, but Peter had rarely been inside this half of the building. They always did their entertaining at Jeremy's house, just as they had when Ruby was alive. Martin's hall was floored with black and white Edwardian tiles identical to those in Jeremy's next door, but here their colour gave the impression of having crept, since the date of their laying, several shades closer to a median grey; though the entranceway was free of clutter its walls were also free of any relieving mirror, print or photo, and the background odour was of footwear rather than lily of the valley. This was a bachelor hall, it struck Peter.

The sounds of Radio 4 were still emanating from the living

room as they entered. It was Professor Laurie Taylor now, his bedside manner as gently astringent to the cerebral cortex as menthol and eucalyptus to the throat. Martin was flat out under a blanket with his feet protruding, naked but for a sprinkling of very black hair.

'Hello,' he rasped. Then, unearthing an arm and waving it vaguely at the room, 'Sorry.'

'Nonsense, nonsense. Don't be silly,' said Jeremy, averting his eyes fastidiously from the wash of tissues, socks and detached pages of the *Financial Times* that spread across the floor from the sofa and adjusting the blanket to cover his lover's feet. 'We've just made a pot of tea next door. Shall I go and fetch you a cup, while Peter stays to invite you to his party?'

'Earl Grey?'

Martin's considerable forehead and what little hair still framed it emerged from beneath the blanket – his temples were lean, like his feet, but the hair here was far more grizzled – and with it a pair of suspicious blue-grey eyes. He was normally a double-espresso man; if it had to be tea, then he liked it wrung from a PG Tips bag.

'Yes, but I could stir in some honey. Honey is excellent for laryngitis, I understand. Documented antimicrobial properties – and very soothing.'

'No,' croaked the invalid. 'Thanks.'

'Well, um, I can see you don't exactly want company,' said Peter. 'But if you're both free on Saturday, that would be great. It's just a bonfire and a few fireworks for the kids, you know. Bottle of wine, something to eat. You know I'm no cook – not like Jeremy.'

This was calculated to please both of them; Martin managed a gravelly noise of approval and Jeremy positively beamed.

'Come on then, Peter, we'll leave poor Martin to his sickroom in peace and quiet, and go and see if that tea is brewed. I may even be able to offer you a Viennese chocolate sandwich.'

Jeremy could manage to make anything sound like a very

particular form of perversion. Or did he select his biscuits especially with innuendo in mind?

As all good hostesses should, Cassie and Kim were putting serious thought into the party planning. At bedtime, with Kim already tucked up and Cassie lingering on the outskirts of her sister's room in her nightie and a pair of her mother's old walking socks, they were bandying menus like a pair of rival *restaurateuses*.

'Sausages. We have to have sausages.'

'And jacket potatoes.'

Not burgers, then. That was something.

'Can we wrap them in foil and cook them in the edge of the fire like we did last year? Sophie Grimwade says they do that at Guide camp.'

'And corn on the cob. Can we have corn on the cob, Dad?'

Clearly they were determined that no finger should go unburned.

'Coleslaw is nice, to put in the bread rolls with the sausages.'

'And for pudding, that thing where you get bananas and slit them open and push in chunks of chocolate, and then cook them in their skins and the chocolate all melts inside and goes yummy. Pleeeease!'

'Toffee apples. I love toffee apples.'

'And flapjacks. We could make them for you. We're good at flapjacks.'

'Good at getting golden syrup all over the kitchen, from what I remember,' was Peter's comment. And ingesting frightening quantities of raw flapjack mix, at least in Cassie's case. 'Come on, now, it'll soon be time for lights out. Or don't you want a story tonight?'

When the allotted chapter was read and the twins closed into darkness in their separate rooms, Peter wandered back to the kitchen where his laptop was accusing him balefully from amidst the scatter of papers on the table. Promising himself he would work later, he hadn't bothered to pack away when he served up the pasties and beans which had been their tea – his as well as the children's – and now there was a spatter of tomato sauce on his photocopy of the demographic data from *Social Trends*. Worse, he spotted several flakes of pastry on his keyboard. Licking his finger, he gingerly dabbed them off, careful not to let any fall into the crevices between the keys. His space bar had once printed *fffffff* for a week following an incident with a pain au chocolat, and the keyboard had only been rescued from the tip by resourceful use of Bev's old hairdryer.

He had just sat down and clicked open the file containing the unsatisfactory beginning of his article when rescue sounded. The telephone. He leapt across to pick up.

'Hello?'

There was no immediate response. Why did he never think to answer with his name, as he would do at work? It couldn't be one of those automated sales call things, because there was no click, and the line remained live. He tried again.

'Yes? It's me. I mean, Peter Kendrick here.'

'Yes, um, hello. It's Mina Heppenstall from Autocare Direct. The motor insurance people, you know.'

A number of things about this caused Peter to be surprised. The first one was how odd it was – and somehow peculiarly reassuring – that she, of all people, should apparently experience nerves on the telephone. It was her job, wasn't it? The second thing was her surname. It was the first time he had heard it and it was so in-congruous. So robustly, ringingly Yorkshire. But of course, why shouldn't she have married a Sheffield boy – perhaps in defiance of her family's wishes, perhaps with their blessing. He pictured a city-centre register office and a white horse tied outside, garlanded with flowers. The one thing which didn't strike him was why she should be ringing him at nearly nine o'clock at night.

'Is it about my claim? Is there a problem? Some further infor-mation you need, or something?'

'N-no. At least, not exactly.' The suggestion of a pause, and then, 'It's going to be OK about your no claims bonus.'

Peter's lungs seemed to be compressed all of a sudden, making it hard to draw breath. Meena's voice came from far off, the tone professional now, making it all sound so routine, so normal.

'Claims within the last five years are not a problem if you were only a named driver on the policy and not yourself driving the vehicle.'

Dimly he registered her kindness in checking up and ringing him back. He would have liked to summon a word of thanks, but his throat was uncooperative.

'I've put it through on the computer, about keeping your bonus. Anyway, that's why I was calling, really, just to tell you that, and –'

And? He had a feeling he didn't want the 'and'. That was why he hadn't told her about it in the first place, that was why he had got off the line. Which he would do right now if he could force his hands to lay down the receiver instead of gripping it drowningly.

'– to say how sorry I am. About your wife.'

There it was. The formal sympathy of strangers, which he had spent nearly four years trying to shake off: because of all things it made him feel the finality of what had happened, casting him as the widower, the bereaved.

'About Beverley, I should say.'

'Bev.'

It was the first syllable he had managed to get out and now he wondered why he had done so. It's just that she hated Beverley; nobody ever called her that.

'Sorry, Bev. I just can't imagine . . . Sorry, that's such a stupid thing to say, isn't it? Of course I can't, nobody could. But I was thinking about your little girls, especially, I suppose. How on earth I would cope if something like that ever happened to me.'

If husband Heppenstall stepped under a bus, leaving her with nothing but his surname. Deflection was less painful, so he asked, 'Do you have kids, then?'

'Yes. I mean, just the one. Sal, my daughter – she's ten.'

Ten surprised him; Meena sounded young.

'Sal, that's nice. What's it short for?' Saleema, maybe? Saleshni?

'Sally,' came the rather abrupt reply.

Peter cringed. Oh, God, she'd think him so blinkered; as if Asian women could only call their kids by Asian names. Why wouldn't her daughter be Sally, especially as Meena had married a white guy?

'Sorry,' he said lamely, but it didn't appear to register: the apology for something inside his own head.

'How old are your two? What were their names, Carrie and Kim?'

'Cassie.' He was touched that she should have remembered – well, almost. 'They're both nine. Twins.'

He waited for the sentimental 'ah, bless' reaction that this piece of intelligence always received, especially from women. It did not come.

'Bloody 'ell. That must have been exhausting when they were babies. And now, too, of course. Poor you!'

Against all expectation, Peter found himself actually laughing. He could tell it was Meena's turn to be knocked off her stride.

'What?'

'Oh, nothing; I'm sorry. It's just that normally I get all this stuff about what a comfort it must be that I have the girls. Something remaining of Bev, I suppose; something to throw myself into – take my mind off my own loss – the arms of my loving family and all that. Nobody ever says how damned knackering it must be.'

'But it is, though, isn't it?' she said, laughing too. 'Well, actually Sal's pretty quiet, no trouble really. Never does anything wild, you know. But you still worry about them, don't you? I find myself worrying that she's *too* quiet, especially at school. Crazy, isn't it?'

'My two are great. Like your Sal, never any trouble really. Worst thing is they don't stop talking. Ever – unless they are actually asleep or eating. In fact, Kim can talk non-stop through her meals as well, but for Cassie it's a serious business, food.'

'Sal is fond of her grub, too.'

'But whatever they're like, it's as you say: impossible not to worry.'

The silence this time was easy and companionable. Until she interrupted it by volunteering, 'I'm on my own, too. With Sal, I mean.'

This ran completely against his surmises. She couldn't surely be a widow at her young age – even if she did have a ten year old? Hadn't she put it in the conditional: *if something like that ever happened to me*? But divorce didn't seem quite right either for a nice Indian girl.

Maybe she picked up on his doubts. 'It's OK, it wasn't . . . what I mean is, there was nothing dreadful like your experience. Not even a messy split-up or anything. It was always just me, all along.'

'Oh?' He really ought to say something, at least. 'Oh dear. Sorry.'

'Oh, it isn't a "sorry" thing,' she said cheerfully. 'At least, it was when it happened, I guess. I was only seventeen and it wasn't what I had in mind, exactly.'

Single and pregnant at seventeen. It was a wonder young Heppenstall hadn't been taught a good lesson by her father or uncles or brothers. Perhaps he had – but then why would she still take his name? Hardly for appearances' sake, in the circumstances. That did seem the strangest part of all.

'I've got my mum, anyway. She's always been great – babysitting and stuff, you know. And there's my kid sister, only she's more trouble than help, to be honest, but it's company, I suppose, after Sal's in bed.'

'That is the loneliest time, isn't it?' he was startled to hear himself admit.

'Well, it's been nice to chat,' she said presently. 'I hope your car will be fixed soon. And good luck, with Cassie and Kim – and, well, you know.'

'Yes, and you. With Sal and everything.'

He heard a click and the dialling tone came back, so he put down the receiver. Then picked it up again almost at once and stood uncertainly, hand hovering over the key pad. He had not really said thank you. Not properly: not for the no claims bonus, nor for all the trouble she had gone to. The documents with the Autocare Direct telephone number were at college on his desk, where he had taken them to post off once he got the estimates. Never mind – he just needed to phone caller ID. He keyed in the four digits: 1471. The number of the last caller began 01143, the Sheffield code. Jotting it down on the spiral notepad, he stared at it blankly. This wasn't the call centre; theirs was an 08-something number.

Abandoning the idea of ringing straight back, he tore off the top sheet from the pad and carried it to the table, still gazing at the number he had written there. It didn't make much sense, but it made more sense than any other explanation: Meena must have been calling him from home.

Chapter 7

The great thing about Sheffield was the hills. Not that Mina appreciated them all the time. Not when she had heavy shopping to lug all the way up to the bus stop from Morrisons because it wasn't on the route of the 27; nor when it was icy and she took her life in her hands slipping and skating down the steep gennel to the newsagent's in anything with a heel. But she had never outgrown the pleasure of taking the toboggan on the bus to Longley Park and careering headlong down its slopes whenever there was enough snow: Mum used to take her, then they'd gone with Jess and most recently it had been she and Sal.

Best of all, though, was Bonfire Night. Last year, she, Mum and Dave had taken Sal on the Supertram out to the Don Valley stadium to see the public display there. It had been good, for sure, and there was something exhilarating about watching fireworks in a crowd: the *phut* of each rocket heading skywards, followed by the brief moment of silent anticipation before the thump or crackle of the starburst and the soft, sighing release of a thousand suspended breaths. But really, what was the point when, by switching off the light and drawing the curtains round behind you like a cloak, you could enjoy your own private display from any upstairs window? For Mina, Bonfire Night meant memories of evenings in Nana's flat at Manor Top, before she died, drinking Horlicks and watching the burst and scatter of multicoloured falling stars across the city from a front row seat on the fourteenth floor. You could see as far as the moors from Nana's windows in the daytime; on Bonfire Night you could watch cascades of light from gardens and neighbourhood parks not just in Gleadless and over towards Norton but as far away as Hillsborough and Broomhill and, the other way, practically to Worksop.

The view from the house in Gladstone Road was not that good, of course, but Intake was still high-lying; the houses on their side of the street were slightly uphill from the ones opposite, which meant that from the upstairs front windows you could see over June's roof and, beyond that, down across the tiny scrap of park and the rest of the estate to a sizeable swathe of the southern suburbs. The best place for firework-watching was actually Jess's room: the one which had been Mum's, and on the odd occasion Mums' and Dave's, before she moved out and Sal got the small back room to herself.

'Why don't you ask a friend round on Saturday,' Mina had asked Sal in the week. 'We could have fish and chips and then go upstairs to see the fireworks.'

It wasn't quite so strange an invitation as it might appear. This was more than Mina's family's private pastime; everyone in Sheffield participated if they knew someone with a decent view. But Sal hadn't seemed keen.

''S all right, Mum.'

'What about that Danielle Markby? She always seems nice.'

Sue Markby worked in the greengrocer's and was always saying Sal ought to go over and play. But Sal pushed her top lip up towards her nose, producing unconvinced wrinkles.

'Nah. Just us is fine.' Then a grin as she added, 'As long as we can still have fish and chips.'

There was no Jess; by the time Mina and Sal came in from shopping and then the chippy she had finished off what was left of the loaf of bread and gone, leaving crumbs on the side and the bread-knife smeared with margarine. Mina wrapped the third portion of cod and Jess's share of the chips back up in the newspaper and put it in the oven, just on low. It was probably no more than a gesture; she would turn it off later when Sal was in the bath.

'Tell you what, let's go up now and see if any have already started. It's after six. We can eat these out of the paper for once.'

Sal gaped at her, hamming shock.

'Well, Bonfire Night counts as a special occasion.'

'That was Monday.'

'Well, you know what I mean. Nearest Saturday is always the best night. Come on – keep your coat on, I would.'

Jess's room was freezing. The council had never put in central heating and, while the gas fire in the sitting room was like an instant furnace if you turned it to high, upstairs the plug-in electric convectors never seemed to make much of an impression. Mina always switched on the one in Sal's room a good half-hour before she was ready to go to bed, and her room was small; Jess's was bigger and besides, she was hardly ever in it, except unconscious under the duvet.

She turned the heater on now and dragged it closer to the window, more for psychological comfort than for any appreciable difference it was likely to make. They didn't put the light on but the room was lit dimly orange by the street lamps. The one just up from June's front path had been broken for weeks but for their purposes tonight this was all to the good: more darkness meant a better theatre for the display.

'Two cod. And I bought us one large chips between us,' said Mina, opening the newspaper and handing her daughter the bigger of the two greaseproof packages. 'Eat what you want and then I'll finish them.'

Drawing the curtains behind them as though it were they who were on stage, they laid their fish supper on the windowsill like a snack bar counter.

'There!' Sal pointed at the first stuttering orange trace, over near the water tower at Norton. It burst tamely, a disappointing handful of greenish sparks.

Mina unfolded the oily paper from around her fish, fingers basking in the release of hot vapour. The batter was warm and brittly dry, but when she broke it open the fish inside was slick and steamy, scalding her fingertips.

'Look there.' Lower to the ground this time and closer to, a flare of fizzing white light between spiked shadows. 'Someone's having fireworks in their garden, I think.'

'Looks like a Silver Fountain,' pronounced the ten-year-old expert through a mouthful of chips. 'Hope they have some rockets later.'

Filching a chip from Sal – 'Oi! You said you'd have yours after' – 'Just trying one' – Mina felt for another piece of fish while her eyes scanned the horizon for flickers of light.

'Yeuch!'

At the side furthest away from her, both paper wrapping and fish were now coldly soggy where, forgetting, she had pushed them into the lake of condensation that occupied Jess's windowsill all winter like – what was it Miss Manning called that stuff in the Arctic – permafrost? Really, she ought to fetch a cloth. Mum used to mop the puddles from all the sills every morning, along with the moisture which beaded the cold metal of the frames themselves. That was probably why, back then, there had been no black mottling on the wallpaper in here, or on the vinyl paintwork in the bathroom.

'Over there, Mum!'

Mina followed her daughter's finger. A rocket trail stretched high into the dark space above Gleadless, slowed, bent left and seemed to peter out. They kept their eyes fixed on the place where it had disappeared and were rewarded by an audible report and a sudden flowering of red and blue, drifting and fading downwards into the night.

'Hope there's some more of those,' said Sal with satisfaction.

Mina nodded, eyeing the chips. 'You full up yet?'

'Go on, then. Share if you want.'

They munched and gazed in agreeable silence, punctuated only by sporadic exclamations as the night sky was studded with bursts of light. Maybe now would be a good moment, thought Mina.

'What about next weekend, then?'

'Hm?'

'Have a friend over. A couple of friends if you like; go shopping, maybe to Meadowhall, come back here for tea?'

Sal picked up a chip, put it down again. 'No, 's OK.'

'We could go clothes shopping. Tammy Girl and New Look; you could try on everything they've got. Fat Face, even, if you want – but only to look, not to buy.'

It didn't seem long since Sal used to beg to be allowed to go into Debenhams and try on all the hats; she always liked the outrageous feathery ones best, the ones that people buy for weddings.

'We could go, Mum.'

'But wouldn't it be more fun if you took someone along, someone from school? I'm sure they all love going round the shops, don't they?'

Sal continued to stare at the skyline.

'Or what about a film?' Mina wished she didn't sound quite so wheedling. 'I could look what they've got on at the multiplex.'

The cinema: the perfect resort of the introvert. Friends grateful to be taken, and no danger of having to talk to them.

'Look, honestly, you don't have to bother. It's fine.'

But it wasn't fine, or at least Mina didn't think so. Not that Sal ever appeared unhappy, exactly, or seemed reluctant to go to school. There were no unexplained tummy aches in the mornings or anything like that. But . . .

'But don't you ever want . . .' *To go out, hang out with your friends, have fun?* As usual, though, she had pushed too hard.

'You finish the chips, Mum. I'm full, and the fireworks aren't that brilliant this year. I'm off to have my bath.'

In Allington, Cambridgeshire, the topography of the landscape was such that nobody could sensibly hope to watch any fireworks much but their own. Since Peter had Jeremy and Martin, the twins had been allowed to invite two guests as well. The smart money had been on Shannon Mahoney and Abby Fox so the final one-two came as a surprise. Shannon, yes, but please could they ask her brother, Diarmuid?

'You've never mentioned she has a brother.'

'Well, he's not at our school.'

'He goes to the village college at Impington.'

So both the Mahoneys were there for the fireworks. Diarmuid, it turned out, was twelve. ('Older man,' mouthed Jeremy with a roll of the eyes.) Trish, who was there as everybody's friend, made up the party.

The bonfire had been assembled in the morning in a flurry of rakes and cold cheeks and laughter, and during the afternoon Kim had kept a constant watch out for hedgehogs attempting to crawl in and immolate themselves, following something Mrs Moore had mentioned at school. They were lucky with the weather; there had been nothing that could be called rain for several days, leaving the tinder as dry as could be expected in the foggy autumn fens. At six o'clock they went out with the box of kitchen matches; by ten past the smouldering leaves around the edges were just beginning to cast the occasional spurt of flame towards the nearest twigs and by quarter past a blaze was definitely established. At half past six, with everyone gathered, Peter opened the first bottle of Beaujolais and the first carton of apple juice. Glassware in a dark garden together with children, spaniel, alcohol and minor explosives seemed one hazard too many, but he drew the line at plastic cups and instead handed round the drinks in breakfast mugs.

'Dad says we're not allowed to do your thing with the lighted sticks because we're not Catholics,' announced Cassie with more than a hint of pique.

Two pairs of quizzical green eyes turned upon Peter, who shuffled in embarrassment, fiercely glad that Jeremy and Martin were in the kitchen doing something with a curd tart Jeremy had brought, and could not have heard.

'Well, it's not because of our religion, exactly – not that we have a religion, even – and of course we respect—'

But the four children had disappeared in the direction of the fire to risk scorched toes and roasted faces by 'checking on' the foil-encased potatoes.

'So what's this with the lighted sticks? Sounds fun,' said Trish, popping up at his elbow, eyes laughing across her mug of wine. 'If I can recite my catechism do I get a go? Knew there had to be something good about that sodding convent.'

He was 99 per cent certain she was ribbing him – that her comprehensive in the West Midlands had not been an RC one. He couldn't recollect the name, but he would have remembered if it had been Saint Somebody-or-other's or the Sacred Heart, wouldn't he? To be on the safe side, he dodged past it. 'Sounds more like a bit of good old-fashioned Celtic paganism to me. Which normally I'd be all in favour of – but not in my back garden, especially when I've got other people's kids on my hands.'

'Spoilsport.'

This time he knew she was joking but he still felt stung into an urge for recklessness, which it took a large swallow of Beaujolais to subdue. 'Come on, let's get the sausages sorted.'

Kim had pricked them for him earlier – a favourite task – and he had them laid out in the kitchen on the wire rack from the grill pan.

'What are you going to do with them?' asked Trish.

'Rake out some ashes at the edge of the fire and lay them across; at least, that was the plan.'

The children were leaning in the doorway, sensing the presence of food. Cassie giggled.

'What if Ollie tries to grab them, like when we had that barbecue in the summer?'

'Then she'll burn her mouth again, like she did then.' Most animals learned quickly about elementary things such as fire; not, it appeared, cocker spaniels.

'What about covering them in some foil?' Trish suggested. 'Might discourage Ol, and also stop bits of ash and stuff from falling on them.'

Jeremy peered over her shoulder at the rows of fat, pink fingers on the rack. 'Quite right, my dear. That way there is also marginally more chance that the insides will be heated above the favoured breeding temperature of the salmonella bacterium before the outsides are burned to a crisp.'

Martin, who had nothing to add to this culinary debate, contributed by finding a corkscrew and opening a second bottle of Beaujolais. His throat was much better but he judged it a wise precaution, if standing about outdoors, to keep it anaesthetised. When Peter had produced the foil and Trish had tucked up the sausages, the eight of them carried the wire tray out to the fire in procession. Peter fetched a garden spade from the shed and used the back of the blade to rake out a flat oblong of embers, on top of which he ceremonially placed the rack.

'There we are,' he said, straightening up with a grin. 'Should be cooked by Tuesday. Now, what about some fireworks?'

'Yes!' screamed three girls' voices at once. Diarmuid, from the masculine eminence of his twelve years, played it cool.

Earlier, Peter had emptied all the contents of his metal tool box on to the shed floor in order to stow the fireworks in the Blue Peter approved manner. Strange how, since being the only one, he had taken on the responsibilities of health and safety. Before, it had always been Bev, while he was the one who used to have them sliding down the banisters on cushions when she was out.

At that moment, Ollie entered busily from the direction of the lane. She had disappeared at around dusk when the first bangs were heard and had been out ever since, answering the call of imaginary guns like a retired warhorse. Olivia/Oliver was an English cocker, not American, and of East Anglian farm stock rather than show-bred, but her legs were still not quite long enough to keep her belly clear of the mud which enveloped Flattery Fen for eight months a year. Contrary to textbook theory about canine loyalty, visitors were always more of a draw than her own pack seniors, so it was towards Jeremy's legs, clad in neatly creased cream chinos, that she made first.

'Down, Ollie,' said Peter, just too late to stop a long, scattered smudge of muddy black from appearing on the hitherto pristine cotton.

'Sorry,' he added, but made no move to fetch a sponge or offer a change of trousers. Jeremy knew where the kitchen was and besides, who wore off-white slacks to a November cookout? Martin, he couldn't help but notice, was also fighting down a smile.

The kids were surrounding the tool box, discussing the relative merits of a traffic light cone and a whistling mortar to kick off the show. Peter gave his casting vote to the cone and, torch in hand, departed for the end of the garden (though keeping a safe distance from the hedge) to set it up. Slitting the adhesive tape with a thumbnail he loosed the twist of tissue paper and string and extended it upwards and to the side, away from the body of the firework. Then he placed the cone down on an even area of lawn, twisting and pressing to give it a firm toehold in the turf. Striking the match required both hands, which meant transferring the torch to his teeth. Then the first two attempts went straight out; funny how the most dully still of evenings could nevertheless produce a puff of wind when you wanted to keep a match alight. Smokers have the knack; I could ask Martin, he thought, I bet he smokes on the sly. But he persisted and the fifth match maintained its flame for long enough for him to apply it to the touch paper – disappointingly black, not blue – and retreat at a smart trot to where the others were waiting near the house, with Ollie attentive at their feet.

A fizzle, some preliminary grey smoke, and then the flare of colour began in earnest, lighting the hedge and lawn an unearthly green. Peter glanced across to enjoy the delighted absorption on the faces of his daughters, holding tightly, one apiece, to Shannon Mahoney's hands. Behind them, he was amused to see Trish looking almost as entranced. As he watched, their faces shaded from green to amber and finally to red, before fading back to their normal colour in the everyday light from the kitchen doorway. Then the girls spun round towards him.

'The whistler – the whistler next!'

After half a dozen fireworks, Cassie and Diarmuid went across to the bonfire to see how the food was doing, while Shannon and Kim tussled at the tool box over a pair of Roman candles.

'This one!'

'No, this one – it says it's a banger!'

'Banger it is, then,' Peter decided. 'What's the point of having sugar beet for neighbours if you can't make some serious noise now and again?'

He made his way back to the bottom of the garden and planted the tall blue-and-gold tube in the grass amongst the litter of spent and blackened cardboard corpses. Diarmuid and Cassie were still over by the fire, so he motioned to them to stay put and crouched down to light the fuse. His technique was almost perfected by now; he managed to grip both torch and matchbox in his left hand whilst using it as a wind break, striking the match with his right. First time! The flame took hold of the black paper twine and Peter turned to make his way back towards the house. The first three canonballs of blue blazed vertically upwards in quick succession to a height of some twenty or thirty feet, each accompanied by a satisfyingly resonant detonation.

That was when things began to go wrong. Perhaps Peter hadn't screwed the base of the Roman candle quite solidly enough into the damp ground; maybe there was simply something defective about the firework itself, some unevenness in how the propellant was packed into its cardboard casing. Either way, the next rapid volley – bang-bang-bang – sent flaming comets out diagonally at an angle of forty-five degrees to the ground, streaking out over the bonfire and lighting the faces of Diarmuid and Cassie: two surprised, uptilted masks of blue. It was the third salvo that had Peter running. The explosions were more muffled this time but the speed of discharge was undiminished, three burning blue missiles skimming the grass at ankle height, straight towards the bonfire and Cassie.

Peter ran. He ran in the opposite direction to that prescribed in the instruction leaflet: he ran towards the lighted firework. He ran fast – but Diarmuid got there first. While Cassie stood rooted by the bonfire, the boy sprang forward with the discarded spade and scooped a clod of earth over the Roman candle, which expired with a wet hiss.

Over the course of the evening, Peter had far too much to drink. Not to begin with; he hadn't wanted to have any while he still had fireworks to light. Just as well – God knows what further disasters might have befallen if he hadn't been sober. When the tool box was empty they repaired to the warmth of the kitchen, there to finish off the lukewarm sausages under the grill. He did have one glass then – or, rather, a mug, in solidarity with his guests – but only one, as he had promised to drop the Mahoneys home at nine o'clock. There wasn't much room round the kitchen table for eight but they squashed up, and Trish insisted on sitting on the pedal bin because there weren't enough chairs, even with Martin in the armchair that was much too low, and the twins sharing. The grill made short work of the sausages, and so did the children, loading them into sesame baps with piles of homemade coleslaw. Ollie's soulful begging from beneath the table had its reward. In fact, of all the party there was only Jeremy who did not fall upon the feast like a sailor on shore leave.

When everything was gone, Jeremy went to the fridge and produced his curd tart together with a spiced fruit compote and a pot of soured cream.

'I am Priscilla, you know,' he announced for the benefit of Trish, who had not heard his favourite joke before. 'Queen of the Desserts.'

That was the signal for Peter to refill his mug. Only a couple of inches. Two glasses of wine and he'd still be fine to drive; it was only the other end of the village.

'Can't they stay just a bit longer?' coaxed Kim when, a little later, he caught sight of the clock and stood up.

'I said we'd have Shannon and Diarmuid home by nine and it's already ten past.'

He knew how he would be worrying if it were him.

'Pleeease, Dad!'

'No. Come on, now. If you get your coats back on quick, you can come with me to drop them off.'

The travellers' site was past the church and the Drayman's Arms and along a bit, down a side road on the right just after the last house. A gaggle of curious dogs sniffed round the Land Rover as he unloaded the two kids and watched them run off to one of the council-provided mobile homes. Not so mobile, in fact, on their concrete blocks – merely cold and uncomfortable, he imagined. Cassie and Kim were still waving to nobody as he backed round and bumped out of the rutted cinder yard.

Their adult visitors were still happily ensconced at the table on their return. Martin was uncorking another bottle and Trish was giggling at something Jeremy had said; clearly they had no intention of leaving just because the formally billed entertainment was over.

'Come on, you two: a quick wash, then nighties and bed. You can have baths in the morning. And Martin, pour me one of those, please, would you? I think I've got some catching up to do.'

And this is what he proceeded to do, with much more application than was advisable, over the next hour and a half. He was not quite sure how much he had had – it was hard to quantify wine in fractions of a mugful – but he knew that he had fetched quite a number of bottles of red from the rack in the laundry room, including a nice Saint-Emilion he had intended to save for Christmas, and he suspected that only Martin was anywhere near to keeping pace with him.

He also knew that when he got to his feet to say goodbye to Jeremy and Martin he needed the edge of the table to steady himself, and that his voice came out sounding louder and more convivial than it was supposed to. When they had gone, he sat down again opposite Trish and grinned.

'Sorry. Lot to drink.'

Actually, perhaps Trish was a little drunk, too, it occurred to him, because she was still perched on the bin.

'Not used to it these days,' he went on. In fact it was ridiculous, really, how little he ever drank any more. 'You know, after Bev— after it happened, to begin with I never used to have a drink at all, even when Kim and Cassie were in bed. I suppose it was in case anything happened, and there was only me here and I wasn't on the ball, to get the doctor or drive them to hospital or whatever.'

She nodded. 'Makes sense.'

But he shook his head. 'Not really. I think it was almost super-stitious, to be honest. Because there'd been plenty of nights before when we'd both been legless and we hadn't worried at all.'

They laughed – companionably, though neither was quite sure at what – and Peter slopped some more wine into both their mugs.

'So no chance of a lift home tonight, then.'

His laughter dried at once. 'God, sorry, Trish.'

He slid his replenished mug guiltily away from him. As if one more or less might make a difference now.

'Just kidding, you twit. I was going to get a bus, but I think I've missed the last one, haven't I?'

Twenty past eleven, said his watch.

'Afraid so; the last one goes at five to. Why don't I call a cab? When you want to go, I mean – don't want to shove you out or anything. I'll pay.'

'But last time it was more than a tenner. It seems an awful lot of money. Why don't I just stay over, like I did that other time? Blanket on the sofa'll be fine. Honestly,' she added with a winning smile, 'you won't even know I'm here.'

He thought that most unlikely – nobody could ever fail to notice Trish's presence – but was too fuddled to argue. Besides, he would rather not be alone with reality just yet: getting his boots on to take Ollie out and drinking pints of cold water and locking up. 'Well, I suppose it is Sunday in the morning.'

'You mean, the library isn't open, so I won't have to be there at eight forty-five a.m. on the dot, double-checking my references?'

She was teasing him again, he knew, but his sluggish brain would supply no appropriate comeback.

'Speaking of sofas,' he said instead, 'it's not the most comfortable in here. Unless you are particularly attached to that bin?'

So, giggling, they stumbled into the living room with their mugs, Peter clutching the final bottle of red, and collapsed together on the sofa.

Presently, Trish raised her nose from her mug and pronounced judgement. 'He's very beautiful, that gypsy child.'

There didn't seem any very sensible reply to this, so Peter kept quiet and took another sip of wine.

'I know we're supposed to say "traveller", and probably "gypsy" is the wrong word anyway, because I don't know if they are Romany as well as Irish. Can you be both?'

He probably ought to know the answer to that, since he was a geographer and they lived in his village, but he didn't, or at least if he knew usually he didn't know now.

'But he looks like a gypsy, somehow. They are both very striking, him and Shannon. With those green eyes and freckles you'd expect sandy hair, and then instead they have that shock of black. But Diarmuid – he's beautiful.'

Was Trish as tipsy as he was? She'd always had a slightly fanciful, romantic streak; it had not been especially helpful, at times, in the construction of her research hypotheses. But was she really waxing lyrical over a twelve-year-old boy with shamrock eyes? He ought to rib her about it, but before he could summon any words, she was saying something that didn't seem so funny. Not so funny at all.

'Your girls are going to be in trouble there, I can see.'

In trouble? What on earth was she implying? This was Cassie and Kim. 'They're nine!'

The indignation in his voice sounded so disproportionate that he found himself grinning with her, in spite of himself. But through the laughter she was shaking her head at him. 'It's a serious business, you know, being nine. Things matter.'

His stomach lurched. As if he needed to be told that. No hardened protective layers yet – every sling and arrow hitting straight home. Every loss, every memory – however much he might try to cocoon them. Tears, alcohol-induced, were not far behind his eyes. She looked at him, held his gaze; she seemed to know the ground had shifted.

'It's OK. They'll be OK.'

For a short, mad moment he wanted to take hold of her hand. Between the open neck of her fleece and the turquoise wool of the scarf she hadn't taken off was a triangle of female skin. He let his fingertips imagine its warmth. *It would be good, it would be very good . . .*

But she wasn't Bev. Even if he hadn't been her supervisor. And anyway, the teasing was already back in her eyes.

'I still say it: that boy is bloody beautiful.'

Chapter 8

'Fancy a cuppa, sweetheart?'

Mina had a cold. It wasn't, unfortunately, a full-blown stay-off-work cold that registered on the thermometer and left you too croaky to speak to callers. Bad enough, though, not to want to venture out in the teeming November rain on a day when you didn't absolutely have to. So on Saturday afternoon Mum had taken Sal into town while Mina rested up at Dave's house. At least, she'd been hoping to rest up.

'Because if so, make me one as well, would you?'

He was only joking, though. Dave wasn't one of those men who expected to be waited on hand and foot. Mum did nearly all the cooking, it was true, but Mum loved to cook and tended to get edgy if anyone else went in her kitchen. Dave made a lovely cup of tea – he left the tea bag in long enough, which most of the blokes Mina had come across lacked the patience to do – and he also didn't think he was the only one who was ever allowed to be ill.

He clicked on the kettle, no doubt still warm from their last brew. 'Tea again? Or would you rather have a Lemsip? I dare say your mum's got some in the bathroom cabinet.'

Funny how men didn't seem to mind their space being taken over, thought Mina. It had been Dave's bathroom cabinet until three years ago; now he had no real idea what was in it.

'Tea is great. Thanks.'

'Wonder how they're getting on.'

As far as Dave was concerned, Mina knew, being dragged round the shops in the city centre, particularly on a weekend, rated somewhere alongside having his root canals done. With the Mondeo off the road again while he waited for a part to be delivered, he might well have been in the firing line; she'd seen his look of relief when Sal was invited to stand in. If he had to lose a valuable Saturday of wet and laden shoppers, she guessed he was at least happy to be allowed to spend it kicking around at home.

'Probably in the library by now.' Mina grinned.

It was a family joke. You might set off intending to look for shoes or take your jacket to the dry cleaner but, with Sal along, within the hour you always ended up at the public library. The way other kids might drag you to the sweet shop – or, at Sal's age, to HMV.

'At least they'll be dry in there. And your mum can't be using her credit card.'

He brought the tea over to the kitchen table and sat down next to her.

'Are you finished with the paper?' he asked, and by way of answer she flipped the *Mirror* closed and pushed it his way. 'Wednesday are away at Stoke,' he added.

It was more of an apology for taking away the newspaper than anything else; the minicab meant he hadn't been able to get to a game in all the time she'd known him, home or away. She knew he still liked to check the team line-up on a Saturday, though. A masculine preserve, perhaps, against female colonisation; like singing 'Delilah' while he shaved. The tea was strong and scalding and sweet. Mum always put one of her own sweeteners in Mina's drinks but Dave knew she preferred sugar, and liked two. Closing her mouth, she inhaled the smoky vapour as best she could through her blocked-up nasal passages, feeling the warmth rise right up to behind her eyes, making them stream pleasurably.

'Dave?'

Probably it wasn't the right moment, but it was so rare to get him to herself like this. Without Mum.

'Hmm?' He was still scanning the afternoon's other fixtures.

'I was wondering, what about if you and Mum came round to ours for Christmas this year?'

His eyes remained on the sports pages but she could tell he wasn't seeing them any more. He was just avoiding looking at her.

'Well, you know, lass,' he said slowly, 'your mum does like cooking. Where would she be without her Christmas dinner to do?'

She'd thought of that one, of course. 'Well, she could cook it at ours, couldn't she? We could do the shopping together beforehand, get the turkey and everything, and then she could be in charge and Sal and I could just peel the potatoes and parsnips like we normally do.'

Mum wouldn't exactly be able to make the excuse about working in a strange kitchen. It had been her own for the best part of twenty-five years, even if she rarely set foot in the place these days. It always had to be her and Sal over at Mum and Dave's – like today, for instance.

'The big roasting pan is here.'

Mina peered at him suspiciously through the steam from her tea. What did Dave know about roasting pans? Or had Mum already been talking to him about it, priming him with all the reasons against having Christmas elsewhere but here?

'And the double steamer for the pudding.'

'Dave!'

He looked up sheepishly, then shrugged and smiled. 'Look, I just don't think you'll persuade her, love, that's all.'

What about you, though? You might. She had hoped for an ally in this, but it appeared that Dave was set to remain carefully neutral.

'Well, then' – it would do no good but she had to ask anyway – 'in that case, what about if Jess came here with us?'

Because they both knew, didn't they, that Jess was what it was all about? Jess was the reason why Mum wouldn't come round to Mina's on Christmas Day, or pretty well any other day, come to that. Dave was staring down at the *Mirror* again but Mina wasn't letting it go that easily.

'Just for her dinner, at least?'

He fiddled with the corner of the back page, his tea cooling unnoticed.

'It's not that she isn't welcome,' he said at last. 'It's only, well, you know how they argue when she's here.'

Dave always just wanted a peaceful life.

'And Christmas is . . . Look, feelings can run high, can't they? Especially if Jess has a few drinks. You know what she's like.'

Yes, Mina knew very well what she was like. She'd heard her stumble in blind drunk; she'd heard her shout and storm and hurl things. But Jess was seventeen, and Mum was her mum, too, and Christmas was Christmas.

The grogginess of cold swept back over her suddenly, depriving her of energy for the fight. Sighing, she pulled another tissue from the box of mansize on the table, blowing her red nose and making it redder. She wondered if Mum would have remembered to get her some of the balsam ones in town.

'Well, maybe if you just mentioned it some time, anyway.'

Dave gave her a look of rather non-committal sympathy. 'Do you want a top-up, love?'

Peter sat in the Drayman's Arms two evenings later contemplating the pint that Rex had pulled for him. The bouquet was free of unwanted soapy notes, but for some reason the beer had not cleared as it usually did once the initial swirlings had subsided, instead retaining an opaque, slightly muddy appearance. He risked a cautious sip. It tasted all right so he took a longer draught and tried to put it out of his mind.

Trish was babysitting again, this time for a purpose: he was having a drink with Jeremy and Martin. Actually, not yet he wasn't, because neither of them was here, even though it was ten past the hour appointed for their rendezvous. He was starting to half wish he had brought some essays with him again when the door of the lounge bar opened and in walked Martin. Alone.

'Sorry, mate. Jeremy was very apologetic. Had some drawings he's absolutely got to finish – tonight without fail. Going to courier them first thing. He'll be along later if he can, but he told me to come anyway. Didn't want to think of you waiting here by yourself. I said you'd be OK, you'd got your beer, but you know Jeremy. I'm better out of his hair. You ready for another?'

'No, no, let me get them. IPA, is it?'

'Not a lot of option round here.'

Martin hadn't bothered to lower his voice; Peter glanced at Rex but he was down the other end of the bar, polishing the redundant guest pump. Peter attracted his attention with a folded five pound note.

'Two pints, please, Rex.'

They took their seats near the fireplace. This time both pints cleared to approximately midway down the glass, but remained sludgy below. If he held it very still, Peter decided, he ought to be able to drink almost half a pint without disturbing whatever inhabited the murky depths.

'Work OK?' inquired Martin presently, after a lengthy swallow of bitter.

'Not so bad. You?'

It was going to be a long evening, if this was the best they could manage. It occurred to Peter that, although he had sat at this table on many occasions with Martin, he had never done so when Jeremy was not also present. Not that they weren't both his friends, but it was Jeremy who had first engaged him in conversation at the gate; he was the loquacious one, the inviter of confidences. Martin was the one who usually rushed in late, straight out of a taxi from Waterbeach station, still in his City suit, and drank more than he talked.

'What are you two doing for Christmas?' Peter asked suddenly, for something to say and with no particular direction in view.

'Think Jeremy said something about doing a brace of grouse. Reckons you can get them on the Internet.'

Peter laughed. 'That wasn't really what I meant.'

It answered his question anyway. Two grouse would not exactly serve a party; it meant Christmas at home *à deux*. Martin grinned back at him. 'Sorry – got you now. Just us. What about you and the kids?'

Something about Martin's staccato style of speech was apparently infectious. 'Same. Just us.'

Just us. Only after the words were out did the discomfort of it become apparent to him, hanging around their table like unwanted cigarette smoke. The pain that Christmas always brought. Not so much for the girls, whose memories were short – or rather were triggered by smaller, less external things. They had not yet acquired the adult habit of measuring loss in months and years. But for him, this Christmas would simply be his fourth without Bev.

Martin drank some more beer, lifted his glass to the light, placed it back on the table with a frown and then surprised Peter by asking, 'Is it four years now? Since.'

Peter glanced up at him, then down again at his pint. 'That's right. Four years in January, in fact.'

January 18. The most painful thing was actually thinking about the Christmas before, the one when they were all together, squabbling about nothing and not appreciating the happiness that was only to last another three and a half weeks.

'It'll be Jeremy's fourth, too.'

This way of putting it struck Peter as a little sad. Was it awkwardness, denial, or simply selflessness which made the loss all his lover's and not his own?

'Ruby died in September, though.'

'Yes.' Of course he remembered the funeral. Back at the crematorium only eight months after Bev, the grounds red and gold in their late summer bedding plants instead of trimly white with frost.

Wearing again the plain silk tie that Jeremy had bought him for Bev's.

'But I don't suppose that makes it any easier. Christmas, that is. I mean, there is always something, isn't there . . .' He wasn't expressing this very well. The way illness and death were always punctuated by Christmases, birthdays, holidays. 'You know: the last Christmas before she was diagnosed and the first one after; the one when you persuaded the doctors to let her come home from hospital for the day . . .'

Peter tailed off, wondering if he was embarrassing the other man. Martin's eyes were on the table but slowly he nodded. 'We'd made such an effort. For her. Especially that last time, as you say. Then the next year, Jeremy didn't want to bother at all. Not even cooking, which wasn't like him. Not worth it, he said, just for us.'

It was the longest and most personal speech he had ever heard Martin make and after it they were both a little awkward, resorting each to his beer. What was remarkable, thought Peter, was how free of resentment his words had been. Not to be worth cooking for cannot have been easy.

'I suppose it's different when you've got kids,' he said.

Not, perhaps, the most tactful observation in the circumstances, but it was true none the less. No chance of getting away without tree, stockings, crackers, turkey and all the works with two young children in the house – much as he might have been tempted to skip it all that first year. Cassie and Kim were his reasons to be cheerful; or, if he couldn't manage that, then at least to pretend to be.

God, what *was* in this beer of Rex's? It seemed to be making both of them most uncharacteristically maudlin. He was fine on his own with the twins; most of the time he was perfectly happy. Wasn't he?

'Must be bloody tough, though.'

Odd, that was the second time somebody had said more or less the same thing to him recently – instead of the platitudes about comfort and having something left to live for. For a moment he was puzzled, unable to place the recollection, before he remembered it had been Meena, the car insurance woman.

He shrugged, then chose to turn it into laughter. 'Complete nightmare! You must know – you've met them!'

Martin relaxed back into his more accustomed mode. 'They're lovely kids. But even so, rather you than me, mate.'

He raised his glass as if in salute, then turned it to and fro, eyeing its clouded contents in distaste. 'What on earth is wrong with this diabolical beer?'

Mina was aware before her conscious mind began to surface, aware before the click that always preceded the first electronic beep of her alarm clock announcing seven a.m. Even in her sleep, she had known it: Jess hadn't come home. It wasn't that she stayed awake until she heard the front door; she wasn't the girl's mother, for goodness' sake. But it was still there somewhere in her unconscious. She just knew.

Nevertheless, she dragged herself up, into her dressing gown, along the landing and into the front bedroom, even before checking in on Sal. Maybe she was wrong; maybe she had slept more deeply than she knew and had missed Jess's creeping return in the small hours. But of course she was not wrong. The bed was empty, unslept in, the bedclothes still flung in the same confusion as the day before. The curtains were open, the lake of condensation on the windowsill not noticeably less for having had no warm body breathing in the room all night. Mina picked her way to the window and looked out, as if half expecting to see her sister walking up the path. It was frosty out. Absent-mindedly she mopped at the pool of water with her sleeve and regretted it at once. She was also suddenly conscious of having very cold feet – she should have thought to put on her slippers.

Wake Sal up first, though, she thought. That way she could get straight into socks and jeans when she was back in her own room.

She needed the reassurance of at least feeling one hot, sleepy form in her arms. But it was stupid to worry, she told herself. It wasn't the first time Jess had been out all night. It was easy to remember, in fact, that very first occasion. It was before Mum left; Jess was only thirteen and she'd slammed out and stayed over at a friend's house after a blazing row. They'd known where she was, that time. And on the odd night in the last couple of years when she hadn't come back, Mina had also had a fair idea of where she was or at least who she was with. Round at that boy Joe's flat, more than once, back in the spring. And with Todd, when she was sixteen, and Kiernan, before that. But these days there didn't seem to be anyone – or not anyone in particular, at least, not since Dari. Sean, then Lewis, then Ed with the motorbike, but none of them serious; none of them had been round to the house more than about twice. Mina had no idea where they lived or even what their surnames were. It wasn't a pleasant thought, but Jess could be pretty well anywhere – with anyone.

Sal was stirring already when she went in, knocking first as she had begun to do recently, more or less as a joke. She couldn't have been properly awake, though, because her reading light was off and her book still lay closed on the floor beside her bed.

'Morning, love.'

Mina knelt down and felt for her daughter in the semi-darkness, drawing her into their customary hug through the bedclothes.

'Tuesday,' said Sal. 'Music, and indoor PE in the afternoon.'

It was a habit she had, this pinning down of her day when she woke up. It went back to when Mina used to say it to her when, at three or four, she was still trying to fix the days of the week in her mind. 'Wednesday, play group this afternoon,' she used to announce, or 'Sunday, lunch at Nana's.' Now it seemed more like Sal's way of having things under control. There certainly wasn't a lot of joyful anticipation about it, most mornings.

'Is it music with Mrs MacLeod in the studio this week, or just normal singing in class with Mrs Edwards?'

'Studio. With the instruments.'

'Hope you get to go on the chime bars, then.'

The chime bars had always been Sal's favourite, that or the tambourine – or in fact almost anything except the despised triangle – but there was no response now. Maybe she was too old to mind about such things.

'Jess is still out.' Mina strove to make it sound ordinary, conversational, matter-of-fact. She was quite pleased with how her voice came out, but Sal was on the alert at once; Mina could feel her tension under the duvet.

'Out where?'

That was the question she had desperately not wanted to be asked. Not only in order to shield Sal from the terrifying admission that, actually, she had no idea, but also because she had been nursing a slim hope that her daughter might have some clue to the answer.

'With a friend somewhere, I'm sure. You know what she's like. She'll be fine.'

The duvet didn't move, so she added, not at all sure she believed it, 'She's a grown-up, you know.'

Dressed and downstairs first, Mina picked up the phone and dialled Jess's mobile, but it was switched off. Mind you, of course it was, at that hour of the morning – Jess never spoke to anybody much before noon if she could help it, on the phone or otherwise.

When they had finished their Cheerios and toast and jam, Mina sent Sal up to clean her teeth and sat down again at the table to write a note.

Jess, hi. Are you OK?

Stupid thing to put. If she was home and reading the note then, yes, chances were she was OK. She tore another sheet of paper off the notepad. Jess hated being fussed over, more than anything.

Jess, hi. There's bread in the bread bin – don't leave the marge out. Call me at work, could you? M.

Propping it by the kettle where it was sure to be seen, Mina had begun to clear the breakfast plates before she had second thoughts, returned to the note and added a PS.

On my mobile, not the work number!

She didn't ring. Not all morning, even though Mina checked her mobile messages frequently between callers, whenever Mrs Gordon wasn't looking. It didn't mean a thing, though, did it? It was exactly like Jess to forget or just not bother. Or maybe the business about the margarine had annoyed her, or the reminder about not ringing on the Autocare line. At break time in the coffee room, Mina called Jess's mobile again. It was still set to voicemail; she hesitated on the verge of saying 'call me' but decided against it. Instead she phoned the house. No reply. Well, Jess was probably asleep. That would be it: she'd come home and gone straight to bed, after being up doing God knows what all night.

In her lunch break she tried both numbers again, with no better luck. But it was the daytime, anyway. She never normally knew where Jess was in the daytime from one week to the next, so why should she worry today? Then her shift was over and it was time to go and pick up Sal, who really was her concern. Something legitimate to worry about, like the three words she managed to wring out of her about school, on the bus.

'Was music fun?'

''S OK.'

'What instrument did you get to play?'

'Didn't do that. Just singing and clapping rhythms and stuff.'

'Was it that "human drum kit" song that you like?'

'No. Some new one. What's for tea?'

What she really wanted to know, she knew she couldn't ask. *What did you do at playtime? Who did you hang out with? Did anyone play with you, chat to you?*

At home, opening the front door, she resisted the urge to call out Jess's name. Sal hadn't asked if she'd rung; Mina chose to believe that was because she wasn't worrying, so didn't want to start her off. She didn't even glance at the stairs up to Jess's bedroom, just made herself walk into the kitchen and put down her carrier bag of groceries as she always did, reaching for the kettle to fill. The note was still propped against it but – oh, wonderful relief – there were crumbs on the work top. She couldn't ever have imagined being so pleased to see the tub of margarine left out, or its lid off.

Now that it was OK, she did go to the stairs and yell up, 'Jess? Where are you? Where've you been?'

Nothing – only, after a moment, Sal's face appearing over the banisters from where she'd been putting her bag in her room. 'She's not here, Mum.'

Been back home and gone out again – well, there was nothing wrong with that. It didn't have to mean she'd be late again tonight. She tried not to admit the next, inevitable thought: *or stay out again.*

By the time Mina had unpacked the shopping, washed her hands and put some chicken drumsticks under the grill, Sal was back in the kitchen and installed at the table with her book. Mina wasn't sure what it was – she had asked and thought she remembered Diamond something and that it was a whodunnit; it meant nothing to her – but whatever it was, it made Sal laugh and the sound was very welcome.

'Keep an eye on these, will you, I'm just nipping to the loo.'

'Sure,' said Sal, though Mina doubted she would be able to tell you what she had just agreed to.

In the bathroom, Mina's eyes slid to the tooth rack where Jess's green toothbrush was in the rack with Sal's red one and her own blue. She might have changed her clothes but she evidently hadn't packed a bag. Ought Mina to be relieved about this? Probably – but Jess had been out without a toothbrush last night and frankly that possibility seemed worse.

There was no time to linger, or to check Jess's bedroom, in case the drumsticks were burning downstairs under her daughter's oblivious nose. They weren't too bad, in fact, though more than due for turning, and before she slid them back under the heat she splashed on some Lea & Perrins, the way Sal liked them. Damn – she had forgotten to boil the kettle for the veg. What was quick? Sliced green beans from the freezer, and she could open a tin of sweetcorn if there was one left in the cupboard. Before her hand reached the handle to look, the telephone rang. *Jess.*

She was across the kitchen and picking up in a second, mind spilling over with all the questions she must not allow out in a flood of blame, so that she was genuinely confused for a moment when the voice on the other end – male and nicely spoken – said tentatively, 'Oh, hello, is that Meena?'

Before she could tell him it was, he had hurried on and a smile was soon creeping into the muscles of her cheeks.

'Look, I really hope you won't mind my calling you at home. In fact, I hope you won't be annoyed that I have your number, because you didn't actually give it to me, I just did the 1471 thing. I'm really not some kind of mad stalker or anything – honestly, I'm not – but after you were kind enough to ring me about my no claims – well, you know, it occurred to me I hadn't really properly thanked you.'

It was funny: something about his diffidence gave her confidence. 'Go on then.'

'Go on what?'

'Thank me. You said that's why you've rung.'

'Is it Jess?' asked Sal through his awkward silence.

'No,' she replied shortly, left hand cupped over the receiver.

'Yes, right, thank you, then,' said Peter Kendrick in her right ear. 'I mean it – it was really good of you. I know you needn't have called, so I really appreciated it, especially when I realised you'd rung from home on your own time.'

Sal was still looking over at her, mildly curious. 'Who is it then, if it's not Jess? Not that Murray?'

'Nobody.'

'Sorry?' said Peter.

'Oh, no, my fault – I was just talking to my daughter.'

'Sal,' he said. It was sweet that he had remembered. 'My two are just in the living room, playing Scrabble. They make half the words up, but they'll allow anything if they can convince the other one it has some mad meaning. They do say, don't they, about twins having their own language. Not sure this is quite what they mean, though.'

'Are they identical?'

'As opposed to fraternal, yes. As opposed to individual and distinctive, certainly not.'

It had the sound of a stock answer he always gave, but the laughter in his voice made her not mind. Kim and . . . was it Carrie or Cassie? She knew she'd picked the wrong one last time, but which had that been? There was a way out of the difficulty, though.

'Are your girls' names short for something?'

'Well, Kim isn't. She's not a Kimberley or anything like that. Cassie, I have to admit, is really Cassandra. Bev's choice, not mine – though I always liked the sound of Cassie by itself all right.'

'They're both very pretty names.'

How lame was that? But he didn't seem bothered by swapping these inconsequential nothings. He was just as bad, in fact.

'And Meena, is that an abbreviation of a longer name?'

'Wilhelmina, I suppose, strictly, according to my birth certificate. But I've never been anything but Mina.'

This provoked not only a prolonged pause but actually what sounded suspiciously like a muffled groan of anguish. OK, so it was a pretty stupid name – there had been plenty of piss-taking at school – but this did seem a rather extreme reaction.

'It's a long story,' she explained. 'There were a few complications when I was born and Mum had to stay in hospital a while, so she sent my father to register the birth. He wasn't even still living with us but he did visit and asked what he could do. Mum wanted me to be Sarah Marie but he must have had some kind of rush to the head. "Could never be trusted to do anything right, that man,"

Mum used to say afterwards. Anyway, it seems he had been reading *Dracula* – the actual novel, you know, the old Victorian one – and there's a girl in it called Mina.'

Sal, who had heard the story many times before, rolled her eyes and continued to read. The phone line still vibrated with silence, so Mina pressed on as brightly as she could.

'He was always reading. According to Mum: I never met him, myself, or not since I was old enough to remember. Nose never out of a book, she says. I always think that's where my Sal gets it from, because she's exactly the same.'

In fact, the scent of scorching Worcestershire sauce had temporarily drawn Sal away from her paperback and over to the grill, where she was saving the chicken from further blackening, turning off the heat and depositing the grill pan on the cooker top before going back to the table with a long-suffering sigh.

Finally, Peter spoke, and his voice sounded odd, almost as though he was laughing again. 'I had imagined it as Meena with a double "e", not Mina with an "i".'

'Oh, right. Like the Indian name, do you mean?'

This time the laughter was definite. Not at her, though, she didn't think – it didn't feel as if he was laughing at her. 'That's right.'

'Well, I must say there's not many white families round here would have thought to call their kids by an Indian name back in those days. Or even now, come to that.'

'No. I should imagine not.'

Then he seemed to pull himself together a bit. 'I wish my two would read more. Trouble is, I suppose, that reading tends to be a solitary activity. Except reading aloud, of course. But it's mostly a thing for when you're on your own, isn't it, and twins don't tend to be alone very often.'

'I guess not.'

'Whereas with Sal being an only child, I imagine she has more time by herself to fill with books? I was like that; no brothers and sisters, so I had no choice but to read.'

If she read less she might be alone less. She couldn't say this, of course, with Sal just across the room.

'Mum,' she said now, turning her book upside down on the table.

'And what about you?' asked Peter. 'I think you mentioned your sister is quite a bit younger?'

'Mum, do you want me to put some veg on or what?'

'In a minute.'

'Sorry?' he said.

'Nothing, just Sal again. Look, do you mind? I think I need to sort out Sal's tea before she starts eating the curtains.'

'Oh God, yes, of course. Sorry.'

He sounded thoroughly rebuked – sort of crestfallen. It was probably mostly to spare his feelings, therefore, that she added hastily, 'But it was very nice to chat again.'

'Me, too. I mean, I thought it was nice, too.'

'And thank you for phoning to say thank you.'

The click as she replaced the receiver cut short his laugh and she was glad to get her face into the freezer compartment to cool the pink and hide her grin from Sal. She put the green beans on to boil and then turned round to where Sal was examining the drumsticks like a dahlia fancier assessing a greenfly outbreak.

'What do you reckon?' asked Mina. 'Have them half cold, or burn them some more?'

Chapter 9

'Dad, Cassie says Diarmuid Mahoney saved her life. But he didn't, did he? Tell her he didn't save her life.'

The three of them were in the living room at home, where they had been detained for most of that Sunday afternoon by incessant, driving December rain. In fact four of them, because in this weather even Ollie ventured little out of doors. Down the lane past the cottage there was nothing much above the height of a beet top this side of Ely to break the path of the wind, which therefore sent the rain veering to the horizontal whenever it blew from the east. It had a tendency to get under Ollie's ears and she didn't like it.

'Dad, Diarmuid didn't really save Cassie's—'

'No, of course he didn't, love. Get off there, Ol.'

Peter prodded the dog gently under the ribcage with one foot, easing her away from the sofa. Ollie's sexual preferences, having been weaned away from the human ankle at an early stage of development, had subsequently fixed more or less exclusively upon soft furnishings. This at least had the virtue of rendering less important the confusion about her gender identity. Sexual ambivalence was of no concern to a sofa cushion.

'Told you, Cassie.'

'But he put out the firework, didn't he? It was banging like anything and zooming straight for me and he put it out.'

'Ooo, were you scared, then?'

A brief tussle ensued on the sofa, on top of which Ollie attempted to climb, tail wagging approvingly.

'Stop it, all of you.'

Peter's best dog-training-class voice had the rare effect of cowing, at least momentarily, both spaniel and daughters.

'Look, fireworks are dangerous, and it just shows how careful you have to be with them, because it's easy for something like that to happen, however careful you are. And Diarmuid was certainly extremely brave. We should be very grateful to him. Although . . .' He didn't want to undermine the boy's selfless act, but really, he couldn't let it go without qualification, could he? 'Although normally the last thing you should ever do is go near a firework once it's lit. Really, he probably should have run away or taken cover, and so should you, if you could, Cassie. Not that I'm blaming you; I mean, it all happened very quickly. Anyway, the thing is, Diarmuid was brave but I think we should try to keep things in perspective. Kim is right, the Roman candle was never going to kill you, however noisy it was. The worst that might have happened is a bit of a sore leg or some trainers with burn holes.'

During this speech, Kim had begun to smirk again rather dangerously, so a change of subject seemed an urgent priority. 'Come on, let's have a game of Monopoly.'

'No-o. Boring game.'

'Takes way too long. We are going to the Mahoneys' for tea, remember?'

How could he forget? The cause of their over-excitement as well as most of the friction. That, and this sodding rain.

'What time is it?' asked Cassie, who had left her watch upstairs.

'Half past four.'

They were probably right that there wasn't time to get through a game of Monopoly, even the truncated *Simpsons'* version. Anyway, there were always arguments over who got to be Lisa.

'Bananahead, then?'

This card game, a family favourite, had been much played by Bev at college for hard currency over bottles of supermarket whisky. When she taught it to Peter they knew it as Shithead; it was after the children came along that it had been rechristened.

'Yeah, OK.'

'Can I shuffle?'

'No, me! You're rubbish at it – you bend the cards.'

'Dad, please can I shuffle? Kim always shuffles.'

'I'll shuffle,' Peter ruled. 'You can take it in turns to deal. And Ollie, leave that cushion alone.'

Honestly, sometimes negotiating his way through an afternoon of cards with the twins was worse than when it was his turn to chair the Geography Faculty's staff–student committee. Militant Student Union reps haggling about photocopying charges had nothing on Cassie and Kim in this form.

'What time is it now?' asked Cassie for the seventeenth time at twenty past five.

'Nearly time to go,' said Peter, adding through the squealing, 'Go and find your pac-a-macs, it's still raining.'

Which fact, besides its being dark, was reason enough for him to run them down there in the Land Rover. The perfect excuse. Because although they were well able to walk or cycle round to friends' houses by themselves now, and frequently did so, Peter always liked to go with them when they were invited anywhere for the first time. It seemed rude, somehow, just to let your kids turn up on some other parent's doorstep when you hadn't even met them. Year 5 wasn't like Infants, when the parents all walked their kids to school so you ran into them in the playground in the mornings. Shannon, like his two, biked to school on her own.

On the other hand – oh, dreadful notion! – what if the Mahoneys imagined he was checking up on them when he arrived with the girls and popped his head in to say hello before he dropped them off? Making sure things were sufficiently salubrious on the traveller site for his precious princesses? Perhaps he shouldn't go after all. But that was ridiculous, he told himself; he should do what he always did and not do anything differently because of who they were or where they lived. And of course he absolutely didn't want to seem unfriendly. And there was the rain.

'Come on then, you two. Jump in the car. Got that jar of jam for Shannon's mum? And gloves – don't forget your gloves.'

Ten minutes later he turned the Land Rover off the road and on to the black cinders of the yard, its scarring of deep tyre tracks now swamped with water. The welcome party of assorted dogs stopped barking as soon as he cut the engine, merely standing watchful. Nor were they the only ones, for over the wooden fencing to the left of the closest mobile home loomed the curious, whiskered faces of half a dozen piebald ponies; all were turned at the same angle to fix their mild eyes on the new arrivals, scarcely bothering to blink away the rain. There was something quaintly traditional about their long, untrimmed forelocks, stocky shoulders and round, feathered feet, matted now with fen mud. They made Peter think of brightly painted wooden caravans from a child's picture book, but this wasn't *The Famous Five Go Camping*. In fact, the ponies seemed somewhat redundant, since the only means of transport visible was a cluster of Irish-registered white vans.

'Oh, look, ponies!' yelled Cassie and Kim, tumbling over each other to get out of the car and over to the fence.

Evidently accustomed to children, the creatures did not shy away from the noisy onrush but stood their ground, nodding their heads in a bizarre caricature of knowing old men and suffering with stoicism the invading pats of four small hands. As Peter came up, the nearest pony was sniffing and blowing inquisitively while the one next to it mumbled suspiciously at the arm of Kim's mac, baring furrowed yellow teeth.

'Can we feed them, Dad?'

'Before they eat your coat, you mean?'

There were rules you were supposed to remember about feeding horses, if he could only remember them. He knew they usually liked Polos, but weren't you supposed to ask the owner first in case it made them fat? In this instance he could not imagine there being any objection – they were hardly thoroughbreds – but it was academic, because they had no Polos. Grass ought to be all right, you would think, but there was even something about grass, wasn't there? About making sure you didn't give them any plants you couldn't identify.

'Pick some of this grass, then. But make sure you only get grass, not anything else in with it.'

'Why?' asked Cassie.

'Don't you know anything?' sneered her sister. 'It's because ponies can't be sick, so if you give them weeds, they die.'

Of course, that was it. No vomiting reflex. 'It's not all weeds that are poisonous. Just don't give them anything you don't recognise.'

'What about dandelions? There are some dandelions over there.'

'Rabbits eat dandelions.'

'Leonie Sivell gives them to her guinea pig, too.'

'So that means they must be OK, doesn't it?'

Peter was slightly out of his depth here. 'Just grass,' he decided. It would not be a great start to poison the Mahoneys' livestock before they had even met. 'And lay your hand out flat, fingers together.' Everybody knew that part.

Even though his conscience was clear as regards animal foodstuffs, Peter nevertheless started when a voice spoke behind him.

'Terrible old cadgers, the lot of them.'

'Brogue' was such an ugly word (a clumpy shoe word) for such a beautiful sound. The rough fondness in her voice, speaking of the ponies, reminded him of Bev teasing Ollie. He spun round.

'Peter Kendrick. How do you do?'

How do you do? Who still said that, except possibly undertakers or old family solicitors? From Shannon, by her side, he thought he spotted a smirk but the woman was smiling openly enough as she took his hand.

'Paula Mahoney.'

Not the most romantically Gaelic of names: he had hoped for a Róisín or at the very least a Kathleen. Perhaps she had been compensating for it when she named her kids. And her hair might be red but she was definitely the source of their green eyes.

'Are you wanting to stay out here feeding these greedy lumps and catching your deaths, or will you come in for a cup of tea?'

The Mahoney trailer was panelled in what passed, under the buzzing generator-powered lighting, for battleship grey. A moveable set of four metal steps with a wooden handrail attached at one side ran up to the front door. The door itself was stippled glass of the kind usually found in bathroom windows, but Paula had hung across it a cheerful woollen curtain checked in blues and yellows, giving an immediate feeling of warmth and privacy which continued as you stepped past it and inside the small living room, with its kitchenette at one end. The rain, which had eased off a little, still sounded drummingly on the roof, reminding Peter of holidays under canvas as a boy, up on the north Norfolk coast with his parents, the three of them nestled in a two-man tent.

'You could stay and eat with us, too, and very welcome,' Paula told Peter from the stove when Shannon had dragged the twins off to see her bedroom.

'Oh, I couldn't possibly – terribly kind of you – but I usually eat later, you see.'

He felt a little ashamed of the polite lie, and the smell of the frying gammon, eggs and potatoes was his punishment, making his stomach rue the hours since their rather too virtuous Sunday lunch of homemade vegetable soup.

'Anyway, my girls would never forgive me if I muscled in on their invitation. Cramping their style, you know.'

'Ach, we're an embarrassment to them, right enough. It's a parent's lot. Shannon's biggest bugbear is my singing, when there's anybody by to hear me.'

This disclosure naturally filled Peter the tone deaf with a consuming curiosity; you could not very well ask your daughters' friend's mother to sing for you on a first casual acquaintance, though, could you?

'Kim and Cassie hate it if I tuck my trousers in my socks, even just when I'm doing the garden. And when I talk to strangers on buses and trains.'

She handed over his mug of tea and their smiles met. He wondered if Mr Mahoney was going to be sharing the contents of the frying pan – he was certain he had heard mention of a dad from Shannon and Diarmuid. There looked to be more than enough for one adult and four kids.

'And your husband . . .?' He let the question drift away open-endedly and, as hoped, she did not interpret it merely as an inquiry into the man's propensity for shaming his kids.

'Gabriel. Working up in King's Lynn at the moment. He and his brother – they lay flooring.'

He nodded, wishing he could think of some intelligent response to this information, and then noticed that the emerald eyes were on the jar of jam he had forgotten was in his hand.

'Ah, yes.' He produced it with less than a flourish. 'This was for you; it's nothing much. Blackcurrant. Homemade.'

Inclining her head in thanks, she took it from him gravely and examined the label.

'Cassie and Kim wrote it. We made twenty-eight jars, and after fourteen times each they've never forgotten how to spell it.' That awkward c-k-c in the middle.

Paula laid the jam on the draining board and stretched up to open a small cupboard next to the one that had housed the teapot, then turned back to him, a small jar in her hand. Fat and round: the kind that would once have contained Marmite.

'If you'll allow me, I'll be returning the favour, then,' she said. 'Bramble jelly; my own.'

He held it to the unshaded bulb the way Jeremy might have done with a fine burgundy; it was both clearer and darker than the garden jam he had brought. Blackberries: wild fruit of the hedgerows. It struck him as a fitting contrast.

Just then the three girls crashed back through the door from the bedrooms, all addressing their respective parents at once.

'When's tea ready, Mum?'

'Dad, you should see Shannon's bedroom!'

'It's so dinky!'

'She's got bunk beds – even though there's only one of her.'

'She sleeps in the top one and has everything else underneath.'

'Can Cassie and Kim's dad stay for tea?'

'Can we have bunk beds, Dad?'

'Please!'

'Please!'

'Please!'

All eyes being now turned on him, Peter decided it was time to be decisive.

'No. Look, I'm really grateful for the offer, Paula and Shannon, but I really must get going. And you two, we'll have to talk about the bunks thing, if you really mean it.'

Not much chance of their persuading him to supply them with two beds each, however, when they barely made use of one apiece.

'Be good. I'll pick you up around eight – if that's OK, Paula? And thank you very much for the tea, and the jelly.'

Outside, the rain had stopped at last, though it still dripped defiantly from prefabricated eaves and from the strings of lights which surrounded the camp like razor wire. The ponies had not moved from their place at the fence but their eyes were closed now under heavily lashed lids, their heads held fractionally lower. Peter caught a movement in the semi-darkness, over by the gateway where the lights ran out. He almost called out but stopped before he made a fool of himself.

The figure was slight and, as it slid off in the direction of the mobile home that Peter had just left, he saw a hand raised briefly in greeting. Cassie's life saver: Trish's beautiful boy.

*   *   *

108

Kerry-Ann Skinner wasn't exactly a friend of Sal's but Lyn Skinner was a friend of Mina's. And Kerry-Ann was at Marksby Road Juniors, too – actually in Year 6 – so it wasn't beyond the realms of reasonable parental expectation, was it, that she should come round and play after school, while Lyn and Mina had a cuppa and did some catching up?

'Still dealing with all those little shunts?'

And kitheads. Lyn had always prized it as one of her best jokes and apparently it still amused her nearly a year after her escape from the call centre. Not wishing to encourage her, Mina merely nodded.

'Gordon the gorgon still keeping you in order down there?'

Another nod, but with half a smile joined on this time. She could almost miss the way Lyn had made the place seem like school. There was something – what was the word for it? – subversive about her friend, which was hard to resist for long.

'How about you? How's it going at that telesales place?'

Lyn stuck out her tongue like a pre-schooler. 'Fine if you want to be insulted all day by posh women in Harrogate for less than the retainer they pay their manicurist. And you can hardly blame them, poor cows. Of course they don't want a bloody conservatory or new patio doors – if they did they'd probably have noticed for themselves and ordered some last month.'

It was true. At least at Autocare Direct people rang them, and generally for a reason. Only about one caller in ten was actively abusive. She giggled – Lyn's effect, again.

'What sorts of things do they say, then?'

'Had some bitch this week threatening to take us to court. Said picking up the phone had made her lose some antique silverware she was bidding for on eBay.'

'Seriously?' Mina could never quite tell.

'Too right. Said she was going to sue us for "loss of bargain". And another one – husbands who are lawyers, the pair of them, I bet – raving on about privacy and the bloody Human Rights Act.

Seemed to think an afternoon phone call was much the same as photographing her in the buff for the *News of the World*.'

'Anything in the script, then, for threats of legal action?'

'Same as for everything else. Smarmy apology and put the phone down sharpish.' Lyn pulled another playground face and slurped her tea. 'Bonuses are good, though. Better than at Oughtocare.'

Another old favourite: *Oughtocare, but we don't.*

'Have a biscuit,' said Mina consolingly, reaching across to her bag for the packet of digestives. Next to the biscuits she tried not to feel the mock leather of her purse, nor to remember that it was slimmer than it ought to have been by one folded ten pound note.

'Thought you'd never ask. I'm starving. And while we're on the subject – rude guests, you know – can I mention I'm freezing my tits off in here?'

'Yes, sorry. One of the heaters has conked out. And we need them upstairs more; the oven's quite often on in here after we get in, doing tea, so it's usually warm, you see.'

'Well it's bloody freezing now. I can't believe the council still haven't done anything about central heating in these houses. It's like the Dark Ages. You must be the only street left in western Europe without it.'

Mina drowned a sigh with a mouthful of tea. The trouble with Lyn was she didn't like to let things lie. A force on the tenants' association over at her own flats, she had fingers in so many pies that she'd forgotten how to keep them out of other people's.

'I think they've decided these houses aren't worth it, to be honest.'

'You mean, they think the tenants aren't worth it. *You're* not worth it!'

Oh, God. Lyn on her high moral horse was the last thing she needed. 'They were going to demolish them, you see. They were "zoned" for it, or whatever it is they say. Ages ago now – when I was a kid. And then the money ran out.'

'I bet it damn well did! After they'd sold everything worth selling and there was no rent coming in any more.'

'Right. But anyway, the thing is that because we're still basically down as scheduled for demolition, that's maybe why they've turned a blind eye to me keeping the house. You know, we've never had a formal transfer or anything; Mum just gave me the rent book and I took over payment and they never queried it.'

Lyn gave a low whistle, spraying digestive crumbs into her tea. 'You never asked them to sort it out?'

'Um, no. Trouble is' – time to lay her cards on the table – 'I'd probably never be entitled to a three-bedroomed place like this, not a house, ground floor with a garden and everything, not just for me and Sal. I don't know if they'd even count Jess, you see.'

Jess was always a bit of an unknown quantity, wasn't she?

'So you just kept quiet,' said Lyn, almost admiringly. But the righteous anger was not at bay for long. 'And because you're scared they'll kick you out, they can keep you living here like bloody Bedouins with no heating, and water running down the walls.'

Mina was wondering if there were many people with ancestors from the Middle East on Lyn's tenants' association, and what they would have made of this colourful outburst, when Sal appeared in the kitchen doorway, open book in hand. Her ten-year-old radar drew her from the page and fixed upon the digestives on the table.

'Can I have a biscuit, Mum?'

Mina handed them over. She had a sinking feeling. 'Where's Kerry-Ann?'

'Dunno. Upstairs.'

The feeling sank further. 'What do you mean, upstairs? What's she doing?'

'My room, I think. Putting on some of that make-up Grandma gave me last Christmas.'

The lecture about the duties of hospitality could wait until they were on their own – if, indeed, there was any point in bothering. Keep things simple. 'Perhaps Kerry-Ann would like a biscuit. And what about a drink for both of you? Why don't you go up and get her to come down?'

111

As her daughter headed off, she added casually, 'And leave that book upstairs for now, why don't you?'

Alone again, Lyn and Mina exchanged grimaces.

'Help herself to anyone's stuff, that one would, without so much as a by your leave,' was the gesture on Lyn's side.

'No. It's not Kerry, it's Sal. She's always like this. Doesn't want friends round, and then if they do come, she doesn't even talk to them.'

Lyn shrugged. 'Well, some kids, you know . . . Can't make her what she's not.'

It was not the greatest piece of reassurance, but for some reason it mollified her. Not for long, though.

'By the way – speaking of kids – my friend Jackie saw your Jess in the Moor. Just by Boots.'

Defensively, Mina took another digestive. 'Oh, yes?'

The pinch of indecision – almost unknown for her – showed in Lyn's face.

'Look, I hadn't really meant to say anything. But if it was me, I'm pretty sure I'd want to know.'

Mina bit her lip and managed not to hurry her on.

'The thing is, Jackie says she's pretty sure Jess was, well, asking for money.'

Begging. The word hovered between them unsaid, before it was chased away by another which was ten times worse. *Drugs.* Begging, 'borrowing' money, that was always what it meant, wasn't it?

When Kerry-Ann mooched in, alone, to inquire about the biscuits, Mina scarcely saw her lopsided features, one eye outlined a gothic black, the other blinking a lurid lizard green. Distantly, she wondered what it was that Lyn was laughing about.

There was no getting away from it now; it had to be. Drugs.

Chapter 10

When the telephone rang four minutes into the brand new year, Peter assumed it was a wrong number. Some drunk, hitting careless buttons in the jostle of a heaving bar. He himself had been drinking steadily since persuading Cassie and Kim to forgo the final two hours of the old year and retire (separately) to bed, and he was too comfortable on the sofa to wish to move. Who could be calling him, anyway? His only living relatives to speak of, Uncle Gerry and Aunty Kath, would have phoned three hours earlier at their midnight, his nine. It was three a.m. now in Riyadh – too late, surely, for even Uncle Gerry still to be up and knocking back the contraband Scotch. Leave it – drunks usually get bored pretty quickly.

When it rang again at 12.09, he cursed under his breath. Alcohol could evidently lead to obduracy, too. *Look up the number if you don't know it properly, you stubborn idiot, and stop calling mine.* He would have let it ring, but was afraid of its wakening the twins, upstairs sleeping shallowly in the excitement of the occasion. How many years' ends could a nine year old remember, after all, even though his own, tonight, seemed countless? Hence it was in blurry irritation that he rose, thumbed down the sound on Jules Holland and guests and seized the receiver.

'Hi, Peter. Just ringing to wish you a Happy New Year.'

The drunk was female – and sober. In fact it was . . .

'Mina here, by the way, I should say.'

'Happy New Year,' he said, meaning it.

Was she going to feel the need to offer, this time, any further explanation or apology for her call? Please don't, he thought, and she didn't.

'You been out, at all?'

''Fraid not. Usually we have friends round here, but this year they were doing the entertaining. Bit of an adult dinner party affair, not the sort of thing you could drag the kids along to. Though we did go earlier and help Jeremy do the canapés. Cassie and Kim are the world's greatest cutters of radish roses and Jeremy tolerates it even though nobody has been known to eat one since 1978. I fear they also managed to consume more *crostini* than they laid out on the trays.'

There was a fractional delay before she laughed, and he berated himself for blathering about canapés but it was OK, because she said, 'Don't you miss the days when they were little and would just go to sleep in a corner and you could carry them home later?'

'Bliss! But I must say it was pretty short-lived in our case. By the time they were about two they would be up all evening dragooning the grown-ups into playing party games.'

'You poor thing! Sal was always a good sleeper – still is.'

'What time did you manage to persuade her to go up tonight, then?'

'Before nine, if you can believe it. But she was reading for quite a while.'

'Oh yes, the bookworm – I remember you said. So you didn't go out tonight, then, either?'

'No. Normally we'd go to Mum and Dave's, at least for a bit – Dave's my mum's boyfriend. But tonight they were out at some posh New Year's Eve dinner dance thing with Dave's younger brother and his wife. He's a policeman – his brother, I mean, not Dave; Dave drives a minicab – and they do go in for these fancy black tie affairs.'

Complete with canapés, perhaps. 'Do they make a big thing of the New Year in Sheffield? I mean, do people turn out in Town Hall Square and count down to midnight and all that?'

'A bit, I guess. Not big crowds or anything. But how did you know I'm in Sheffield?'

Ah. How *did* he know, in point of fact? Call centres, with their anonymous 0870 numbers, could be in Timbuktu and quite frequently were. 'Well, when you phoned me from home, last time, and I got your number, I recognised the dialling code. And, actually, by your accent, too. It couldn't be from anywhere but Sheffield – or nowhere east of about Rotherham, anyway.'

'Oh, do you know Sheffield then? Do you have friends here or something?'

She sounded so delighted that he couldn't be wholly sorry he had backed himself into this corner. He attempted prevarication. 'It is a great accent – really warm and homey. If you don't think that's a bit patronising.'

'No, you're dead right. We once went on holiday to Cornwall when I was a kid, a coach tour, and we were looking round some castle, I forget where, and bumped into this family who were having a row in full-on South Yorkshire. We rushed up and greeted them like long-lost friends, and they forgot all about whatever it was they'd been arguing over. The mum said, "We're from Donny" – as if all the world should know where Donny is. Always makes me smile.'

Just when he was beginning to think he might have got away with it, she added, 'So, go on, what's your Sheffield connection?'

'I had a friend who lived in Eccleshall.' Strictly speaking it was true, although he had never been invited back to Tom's house there; they had only ever met at the University, pooling the results of their field work. But how to explain to somebody that you were familiar with their home town only as the subject of a research project? It was nearly ten years ago, now, in any case.

'Well, Eccleshall is quite a different kettle of fish from where I live. Have you ever been to Intake?'

It may have been the hopefulness in her voice that tempted him to abandon the resolution of digging his hole no deeper. Whatever the reason, it was out before he could stop it. 'Intake! Yes, I met quite a few families in Intake. Living just south of the Mansfield Road, mostly.'

'But that's just a stone's throw from ours! Who do you know?'

'Oh, I'm sure they wouldn't remember me. It was a long while back now.'

But then he felt a miserable heel, for putting down the shutters on this connection that she was so happy to have found. 'I was just conducting interviews, you see. For my work – a research project.' *Stability or Stagnation? A Comparative Study of the Populations of Unredeveloped Estates in Sheffield and Glasgow.*

'So my neighbours were your guineas pigs?'

Grateful for her amusement, he asked, 'What about you? Have you ever been to Cambridge?'

'Just once, yes. We came down on the coach when I was a teenager – me and Mum and Jess in the pushchair.'

'And I suppose you did the sights, did you? King's College chapel and all that?'

The line seemed to crackle briefly. Then, 'Well, you know, it was only a day trip. There wasn't time to do everything.'

It was true. There were only so many colonnaded stone court-yards you could fit into one day. 'I'd like to bet you didn't get round to visiting my college, anyway. It's by itself, not with the others along the river. Nobody ever makes it that far. Which at least means we get some peace and quiet, even in the tourist season.'

She laughed at that, a not entirely comfortable laugh, though he thought he also sensed some release of tension. 'Not really a problem we have at Autocare, strings of Japanese visitors with camcorders. Just as well, probably – we're most of us not very photogenic. Good faces for the telephone, my friend Lyn used to say!'

That, of course, made him wonder what she did look like but he got nowhere with it; he still could not seem to shake himself out of the image of oiled black hair and almond eyes.

'Anyway, look, I'd better go, that sounds like our Jess coming in and I don't seem to have caught up with her for days. But Happy New Year, again.'

'You, too. Let's see if I can manage to get through this one without crashing my car.'

'Autocare Direct Motor Insurance. My name is Mina, how may I help you?'

January 2, 8.31 a.m. and the new year at work began exactly as the old one had left off.

'I want to report an accident. But it was all the other joker's fault, so the claim will be on his policy, won't it, not mine? I'm really not intending to lose my no claims on account of some prat in a BMW roadster driving like a pigheaded maniac!'

Nothing very new and original about any of that either.

'Of course, sir, if the fault was entirely with the driver of the other vehicle, then you have no reason to be worried about your own no claims bonus . . .'

The soothing lines from the script tripped out pretty much by themselves by now, leaving Mina's mind free to wander – and to wonder. Specifically, to wonder whether Peter Kendrick had noticed when she fobbed him off like that, on the phone the other night, about her trip to Cambridge? And if so, whether he had minded, because he hadn't sounded as though he did.

'Now, could you start by telling me your policy number, please?'

The thing was, the allure of mouldering old architecture wasn't that strong when she was thirteen – if it even was now. Nothing compared with the pull of the shops of Cambridge city centre. She seemed to recall having spent most of the day in a Virgin mega-store. But she couldn't very well have told him that, could she? He probably loved all those chapels and cloisters and things. They were his place, after all. 'My college', he'd said; so Dr Peter Kendrick wasn't a medical doctor after all but the teaching kind, a PhD.

'And please could you confirm the make and registration of your vehicle, Mr Bostock?'

They were his place. Not hers.

'Thank you. OK, so where exactly did the incident take place?'

This part did require a greater proportion of her conscious mind and, midway through his description of the accident itself, it temporarily claimed all of it.

'. . . kept coming straight towards me, even though he could see me there perfectly well – one o'clock on a bright afternoon. Just kept his toe down and refused to stop. Ran smack into me, head on.'

'Really, sir? That sounds unusual. You're sure there's no way he can have failed to notice your vehicle in the road in front of him? No lapse in attention or anything? Using a mobile, turning round to talk to passengers in the back?' *Playing charades.*

'No chance. He was on his own, and looking right at me. I saw the bloody whites of his eyes, the nutter.'

'Well, in that case it does seem as if it'll be hard for his side to deny liability. Are you certain that your vehicle was within your own side of the road when he hit you? Was there a broken white line up the middle of the street where the accident took place? That always helps, in case he tries to argue it was you who was too far over and not him.'

Though she didn't see there could be much doubt, if it was really a head-on.

'Within my own side of the road? Of course I wasn't, how could I be? There was a whole bloody row of parked cars right the way along my side. I have to get past them, while laddo in the flash convertible just keeps coming at me, like he thinks I'm going to back up or something.'

Mina was visited by competing urges to laugh or cry. 'And did you stop or attempt to stop, sir?'

'Stop? No way. I was almost past the whole row of them, which he could see perfectly well.'

She summoned her most patient manner. 'The thing is, Mr Bostock, that if you were on his side of the carriageway then technically it is you who should have given way and not the other driver.'

118

Instinct sharpened over the years told her to remove the receiver from her ear by half an arm's length for a few seconds before she resumed taking the details of the claim.

'You might say so, sir, but I'm afraid it wouldn't be the view a court would take . . .'

Nor was it the only time she had to take evasive action to protect her eardrums that morning, listening to tales of unfestive seasonal mishaps; by half past ten her head was starting to pound, her throat was dry and she was more than ready for her twenty-minute coffee break.

Debbie was there before her, and Fran, sending another two Diet Cokes tumbling into the drawer at the bottom of the machine. Mary, Nupoor and Gwen were in the corner, all hard at it on their mobiles. You'd wonder how that could seem like a break, just more talking on the phone. But it didn't always follow, did it? Dave was always offering to drive her and Sal anywhere and everywhere on a weekend; in fact, he seemed positively to enjoy it.

Fran pocketed her Cokes and turned to Mina and Debbie.

'Had time to get to the sales much, yet, then? Such a pain having to be back at work. Yesterday was jam-packed at Meadowhall; I'm sure today would have been much easier. I tell you I was this close to ringing Mrs G and saying I was sick.'

Debbie grinned at her. 'You should get Stu to call, say your voice has gone completely. 'S what I do.'

'Doesn't mean she believes it.'

They were all talk. Mina could not remember the last time either of them had missed a day; like her, they needed the money.

'Anyway, what did you get?'

'Well, like I say, it was dead crowded, had to fight your way over bodies to get near anything. But I did get these boots I've been eyeing up for ages. In Ravel, they were. Mid-calf with a dinky little heel and tassels on the side. Proper suede and I only paid a couple of tenners, down from £59.99, would you believe?'

'Will you wear them tomorrow so I can see?'

'What, risk getting them wet just to wear them in this place?'

'The ones I'm after are in Hobbs – like I can afford to shop there. But they're gorgeous. Little black slingbacks with a kitten heel. I'd have to wait for them to come down a mile before they'd be in my league. But they'd look so good with my new pencil skirt, or with skinny jeans and a silk blouse.'

It wasn't that Mina didn't like shoes. She was extremely fond of her pointy-toed boots. But sometimes . . . well, she missed Lyn, for a start. Lyn used to sort out the world's problems over coffee break, from American foreign policy to the latest failings of the Autocare management.

'I tell you what would look good with your pencil skirt as well, Deb. These knee-length zip-ups I saw: shiny plastic, and you can get them in black or a kind of mauvy grey. Sort of eighties retro look, like something out of *Cagney and Lacey* when we were kids.'

Somehow she didn't suppose Peter Kendrick had to spend his coffee breaks listening to people wittering about shoes. Although she found it hard to imagine what people in universities did talk about – if indeed they bothered with such mundane things as coffee breaks.

'Oh, I think I've seen them. In that funny little shop in the city centre that looks like it sells bondage gear?' said Debbie.

Fran snorted. 'Tell me about it! Half the stuff in there is PVC or has chains on it. It's some kind of punk revival thing, I guess, but I can never go in there without a quick glance to make sure there's nobody I know to see me.'

Neither the caffeine nor the short respite from the telephone made much difference to Mina's gathering headache, and well before noon it had settled into a persistent mind-numbing thump. Her how-may-I-help-yous were sounding increasingly brittle and insincere.

'I would like to report a theft from a vehicle, if I may.'

'Certainly, sir. Do you have your policy number there, please?'

He told her, and the computer called up the details of Mr

Mohammad Ali Shah of 108, Tennyson Avenue, Leatherhead, Surrey.

'Now, Mr Shah, please could you tell me exactly what was taken?'

'My golf clubs. They were on the back seat, you see, and . . .'

Most of a ham. Mina was used to things not being in the fridge when she came to need them – a few eggs here, a bit of cheese or bacon there – and Jess was always finishing off the bread, but most of an entire smoked ham?

'And what would you estimate the value of the stolen property to be, please?'

'A whole set of clubs, it was, including a customised hybrid wood and a sand wedge, not to mention the leather trolley bag. Only bought them last year. I believe I paid something over twelve hundred. I'll be able to check it on my old credit card statements for you, if you need the exact amount.'

Mina had boiled the ham to take over to Mum's on Christmas Day as her contribution, and all they'd done was have a few little slices off it with their cold turkey at teatime, because nobody was ever very hungry by that point, were they? And then her mother had insisted she wrap it in foil and take it home again, and she'd gone along with it because she felt sure Mum was thinking of Jess getting to try it, though of course she'd never say so. Well, she'd got to try it all right. Gone – the whole thing, foil and all, disappeared.

'And where exactly was the vehicle parked at the time of the theft, Mr Shah?'

'It was just on the drive outside my house.'

Tapping in the details as he spoke, Mina's errant mind just couldn't make sense of it. She was tempted to hope this meant it couldn't be heroin. Weren't smackheads supposed to be seriously skinny? They must hardly eat at all. Hunger on this scale made her think of dope – but she'd never heard of anybody begging in the streets to support a marijuana habit.

'. . . how soon do you think I might receive the cheque?'

121

'Of course, that will depend on whether your possessions are recovered. If the police make an arrest they may be able to track down your golf clubs fairly quickly and return them to you. If that hasn't happened within sixty days then we would normally proceed to process your claim and a cheque would be issued at that time.'

And besides, nearly a whole ham at one sitting? That was a major attack of the munchies. If only she had someone she could talk to about it. She'd even chickened out of sharing her fears with Lyn. Mum was the last person, of course, and Dave . . . well, it was tempting but it wouldn't be fair to ask him to keep something so big from Mum, would it?

'Oh, we know who it was, all right.'

'Sorry?'

'I know who stole the clubs.'

Mina closed her eyes for a moment, drawing the forefinger of her free hand wearily across the lids. 'So who . . .?'

'It was my wife – my ex-wife, I should say. She's got them.'

On Peter's first day back in the Geography Faculty he ran into Trish in the coffee room. Almost literally, in fact.

'Hey, sorry!' he said, catching the edge of the toppling pile of paper in her arms and setting it back to rights, hoping she hadn't noticed the accidental brush of his fingers on her wrist as he did so, nor the way he jumped at the contact.

'No, no, my fault. Not looking where I'm going. It's you I was looking for, anyway. This lot's yours.'

'Ah. Yes, great. Thanks very much.'

Avoiding further hand-touching, he took from her the sixteen hundred wholly unnecessary pages of photocopying with which he had wasted a portion of her morning, and tried to ignore the stab of guilt: a temporary credit to Trish's subterranean bank balance but an irredeemable debit to the environment.

'D'you need a hand with them?' she asked, and despite his

assurance that he would be OK, thank you, she followed him along the corridor in the direction of his office.

'I got quite a bit done over the vacation. On the old PhD, I mean.'

'That's good.' He wanted to show a supervisorly interest but to ask questions might have smacked more of inquisition than polite inquiry. That she was working conscientiously at the final polishes he knew; that she felt under pressure was self-evident. By tacit consent, submission dates were never mentioned between them. But Trish, it seemed, was in conversational mode.

'I've dug out all those missing page references now. Took me the best part of the week before Christmas. Mind you, it was a good time to choose: it probably went much quicker because I was the only one left in the library by then.' The virtue in her voice made him smile. 'The woman at the desk in the UL Reading Room had nothing to do but fetch the books as soon as I handed her the slips. But for me, she'd just have been whistling "Jingle Bells".'

'Good.' He'd already said that. 'Er, great. That's great.'

She dodged past him to open the door of his office, narrowly avoiding setting the whole stack of papers back on the slide. Wedging them in place with his cheek and stumbling past her to precipitate the collapsing pile towards the top of his desk, he caught sight, irrelevantly, of her shoes. In fact, really, you could hardly miss them. Trish was usually a scuffed Timberlands kind of girl, but today, below the perpetual jeans, her feet were indulging a taste for frivolity. Lime green and pointy, like something Audrey Hepburn might have worn in *Roman Holiday*, thoroughly inappropriate for riding a Vespa.

She had seen him notice, so some kind of comment was inescapable. 'Nice shoes.'

'Thanks. I got them in the sales; went into Birmingham with my sister while I was home. She made me get them, actually. Half price, though – a real bargain.'

Even knocked down, they must have added up to a mountain

of redundant photocopying, but he fought the urge to feel frustrated with her. Small-scale financial patronage hardly bought him the right to begrudge her a pair of new shoes.

'Anyway, since I got back I've been refreshing some of the theory sections. The literature review in chapters two and three, you know.' Behind him, she had settled herself familiarly into his armchair, obliging him to go through a show of shuffling the photocopies into purposeful-looking heaps.

'Oh, yes?'

'Trouble is, there's masses of new stuff that's come out since I wrote those sections. "Refreshing" is hardly the word for it. Rewriting from scratch is more like it.' Laughter glinted through her grumbling tone. 'Bloody academics. They will insist on writing new stuff all the time, won't they? Don't know when to stop, some of them.'

'I blame the Research Assessment Exercise.' He grinned down at his heaps of paper, though not without an edge of discomfort; lately, he couldn't exactly be accused of overproduction.

'Social exclusion seems to be the hottest topic in urban geography. The journals are full of little else. And it's all so sodding relevant.'

He had to turn round and laugh, then, leaning back against the desk. But, cockeyed Trish logic though it appeared, what she was saying held a recognisable truth. In the early stages of a project, finding material right in the zone was what you hoped for; towards the end, it was a curse.

'Anything in particular on your cities?' Manchester, Belfast and Bristol were the case studies Trish had chosen for *On the Edge: Urban Poverty and Marginalisation in the UK*. Sexy titles were the order of the day, but hers always sounded to him more like something billed in the *Radio Times* as gritty drama than a doctoral thesis.

'Not really, except a few brief mentions in passing. But there was a big piece all about Sheffield in *Urban Studies* at the end of last year, and it parallels a lot of my findings. I'm going to have to work it in.'

Sheffield. The name gave him a similar start to the one occasioned by brushing hands with Trish. Sheffield meant Mina.

'That sounds a good idea. And of course you do need to make sure your review of the field is up to date, with no major omissions. But try not to get too stressed about it. At a certain point, when you're ready, you're going to have to draw a line.'

'"Correct at the moment of going to print", sort of thing?'

'That's it, exactly. Otherwise your dissertation would be like the Forth bridge.'

Stretching her legs out from his chair and crossing lime-green-strapped ankles, she cocked a winning smile. 'A magnificent edifice, you mean? Forging a vital link, spanning hitherto uncharted waters?'

'Absolutely,' he agreed. 'Not at all rusty or in need of a lick of paint.'

Satisfied, apparently, with this student–supervisor consultation, Trish rose to leave. 'Back to the bookstacks, then.' From the door, she cast a hopeful eye back towards the photocopied piles. 'Unless you've got anything else for me to do at the moment?'

'Oh. No thanks, not just now, I don't think. But' – he kept his eyes on her face and well away from the resplendent shoes – 'why don't you come over for supper one evening? Cassie and Kim will want to thank you properly for the lettering set, and they are avid for victims to show off the rest of their Christmas haul to, as well. I'll do spaghetti.'

Her feet might be living the high life, but she still needed to eat, didn't she?

Chapter 11

There had been something perceptibly different, this past week, about the stereophonic broadcast from the Land Rover's back seat. It still began, even before seat belts were fastened and doors closed, with the usual muddle of white noise.

'Mrs Moore was off sick –'

'Jason Scrivener kicked his football on the roof of the infants' toilets –'

'– so we had a supply teacher called Miss Beesley and she was really strict –'

'– and Mr Edwards said he wasn't going to fetch it down because Jason's a Year 4 and shouldn't have been in the infants' playground in the first place –'

'– and Abby called her Miss Beastly, because she is, she's horrible, and we might have her again tomorrow. Do you think we'll have her again tomorrow?'

'Dad, what's for tea?'

But in due course, instead of the two voices falling into step around a single story, one twin at once held the stage while the other, each in turn, lapsed into a most uncharacteristic silence. It was Cassie who took the floor first.

'I hurt my leg really badly at playtime. I was on the big climbing frame doing a flip over on the middle bar and my hand slipped and I came right off. My knee hit the metal side bit and it really, really hurt. I had to go and see Eve – Shannon came with me to help me along – and she put a cold compress on it but she says I'm going to have a massive bruise. It swelled up and everything, but it's gone down now. Do you think I will have a bruise?'

'I'm sure you will,' he soothed, a sufficiently experienced parent to know that this, and not the contrary, was the reassurance she sought. 'I'm sure it will look dreadful in a couple of days.' But why had it fallen to Shannon, and not her sister, to accompany her to the medical room? Kim, indeed, had listened to the whole tale with an expression, from what he could make out in the driving mirror, of lofty scepticism.

Then it was Kim's turn to speak, and Cassie's to stare pointedly out of the window.

'Leonie Sivell lost her Tamagotchi. She had it stolen.'

'At school, you mean? I thought you weren't allowed to bring electronic games to school?'

'We're not, but she just had her Tamagotchi in her coat pocket because she was going to her dad's house after school and she says there's nothing to do there. He doesn't even have a telly.'

With amusement he caught her small shudder at this outlandish form of deprivation. 'So, what happened?'

'Leonie left it in the cloakroom and one of the traveller girls took it. Miss Beesley caught her with it at lunchtime and she had to go and see the Head.'

Peter tried not to cringe too visibly. 'Doesn't she have a name?'

'Who?

'The girl who took the Tamagotchi.'

'Course she does. Everyone has.' *Dur.* 'But I don't know it.'

'So then, how do you know she's a traveller?'

'She's got red hair. And she has free dinners, and comes on the travellers' minibus.'

The trappings of well-meaning social provision, marking out its recipients from the crowd, like a sizzling letter T on the forehead.

'All right, but I don't think you should refer to her as a traveller girl.'

'Why not? You said we had to say traveller, because we don't know if they're proper gypsies, and anyway that's an old-fashioned word, and some people think it's insulting, like coloured and fat and beggar and tramp.'

Oh, God: this time the wince was all too evident. Had he really said those things? Certainly he recognised most of them as versions of things he had attempted to explain. Pulling himself together, he tried again.

'Yes, traveller is the word we use for the Mahoneys and their friends. But what I mean is, I don't think you should say "a traveller girl" when you're describing someone.'

'But she is one, so why can't I say it? Should I call her a ginger girl instead?'

'Er, yes, I suppose that might be better,' he said, not at all convinced of his own argument. The problem, of course, was the context. *Traveller girl steals Tamagotchi*. How to convey this to a nine-year-old, who was wholly innocent of the pernicious newspaper headlines of Peter's youth, reporting frequently and with perfect accuracy *Black man on assault charge*, but never, never *White man gaoled*?

They were bumping along the lane, now, past the Dorlinsons' driveway and into the unlit blackness beyond, Peter slowing by ingrained habit just a second before the bounding form of Ollie launched herself in front of their tyres, ears and topknot flapping ghostly pale in the headlights. Having been at home to witness it himself sometimes, when the girls came home from a bike ride, he knew the speed with which the spaniel could pass from comatose in her favourite chair to the whole-bodied excitement of greeting, and now, bending to caress her as he stepped down from the driver's seat, he was not surprised to feel her flanks still trailing the warmth of sleep and meet fuzzy disorientation in her blinking eyes. Then she turned to lollop through the pet door, chased by Kim, while Cassie materialised at his side, asking again, 'What's for tea?'

The inquiry was not unusual, and nor was her request to help him with chopping the onions, because she took a perverse enjoyment in making her eyes stream, and liked to winkle out and munch the small, sweet, central circles. What was strange was the disjointedness; the lack of her sister hovering at the table, watching operations and pinching her nose against the smell. Kim had flung through the kitchen at high velocity, depositing her lunchbox in the sink as usual and heading for the television without a backward glance. Alone.

'Let's see this bruise, then,' said Peter with slightly false cheer after the onions were dispatched into the frying pan to soften for a pasta sauce.

Cassie rolled up a stretchy school trouser leg to display a slightly reddened patch to one side of her knee. 'It hurts, still,' she said proudly, prodding a finger into the centre to make a dimple and watching in quiet satisfaction as the livid white point faded slowly back to pink.

'Should be starting to turn blue by the morning, I should think. Do you want some ice on it?'

Usually they both enjoyed the application to some wounded area of a bag of frozen peas, thinly wrapped in a tea towel, but today Cassie was stoical. 'It'll be fine.' Then, 'Dad, can I go to Shannon and Diarmuid's after school tomorrow, to play?'

The request was so far from unusual that he wondered at the slightly breathless tumble of its delivery. 'Of course you can, love. What, and stay for tea?' Maybe he could stay in college and get a bit of work done before they came home. 'What time would you want picking up?' Then a thought struck him. 'But it's Thursday tomorrow. Hasn't Kim got her flute lesson?'

Maybe that was it. The desire to play the flute – in addition to the piano lessons at Miss Frobisher's they had had since Bev was alive, sharing the hour and the piano stool – had been a surprising flight of individuality on Kim's part that he had met with encouragement, back in November. Was she going to start to pull out, so soon?

'I think Kim should go to her lesson,' he said gently. 'It's only been a couple of months, she ought to give it more of a chance.' This was a habit of his that he had found to be effective: treating them as interchangeable when anything needed to be said. But Cassie's eyes were averted; she was still poking her bruise.

'Not Kim.'

Not Kim, what? Not Kim, cut out to be a flautist? 'I think she should give it a little longer before she gives up, that's all. I've hired the flute from school until the summer; we've booked the lessons. Two more terms.'

'It's not Kim, just me. The Mahoneys – they've only invited me.'

'Only . . .' He stared at her. 'But why? Has Kim fallen out with Shannon?' Girls did that, didn't they? Squabbling over partners in PE and who would be whose best friend. But somehow, having each other, his two had seemed somehow immune.

'Not exactly. They didn't invite her, that's all. And she said she didn't want to go, anyway.'

There was a defiant jut about his daughter's chin which he did not like the look of one bit. But then he smelt the onions burning and had to leap to the frying pan and unstick them, browner and more caramelised than he wanted for his tomato sauce. Best let it drop, he decided; whatever the problem was, it would come out soon enough of its own accord.

'If you've finished admiring your injury, do you think you could fetch me a tin of tomatoes from the cupboard, please? There should be one next to the baked beans.'

Supper and Bananahead were amicable enough, though there was no mention from either sister of the Mahoneys or the next day's visit, and when Kim went up early, he took little pleasure from her sudden apparent absorption in practising her flute. Because something was wrong, and he had known it that morning, though he had dismissed it from his mind as foolishness at the time. He had known it as soon as he got up; as soon as he went along the landing to Kim's room and opened the door, his cockerel greeting faltering from cheery crow to uncertain gurgle as his eye fell on the bed. And, beneath the rumpled duvet, the shape of just one sleeping twin.

*　　*　　*

130

The trouble with January Sundays was that they ended before you had even washed up lunch. Mina had never acquired the brisk efficiency with these same pots and pans that had always appeared so effortless in her mother; roast pork and all the trimmings, even with bought apple sauce, still took her the best part of the morning to prepare, and the rapid winter dusk was on its way down before everything was free of grease and back in its place, catching her unawares and bringing with it a mild sense of panic, of things unachieved.

As the light faded, she shooed Sal outdoors into the grey garden, determined that one member of the family, at least, should see daylight today. Mum and Dave, she supposed, must have crossed from porch to Mondeo at Dave's house, as well as walking up her own front path shortly before noon; but Sal was young and Mina had a trust in the magical properties of fresh air just as she had in vitamins and regular dental appointments. There had been no show of reluctance; indeed, it might have been nice if Sal had occasionally given a hint of the scornful dissent displayed in bus queues and supermarkets by other girls her age. What Sal was doing now, as Mina forgot scouring pad and roasting tin to watch her from the kitchen window, was spinning. She used to spin in just that place on the grass years ago, at the age of six or seven: giddy and giggling, arms flung wide, winding herself into dizzy oblivion. But this was different, this slow, absorbed turning on the spot. Her eyes were not screwed shut but open and blind – except, Mina suspected, to images from the book which was zipped inside the breast of her bomber jacket.

Persuading Mum and Dave to come over here for lunch, instead of her and Sal going there, had seemed a small coup. First time in ages – since way back before Christmas. And then coaxing Jess out of bed and downstairs to eat lunch with them at the table in a shadow play of family unity; even keeping the surface chatter going with Dave's obliging aid, while Sal munched her crackling and watched them all narrowly, and Mum and Jess looked anywhere but at each other. But how far had it got them, really? Jess had gone straight back to her room with a grunt as soon as she'd finished her rhubarb crumble; Mum, her offer to help with the dishes declined, had gone to watch TV with Dave, and Mina's sense of triumph had subsided along with the detergent bubbles in the sink.

Leaving the last of the saucepans to drip on the draining board, Mina dried her hands, summoned a smile and went through to the sitting room.

'Gibraltar,' Mum told the quiz contestant on the screen. 'All done, love? Shall I make coffee while you have a sit down?'

But Dave was heavily asleep against her shoulder, his hand still loosely wrapped round hers, and Mina had no heart to disturb him. 'Let's have a cup of tea later, shall we, when he wakes up?'

Mum nodded. 'We won't stay long, though,' she said, settling back comfortably. 'Eric Clapton. Wasn't it Eric Clapton who sang "Layla"?'

'How's Mrs Warburton? Did you say she was coming out of hospital yesterday?'

'That's right. Well on the mend. They've got this hip replacement business down to a fine art these days. Only in for four days this time, and it was more like a fortnight last time.'

'That must be ten years ago, though, Mum.'

'Twelve.'

Still less than half of the quarter-century Mum had worked mornings with Mrs W at the chemist's in the arcade. Long enough to drop by the hospital every day with gossip and magazines but not long enough to call her Peggy. Not with Mr Warburton being the pharmacist; Mum could be old-fashioned about some things.

'When's she likely to be back at work?'

'Another couple of weeks, probably. There's a lot of standing up, of course, but that's better for it than sitting, she reckons. Derek and the Dominoes? I thought it was Eric Clapton.'

Sal, who had drifted in from the garden during the Mrs Warburton exchange, was tucked in an armchair and finding her page. 'Derek and the Dominoes was Eric Clapton. His band. That's what they were called.'

How did a ten-year-old come by this knowledge?

'Wonder why he called himself Derek,' her grandmother said. Dave's older brother was a Derek. A paunchy, affable man, worked in van hire; far from rock legend material.

'Well . . .' Mina glanced at Sal, but she was reimmersed. 'Because it begins with D, I suppose.'

'But why Dominoes? Why not Eric and the Eski—'

There was no need to turn and look behind her to know that Jess stood in the hall doorway. It was clear from her mother's compressed lips, the gaze fixed back on the television.

'I'm just off.'

Where to? But she could almost hear Mum's voice saying it. Absolutely the wrong thing. 'Going out for a while?' she asked; a marginally more placatory wording, at least, than 'When will you be back?'

Jess eyed the carpet and answered a different question. 'I'm going into town.'

'Have you got . . .' The bus fare to the city centre was £2.95 and Mina knew for a fact that Jess had split her last fiver on Friday.

'I'm fine.'

Both sisters were looking studiedly away from their mother; Mina conquered a desire to whisper. 'Only, if you need—'

'Really, I'm fine. I've got a twenty.' The last phrase was spoken on a rising tone; the set of Jess's mouth – the same but also very different – suddenly reminded Mina of Sal.

'Oh, right. OK then.' A twenty: the bravado could not be directed at her, therefore. There had only been a fold of four tens in her purse, plus some loose change.

'No, it's not OK.' Mum was still facing the quiz but there was steel in her voice. Neither of her daughters spoke; both waited. 'It's not OK to keep taking money from Mina.'

Jess drew in breath to speak but Mum finally turned her eyes

133

upon her, blazing her to silence. 'Taking, wheedling, borrowing –
it's all the same, and it's not right. Your sister works hard for the
money she brings home – Lord knows it's little enough any of us
can make – and she needs it for herself and Sal. You insisted an
staying here when you could have had a home with us. Mina already
feeds you, gives you a roof over your head. You might have the
grace to be grateful for that, and not bleed her dry just so you can
go gallivanting into town with your good-for-nothing friends.'

That was it. The day, lunch, had all been worse than a waste of
time. Worse than not bothering. Her mother was in full flight, and
Mina did not care at all for what looked like the beginnings of a
smirk twisting Jess's lips.

'When do you think your sister last had an evening out on the
town? She takes her responsibilities seriously. She works all hours
in that call centre. It's a regular job and she's stuck at it: for Sal.
For you, if only you weren't too wrapped up in yourself to notice
it. But you – when have you ever stuck at anything in your life?'

'The *Cutty Sark.*' Sal addressed the TV doggedly from behind
her paperback. *My Family and Other Animals,* Mina noticed.

'How long before you're going to wake up? When are you going
to get yourself sorted out, realise the world doesn't owe you a living?'

Still slumped against her, Dave stirred. No doubt the antipathy
bristling from her shoulder had served to wake him; perhaps for
the same reason, his eyes remained firmly closed.

Jess, alarmingly, was close to grinning. ''S not Mina's.'

Their eyes were locked. Mum said nothing.

'The twenty. It wasn't Mina that gave me it.'

Please, no, prayed Mina silently. Jess was looking dangerous,
almost exultant. 'Want to know where I got it?'

How do you like having a beggar for a daughter? Or worse.

But Mum wasn't ready to listen to it. 'What difference does it
make? It might not be Mina's money this time, but often enough
it is. Do you think I'm blind? I know how she bails you out, week
after week. If I had my way, you wouldn't get a penny, not until

you start to make some effort. Find yourself a job, or at least sign on at college, do a course or get some skills, instead of idling your life away. Not a penny.'

'It was Dave.' The triumph was now undisguised. 'Dave gave me the money. Just now. Upstairs, after lunch.'

Mum's shoulder, already stiff, became positively rigid. Dave's eyes stayed resolutely shut. Jess stood staring at her mother for a moment, as though considering some further comment, before spinning on her heel.

'See you, Mina. Sal, Dave.'

Seconds later the window frames danced to the slam of the front door.

'World Cup-winning England manager Sir Alf Ramsey also managed which football league club?' demanded the TV quizmaster into the silence which followed.

Sports trivia of the 1960s apparently not among her specialist subjects, Sal remained buried in her book. Mum's gaze was straight ahead. The only member of the party who might have known the answer was oblivious of the question; no longer feigning sleep, he was fretting Mum's fingers between his own and studying her face pleadingly.

'It was only a few quid, sweetheart.'

But Mum was suddenly brisk. 'I think we should go. Dave's working tonight, anyway, and I've got a dozen things to do. I'm sure you have, too.' Then, unwinding a little, 'Thank you, Mina, love, it's been a treat. Lovely piece of pork, and you'd cooked it to a T.' There was even a smile, barely forced, as she added, 'Almost as good as I do it at home.'

When they were going up the path, though, Mina pulling closed the curtains heard the argument begin: Mum fulminating again and Dave's voice, quietly reasonable, saying something about family.

The time went slowly until Sal's bedtime, even though, for once, she could be persuaded to a game of draughts after their cheese on toast. The house now empty of its afternoon of friction, Mina found that she was craving her own company as she hadn't since the place first became hers. Just to be by herself: that's what she told herself it was. Anything else – anyone else – was nowhere close to an expectation, hardly even a fully formed hope.

Half past eight. 'Come on, then, Sal. School in the morning; time for bed, now.'

'Do I need a bath?'

'No'. Better not: the Gerald Durrell was a library book. 'You can have one tomorrow.'

New Year's Eve had fallen on a Monday night so that it was a few minutes into Tuesday that Mina, on a whim born of festive loneliness, had telephoned Peter Kendrick. It was at a more polite hour of the evening that, quite unanticipatedly, he'd returned the call the following week, this time on a Sunday. But there was no reason to imagine she had set a precedent when she'd tentatively reciprocated last week, and rung him to share philosophical nothings on Sunday evening. Absolutely no reason to suppose that he would call her tonight.

Five minutes later she was gathering to herself two skinny armfuls of warm flannelette, ticklish curls and peppermint breath. Closing her eyes, she inhaled deeply the scent which, evolving but still essentially unchanged, had first intoxicated her in the maternity ward.

'Go on up, then, love. Bed.'

'Can I have my light on and read for a bit?'

Philosophical nothings. Yet somehow, exchanging the small terrors and joys of parenthood with Dr Peter Kendrick did not seem like nothing. Maybe it was the gulf between their lives which, perversely, made connection seem possible. Maybe it was something else: just Peter. Either way, she had no sensible basis for believing he might phone. But she found herself dearly hoping that he would.

Settled in an easy chair with the ears of the recumbent Ollie draped over one arm and the telephone receiver resting on the other, Peter felt a double pang of guilt. Not only had he turned down Jeremy and Martin's hospitality on the shallowest of pretexts – something about lecture notes that had sounded rickety even to himself – but his refusal had cost Trish twenty pounds in *bona fide* babysitting earnings. What made it somehow worse was that, unusually, the invitation had been delivered by Martin, stopping off on his way back from the station on Friday with a tartan muffler of Ruby's over his City suit and tie. (Peter pictured it wound round tenderly by Jeremy that morning, in one man's hall or the other, against the early chill outside.) Entertaining arrangements normally fell to Jeremy's part and Peter, heedful of the uncomfortable date, was reminded of his night with Martin in the Drayman's before Christmas.

'It's nothing much. Couple of friends of Jeremy's. He's threatening to make profiteroles.'

'Oh dear, now I'm seriously sorry to be turning you down. Jeremy knows how all the Kendricks feel about his choux pastry. If it had been any other night. But Sunday . . .'

What was it about Sunday, anyway? Only that it was a night she appeared generally to be in. Not – certainly not, surely? – that she could possibly be expecting his call.

Pillowing the phone on the rise and fall of a woolly flank, he keyed in Mina's number. For some reason he hadn't transcribed it into the big leather-bound address book on the kitchen windowsill; he would have felt self-conscious writing her in under H for Heppenstall, next to Dan Hoskins from the garage, hobbler of lawnmowers. The number was still on the scrap of paper on which he had first jotted it down – though he no longer had to go upstairs and look for it, somewhere there in his bedside drawer.

She answered on the second ring, which he forced himself to ascribe more to Autocare drilling than to any question of anticipation.

'Hello.'

That had him smiling already; workplace habits did not spill over into identifying herself to callers when she was at home. Experimentally, he responded in kind: 'Hello.'

And was rewarded. 'Peter. I wondered if it would be you.'

'Well, it is.' Not only was this utterly inane, but he feared the satisfaction might have shown in his voice. 'Weekend,' he mumbled on, with more haste than coherence. 'Did you have a, er, good weekend?'

'I did Sunday lunch. Had the whole family over.'

Something about her voice tipped him off. 'So, that'll be a no, then.'

Her laughter, which always seemed to come so freely, nudged him into the strangely easy intimacy that characterised their conversations.

'What was it? Sal?' Though from what he had heard of the child, she didn't sound the sort to shipwreck a family Sunday. All the concerns about her seemed to be of the insidiously slow-leaking kind, well below the waterline.

'No. Jess.'

'Your sister?' Mina had not said much about the teenage sister, except in relation to her disorganised eating habits and her un-reliability as a babysitter. Perhaps not ideal aunt material, but it had all sounded pretty normal for seventeen.

'Yes. She lives with me here, you see.'

'Not with her mother – your mother, I mean?' Obviously not, if she lived with Mina. Stupid question. But politer than a general demand for information – and equally successful, as it turned out.

'It's a long story. She and Mum, they don't get on. Never have, not since Jess was at junior school, and decided she could start ignoring Mum. Taking no notice, doing her own thing. Or answering back. Started way back, when she was about eight or something.'

Soon after Sal was born. It can't have been easy with a baby in the house. This was hardly a thing he could say, though.

'It was non-stop arguments, and it got worse and worse as she got older. By the time Jess was twelve or thirteen they were like cat and dog every evening. And then Mum was going out with Dave, and she and Jess both started staying out, avoiding the fights.'

'Leaving it to you.' He said it gently, sympathetically, but he felt her reaction. An instinct of denial, defensive of her mother.

'It wasn't like that. Mum's still hurt that Jess won't live with her – I know she is, though she'd never admit it. But they're too much alike. Mum used to take her on. Always said the wrong thing, wound her up more. Still does, every time. Like this afternoon: she can't resist having a go, even though she must know it'll only make things worse.' Then he was pleased to hear her chuckle. 'They're both as bad as each other: stubborn as a pair of old ironing boards, as my nan would have said.'

Peter, who had had his struggles with a recalcitrant one of his own, shared her enjoyment of the simile. 'And what was it about today, then? The argument?'

'Oh, anything and nothing.' Warned away, he felt a tug of disappointment; but then she appeared to relent. 'Money. Well, amongst other things. It's often about money these days. Jess never has any, so she's always borrowing it.'

'From your mother?' It was a stab, and her rueful laugh told him it was some way off target.

'Some chance! No. This time, from Dave.'

'Ah. I can see that could be sticky.' They both contemplated the matter in silence for a moment. Poor Mina, thought Peter – and poor Dave. 'Is she still at school, then, Jess?'

'No. She was out of there as soon as she could, straight after GCSEs.' There was a downward inflection to this, a tinge of something he could not identify. Apology, perhaps, or regret? Or merely resignation? 'No, she gets her giro, so she ought to be able to make do all right. But, well, you know.'

He didn't know, not at first hand; he'd never had trouble finding holiday jobs even when he was a student, and had walked straight from his PhD into a Fellowship. But he could imagine. 'I don't suppose it goes very far, does it? Not after what she gets through in food.'

He'd clearly got it wrong again, though. There was a sort of snort in his ear. 'Oh, I feed her. Not that she'll often let me cook for her, but it's me that fills the fridge, and she helps to empty it. And the biscuit jar.'

This was more familiar turf. 'Tell me about it. My two are like locusts if I ever buy biscuits, especially anything with chocolate on.' My three, in fact, he corrected inwardly, tickling a finger beneath well-covered spaniel ribs. 'You turn round and there's nothing left but a few crumbs. I've resorted to keeping a secret stash on top of the kitchen dresser in case any of my friends come round.'

She had stopped laughing now; the line was quiet, so he asked, 'Where do you think it all goes, then?'

'I don't know.' Her voice was quiet, anxious. 'That's just it, really – where does it all go? She's out such a lot, I hardly see her to talk to, it's hard to know how she's spending her time, or her money. But if I try questioning her, she'll just explode, the way she does with Mum.'

Seeking to reassure, he latched on to the most tractable thing. 'Well, if she goes out all the time, won't that be it? If she's drinking in pubs and clubs in the city centre, it can't be cheap. You buy one round, even in my local in the village here, and there's a tenner gone, just like that.'

'Well, maybe. You might be right. Someone at work said there's a bar in Angel Street charged her eight quid for a small gin and tonic and a packet of cashew nuts. She was annoyed because she doesn't even like cashews, but apparently they don't sell plain old crisps or peanuts.'

The anxiety was submerged rather than dispelled, and he knew they had glanced away from its cause. Gingerly, he tried another approach.

'So, it must have been messy when your mum moved out. Was there a big bust-up?'

The pause seemed not so much a holding back as a thinking space. 'Oddly, no. Or not exactly – no big, blazing row, as such. Nothing worse than the way they were all the time.'

'But – when Jess moved back in with you . . .'

'She didn't. It wasn't like that. She never went.'

At, what, fourteen? Kim and Cassie in five years' time.

'When Mum moved in with Dave, she expected Jess to go with her but Jess dug her heels in and said she wasn't going; said why should she up sticks and go and live with Mum and her new lover-man, and be the gooseberry? So Mum ranted and raved but in the end she had to give in. When Jess makes her mind up, there's no budging her. And honestly, it was the best option.' He heard her draw in breath, mustering the power to make him understand. 'It's like they were locked in this constant, destructive battle, that Jess needed to get away from. It was sending her wild, making her do crazier and crazier things. Driving her away. And I was going to be here anyway, with Sal. Jess and I got on OK. We could all see it was the best solution for Jess. Best all round, in fact.'

Best all round! Sal would have been seven; Mina twenty-four, and saddled with an angry teenager. Surprised at the fierceness of his protective response, he was trying very hard not to judge the mother. Mina, perhaps intuiting it, was defensive in her turn.

'It worked well, honestly – much better than when Mum was living here. She came round loads. Picking up Sal when I was working, bringing casseroles, bits of shopping. She and Jess got on better, at least for a while. Not being together all the time helped. Breathing space, you know.' Then, he could hear it, she was smiling again. 'Like people who can put up with their ex much better once they've split up.'

This was simpler, something he could understand and agree with. 'More distance. Less tension.'

'Exactly,' she said, and her relief at his imagined understanding prickled him with guilt. 'You know, I don't normally tell all this stuff to— to new people.' His heart leapt absurdly to fancy that

the excised word might have been 'boyfriends', or at least 'men' –
then plunged with equal foolishness to think it was more likely
'strangers'.

He cleared his throat. 'It must have been tough for you, though.
I mean, it's a lot to take on, a stroppy teenage sister, and with a
daughter of your own as well. Does she argue with you, too?'

'Not really, no. I suppose I'm less of a threat or something. Less
of a wall to kick against. Mum always tries to lay down the law,
and Jess can't stand that, it just gets her spoiling for a fight. I haven't
tried to tell her what's what, or how she should live her life. I mean,
how can I, to be quite honest?'

There was a change of inflection in these last words which made
him diffident as he asked, 'Why? Because you're not her parent,
do you mean?'

A short, mirthless laugh. 'What am I going to say to her? Go
to college, get yourself trained. And whatever you do, don't get
knocked up at seventeen like I did and wind up working in a
bloody call centre all your life.'

Torn between shock, embarrassment and a desire to hug her to
him like one of his daughters, he was relieved instead to find that
she was laughing again, but properly now, and joining in was suddenly
easy and the right thing to do, and camaraderie was restored.

'How about you, anyway? Here's me moaning on about my lot
and I haven't even asked about Cassie and Kim.'

'Oh, they're fine.' He regretted at once the polite reflex which,
usually no more than a conversational shorthand, was today accompanied by a guilty lurch.

'So what did you get up to this weekend? Anything nice?'

'We went for a bike ride.'

'Bikes?' It was hard to decipher the short syllable, but whatever
the intimation, he felt certain that Mina and Sal – let alone Jess –
never went out cycling for pleasure.

'Well, it's a bit flatter round here than in Sheffield. Less taxing
on the leg muscles. We're pretty sedate.'

Apparently, though, she had not been picturing skintight Lycra. 'I was just thinking, you know, a Cambridge lecturer, of course you'd have to have a bicycle, wouldn't you?'

He laughed, even as he defended himself. 'It's true I do have one at work, to get me to lectures and the library. Everything's pedestrianised, and the timetable doesn't factor in time to walk. But this is my home bike.' Less upright, broader-wheeled, and an awful lot more muddy.

'You actually have more than one bicycle?'

The incredulity seemed rather unfair, since she must deal daily with people who owned more than one thirty thousand pound car, but he pressed on past it.

'There's hardly any traffic on a Sunday, not on the back lanes.'

'Where do you go?'

'Sometimes to a pub, for a sandwich, or just a lemonade.' Sitting in a beer garden, in the summer, or by a log effect fire in winter, with Ollie lying flat out under the table, ribcage heaving as if heart or lungs must give out from her headlong gallop after their wheels, but tail still gamely thumping the floor. 'Or else the woods. We go blackberrying there, in the autumn. And the girls are not too old for hide and seek among the trees – except that the dog always gives them away by running over and barking. Other times we just go out and ride, to nowhere in particular: as far as we get and then back again.' The twins two abreast behind him, pink and united and laughing at nothing. *But not today.*

'It sounds fun. Mum had an old bike – I think it might still be in the garage at Dave's – but I never even learned to ride. Nor Sal, either.' She giggled. 'Blame the city council – the buses are too good! But anyway, which was it today? Underage drinking, or a round trip to where you started from?'

'Actually, they couldn't decide. They – well, there was a bit of an argument.'

'Ha! So, join the club.'

'They did rock, paper, scissors.'

'Very civilised.'

'Yes, but . . .' How could he begin to explain? 'The thing is, it's always been a sort of family joke. Rock, paper, scissors: it doesn't work with them.' It had even been a bit of a party piece at one time, an act to impress occasional house guests and upstage birthday conjurors. 'They always come out with the same thing. I don't know how – don't think they know themselves – they just do.'

'Really? That's, er . . .'

'Freaky. It's OK, you're right, it is weird. Only today, they didn't. Didn't do the same, I mean. Cassie won first time.' Her emphatically flat-fingered paper, curling to wrap Kim's stony fist.

'Oh,' said Mina, though he felt she would have said more, had there been anything more to say. 'And, um, where did she choose for your ride?'

'She wanted to go round by the travellers' site to pat the ponies, and Kim was for going to the woods. Since Cassie won, ponies it was.'

'Doesn't Kim like horses? Can't say I blame her – they scare me to death. Sal used to want to stroke police horses, when she was younger. You get mounted coppers around town on a Saturday sometimes if United or Wednesday are playing at home. I was always convinced they'd have her hand off. Teeth the size of a cake server.'

Grinning, he assured her, 'Actually, she's pretty keen on them, too. Though I'm rather with you on it; they are alarmingly large.' Bev had been the horsy one. 'No, it's more because Cassie is friends with a couple of the traveller children. It's a recent thing, a bit of an infatuation, and Kim feels excluded, I guess.' The grin had unravelled and slid away. 'It's funny, really. I used to worry about them: worry they spent too much time only with each other, wish they'd have more separate friends. But now that it seems to have happened, it isn't at all how I'd imagined it. In fact, to be honest, it feels pretty horrible.'

Into his mind reared the picture of Kim, dismounted and

clutching her handlebars like a barricade as she hung back in the shadow of the hedge at the site entrance, refusing to follow them in. The knot of piebald poines at the fence had looked lumpier than before in their mud-caked midwinter coats; on the cold air they blew up a storm of breath at the approaching Cassie like cartoon bulls at a toreador, an image at odds with their quiescent solidity. He had stood uncertain, torn between the two girls, while the dogs sniffed incuriously at his trouser legs; he was caught there in no man's land by Paula Mahoney, drying her hands on a checkered tea towel as she hallooed from the steps of her trailer, inviting them in for a mug of something and a warm-up by the gas fire. Shannon and Diarmuid, she explained, were out, gone along with their father to a job over at Littleport ('just for the ride, mind you, for they'll be little help to him, sure enough'). Peter could almost have forgotten himself and called over to Kim: *It's OK, they're not here.* Instead, of course, he had spurned the proffered hospitality, too awkward to indicate his other daughter, stranded with her bicycle by the gateway.

'They are hardly speaking.' It was only as he said the words out loud that he realised the truth of them. 'Normally, they talk all the time. To me, if I'm there and prepared to listen, but if not, then to each other.'

Except that wasn't quite right, or at least it didn't quite convey it the way it was – or used to be. 'Talking is the wrong word for it, but when they're on their own together, they're always, I don't know . . . interacting. It's not necessarily a conversation. They often don't do anything – you know, play a game or anything like that. They just hang out.'

'That's what kids do, isn't it? I wish Sal would just hang out more, with her friends, instead of burying herself in books.'

'But they're not gossiping or even exactly chatting. It's like . . .' It was like him and Bev, at the beginning, those first few months. 'It's like when you're in love. As if the rest of the world exists only at a distance; there's just the two of you. They can just giggle for hours about – God, half the time I don't even know what it's about.' Even when he listened he was an outsider to their arcane lovers' dialogue: a word here, half a phrase there, a renewed spurt of laughter. Until recently.

'Now, though, these last few weeks, it's different. Normally, if they're in the same room, there's always a connection.' Almost tangible: taut and alive, like wire. 'But these days they're just sort of separate. Like two completely separate people.'

It was a few seconds before she responded: diffidently, unfamiliar with these mysteries. 'And isn't that a good thing?'

'I suppose so.' Trying for stoical, he succeeded in sounding merely miserable. 'It just doesn't feel that way, that's all.'

Separate people. It was what he had always wanted, what he'd worked towards, wasn't it? But the reality was very different from the bookshelf abstraction. The whole house seemed out of kilter: two bodies thrown off their trajectory, jolted into separate orbits, closely tracking but no longer intersecting.

'Growing up, growing apart. It's not going to come without a bit of pain, is it, I suppose?' She groaned. 'Sorry, that sounds so corny, doesn't it? Like the problem page in one of the magazines the older women read in coffee break, at work.' Then she was laughing again, wryly self-deriding. 'Next, I'll be telling you all they need is to take up a new hobby, or get out more.'

'Actually, no, you're quite right.' He spoke seriously: to hell with avoiding embarrassment. 'Talking to you is a great help.'

'Aunt Mina's telephone advice service. Dial up for a dose of homespun wisdom.'

'Well, I'm just as bad. Peter's Parentline: no homily too glib. We should go into business together.'

'Might pay better than flipping car insurance.'

His smile was showing no signs of fading when he replaced the receiver a short while later. Ollie, who had already taken her cue to yawn and stretch from the return to briskness in their good-byes, sat up and regarded him with brimming eyes.

'OK, no need to look so tragic about it. It's not that late, I'll take you out now. The rabbits won't be in bed yet.'

It was this fresh piece of manufactured guilt which led back to his original train of thought, when he had sat down to make the call. Odd, it now struck him, that all his compunction had been towards Jeremy and Martin, and Trish, and none of it towards Bev.

Man and dog stared at each other for a moment, silent co-conspirators. Then Peter keyed up the speed dial list and logged in Mina's phone number.

Chapter 12

It was the leather jacket Mina couldn't understand. Battered to suppleness, it had been given to Jess by that boy Kiernan she'd gone out with for the best part of six months, back when she was fifteen; a trophy, no doubt once treasured for smelling of its owner, then kept, unreturned, in partial reparation when he dumped her for the spike-haired girl from their Design and Technology class. Why would Jess part with the jacket?

Not that much sense was to be made of anything, lying stiff-limbed in the unbounded darkness, which could not even be measured into hours without the risk of waking Sal as she raised herself to squint at the alarm clock. It was one of the nights when her daughter had crept into her arms with a tale of funny creakings in the roof, and Mina permitted herself a shallow sigh as Sal shifted further over on to her stomach, away from the confines of her mother's embrace. Her flatter profile and the widened distance between them allowed Mina sufficient leverage to lift her head and shoulders a few inches from the pillow, craning to make out the floating digital display. 2:27. Scarcely even a late night for Jess and her friends; certainly far too early to be counting down to the dawn. Sal had been here maybe an hour; if Mina had put her light out at eleven thirty that meant she had so far managed less than two hours' sleep. Not enough; not nearly enough, with eight hours of claims calls ahead of her and fifty other things to do before she could lay her head down again. She should close her eyes again; there would be no getting to sleep with them open like this. Clock-watching was too tempting – and thoroughly destructive. Already it had flicked on to 2:30: three more minutes of lost repose.

When the other clothes had begun to disappear, she had ignored it, dismissed it from her mind. True, it was usually Mina who ran them through the machine with the rest of the wash; as often as not, she folded them, too, and returned them in a pile to the end of Jess's bed. A few things, she had even bought herself: a warm fleece last winter, a pair of new trainers. But they weren't known the way Sal's clothes were known, more intimately than her own. It's not that she'd ever been one of the pink-socks-on-Tuesdays kind of mums, matching knickers to T-shirts, but she could remember exactly where each item of Sal's had been purchased, had by heart every resewn button, every felt-pen mark that wouldn't wash out, every place where the toes were wearing thin. Jess's wardrobe, though, was a ragbag of cheap sale bargains and charity shop gleanings, supplemented by borrowings from friends, and things had always disappeared in the opposite direction, as clothing circulated like coinage. It was only recently, when the lessening of the heaps could no longer be denied, that Mina had been forced to take notice. And now the leather jacket was gone.

2:43, and her eyes were now so used to the darkness that she could see the detail of Sal's sleeping back and not just its outline. The small, disconnected marine creatures — royal blue starfish and turquoise seahorses — appeared the same shade of dim orange-grey in the curtain-filtered light from the street. The sleeves were getting short, and the legs must be the same; the label, she knew, said 'age eight to nine'. There were only really the pink candy-striped ones that fitted properly now; perhaps she should take her shopping for pyjamas on Saturday, with the bribe of a library visit afterwards. That would be her daytime daughter again, the ten-year-old one, ironic and contained. How could Sal be so self-sufficient during the day, but come crawling under the duvet like a toddler, so needy at night?

Maybe it would have been different if she had ever seen her father. But she never had, so the notion was far-fetched. That door had been closed, firmly and finally on both sides, before Sal was even born — to little beyond mutual relief.

Jess wouldn't give the jacket away, of that Mina was almost certain. Except maybe to a boy, in a rush of fondness or the need to impress. But she hadn't even seen Jess with a boy, not since Ed with the bike. Of course, she might have sold it. Debbie at work had bought a leather jacket on eBay and seemed to think it a steal at thirty pounds, and there was no denying Jess was always short of cash. But Kiernan's jacket, the beloved jacket? Somehow it didn't seem likely.

So if she hadn't lent it to someone and she hadn't flogged it, what possibility did that leave? The jacket had to be wherever it was the other clothes had gone, along with the tins of soup and corned beef that were missing from the kitchen, the smaller of the two enamel saucepans and – Mina was almost sure – a couple of spare blankets from the airing cupboard. It was the only explanation. By slow degrees, returning daily to raid the fridge and pick up clean laundry and never saying anything, Jess appeared to be moving out.

Mina was not the only insomniac that night. At around three a.m., Peter was standing at his kitchen sink with a sweater on over his pyjamas, downing a pint of water. The central heating was timed to go off at eleven and in the intervening four hours the temperature in the house had fallen by more degrees than he would have believed possible, so that he felt a need to lift the toes of his bare feet out of contact with the quarry tiles for fear that they would adhere, like a wet tongue to ice. Ollie stood watching him from the doorway, tail lashing optimistically in the bewildered hope of a walk, but clearly remembering with fondness the warm hollow she had left in Bev's pillow upstairs. Alcohol always had this effect on him now: sleep claimed him as soon as he fell into bed, only to wear off far too soon, leaving him wide awake and dry-throated two or three hours later.

'Go back to bed, we're not going out,' he told the dog, but she continued to gaze at him expectantly, with only a marginal slowing of the wag at the rear end.

Drinking had not been an anticipated feature of the evening. Indeed, when the Finance and Estates Committee meeting in college ended earlier than usual at half past nine, he had rejected the offer of a quick beer down the road with a couple of his younger colleagues, pleading the need to relieve the babysitter, and driven home in the fullest expectation of being in bed before eleven, clear-headed and Ovaltined. The subversion of his righteous intentions was down to Trish, whom, upon his return, he found running a gambling lair in his sitting room. They had been playing table tennis, she explained with a look of apple pie virtue, but she'd wanted to settle them to something quieter before bed. The fact that it was five to ten, almost an hour and a half past designated lights out time, seemed not to dent her aplomb in the least. Nor did the bottle of whisky – his whisky – standing open at her elbow.

Not that he begrudged her access to anything the cottage offered in the way of food and drink, of course. And when, shifting along on the sofa to make room for him at the card table, she sloshed a generous measure into the bottom of Kim's empty orange-juice glass and pushed it his way, he did not demur.

'It's OK.' Trish's eyes danced in mock innocence over the rim of her own tumbler. 'They cleaned their teeth again after the juice.'

The three piles of coins, though, he almost decided to mention. It was one thing for him to have taught them pontoon as a means of practising addition up to twenty-one, but they had always played for tiddlywinks. Stud poker for the contents of their piggybanks was a somewhat different matter.

'It evens things up,' offered Trish by way of clarification, waving her Scotch in the air.

Cassie elucidated further. 'Otherwise it's not fair, kids playing a grown-up, so Trish has to be squiffy. It's like the ping-pong. Not whisky for that, I don't mean. But she always beats us if she uses a bat, 'cos she's bigger, so we have the bats and she has to play with a saucepan.'

'A saucepan?' Peter was struggling to keep up.

'Oh, not the scoopy pan part, that was hopeless. It made the ball zoom off all over the place. She used the back bit, where it's flat. It makes such a funny noise, honestly, Dad, you should hear it.' She rocked back on her heels where she was kneeling at the coffee table, and tipped her head back, mouth a perfect circle. 'Bop. Bop.'

Kim, folded in the armchair, shook her head, cheeks puffed wide. 'More like "bock".'

Scooping up the cards to shuffle, Trish stepped in pacifically. 'Surprising how it cuts down on manoeuvrability, anyway. It's the extra weight. Probably good for the wrist, though: better than the gym. Shall I deal you in, Peter?'

Dumbly, he could only nod.

'OK, girls. Two p in if you want a part of the action. Ace to five low, jokers wild, and a pair of one-eyed jacks beats all. Cassie to open.'

He had allowed only three hands before dispatching the twins to bed: just long enough for him to let them win back some of their pocket money. They had gone up all right, with very little protest; Kim, in particular, was very quiet, though he was unsure whether it was exhaustion or if she was just out of sorts. Either way, when the departing Cassie fired a closing shot of 'Will you play ping-pong with us tomorrow and use a pan, Dad? Please!' Kim did not even join in.

By then his resolution had evaporated in the smoky fumes from his glass, and they had played until after midnight, as Trish repeatedly topped up their drinks and Peter found it took progressively less effort to fulfil his determination of letting her win all his money. Several times he was on the point of asking her how she'd found them tonight. *How were they? Did they seem different to you?* But then she would deal another hand, and have to explain what she meant by 'spit in the ocean', and the moment would pass; if she'd noticed the girls being unhappy or at odds, she volunteered nothing. He had settled instead to watching her slim wrists and long fingers as she riffled the deck to interleave the cards; she was good at it, and it gave him pleasure to see, although there was no inappropriate desire shot through it this evening, more a formless kind of nostalgic yearning, which he put down to the whisky.

Both the bottle and his pockets were seriously depleted by the time she said she must make a move. For once, she let him call a cab, and he had to go and fetch his other jacket to find the twenty pound note to press on her, in addition to her other winnings. When they heard the diesel engine and the groan of suspension in the rutted lane, they went through to the kitchen where, on the doorstep, Ollie lifted her muzzle to test the night air and Peter thanked his babysitter one final time. Trish, flapping a hand to indicate to the driver that he'd found the right house, was close enough for him to inhale her female scent. *The wrong scent.* But what had loomed in his mind instead – what rose there now, as he rinsed his glass and placed it upside down on the drainer – was not Bev's face. It wasn't any face at all, in fact, but only a name, and a voice down a telephone wire.

Mina. The suprise of it caught him in ribs like a physical blow: quite how badly he wanted to meet her.

'What size did you say she was – twos?'

Mina knelt up to squint back towards Lyn's disembodied face, framed in the square opening of the loft hatch, and almost cracked her skull on a rafter.

'Yeah. Kerry-Ann's always had tiny feet. Used to buy her shoes in the Baby and Toddler section at Tesco's until she was about five. I used to threaten to put her in bunny rabbit booties, even when she was starting school.'

Mina grinned. 'Evil mother.' Rubbing her head, she turned back to the row of assorted boxes and ancient suitcases that headed off into the darkness under the eaves. 'Sal's got clodhoppers. Five feet nothing and skinny as a rake, but she's been wearing size sixes for a year. Dave says if only she had less turned up at the ends of her legs she might be a bit taller.'

'And what does she say?'

'Threatens to kick him with them. Look, are you sure Kerry's really going to want these pumps if we find them? It must have been when Sal was in Year 3. The height of her fairy tale princess phase. They're pinkest of baby pink; you know how she still likes pink, and Kerry-Ann is such a little mini-goth.'

The head in the trapdoor gave a snort of laughter. 'Is that like a what-d'you-call-it, a Visigoth or something? Marauder causing havoc with an axe? Because if so, you're bang on the nail.'

'She had them to go with a party dress Mum bought her for her seventh birthday. Hardly worn. But Kerry'll turn her nose up – they won't go with anything she's got.'

'It's OK. She's going to dye them black, she reckons.'

'Oh, God. What, in your kitchen?'

'Outside with a bucket and some newspapers down. Let her freeze. It doesn't bother her when she goes into town in a miniskirt and bare legs when the temperature's below zero.'

Mina wasn't sure whether she should be pleased or concerned that Sal could still be persuaded to wrap up warm.

'Trouble is, I've no idea which of these boxes they're in. There's so much clutter up here. Half of it is Mum's, or Jess's stuff from when she was little. My old school reports are even here some-where, I think. She didn't want to swamp poor Dave when she moved over there.'

Leaning over to pull another box towards her at random, she breathed in an uncomfortable throatful of dust, and with it the unmistakable scent of primary school. Not Sal and Kerry-Ann's, not Marksby Road Juniors, but her own. Cow gum, she thought, as she lifted the cardboard flap; sugar paper. And poster paints, the kind you used to mix up from big tins of powder kept in the teacher's stock cupboard: strictly out of bounds. Opening the eyes that she'd closed in order to inhale, she saw only the top sheet – a collage snow scene which she dimly recognised when she ran her fingers over the slices of tin foil and paper doily – before she buried it again with a private smile.

'All sorts of crap. No idea why she's kept it all.'

Behind the first line of boxes were others, pushed beyond the point where the floorboards ended, so that they balanced precariously across between the joists. One old, sagging carton, proclaiming itself as having once contained baked beans at $7^1/_2$p a tin, had given way under the burden of years, tipping a scatter of old Christmas cards into the dark space below. Mina shuffled forward on her knees to the edge of the flooring and reached down to retrieve them, pulling her hand back in distaste as her fingers brushed glass fibre insulating fleece, prickly and damp, setting her teeth on edge like chalk on a blackboard.

'Might be further along. I'm pretty sure there were some bags of Sal's old things. Chuck me the torch, will you?'

The head rose and behind it appeared Lyn's shoulders and torso, swaying slightly. 'You sure about this stepladder? Feels pretty dodgy to me.' Letting go of the rim of the hatch rather reluctantly with one hand, she rolled the torch she was holding towards Mina.

'Ta.' Mina clicked the switch and directed the fading beam along the narrow strip of boards between the boxes. Ah, yes – here on the left. Several large carrier bags, the kind you bring back from department stores in the sales. But next to the bags there was a gap. An oblong of bare floorboard where a box should have been. Two boxes, in fact; maybe three.

'That's odd.'

Hardly aware that she'd spoken aloud, she worked her way to the next box, the one beyond the empty space. Beneath the sheet of newspaper, dry and brittle now, which had been tucked into the top of the box were files of notes. And a textbook: *Introduction to Business Studies*. The remnants of her aborted A-level course. Hastily, she replaced the newspaper. She trailed her fingers across the empty patch of floor and then examined them closely in the torchlight like a TV police inspector. She couldn't see any dust – but then she couldn't see much at all with any certainty up here in the gloom. The torch, as if reading her thoughts, wavered and gave out. One thing she did know for certain, though: she knew what was in the missing boxes.

It had always struck her as contrary that, for all the grief Mum had given Mina about her pregnancy – the stormings about ingratitude and how she'd ruined her life – she had not only thrown herself into it, long before Sal's arrival, with the gusto that was like breathing to her, but afterwards had folded carefully to 'put by' not only Sal's tiny bibs and playsuits but also Mina's maternity clothes. Mina might be partnerless, a no-hope single mum, but Mum was evidently not quite proof against the hankering to be, one day, a grandmother again.

'What is it? What've you found up there? Something mouldering? Bats in the belfry?'

'I haven't found anything. The opposite, in fact.'

'What d'you mean?'

'Something that's not here and should be.' Sitting back on her heels and banging the torch on the floor, she produced a flickering resumption of light, sufficient to find her way back to the carrier bags. 'But I think I've got the pumps, anyway. In here with her old sweatshirts from infant school. Look out, I'm coming down.'

With no room to turn, she crawled backwards on hands and knees towards the hatch, dragging the bag of clothes after her. Lyn held the bottom of the stepladder, reaching and taking the bag from Mina to ease her descent.

'Is this them?' She fished out the shoes and scrutinised them. 'Little silky numbers? Kerry's going to go crazy for these, once she's turned them black, like everything else she possesses.'

'Have you got time for a cuppa before you go?'

Lyn glanced at her watch. 'Better not. Tenants' association meeting this afternoon, and I've got to get Kerry-Ann to her dad's. He's babysitting for once. Small bloody miracle.'

The two girls were down in the kitchen, though scarcely together. Kerry-Ann was crouching to apply lip gloss in the glass of the microwave; Sal looked up, at their entrance, from the inevitable book.

'Thanks for these, anyway. Look, Kerry, what d'you reckon?'

Kerry-Ann picked up one of the pumps and held it away from her, eyes narrowed, as if trying to get past its pinkness. Then pronounced her verdict. 'Yeah. Yeah, they're cool. Thanks.'

This last word was directed at Mina, who suggested rather half-heartedly, 'Thank Sal,' and sat down next to her daughter, one hand sliding to squeeze her knee under the table, the other falling distractedly on top of the folded clothing in the bag. The smell of fabric conditioner lingered behind the must. She lifted out a laundered sweatshirt, bottle green as required by St Margaret's C of E Infants. Not that the C of E ever seemed to come into it much – except that Sal did always love the Christmas carols.

Kerry-Ann, her slick cherry lips parted in delighted mockery, leaned across to seize and hold aloft the diminutive garment. 'Ah, bless! Weren't you just the cutest little thing in this, then? Mummy's little angel.'

Sal made a grab for the sweatshirt, but Kerry snatched it away and held it up against her own chest, thrusting forward her buds of breasts and pouting like a glamour model.

'Stop that,' her mother barked at her, but Mina, for once, was oblivious of Sal's discomfiture. She was looking at the green top, but her eyes were seeing something quite different. Smaller clothes. Tiny dungarees and T-shirts and fleecy flannel sleepsuits. It was possible – just about possible – to imagine Jess selling Kiernan's leather jacket for hard cash. But baby clothes? And, more shameful of horrors, her own stretch-top jeans and billowing maternity smocks?

Not to be deterred, Kerry was burrowing back down into the contents of the carrier bag, where she soon lighted upon pink satin among the school greens and blacks. 'Oh yes – this is the best! Wow, Sal, you must have been the sweetest little cutesy-pie in this. Bet all the other girls were dead jealous. I know I would be.' Her grin was accompanied by extravagant puking gestures, finger to open mouth, over the frilled bodice and puffed sleeves.

To Mina's surprise and pleasure, Sal returned the grin. 'Grandma gave it to me. Isn't it fab? I wore it to about five parties in one month. Had little white lacy tights to go with it and everything.'

'She didn't want to take it off, the first time,' Mina told them, joining her daughter in playing to the gallery. 'It was her birthday – she was seven – and she actually wore it to bed.'

'What – and the frilly tights as well?' crowed Kerry-Ann.

The visitors left soon afterwards, and Mina said, 'Lunch?' But instead of getting up to see about making them a Saturday sandwich – cheese, or ham if there was any left, and always some pickled gherkins on the side – she sat at the table a little longer, busying herself with refolding the old clothes and returning them to order in the bag. Sal had opened her book again but, eyes on the page, spoke with casual defiance. 'I loved that dress, Mum.'

'I know, love. So did I.'

So the money had never been for drugs. She tried to make herself experience this as a relief. And the moving out, the nesting, that now began to make some sense. Though where? And with whom – or was it alone?

'Can we have tomato in with the cheese, if there are some? And can I have salad cream in mine, too?'

'I'll see.' Mina folded the top of the carrier bag neatly over and rose to her feet. 'Get the gherkin jar out, could you, please?'

Oh, Jess. I can see why you'd find it hard to go to Mum, but you could have talked to me.

Chapter 13

It was six nights later, on the Friday, that it happened, and the crisis might have been avoided had Ollie not regarded herself as off duty in the evenings. Once the junior pack members had gone up to bed and Peter had settled in the sitting room to work or leisure, Ollie always closed her eyes and collapsed on her back on the carpet, legs floppily askew above her in a parody of the chase. Even so, it could have turned out differently if he had heeded the stirrings of conscience and made a start on his weekend's marking, instead of slumping wearily on to the sofa and turning on the television. Then, just possibly, the sound of movement in the kitchen, followed by the soft click of the back door, might have registered on Ollie's slumbering spaniel brain.

The film ended at eleven and before the closing credits had begun to roll, the dog was on her feet and stretching, demanding her walk. Switching off and picking up her lead, he followed her out into the moonlit lane, where the air had a metallic tang perceptible to man as well as dog; the mud had already lost its give underfoot and would be glittering with frost before dawn.

'Brrr. Hurry up, Ol, I'm cold.'

When she continued her sniffing in the hedge opposite, he stamped his feet – cold in loose, unlaced boots – and brandished the lead at her. This far from the main road he carried it only as a threat, but to show her it was generally sufficient; sure enough, she ceased her rootling quest, squatted to empty her bladder, girl-style, and trotted obediently back to him, battering his legs briefly with her tail before heading into the kitchen before him. As he locked up, his fingers felt that the door was, unusually, on the latch,

159

without its registering on his conscious mind; nor did he notice
the space in the row beneath the coat hooks where the third pair
of wellingtons should have been, not even when he kicked off and
stowed his own boots.

A quick, automatic check round, the turning out of lights, and
he made his way upstairs. Even then, while Ollie scampered straight
for the bedroom to stake her place on the duvet, he went first to
the bathroom to brush his teeth and pass a flannel over his face
before looking in on the twins. Cassie's room was the closest. As
he pushed open the door and squinted towards the bed in the
gloom, the covers appeared rumpled but flat; when he crept nearer,
the impression was confirmed: the bed was unoccupied. Perversely,
therefore, it was with a lightened heart that he closed Cassie's door
and opened Kim's. For the first time in weeks they had not stayed
in separate rooms. Back together: back to normal. Kim's room was
darker than Cassie's; the window was small and faced out over the
lane, away from the main road and the village and the distant glow
of street lighting. He was already beside the pillow, touching the
tangled sprawl of hair that was all that was uncovered of his sleeping
daughters, before he realised; it was longer still before his baulking
brain could be forced to process the information. The balled shape
beneath the duvet was certainly too small for two children. Indeed,
it seemed to him, as his fingertips traced its bumpy contours, it
was almost too slight for one.

He didn't wake Kim straight away. First, his incredulous feet took
him back to Cassie's room to check that he had not been mistaken;
then he had to make sure that she wasn't in the bathroom, that she
hadn't taken it into her head to go to the downstairs loo, or wandered
to the kitchen in search of a drink, somehow missing him while he
was cleaning his teeth. All dark; all empty. The sitting room, too,
where she might have come looking for him, perhaps for comfort
after a nightmare; and finally the dining room, which he checked
only for the sake of completeness, and for something to do. Because
by now he knew he was only delaying the inevitable, the confron-

tation of the unconfrontable truth. The image of Cassie's missing wellies, which must somehow or other have imprinted itself at the time upon his retina, now took shape in his mind, emerging like a photograph from developing fluid. He walked unsteadily back to the kitchen; he looked; they were not there.

A cursory search revealed that her duffel coat was gone, too, and her longest scarf, hand-knitted in scarlet by Aunty Kath in the Saudi heat and matching Kim's blue one, which now hung alone on the peg. For a moment he had room for an absurd stab of relief that she would not, at least, be too cold out there. Not at first, anyway. His logical mind warned him of the urgency of the situation – that she could already have been gone an hour, two hours; that every minute was precious – but somehow his imagination would not take hold of the notion and he returned to his own bedroom on legs to which he felt only distantly connected. Ollie had not stirred during his peram-bulations, and remained blissfully unaware that anything was amiss. He plunged both hands into her warm, grey fur, noticing that his fingers, by contrast, were like ice. With the return of feeling came a wash of pure fear. It caught him by surprise, as physical as vertigo or nausea, tingling the soles of his feet and making him want to pee. The spaniel raised her head and gazed at him mournfully.

'Cassie,' he told her, and speaking the name clicked something into gear inside him. In three strides he was back at Kim's door. Picking up her fleece off a chair he squeezed her shoulder gently through the quilt.

'Come on, love. I'm sorry, but we need to get you dressed. No need to take your 'jamas off, just put your fleece on top, and some warm socks.'

He left her and went to rummage in the top drawer where her socks lived, looking for the stripy pair she wore with her wellies when it snowed and finding instead Bev's hiking socks, the ones she and Cassie always fought over. When he turned round again she was out of bed, pale and blinking against the light, a crease of pink indenting one cheek where the seam of the duvet had lain.

161

'Where are we going? Is the house on fire?'

He folded her into a hug and tried to block out her five-year-old face, here on the same spot. *Mummy? Why? Where is she?* Except it had been two pale faces, then, and two pairs of wide, bewildered eyes.

'Kim, sweetie.' He spoke into her hair, quietly, without loosening the hold of his arms about her. 'Did Cassie say anything to you? Anything she was planning, like a game, or an adventure?'

Maybe he had forgotten she wasn't a small child any more, but nine years old: nine, and a twin. Her fists were on his chest at once, pushing him away so that she could see his face.

'Where is she? What's happened? Where's Cassie?' Her voice, rising almost to a wail, had already told him everything he needed to know, before she added in a whisper, 'She doesn't tell me anything any more.'

Neither of them looked towards Cassie's open bedroom door as they passed along the landing towards the stairs, a confused Ollie at their heels.

'Uncle Jeremy's.' He made his decision only as he said the words. 'I'm taking you to Uncle Jeremy's, and he and Uncle Martin can look after you while I go and find Cassie.' *Uncle.* The girls hadn't called them that in years.

'But I want to—'

'Absolutely not. You need to be a good girl and stay with Jeremy and Martin until I get back.'

We get back. He should have said 'we', but it would make it worse to correct it now.

On the way to the door he glanced towards the telephone, but looked away again at once. Probably he ought to ring the police but it was too soon, too irrevocable a step. A numbered missing person file. He wasn't ready. Besides, it would upset Kim, he told himself: he could make the call later, from his mobile, when he was alone.

'You stay here, Ol.' Another decision motivated by fear: the image of sniffer dogs and men, spread out in a slow line across the beetfields at dawn.

They put on their boots and he wound Aunty Kath's blue scarf round Kim's neck and checked she'd got her gloves – had Cassie remembered gloves? – and bundled her into the Land Rover. The passenger seat, for once: they could both do with the company, and he didn't want her sitting next to the empty left hand seat in the back.

He was surprised to see lights on in Martin's house when they reached the villas, and even more so, consulting his watch, to see that it was barely half past eleven. Only half an hour since he had been watching the film. It made knocking them up less of a drama, but Jeremy, coming to the door after some delay in a purple silk kimono and matching slippers, could not quite disguise his startlement before, seeing Kim, he smoothed it into welcome.

'Hello, hello. Now here's a delightful surprise. Two visitors, one of them in extremely smart polka-dot pyjamas, if I may say so. Very this season – though I'm not sure they were quite designed to go with the wellingtons. To what do we owe this unexpected pleasure?'

Peter, telegraphing his thanks across Kim's bent head, ushered her forward into Martin's austere hallway, where she looked up at Jeremy and told him admiringly, 'You've got Chinese dragons on your feet.'

Rippling his toes to make them dance, the owner of the dragons turned an apologetic smile to her father. 'Martin's asleep. Hard week – he was completely bushed. Often is these days, on a Friday. Can't take the pace any longer, poor lamb. But I am fully at your disposal.' He said no more, but raised an inquiring eyebrow.

'Look, it's probably nothing.' Peter's hand crept across Kim's shoulder. 'Fun and games, some crazy lark. Kids, you know.' His improbably chirpy tone, he was sure, convinced none of the three of them. 'Cassie has decided to go AWOL. Some kind of nocturnal jaunt. I need to go and join in the hide and seek, so I wondered if you could have Kim for a bit. She could just curl up on the sofa or something.'

Jeremy opened his mouth, then closed it again. Then spoke decisively. 'No.'

No?

'No, Martin will look after her. I'll wake him up, the lazy slugabed. No business being tired, anyway, while the night is yet young. He can get up and make himself useful. I'm coming with you.'

'That's very kind of you, Jeremy, but there's really no—'

'Nonsense, nonsense. You can't go out there all on your own; you need someone to hold your hand.'

He steered them into Martin's living room, patting the leather sofa for Kim to sit, which she did for fully two seconds before bouncing up again. 'It's not fair, why can't I—'

'No!' Strain cracked through into Peter's voice, making it sharper than he'd intended. He tried to clear his throat, but found it too dry. 'No, sweetheart, you need to sleep. It's very late.'

'Your dad's already got one daughter out playing will-o'-the-wisp in the night. What he really needs is for the other one to be a good girl, and stay tucked up here until he fetches Cassie home. You'd be comfier at my house, of course, but I suppose that undomesticated man of mine must at least have a spare blanket or two somewhere, and maybe even a pillow. I'll go and get him up, and we'll soon have you settled.'

When Jeremy had departed the room, Peter was consumed by a sudden impatience with bedding and other trivia; he wanted to be off, to be feeling he was doing something. It took a major effort of will to seat himself stiffly on Martin's sofa and pull Kim down next to him.

'It'll be fun – like camping out for the night.'

'I'm not sleepy.' Her tone spoke exhaustion and intransigence in equal measure: a fatal combination. At home he might have resorted to putting on a DVD, but the shelves behind Martin's television offered little assistance; *Taxi Driver* and *Full Metal Jacket* seemed unlikely to induce peaceful childish slumber.

'Well, maybe Martin will make you a cup of cocoa and you can have a midnight feast or something.' Though jelly beans and the wherewithal for chocolate sandwiches seemed almost as unlikely here as *Piglet's Big Movie*.

When the master of the house appeared, however, looking dutifully awake and attentive and wrapped in a dressing gown Peter was certain belonged to Jeremy, he bore not only an armful of blankets and cushions but an old copy of Belloc's *Cautionary Tales*. He had Kim tucked up and listening agog before Peter and Jeremy were fairly out of the door – the former trying to remember whether any of the poems featured incorrigible Cassie, who ran away from her family and was eaten by bears.

'She'll be all right, you know,' said Jeremy, as he clambered into the Land Rover beside Peter.

'Yes. Thanks.' Peter was not quite sure which twin they were talking about and Jeremy, perhaps realising his mistake, added more firmly, 'They both will.' He had one of Martin's spare blankets folded on his knee, for all the world as if they were heading out on a picnic.

Jeremy hadn't asked anything about where they were going, and indeed Peter had hardly applied his mind consciously to the question, but now, as they reached the decision point at the end of Flattery Fen and had to turn either left or right at the main road, he began to think aloud.

'They're always with a friend, aren't they? At a friend's house, I mean.' Though wasn't that when they failed to come home from school on time, not when they stole out in the darkness after they were supposed to be asleep? Surely, anyone's parents, finding a nine-year-old on their doorstep at this late hour, would have been on the phone at once – would, in fact, have run her straight home. *And nobody had called.* Needing to think about what was most likely to have happened loosed by a fraction the grip he'd been

165

keeping on the other possibilities. Cassie not holed up in a friend's bedroom watching illicit late night TV but outside alone in the dark and the cold. Cassie hurt. His mind flowered into the jargon of TV medical drama: *exposure; shock; loss of blood.* A knock on the head: *subdural haematoma.* Worst of all was the thought of Cassie not alone – but not with a schoolmate either.

Scarcely aware of what he was doing, he flicked the indicator, brought up the clutch and swung the nose of the Land Rover left into the High Street, towards the centre of the village.

'Who are the likely contenders, then?' asked Jeremy. 'For partner in crime.'

'Well, there's Leonie Sivell, but she's at her father's house most weekends, on the other side of Cambridge, and I think she usually goes over on Friday night. Abby Fox is a possibility. Or Sophie Grimwade: Sophie's in the Guides.'

'And Girl Guides these days would stoop to harbouring a fugitive – leading the innocent astray?'

Incapable of laughter, Peter was nevertheless grateful for his friend's resolute buoyancy. 'I was thinking more about camp. Guide camp, you know: Sophie has been several times and I know my girls are envious. Maybe they've got some idea of having an impromptu one of their own. Couple of apples apiece and a makeshift shelter in the woods, very *Swallows and Amazons.* They're probably swigging ginger beer and calling it "grog". Trying to light a fire with sticks.'

'Well, I must say I think August might have been a better time to pick for it than February. I'd be wanting my hip flask, never mind ginger pop. She didn't take any animal furs with her, did she, and perhaps a dog sleigh?'

Jeremy spoke lightly, but Peter knew he was being warned out of his wishful fantasy. This wasn't *Just William*, and Cassie wouldn't be disappointed to find she'd come home again before the grown-ups had even missed her.

'Maybe I should ring first, anyway.' They could have done that

166

from home. But he needed to be on the move, he needed to be out of doors, closer to wherever his daughter was. 'Or is a knock on the door better, if you're going to get people up in the night and scare the wits out of them? The personal touch.' Like the two police officers who had come about Bev. The sergeant whose rank meant he had to do the talking, and the young WPC who couldn't meet his eye.

They'd already passed Sophie Grimwade's door, though, and had driven straight past the top of the cul-de-sac where Abby Fox and her family lived. Past the church; past the Drayman's, where Rex had long since cashed up, cleaned the pumps (with too much detergent) and switched out the lights. Talk of other friends was simply that: talk. There was only ever one place to go and look first. As he reached the last house he slowed and indicated right, pulling the Land Rover towards the centre of the road and half halting before turning across and into the narrow lane. Into the beam of the headlights swayed the open gate and the cinder yard beyond.

Jeremy kept his eyes straight ahead as he recited quietly, '*My mother said that I never should...*'

'Shut up, you old bigot.'

It wasn't only the usual welcome party of dogs that was summoned to the vehicle's approach. In the doorway of her mobile home appeared Paula Mahoney, face reduced by the headlights to a pale, flat disc, her green eyes darkly colourless.

'*And here comes Sally with a tambourine,*' was Jeremy's comment, but Peter was out of the driver's door and halfway to the steps, where she met him breathlessly.

'Well?'

She didn't look into his face, which would have told her all she needed to know, but past the side of his head to the Land Rover, trying to make out the second figure stepping out behind the glare of the lights. Sparing her the painful hope, he said, 'Look, sorry, it isn't Shannon. It's just my friend Jeremy, come to help us look for them.'

'Shannon?' Now her eyes did flick to his. 'Shannon's here with me and Gabriel. It's Diarmuid. I thought you might be bringing my Diarmuid home.'

'Diarmuid?' The conversation was beginning to take a circular course; he took a firmer grip. 'It's Cassie we've lost. I guess she must have crept out at about nine thirty or ten o'clock. Do you think they're together somewhere?'

Jeremy, emerging into the light, inclined his head graciously to Paula. 'When did you miss your son, exactly?' he asked.

There was no defensive shuttering down, in fact she turned to this stranger with something close to eagerness. 'He went out to look to the ponies, just short of nine, it must have been. He does their hay nets about that time, and checks the water trough. Bláthnaid has been lame and got a bandage on her, so he'd have been seeing to that, too. We didn't miss him for quite a while – he's often out there talking to them all hours, or off walking by himself. But when he wasn't back by eleven I started to worry, and Gabriel went out to call him in. That's why we know he's taken off. He found a saddlebag missing.'

'A saddlebag?' Peter's mind reeled. 'You mean he's taken a horse?'

Her laughter rang like a bullet round the frosty camp, metallic and shocking. 'A horse, no, Lord bless you! The saddlebags unhitch, they're just leather holdalls with pockets, and straps you can sling over a shoulder.'

'And do you know what else he took? Clothes or food or blankets or anything?' Not that he'd had the sense himself to check at home and see what Cassie might have taken with her. Apart from the wellies and the red scarf. 'I mean, does it look as if they were planning to stay out – stay away for a while?'

'Or is there anywhere you know of that he might have gone?' broke in Jeremy. 'A bolt hole, somewhere he might camp – or else a friend or relative, another person he might have gone to, and taken Cassie with him?'

She shook her head, more in perplexity than denial. 'Diarmuid has so many places. But he always rings, right enough, or else comes back before it gets late.' With insistence, she added, 'He's a good boy.'

'So he's got a mobile phone, then?' Peter clutched at the idea as at the promise of redemption.

This time the shake of the head spelled apology. 'He's had it turned off the whole time. Or else they've got themselves some-where with no reception.' She glanced back over her shoulder towards the door of the trailer, which still stood slightly ajar. 'Here now, why don't you come inside for a minute? We don't have to talk out here in the cold.'

She led them up the steps and pulled aside the checkered woollen curtain. The living room seemed more confined than on the previous occasion; Peter sat down hurriedly to avoid crowding the small space and, at a wave from Paula, Jeremy followed suit.

'Gabriel,' she said, still standing and reaching to light the gas beneath the kettle. 'My husband.'

He was a tall man, judging by the uncomfortable angle at which his legs were bent to accommodate the low level of the padded bench seat; a man who looked out of place within doors. His hair was as black as his son's, but his eyes were a dusty grey. From beneath the crook of his arm Shannon stared up at Peter, her own eyes red from tiredness or crying.

'Hello,' said Peter. 'It's, er, my daughter.' He wasn't sure how much they would have heard from inside the trailer. 'Cassie. She seems to have gone walkabout with Diarmuid.'

The other man nodded slowly but said nothing, and Peter hoped it didn't sound like an accusation when he found himself adding. 'She's only nine.'

Jeremy coughed discreetly. 'Would it help if we were to have a drive round, take a look, do some asking about?'

'We've already been round the obvious places in the van,' Gabriel said. ' Me and Michael – my brother. Nobody's seen hide nor hair of the boy.'

169

'Do you think it might be time that we called the police?' asked Peter.

Following the turn of Paula's head, he was in time to see Gabriel's eyelids flicker.

'It's not normally the first thing we do, round here, call the police,' Paula said, handing a steaming mug of tea to Peter, and her eyes held a caution as well as an apology.

They had little choice, then, but to drink their tea and rehearse again, with less conviction each time, the events of the evening and the possible places where the runaways might be; Paula spoke little and Gabriel less, while Shannon seemed to be drifting into sleep on her father's lap. Their mugs emptied, there seemed nothing to do but thank the Mahoneys, exchange promises to contact one another immediately should any information come their way, and rise to leave. As they did so, Gabriel seemed to rouse himself to some kind of effort of reassurance, perhaps for himself as much as for the visitors. Peter wondered if he was aware he was echoing Paula's earlier words.

'He's a good boy, is Diarmuid. He knows how to look after himself, sure enough – they'll be all right, the pair of them.'

Following them out into the yard and closing the door behind her, Paula laid a hand on Peter's arm.

'Don't you be minding Gabriel – you call the police if you want to. It may not be how we're used to sorting out our problems, but we do understand. We know it's what other people do.'

He managed to produce a smile. 'Right. Thanks.' And, he thought but did not say, they might actually take notice if it was a nine-year-old girl he was reporting missing – not just a twelve-year-old traveller lad.

When they were back at the villas, though, and he had checked on the peacefully sleeping Kim, tucked up on Martin's sofa, he didn't reach for his mobile. Stepping back out of the front door and over the box hedge he got as far as taking it from his pocket and pressing the nine twice, before flicking it closed again.

He wasn't sure if he was sparing Paula a difficulty or merely being a stupid, blind coward on his own account. Police on the doorstep in the night – he'd been there before and was too scared to face it again just now.

Jeremy was waiting in his own hall.

'I'm going back to the cottage,' Peter told him. 'To see if she's come back.'

'Then I'm coming too.'

Ollie was groggily pleased to see them, winding herself catlike around Peter's ankles so that she almost had him over on the kitchen floor. It would have been nice if she'd shown a little more consternation at seeing them return alone, but no doubt that was projection. Squatting beside his dog, he was suddenly aware of how exhausted he was – and to how little avail.

'Well, since we've been out, we've done precisely nothing,' he told her.

That brought Jeremy's hand to his shoulder, gently admonitory. 'I'll put the kettle on. You go and sit down.'

The sitting room is what he'd meant, but instead Peter went upstairs to the two empty bedrooms. Just to check, he told himself. But there was Cassie's duvet, still rumpled into the same shapes as when he had found it empty three hours ago. It would have been consoling to crawl under it; he half wished now that he'd allowed selfishness to overcome fatherly good sense and woken Kim and brought her home, so that he had a human form to hold close.

Back downstairs, Jeremy had made a pot of tea; thoughtfully, he had also rooted out a bottle of single malt and a couple of glasses. Peter subsided on to the sofa, where Ollie didn't need asking to jump up with him. The spaniel was soon unconscious, snug against his midriff like a hot water bottle: as with the scald of the scotch, a palliative but not a remedy for the pain.

Jeremy's face was grey and Peter had time for a distant pang of guilt.

'You should go home.'

But his friend just shook his head, and lay back in his armchair with his tea, the whisky untouched. They didn't talk much after that, and as Peter contemplated his next move, his mind played over and over the half-forgotten lines:

> *I went to the sea – No ship to get across;*
> *So I paid ten shillings for a blind white horse;*
> *I was up on his back and off in a crack.*
> *Sally, tell my mother that I'm never coming back.*

Cassie. Waiting for the phone to ring on Sunday evening, trying to settle finally to the weekend's backlog of neglected essays, Peter had been full of Cassie. So full that he could hardly force his eyes along the word-processed lines, still less take in their sense, or how they related to his question on brownfield regeneration. When it did finally ring, he picked it up brimming with the need to tell his story.

'Mina, hi. You won't believe what happened here on Friday night. With Cassie. God, she had me worried.'

'Cassie? Is she OK? What's she done?'

But suddenly, as he tried to find the words to use, events that had seemed so momentous took on an air of picture-book unreality.

'Oh, well it all turned out to be nothing very much, though she had us in a pother for a while. She took it into her head to run away from home, like they do in all good children's books. But she was back first thing in the morning.'

Mina's voice, when it came, was bright with shock. 'In the morning? You mean she was out all night – missing all night? Jesus, Peter, what happened? Where was she? Is she all right?'

Holding on tightly to his Enid Blyton images, he spoke lightly, but his hand on the receiver was shaking. *Nothing very much* – but at the time, everything.

'She was with a boy she knows. They went to a marina, a couple of miles away on a cut of the river, where lots of boats are moored up for the winter. Cruisers, you know: small houseboats. Nobody goes up there much at this time of year. They broke into one, and they were going to camp out there. Not that it took much breaking and entering, I gather, more just a case of lifting a tarpaulin and opening a window. But they were seen by someone out walking a dog on the towpath and the police were called, picked them up and brought them home.'

It had only been perhaps ten seconds, no more. From when his sluggish waking brain had first received the imprint of flashing blue behind the curtains until he'd made it off the sofa and over to the window with Ollie tumbling at his heels and Jeremy stirring in the armchair and had seen Cassie's slight figure in the drive outside, half drowned under a standard issue blanket of police grey like a suspect being bundled from the back door of a courtroom, and his chest had tightened with a silent shout of joy. But in those ten seconds he'd had time to live it all through, just the way he had four years before. *Sorry to disturb you, sir, but are you Dr Peter Kendrick?*

'God, if Sal ever did that to me, I swear I'd kill her.' The irony of Mina's words had neither of them laughing. 'How was she when you got her back? And how is she now? How did she . . . why . . .?'

All the questions, of course, with which he had been carefully not bombarding Cassie with; not bombarding himself.

'I don't know, really. She's definitely contrite. And clingy; she's hardly left my side – hardly out of my arms, in fact. They've both been the same. But she hasn't said much.'

Not to him, and not to Kim. The sisters had ended Friday night in the same bed, but the bed had been Cassie's not Kim's, and in the daytime they seemed to be circling round each other uncertainly. He'd noticed a lot of eye contact between the two of them – something they didn't normally need.

'Give it time,' Mina said quietly.

'I know: don't push it, let her talk when she's ready.' It's what the bereavement counsellor had told him, too. But thenit had been different. Their silence had united the sisters: a closed, grieving unit.

'It's funny, at first, all I wanted was to get the police officers out of there so I could have her back to myself.' Like Jeremy who, as soon as she was home and safe, had shaded out of the cottage like a cat. 'But I had to offer to make them a cup of coffee, because it was six o'clock on a Saturday morning and perishing outside and they'd just brought my daughter home, and they said yes – it was two youngish blokes, and I think they hoped there'd be biscuits, but by then my good manners were wearing thin so they didn't get so much as a plain Rich Tea, but they took an age to drink their coffee, and seemed to think we wanted entertaining with lurid tales of accidents on the A14, and Cassie was sitting at the table looking more and more disconsolate.'

'Probably waiting for you to kill her when they'd gone.' This time he knew she was smiling; he tried to join her but couldn't manage it.

'Right. Maybe that was part of it. But while they were there and I was wishing them gone it never occurred to me . . . the awkwardness. I held her tight but it felt unnatural. I suddenly didn't know what to say. As if I was removed from it all, looking in from the outside.'

He had breathed her in, his Cassie, and it hadn't been her own familiar scent he inhaled but engine oil and canvas and crushed winter grass. A lingering antiseptic tang from the police blanket. Never touch the baby bird or rabbit that you find in the lane, Bev used to tell the girls; it won't smell right when it gets back to the nest or burrow, and its mother will reject it.

'She'll come back,' said Mina, the apparent incongruity making perfect sense to him. Then, after a pause, she asked, 'What was it like? I know it's a stupid question, but I just can't imagine it at all – if Sal went missing, you know. I mean, Jess stays out sometimes, but that's different. I can't get my head round what it would feel like if it happened with Sal.'

'It's not a stupid question.' Just not one that many people would ask – though every parent must want to know. 'But you might think the answer is stupid.'

'Try me.'

It had in fact taken him a while, sitting beside Jeremy in the Land Rover in the early hours of Saturday, to place where he'd felt the same dislocation of panic before. Not after Bev's death; it stood as a permanent strike against his record as a father that, though anxiety for his daughters' grief had loomed large in his mind, the loss of his wife, at its most visceral, he had experienced only for himself. The connection, when he made it, was a surprising one. Two years ago: a theme park in the West Midlands. A rattling death-trap with some name of biblical terror – Armageddon, or Apocalypse.

'I know it'll sound like the worst kind of cliché, but I can't help it: it's how it was. It was like being on a rollercoaster.'

She didn't laugh, for which he was grateful. 'Go on.'

'Not the up and down thing, the usual image, that's not what I mean. Have you been on them? The big ones, you know, like at Alton Towers or Thorpe Park?'

'Yes. Once, at Blackpool, on holiday.'

'Me, too, just the once. I'd never been on one before, not as a kid or anything. They look quite fun from the ground, don't they? But then there's that moment: the moment when it stops climbing.' When the slow, juddering ascent levels out and the traction continues to draw the car forward to the brink of the abyss. And then all at once nothing – except for a swooping, plummeting certainty. 'Quite crazy, of course, but I was convinced the girls were going to die. They'd be dashed to their deaths, and there was nothing whatsoever I could do to prevent it.'

He was laughing himself now; but Mina still wasn't, which helped him to stop. 'Well, Friday night was the same. The same certainty – the same helplessness. And the way everything else, all the ordinary things, just stopped existing.'

Her slow nodding was almost tangible, as if she were in the room with him. 'That's the weird thing, isn't it, about those rides? There's all this stuff going on all around, families wandering about eating their chips and enjoying the sunshine and moaning about the length of the queues, and it's so *normal.* And then you go up in the air and get flung about till your head feels like it's going to explode and your legs don't work any more and the world is miles away and upside down and inside out. When you come back down to the ground you can't quite believe it's still all there, just as before.'

'That's it, exactly.'

'Vomit,' was her next observation. 'That, and a few kids with green faces, is the only sign of what you're in for, until you get up there and it's too late.'

'Right. And those notices warning you off if you've got a bad back or neck problems or you're epileptic or anything.'

'Or pregnant.'

There was something about the way she said the word that brought Peter up short.

'Mina?'

There was a soft expulsion of breath, which might have been a sigh.

'It's Jess. I think she's pregnant.'

'Bloody hell.'

Not the traditional sentiment, perhaps, with which to greet the tidings that a friend was to become an aunty; but it was Peter's first reaction and, as it turned out, it seemed to be the appropriate one.

'I know. I mean, she's only seventeen, for God's sake.'

The same age as you were, with Sal. 'But are you sure about it? You say "you think". If she hasn't said anything, how can you be certain?'

'What else would she be wanting with baby clothes?'

'Ah.'

'Yes. A whole lot of them, missing from the attic. And some of my old maternity clothes, too, if you can imagine. Well, actually, please don't imagine.'

He felt a grin gathering. 'Bev was enormous, at the end. With two of them of course, you know. I think she had to shop in Millets. The camping section: I distinctly remember one outfit that had storm guys.'

He seemed to be saying all the wrong things tonight – and then they were turning out to be the right ones. Mina was laughing; he caught the skipped beat in her voice.

'So there can't honestly be any other explanation, can there? And it does account for some things. She's been out a lot – away, you know – and when she has been here, she's been very un-communicative. Not just the usual teenager business of grunts and silences. I'm talking about really secretive. She used to tell me things; even things about boyfriends. Maybe because I wasn't Mum. But these last few months, it like there's been a wall come down.'

'Hurts, doesn't it?' he volunteered, though it was neither Mina nor Jess who was in his mind.

'I just don't know what's going on with her any more, not the big stuff, the stuff that matters. And things don't come much bigger than this, do they?'

'The money.' He called his ambulant thoughts back to heel. 'You said she was always borrowing money. I suppose this is the reason, is it?'

His reward was the flash of gratitude in her next words. 'That's right. And after I'd been imagining all kinds of things.'

'Crap shoots and opium dens?'

The flash kindled to a glow. 'Exactly. And after all that it turns out to be something so . . . well, so mundane, really. So ordinary. But so bloody devastating, too.'

It was true. Being pregnant wasn't like being a junkie, meeting dealers in dark alleys, shooting up with dirty needles. Pregnancy was normal and human and healthy; it didn't leave you dead in a ditch. But it turned your life inside out, just the same. And not only Jess's own life, either.

'Do you think she'll let you get involved? What I mean is, she might feel differently when the baby comes, mightn't she? Just because she's blocking you out now doesn't mean she won't be grateful for your help later on. Unless . . .' Maybe he was making assumptions. 'Is there a father in the picture, do you think? A boyfriend?'

'God knows. But actually, no, I don't think so. I think if there had been I can't see her being so cloak and dagger about it all. He'd have been round at the house; they'd probably have been showing off about it, in fact. How clever they'd been, how grown up, how they were going to be a family. Cooing over the Mothercare catalogue and talking about repapering her room in either pink or baby blue as if it was all some kind of game. That's just how blind and stupid she'd be about it, our Jess. That's why, that's why I wish she'd let me . . .'

There was a pause during which Peter politely averted his ear from the muffled sounds at the other end of the wire and felt more than usually inadequate. Then the noise resolved itself into a cough.

'Sorry. Ignore me. Anyone would think I'd welcome the idea of another kid in the house – no sleep for wailing at nights and piles of nappies in the bathroom.'

'Yes. I mean, no.' *I mean, I understand.*

There was no response from the other end of the line, so he tried again. 'Look, sorry, Mina, there was me babbling on about Cassie's little scrape as if it was the end of the world. And here's you—'

'Oh, don't worry. It's not me that's on the bloody rollercoaster this time, is it? And if Jess doesn't want my help, then she'll just have to ride it out by herself.'

Chapter 14

When the whistle blew at ten to nine and the lines of children rippled and shunted into the building like so many lumpy centipedes, it was also the signal for a corresponding movement of adults in the direction of the school gate. The junior playground, which had been thickly populated with knots of women, rooted and deep in conference, took on a different focus, as toddlers were called to heel, pushchair covers adjusted and goodbyes called; mums in suits checked their watches and strode, businesslike, for their cars; grandmas, pressed into service for the school run, set off homeward with sprightly step, secure in the knowledge of their indispensability. By eight minutes to nine the knots had disengaged as each person headed out separately towards the rest of her morning; by seven minutes to the initial trickle had become a flood but by five to it was back to a trickle again. By nine o'clock the non-slip tarmac was empty but for six people. Four mothers had re-formed into an informal caucus and were talking again. Two figures stood apart: Peter Kendrick, uncertain, by reason of his gender, whether or quite how to attach himself to the group, and, over by the climbing frame, a fellow outsider, Paula Mahoney. He hadn't spoken to her, he realised with a guilty jolt, since he and Jeremy drove off from the cinder yard into the night. Catching her eye, he smiled and went across to join her.

'Can you believe they need six of us just to walk two classes of nine and ten year olds round the village?' she wondered.

'Mrs Moore said the maximum is seven kids to each adult. Fifty-five kids. Two teachers and six parent helpers makes eight grown-ups: seven eights are fifty-six.' Why was he spouting arithmetic?

'Did she make you sign to say you'd read that blessed piece of paper – about loose paving slabs?' Her voice was scathing but amusement lit the emerald green.

'Oh God, yes! The risk assessment sheet.' All adult helpers on excursions beyond the safety of the school gates were obliged to read and note the list of hidden dangers which lurked beyond. In this case, the perils of crossing roads – roads that the Year 5s were used to negotiating, alone and unshepherded, a dozen times a week on their way to and from school, sweet shop and recreation field. And that was the sensible part. 'The hazards of those kerbs and bumpy bits of pavement; just asking to be tripped over. Not to mention stinging nettles in the hedges. I can see this morning is going to be life on the edge.'

The title of Trish's thesis, he reflected – and something Paula knew far more about than either of them.

There was no sign of movement from behind the criss-crossed safety glass of the double doors which led into the Year 5 cloak-room. Peter, who – like Paula, too, perhaps – had been steering his mind away from the night of their children's midnight flit, decided to take the plunge.

'How's Diarmuid?' seemed like a relatively safe and non-incriminatory way to raise the topic.

'Bloody well grounded, is what he is,' came the truculent reply, leaving him uncertain quite how to continue.

'Cassie was pretty excited about having a ride home in a patrol car,' he tried. 'Well, not at the time, of course, but the next week she took great delight in telling all her friends about it.'

'Excited?' She was staring at him with something unfathomable in her expression. Something that made him wish he had gone to work this morning after all.

Unable to pinpoint the problem, he backtracked at random. 'Of course she was scared, too. Cold and scared and worried about the trouble she was going to be in, and regretting whatever crazy impulse took the pair of them off like that . . .'

He tailed off; the green eyes remained impenetrable. Then she spoke, and there was a caustic edge to her voice he hadn't heard before.

'Exciting isn't the word I'd apply to Diarmuid's spending half the night and all the next morning in a police cell.'

It was several seconds before he found even the voice of halting idiocy. 'W-what?'

'Well, half the night in a cell, and most of the morning in an interview room, with the duty solicitor and some plummy-voiced woman from child services, and me stuck there like a spare part when I should have been at home with Shannon, because Gabriel had to go out on a job. He went as soon as we heard the boy was safe – and anyway, the last thing we needed was him down there saying his piece and making everything worse than it was.'

'I had no idea.' As if that was any excuse. 'I – I should have phoned.'

'There'd have been no reply if you had. I left Shannon with Mary in the next trailer, and it's hardly chatting on my mobile I'd be doing, sitting there on a metal chair and listening to the blessed lecture. The sanctity of private property and the slippery downhill path to a life of crime.'

'But . . .' But what? It was true that the kids had broken into somebody's boat. Maybe what was surprising was that it had never crossed his mind that they might question Cassie. Their job – he'd accepted it without question – was to bring his missing daughter safely home.

'There wasn't any damage, was there? I mean, they didn't have to force a door to get in or anything?'

A brief shake of Paula's head.

'And they didn't leave a mess?'

'Not that I know of. And I'm sure they'd not have been shy about mentioning it.' The way she was looking at him made him feel as if he'd just taken out his cheque book and offered to make things good.

'Maybe it's because he's older. Because Diarmuid's older than Cassie, that they brought her straight home and kept him in.' Although they both knew that wasn't why – or not the only reason.

'He's twelve years old,' she said, without inflection or emphasis. A child; her child.

It was inadequate, but he said it anyway: 'I'm sorry.'

Her nod of acknowledgement was brief; he could almost have called it curt.

'Diarmuid, is he . . .?' *OK?* Of course he wasn't. 'How is he?'

'He's grounded,' she said again. And this time her expression softened and the laughter was back; it gleamed not far beneath the viridian surface as, catching a movement, she turned her glance towards the cloakroom doors. 'Ah, that'll be them coming now.'

First out was a five-a-side of noisy boys, jostling in the doorway to get to the fresh air, shouting about nothing; then quickly ensued the main throng, a dense cluster of chatter and clumping trainers. The girls, for the most part, followed in a straggle of twos and threes, more focused on one another than on freedom. Cassie and Shannon came out together, arm-linked and heads bent, both talking at once. As they reached the outdoors, Cassie looked up and scanned the playground, spotting Peter and giving a peremptory wave; Shannon's gaze followed, and the Mahoneys, mother and daughter, locked eyes for a short moment, before Shannon tugged at Cassie's sleeve and the tête-à-tête resumed.

The stream seemed to have dried up when Mrs Moore emerged and with her Miss Lovatt, the other Year 5 teacher, chasing out before them two boys still flushed from the dispute which had delayed them in the cloakroom; the smaller one aimed a surreptitious kick at the back of the larger's ankle as soon as their teachers' attention had passed on. Paula, in common with the group of other mums from the opposite side of the playground, began to move towards Miss Lovatt and Mrs Moore, who had set up standard beneath a netball hoop and were shuffling clipboards importantly. Only Peter continued to watch the door with a clutch of anxiety.

It hardly lessened when finally Kim trailed out alone, concentrating fiercely on buttoning up her coat. She seemed as unaware of Cassie's whereabouts as Cassie of hers, as she edged to the periphery of the gathered circle around the goalpost. Wrenching synonyms invaded Peter's head: disconnection; dislocation; disjointure. As he approached, he could hear Miss Lovatt telling the children how tidy lawns and well-stocked flower beds were a naturally occurring feature of the landscape, but it scarcely raised his geographical hackles. He laid a hand on Kim's shoulder and, as she turned and threw her arms round him, pulled her in tight to his stomach and chest.

'Cassie's not in my group,' she told his jacket in a classroom whisper. 'She wanted to go with Shannon and her friends. I haven't got a partner.'

Seven eights are fifty-six: eight groups of seven, each with an adult.

'Don't worry, sweetheart,' he said. 'You can walk with me.'

Mina stood by the wall bars waggling her toes and trying not to notice the clock. There was a hole in her tights, she saw. Just a small one in the vicinity of her left middle toe, no issue at all when her legs were under a desk all day and her customers a hundred miles away at the end of a telephone line, but large enough to show her up at a parents' evening. It was her own stupid fault; she had been meaning to file her toenails for days. But then, she would normally have expected to be meeting Mrs Edwards with her shoes on.

The worst thing about the clock in the school gymnasium was the second hand – there, presumably, to allow for the timing of sprints, sets of press-ups and the like. That, and the overlarge face and bold hands, designed to be deciphered by infants and visible even through a haze of junior sweat, combined to make the passage of time very difficult to ignore. Five past eight; she had been here twenty-five minutes already and was no nearer to reaching the floor cushions.

Mrs Edwards was a talker. Her parent consultations always ran on well past the allotted ten minutes, so that any appointment later than six thirty meant you were sure to have to queue. Not like Mr Grossman in the far corner; Mina had been watching him shave his sessions down to nine minutes thirty, and just now, four minutes up on schedule and with no one waiting, he had slipped out for what she was certain was a crafty cigarette by the Reception sandpit. Sammy Bahia's parents weren't helping matters, either; Mr Bahia had sensibly been confining himself to smiling and nodding since eight o'clock, but Harjeet had settled down comfortably cross-legged and seemed to be telling her son's life story. Usually, they were at least in the hall, where a row of stacking chairs would be unstacked for the convenience of those waiting, but preparations for an imminent performance of *Bugsy Malone* had tonight relegated them to the gym, where the cork flooring prohibited the presence of scuffing furniture. Hence the clusters of floor cushions. It was also the reason for her disgracefully stockinged feet, and why the corridor outside resembled the entrance to the mosque in Wolseley Road on a Friday morning.

Eleven minutes past. Sal had been out there in the playground since twenty to. It was the first time she'd brought her along to one of these things. Other mums did, sometimes – single mums, probably, like her. She had passed a short line of Year 3 girls dangling mournfully upside down on the climbing frame outside when she came in. Younger ones, as well: several mothers had parked sleeping babies in buggies by the row of shoes, or were talking with desperate animation to toddlers, grizzly from being out past their bedtime and forced into idleness. One small boy of three or four had made it to within two feet of the top of the wall bars before being plucked off, wailing. But Mina always left Sal at home with Jess, or took her to Mum's. Mum had never taken her along to a parents' evening, not once that she could remember, and that seemed like the way it should be. It was private and grown up and mysterious, Mum talking to the teachers; to have to hover outside to hear the verdict was undignified, somehow: like a petty offender on a bench in a courtroom corridor. Tonight, though, there'd been no option. No Jess – there was never a question of Jess these days – and Mum and Dave were committed. It was Derek's birthday, and on birthdays Dave's family always went out for a steak; Dave was supposed to be watching his cholesterol but five times a year he permitted himself a twelve-ounce fillet steak and a stiff-peaked Irish coffee, and nothing was going to make him miss it. Mum couldn't be dispensed with, either; these were the only occasions when she was allowed to drive the Mondeo home, while Dave sat in the passenger seat and gave his full attention to digestion.

Harjeet Bahia leaned forward and emphasised some virtue or failing of Sammy's with a flourish of bangled wrists, as the toytown clock ticked past the quarter hour. *Why don't you go in and watch the rehearsal?* she had urged Sal. Lots of the other Year 6s were in it. Kerry-Ann Skinner was Tallulah, she knew, because Lyn had been scouring the shops for sheer, cream-coloured tights, small enough not to slip down and wrinkle on Kerry's calfless prepubertal legs. And the girl, Izzy, from the paper shop: she and Sal used to be pretty friendly when they were in Miss Ayling's class. At least it would have been warm in the hall, and there would have been something to watch. Not that Sal would be bored, she'd got her library book with her; it was just . . . why couldn't she have at least done scenery? Sal was handy with a paintbrush, and she always used to enjoy mucking in with the props.

At last, Mrs Edwards and Mrs Bahia seemed to have run out of things to say and, with a smoothing down of skirts and kameez, both rose to their feet, assisted by an arm apiece from Mr Bahia. Mina stepped forward hopefully, but only by a step or two, as the threesome continued to stand around the heap of cushions like bargainers at a street bazaar. She approached a little closer; not past the invisible line of privacy, of course, but near enough to be palpably hovering. It might not be politely British, but it did the trick. Hands were shaken, smiles smiled, and Sammy's parents took their leave.

'Mrs Heppenstall, so sorry to have kept you waiting.' The words were spoken with a cheerful lack of remorse. And why was it always 'Mrs' at school, Mina wondered, like an honorary title proceeding from parenthood? She still sometimes struggled not to think they were making a point. Mrs Edwards swept an hospitable hand over the assemblage of bean bags and scatter cushions. 'Take a pew,' she invited, with an apologetic smirk, again empty of all apology. 'Or maybe I should say, take a hassock.' The smirk had widened into a beatific smile; Mrs Edwards was a Christian and she didn't mind who knew it.

'Thanks.' Mina punched the nearest bean bag accusingly, before lowering herself into the resultant hollow.

'So.' The class teacher seated herself and tucked her plaid skirt round spreading knees. 'How has Sally been getting on?'

'Sal.' She must know that Sal was never Sally: hadn't been since she was at play group. Besides, shouldn't Mrs Edwards be the one telling her how things were going? A provisional answer seemed wisest. 'All right, I think.'

Mrs Edwards said nothing: Mina squirmed in the beam of her benevolence. 'That is, she seems to get through her homework OK, never has much of a struggle with it. And she hasn't mentioned any difficulties with her work in class.'

'Right. And does she look forward to school?'

'Well, she gets herself up and ready, we never have a battle in the mornings.' Not like it used to be with Jess. 'She hasn't been late once this term. She knows I have to be at work, you see; she's a good girl, thoughtful that way.'

'But does she seem happy to be going in? Is she enthusiastic?'

It wasn't only good works, it seemed, but a cheerful heart that Mrs Edwards's God required of her pupils.

'Well, you know kids that age. There's no need for a shove, as such, but she's not exactly dashing to the school gates, either. They like to play it cool.'

They both knew this to be a bluff; cool was hardly in Sal's

vocabulary. Mina pulled her laddered toes closer beneath the concealing bulge of the bean bag and went on the offensive.

'How have her spellings and tables scores been this term?' As if she didn't already know. Twenty out of twenty every Monday; twelve out of twelve every Friday.

'Very good, certainly. Very creditable indeed.'

'And her progress in literacy?'

'Again, very satisfactory. Her reading, as you know, is some way ahead of her numerical age, and her writing is generally fluent and accurate and shows signs of considerable imagination at times.'

Nodding bolsteringly, Mina pressed on.

'And science? She's always talking about what you've been doing in science.'

'Yes. I have no complaints there at all. She's attentive, she takes in the information very readily, and is able to think for herself, too. And she's never shy to put her hand up in class – always contributes plenty of ideas.'

So why was there more patience than warmth in the smile? Maybe it was maths; not the tables but the complicated stuff, those problems with brackets and x's and y's that Mina knew she could never have helped her with. Sal never appeared too taxed by them, but maybe she'd been getting them wrong?

'How about her maths? Is that going OK?'

'It's fine.'

'I mean, I know she doesn't care so much for sums, she'd really rather be reading than anything. Every waking hour, if I'd let her.'

Now it was Mrs Edwards's turn to nod – sagely, almost sadly. It brought to mind images of a priest in the confessional, though in truth Mina had no idea what that would be like; come to think of it, she wasn't sure you'd be able see the priest at all. Didn't they sit behind a grille?

'Ah yes, reading.' She pronounced it like a sin: as if it were one step from self-abuse.

Mina strove to ignore the tone. 'I don't know quite where she gets it from. I used to read when I was a kid, of course, but somehow these days I never get the time, or else I'm too tired; I start a book and it sits by the bedside for months. But with Sal, I haven't needed to encourage her at all, never have. She just devours books like they're jam butties, that's what Dave says. He's Sal's granddad – at least, he's my mum's partner, you know, and he's like a granddad, the nearest thing she has.' Once launched upon this stream of blather, she found it was hard to stop. 'Funnily enough, though, she might get the reading from her real grandfather – my dad – because I know he was a bookworm, too. I'm called after someone out of the *Dracula* book; that was down to him.'

Literary family reminiscences, however, were not to be allowed to deflect matters; a teacher could spot a prevaricator.

'It hasn't occurred to you that all this reading might be something of a defence mechanism, in your daughter's case? You know, we often use books to escape, don't you think? From our lives, the world, the daily round.' A pre-scripted pause. 'Maybe from unhappiness?'

Twenty excuses and denials danced around the edges of Mina's mind. But a certain truculence – or maybe it was just foreboding – kept her silent.

'There's nothing wrong with Sally's school work. I have no concerns on that score, no concerns at all. But I am rather worried about the social side of things. Her peer relationships.'

'Sal,' was all Mina could trust herself to say. Part of her shouted that it was none of Mrs Edwards's business. If Sal had been managing the flipping algebra all right, then what was her problem? Surely, in school world, reading was meant to be a virtue. But another part of her – linked to somewhere tight and uncomfortable below her ribcage – was repeating, *peer relationships*. And then other phrases of professional vocabulary. *Behavioural issues; educational psychologist.*

Mrs Edwards had stopped, the smile replaced by a look that radiated concern; she seemed to be waiting for Mina to speak.

'She hasn't – that is, there haven't been any specific problems, have there? Incidents, I mean, with the other girls? Sal hasn't got into a scrap with anyone, or anything?'

A sorrowful shake of the head. 'Nothing like that. Nothing physical; and even if, from time to time, the other girls say cruel things, your daughter rarely responds in kind. No, that's not the problem at all. There is little outward friction, because . . . well, to be frank, Mrs Heppenstall, there is very little interaction there at all. In my opinion, I would say that Sally is almost completely isolated.'

It wasn't something Mina didn't know already, when she ever chose to face the fact: but there was something sickening about hearing it voiced in this setting, its formality undisguised by the spurious domesticity of the floor cushions.

'She's always been quiet.'

The smile was back. 'Many pupils are "quiet", but they find their own niche, with other quiet children. This is different.'

Mina swallowed the urge to argue. Better to play along: better for Sal.

'What do you think I can do to help?'

That seemed to strike the right note; the confessional became the vicarage discussion group.

'Does she have classmates round to the house? I know sometimes children who find socialising difficult in the school playground can relax and make friends more easily at home. Perhaps you could invite one or two girls over, talk to their mothers, you know. Two at once is often better than one, it can take off some of the pressure.'

Talk to their mothers? Sal would kill her. And two rather than one? Like that day last summer: Stefi Janiak and Kerry-Ann Skinner thick as thieves in Sal's bedroom, squawking over rude 'knock-knock' jokes, while Sal sat on the back step, kicking moss tufts from between the cracks in the paving. Mina felt a resurgence of defiant resolve.

'She's happy,' she said, trying to be sure it was true. 'Sal's happy as she is.'

Outside, shoes retrieved and coat rebuttoned, she ran into a gaggle of underage gangsters: boys in pinstripes wiping off pencil moustaches with the backs of their hands, and chorus line girls, pale and shivering in silk slip dresses, awkward on their unaccustomed heels like day-old thoroughbreds. Her eyes caught Kerry-Ann's, islanded in a sea of white foundation beneath her sequined bandeau, but there was no acknowledgement; Kerry was with her friends. Threading a path between chattering hoodlums and their molls, Mina made her way by instinct past the corner of the school hall and round into the infant play area.

There, perched astride the bowsprit of a wooden pirate ship, sat Sal, reading *Robinson Crusoe*.

At about the same time that evening, Peter was pushing his way into the Drayman's Arms, grateful for its stale, beery warmth after the chill of the car park, to discover that one of his friends, but one only, was there before him. Martin was perched on a bar stool talking to Rex, and turned in relief at his approach.

'. . . might have had a decent forward line if Benitez would look at anyone who's not Spanish,' Peter heard the landlord opine, and grinned. Rex's knowledge of football, as of the weather, was based almost entirely on hearsay; the Drayman's did run to a television and it was even occasionally switched on, but it was angled away from the bar and he'd never known Rex to pay it any heed. Nor did Peter have Martin down as a sports fan; the exchange was apparently for form's sake on both sides.

'Hello, mate. What are you having?'

As usual, his pint was already foaming into the glass before he'd had time to say 'IPA, please', let alone 'thanks'.

Martin, he noticed, had taken the coward's route, eschewing the vagaries of Rex's draught bitter in favour of a pint of Stella.

'Jeremy sends his regrets again. Work crisis.'

They moved their drinks to a corner table and sat down, and Peter began the long wait for his beer to clear.

'Thought I might not make it, either,' said Martin. 'Some problem on the line. Sat in a cutting near Baldock for nearly an hour.'

Peter nodded, but he was visited by a moment of doubt. A City equities analyst and a children's book illustrator who worked from home – and which of them couldn't make it due to pressure of work? Even discounting the caprices of First Capital Connect, there was something fishy about it.

'So what was it with Jeremy, exactly? Sudden watercolour emergency? I suppose you never know when someone might not need a pen-and-ink hedgehog or two in a hurry.'

Luckily, Martin heard no bitterness in the jibe, but fell into step with a grin. 'Constantly on alert with crayons at the ready, he is, just waiting for the call. Except it wasn't hedgehogs. Hedgehogs aren't the thing. It was some post-modern princess – all girded up in armour and feminist dogma.'

'Ah yes, I know the type.' Bev had had a soft spot for books like that. 'Any prince kisses her before he's invited and he turns into a frog on the spot.'

'Or she slaps him with a sexual harassment suit.'

'Fairy tales ain't what they used to be.'

So far it was going better than expected. Nobody had had to ask about work. The silence, while Martin slugged his Stella and Peter peered at the settling contents of his glass, was barely awkward at all.

'We bought our girls a lot of books about twins. It was mainly Bev, in fact.' The reference books on the subject were mainly him, but the kids' story books were all her. 'You'd be astonished how many there are of them on the market. I don't think I remember having any myself, except Mary Plain. But Bev tracked them down everywhere, and read them to the girls: twin penguins; twin baby elephants; twins playing practical jokes at school; twins separated at birth and reunited in freak circumstances, one a princess and one a scullery maid.'

191

'I think I had one about a pair of twin magpies.'

Smiling, Peter nodded. '*Two for Joy*. Got it. Twin beavers, even, if you can believe it: Chilawee and Chickanee, in *Sajo and the Beaver People*. That one always made them cry.'

Martin sipped his lager thoughtfully. 'So, what was the idea? Make them feel normal?'

Perhaps it might have been more tactfully put: but, yes. 'That was more or less it, I think – what she claimed, anyway. Though actually I think she just loved reading stories about twins. I was always worried it might go the other way – reinforce their sense of being different, or something. But of course Bev was right, as usual.'

Children being children and the centre of their small universe, they needed very little prompting, especially when they were very young, to see the way things were for them as the very barometer of normality. Non-twin children were the oddities.

'When they first started nursery school, they had a thing about "Once-lers". They got it from Dr Seuss, you know. It was their word for children who didn't have a twin.'

'So, all the others, basically?'

Peter laughed. 'Well, as luck would have it, there was one other set of twins at their pre-school. And sometimes kids with a sibling close in age counted as honorary Twozlers. But Once-lers were the rest – the lonely, self-sufficient mass.'

'Don't remember Once-lers. What are they in – *The Cat in the Hat*?'

'No – a book called *The Lorax*. It's just him – just the one of him. And you never see him, except for a pair of hands.' The top half of the IPA looked safe to sip now. So he sipped it. 'Mind you, there's no need to feel too sorry for him. He's only on his own because he's committed environmental genocide. Chopped down all the truffula trees.'

Over the rim of his pint, Martin nodded seriously, making Peter wonder if he was being humoured. Why was he blathering like this? But he didn't seem to want to stop.

'So, anyway, Cassie and Kim were Twozlers, like all the twins in their books.' Slightly fractured Twozlers, perhaps, these days – but still Twozlers, for all that. 'Everything and everyone, for them, seemed to fall into twos. I suppose relatives often bought them matching teddies, matching dolls – but all the contents of their toy box had to be neatly married off. I think we coloured it, too. Bev and I were Twozlers as well, you see. We came as a pair, as far as the girls were concerned.'

But not any more. That was how it had felt – how it still sometimes felt. People talked casually of 'other halves', but it was only when you lost yours that you realised how true it was. He'd felt distorted, incomplete; perhaps he still did. A conker with one flat, exposed side. What was it about Rex's beer? It had barely wetted his lips and the melancholy had set in. He sighed. 'I don't think nature intended me for a Once-ler.'

The silence that followed this confidence was pregnant, forcing him to look up from his beer, into which he had been staring moonily. Martin: this was Martin he was talking to, he reminded himself, not Jeremy. The poor man had the air of a cornered rabbit, cut off from its burrow. But maybe Peter had mistaken the case, because now his companion leaned back in his chair, head brushing Rex's rustic brick-effect wallpaper, and said, 'Nor Jeremy, either.'

Peter looked at him inquiringly.

'He's much too gregarious. Natural born Twozler.'

Or possibly even a Threezler, speculated Peter, though he instantly repented this piece of rather invasive levity.

'I mean, he's a fastidious old sod, doesn't like other people's mess. But when it comes down to it, he was never meant for a Once-ler.'

Slightly awkward, they both picked up their glasses and drank. But Martin hadn't finished.

'Trouble is, I suspect that I am. Really quite a Once-ler, to be honest.'

It was Peter's turn to nod, and to find nothing to say. Maybe,

193

he pondered, it was Ruby who had somehow kept the balance. Maybe that had been how it worked. Maybe it was harder for them, in this way as in others, without her there. Surviving without Ruby . . . Surviving without Bev . . .

Without conscious forethought he suddenly found himself saying something. Something undoubtedly stupid.

'There's this woman.'

Stupid, unguarded, inappropriate, embarrassing. Almost certainly deluded. He had Martin's full attention, but didn't meet his eye.

'It's nothing, really. Just a new friend, I suppose. Except that sometimes . . .'

What was he prattling about? It really must be the beer. Into the trailing end of his words, Martin inserted a cough.

'Look, I'm not the one to advise you about women, mate.'

Then he grinned, and the tension was broken as he added, 'On several counts.' He swigged at his drink, then pulled a face. 'If it's relationship counselling you're after, then Jeremy's your man. Fancy some crisps? This Stella tastes of disinfectant.'

It was while Martin was at the bar fetching two bags of cheese and onion that the pub door swung open and Jeremy walked in. He approached the bar, nodding to Rex and skimming a hand briefly across his partner's back, before hailing Peter and coming across to the table.

'So sorry to abandon you both. But my toils are over now, and my thirst is great.'

'You've finished the illustrations, then?' Peter moved his jacket from the third chair for his friend to sit down.

'Finally, yes. All packed up into their padded envelope and ready to be entrusted to the courier at dawn's first light.' Stretching out his legs as expansively as the pedestal feet of the small table allowed, he smiled his broadest smile. '*The Perils of Penelope the Peregrinating Princess*. She put up quite a fight, I can tell you. A doughty campaigner. But at last I have her corralled; she is home from her travels and safely back in bed at the castle.'

Was he being mocked, he wondered? As Martin came over with the crisps and Jeremy's gin and lemonade, and Peter caught a fleeting expression on Jeremy's face, the suspicion he had entertained earlier took hold again and began to harden. Drawings or no drawings, he was sure of it. Jeremy had set the two of them up.

It was neither Sal, friendless at school, nor Kim, sisterless on the geography walk, who couldn't sleep that night. Rather, it was Cassie who came down in dressing gown and polar-bear slippers, seeking parental reassurance. Peter, having dispatched Trish back to Cambridge in a taxi, had one eye on late night television and one on the *Planning and Environment Review* when he heard the wooden clunk of the kitchen door latch. He waited until sound gushed in the pipes behind the wall, giving whichever twin it was time to establish her cover: the compulsory drink of water.

As he came in, she turned gratefully, poised with one polar bear denting the other's snout – and then back to the sink, not quite in time to cut the flow of water as it spilled over the rim of the glass and down her wrist. Ollie, who had padded through to the kitchen behind him, made for her bowl and began, noisily and with a lack of accuracy which defied evolutionary logic, to slop water towards her mouth with her tongue. All for one, thought Peter; he picked up the kettle and joined Cassie at the taps. The heat she had brought with her from under the duvet fuzzed the air above the collar of her dressing gown but still, out of habit, he asked her, 'Cold?' His question, and her shrug, were sufficient excuse for him to wrap an arm round her shoulder, fretting at the soft towelling with his hand. She responded with pleasurable 'brrrr' noises, and she was four years old again, and he was rubbing her dry on a windy beach.

There was an armchair in the kitchen. Its calico worn to slippery silk, it had once belonged to Bev's grandmother and had stood in the corner of the guest bedroom when they first moved in and still boasted such a luxury. Bev had moved it down when she was nursing the girls, so that she could feed them, propped into position with cushions for lack of sufficient hands, while she watched Peter cook their supper; somehow it had never gone back. The kettle filled and set to boil, he sat down in the chair now. It was all the invitation necessary; Cassie ceased her hovering, forgot her drink and planted herself at a comfortable right angle across his lap, bottom wedged firmly against one chair arm and slippered feet dangling over the other. Funny, he thought, how a piece of family furniture provides such a physical measure of passing time. The two girls together had once fitted endways within the span of those arms: his hands to left and right cupping their crowns to guard them from the cool, taut fabric, their curled toes nudging together in the centre of his lap. Twenty toes; he remembered thinking it unimaginably many. And now she was so very long: long-armed and long-legged – too big for this, really – though the weight on his thighs remained slight. What did she weigh now? Five, six stone? He had little idea; mercifully, children's clothes were sold by age and not by centimetres. But Bev would have known, he was sure. Not, perhaps, in the charts and percentiles way she would have known it when they were small, but still she would have known.

Cassie's head lolled sideways against his chest; her breathing was shallow, insufficient to create even an imagined lift and fall in the arm he had folded about her. She said nothing, and he wondered whether she had fallen asleep there, as she and Kim both used to do sometimes when they were half her size, while Bev sang Gershwin numbers as she rinsed cocoa mugs at the sink. In fact, he may have been half dozing himself, because when she spoke, it took him a moment to place himself, and several more to understand what she was telling him.

'I thought it would be exciting, but it wasn't.'

'Exciting . . .?'

'It wasn't. It was cold.' She hadn't raised her head, and the words tingled through the wool of his sweater. 'And when we got to the place – with all the boats, you know – it was even wetter and muddier and colder than anywhere else. You'd think it would be nice, a boat, like those old-fashioned ones you see on telly, painted all pretty colours with horses pulling them. I thought there'd be bunk beds and a dinky little kitchen and everything, and a kettle, like in his mum's caravan, but there wasn't anything, just two benches covered in slippery plastic stuff, and some ropes and stinky old fishing baskets, and loads of water in the bottom so everything got soaking wet as soon as you put it down. Diarmuid put the bag down, and it got in the water and he said the f-word.'

The rush to confide seemed to have spent itself, and he felt Cassie's nose burrow closer into the lambswool comfort of his chest. He hugged her close, and murmured the universal mantra of reassurance, in which individual words were not important. His own Cassie, his own little baby, safe now, safe here with him. And then relieved of her burden, she was shepherded readily back to bed. Very soon, leaning motionless on the landing wall by the crack of her bedroom door, he heard the familiar, snuffling sounds of her sleeping breath.

Chapter 15

On the Saturday at the end of a long Lent Term, Peter could have done without his college supervisors' garden party. For one thing, mid-March was a peculiarly optimistic season for outdoor entertaining, and after an hour of huddling in well-muffled groups on the windswept Fellows' lawn, the attractions of the daffodil backdrop had paled and hosts and guests alike had fled to the comparative warmth of the Senior Parlour. For another, the last nine weeks of intensive teaching and administration had drained him of enthusiasm for the company of his colleagues. After eight weekends when he had too often had to say 'no' to them, he wanted only to be at home with Cassie and Kim, taking them for a bike ride, or getting messy with cardboard and glitter glue. He also hated that the event began at two o'clock. A lunch or a dinner had a naturally confined time frame, but an afternoon party had no natural end; this one, gloomy past experience reminded him, tended to drag on until the last of the circulating trays of canapés was empty and the last of the wine bottles drained – or the serving staff drew stumps and went home. Luckily Trish hadn't supervised for him this term. When in the past she had done so, she had enjoyed her free drinks with the best of them and been among the last to leave; her absence this afternoon, however, meant she was available to babysit, feasting not on chicken satay and crab puffs but the large plate of corned beef sandwiches he had left in the fridge for her to share with the girls.

It was after five when the last Geography supervisor gathered his coat and scarf and Peter was able to head home. During the early stages of the party, he had almost regretted the intemperance that had led him to leave the Land Rover in the drive and catch the bus in, but as the long hours unrolled he had increasingly found that the mid-list college white wine was the best way to get through things; it was surprisingly palatable, in fact, he realised – and after all, he had to justify not driving.

There was a queue at the bus stop. He had once heard somebody on a smug Radio 4 chat show saying that any man over the age of thirty travelling on a bus must have failed in life; at the time he had yelped and banged off the radio, but now as he boarded the bus, lone male among so many women laden down with toddlers and Saturday shopping, he couldn't help smiling. Maybe it was the Sauvignon de Touraine making him sentimental, but his mind turned to Mina on the number 27. Why did he remember the number of the bus she caught – like so many other small details of the life she described? Saturday: she would be ringing him tomorrow. He could entertain her with stories about the bloody garden party.

Back at the cottage, Trish was stretched full length on his sofa with the *Radio Times* open across her stomach, Ollie somnolent across her ankles and her eyes closed. But they snapped open at his approach.

'I'm thinking about my footnotes.'

He grinned. *Not*, as the twins would say. Where were they, by the way, while their minder dozed unheeding? The rest of the house was disconcertingly quiet.

'In fact,' sitting up, Trish pushed a hand back through her fringe so that bits of it spiked crazily upwards before toppling back to join the unruly mass, 'I was thinking about my conclusion. I think I might need to rework it a bit, to take account of those new insertions in chapter three . . .'

He held up a hand, less a red light and more a white flag. 'Not today, Trish. Please, no more shop talk today.' And then in propitiation, because he hated nothing so much as dented enthusiasm, 'How about coffee?'

Obediently, she followed him through into the kitchen, saying nothing but still, he rather feared, thinking about geography.

'How have the kids been?' he asked. It may have been partly a diversion from her thesis, but these days the question was more than just a formula. They both knew it; he caught her glance towards him and then away again before she shrugged.

'Oh, OK. Great. They're never any trouble.' Which she was well aware was not the issue. Taking down two mugs while he put the kettle on, she added, 'We played Scrabble, because Kim didn't fancy cards. I gave them both a hundred point start – because, as you know, I'm a demon – and, actually, it was Cassie who won. They were bickering a bit, because Cassie got rid of all her letters at once with FLETCHER going across my ZLOTY, and Kim said names aren't allowed. Cassie pointed out there's a girl in their class called Fletcher and it means a person who makes arrows, and I had to admit she was right, so Kim went into a sulk; but she carried on playing, and soon cheered up again. They've been fine.'

'Where are they now?'

'Just gone upstairs. Cassie said she wanted to read a book.' She held out the mugs for him to take, stopping just short of digging them in his ribs. 'Honestly. They're fine.'

More in gratitude than conviction, he nodded and took the mugs, spooning in the guilt-free granules. Fair trade, organic and decaffeinated: the full set.

Trish was looking at the jar, too, in some scepticism. 'Decaf? I might want to be up working late tonight, you know.'

'Like you were working when I came in?'

This produced a pout, but he knew she was pleased with his teasing by the way she switched the subject.

'Do you think the twins'll want another drink? They had some juice at about four o'clock. Shall I call them down, or are you going to go up and say hi?'

He always went up. Even when she babysat late, and they were in bed when he came home. It mattered to him that Trish had never shown the least surprise at his habit of saying goodnight to his nine-year-old girls when they had been long asleep and would not know he was there, blowing a kiss from the doorway and whispering that he was safely home. But now he prevaricated.

'Oh, they'll come down when they're ready. It's rare enough for them to be reading without coercion – let's not interrupt them.'

What was it he had he told Mina? *Reading tends to be a solitary activity.* That was the real reason he didn't want to go upstairs: he knew he would find them curled up on two separate beds.

'Do you have to get straight back, after this coffee? Or stay and have supper with us?'

'Well, I really ought to be working on that concl—'

'Shut up. I've said: no work talk tonight.'

Back in the sitting room carrying both mugs, he had to use his foot to shoo Ollie off the sofa, where she'd appropriated the place warmed by Trish. 'You know you're not allowed on the furniture,' he said weakly, the lie convincing none of them. The spaniel gave him an old-fashioned look and settled pointedly at Trish's feet when they sat down with their drinks.

'Perhaps I should give you a game, then, before I put the fish fingers on?' Peter nodded at the Scrabble box, which was still out on the coffee table. ZLOTY, he thought, smiling. 'Do you play for money?'

She was flashing her teeth at him like a shark at its dinner and unfolding the board when the telephone rang. Peter picked up the handset from under the spill of square, cream tiles. Trish always brought it in here when she babysat: in case he rang in for any reason, he assumed, and not to make calls to relatives in the Antipodes.

'Peter, is that you?'

Mina. The first thing to register on his alcohol-slowed brain was a mild, formless irritation: not at her, exactly, but at unruly circumstance. It wasn't her night, and it was too early; she was meant to call on Sundays after the kids were in bed, when he was comfortable with a beer and something on which to rest his feet – and when Trish wasn't here. The second thing was why she would wonder if it was him. Of course it was – who else could it be? And why did she sound so distracted?

'Yes. Hello. It's me.'

'Oh, Peter, I'm so glad you're there.' More than just distracted; she sounded . . . well, he wasn't quite sure what it was but it made him regret his own slight note of irony. Not that she seemed to have noticed. 'Can we talk?'

The oddness of the question made him shoot a furtive glance at Trish, busily flipping Scrabble tiles letter side down.

'Of course. What's the matter?' Because by then he knew for certain that something was; but still he was taken aback when his recognition of the fact brought a sound from the other end which could only be a poorly suppressed sob. Was it Jess? She'd been so worried about pregnant Jess.

'It's Sal. She's disappeared.'

'She's what?'

'Well, maybe that's putting it a bit strongly. I really don't want to sound like it's some big drama, not like with your Cassie; I mean, with Cassie it was at night, and Sal's a year older, and it's still just the afternoon.'

At the moment. He could almost hear her thinking it, and glanced involuntarily at the sinking sun beyond his own window.

'It's actually only been an hour or so. I called Mum, but she and Dave are out somewhere, and they're hopeless, they never have their mobiles switched on. When Dave's not working, you know: says he doesn't like to feel on call. Even Jess isn't here – not that she'd be much help. Anyway, I just thought, you know, after what happened with Cassie, you'd maybe know what to do. But I'm sure I'm being silly, and just worrying about nothing.'

She drew a breath, and he stepped in firmly. 'No, you're not.'

'Sorry?'

'You're not sure at all, or you wouldn't be phoning me like this.'

'I . . . No.'

More gently, he said, 'So tell me.'

Something in his voice overcame the politeness that had kept Trish's eyes down on the plastic letters; she was watching him in open concern, making him unaccountably uncomfortable as he listened to Mina's story. But he could hardly walk out into the hall as if it were a confidential work call and she were a roomful of undergraduates. Getting a grip, he gave the narrative his full attention.

'. . . round at a friend's house. Well, not even a friend, really, just a girl in her class but her mum works in the greengrocer's and she's always asking me if Sal wants to go round and play. There was another girl over this afternoon, too, so I talked Sal into it, though I know she'd rather have been at home with a book.'

So many opportunities for self-blame: an inescapable incident of parenthood. 'What time was this?'

'She went round at about two o'clock. It's only just round the corner, this Danielle's house, so she went off on her own and I was expecting her back about half past four. She wanted to do some work on her school science project before tea. I didn't worry until five or so. I was actually pleased – thought it was a good sign, you know, that she was getting on with Danielle and the other girl, Carly, having a good time and forgetting about her project.'

More blame. The sympathy made him wince. All too visibly, it seemed, because Trish, kneeling at the coffee table and still rummaging absently through the tiles, now raised her eyebrows in a parody of exaggerated curiosity. Peter kept his face stony, refusing even in friendly irony to treat Mina's distress as soap opera.

'In the end, I put on my coat and walked round there, thinking to fetch her home for tea, but Danielle's mum said, wasn't she already back? Danielle and Carly reckoned she'd left at four o'clock. They'd been playing outdoors, the three of them, out on the estate; Sal had got bored, they said, and told them she was going home.'

More like two hours than one, then. But it wouldn't help to let his anxiety show. 'What did you do? Where have you looked?'

'Well, first of all I came back here. In case we'd missed each other, somehow. I know that doesn't make much sense, but I couldn't believe it, I suppose – just kept thinking she must be at home after all. Then when she wasn't – of course she wasn't – I went back out and had a good walk round the estate – the shops, and the little park. She likes to hang about on the swings there sometimes when it's sunny, reading or day-dreaming.'

'Did you ask in the shops? Whether they'd seen her?'

'In the newsagent's I did. Mrs Sharma likes Sal; she used to give her lollies when I took her there in the buggy. She hadn't seen her. The chemist's, where Mum works in the week, closes early on Saturdays. And, well, I didn't like to ask the others.'

Too much like a house-to-house, perhaps?

'I mean to say, she's not likely to have been in the butcher's or the launderette, is she?'

Guiltily, he swallowed a laugh; that she could joke about it didn't mean he was allowed to. 'Right. And have you spoken to anyone else? Asked around, I mean? Contacted neighbours, and her other friends?'

The hint of a pause. 'Well, she doesn't exactly have many friends just round here.'

He had run out of the questions it felt safe to ask, so that after another silence it was she who bit the bullet.

'Do you think I ought to call the police?'

The first few hours are the crucial ones, intoned a mournful detective inspector in Peter's head. Before the trail goes cold. Not that he had been brave enough to act upon it in his own case.

'I don't know.' The trouble was that all the persuasive arguments from caution and common sense were driven out by the desire not to cause Mina more alarm.

'Nor do I. Maybe I won't, not quite yet. Like I say, it hasn't been long. And the thing is, what would they be able to do at this stage that I can't do myself? If it comes to asking round the neighbours' houses and so on, as you suggest, going back and checking all her usual haunts – I can do all that just as well as they can. Can't I?'

He heard the note of appeal and he knew all the sensible things he ought to say. Call the police. Call the hospitals, if only to reassure yourself. Call your mother again. Instead, from nowhere, he found himself saying something completely different.

'I could come up there. Help you knock on doors, make calls; help you decide what to do.'

Maybe it was tipsiness; maybe it was something else. But the idea grabbed him and wouldn't let go.

'It'll only take me two hours to get there – less than that, probably, it's straight up the A1. Just stay where you are; I'll come.'

He didn't need Trish staring at him agape to know how ridiculous it was, how absurd and nonsensical. Which Mina would surely tell him, wouldn't she, any moment? Once she had recovered from her embarrassment at his lunatic offer. He began to shuffle his arguments.

Instead, she just said weakly, 'Tonight?' and already he was calculating times and distances and wondering where he had left the road atlas and when he had last filled up with diesel.

'What's your address? How will I find it?' he asked, and Trish wordlessly passed him a pencil and a Scrabble scoresheet.

The necessary instructions communicated by a dazed-sounding Mina, he was about to ring off when she halted him, belatedly questioning the utility of his mission, and its practicability. 'What about your girls – Cassie and Kim? What will you do about them?'

'Oh, that's OK.' He looked hard at Trish. 'I've got friends who can hold the fort here.'

'But I'd hate you to come all the way up here on a wild goose chase. She'll probably turn up any minute now, wondering what all the fuss is about.'

'I'll give you my mobile number. If she reappears before I get there, just call me and I'll turn straight round. Not a problem.'

That seemed to exhaust her objections, so he told her the number and she repeated it back to him, her voice automatic, as if she were in the call centre. A quick double-check on the number of round-abouts, and he was telling her he'd be with her very soon when she interrupted again to say, simply, 'Thank you, Peter.'

When he clicked the 'end call' button he was surprised to find himself already standing up. Trish, however, remained stubbornly rooted to the floor at his feet.

'I don't think so.'

The fact that the words were offered in a light, conversational manner didn't fool him for a moment. 'Sorry?'

'No way. Not gonna happen. If you think you can leave me here with your neglected offspring while you jump in the car and head off to God-knows-where at breakneck speed, to spend all night, like as not, sorting out some crisis for a friend of yours whose address you don't even seem to know, then I can promise you, you've got the wrong girl.'

Not for the first time, he wished he could be sure when Trish was joking. She might be mocking him – but there was no mistaking a certain resolution about her chin.

'I know her phone number,' he contended, irrelevantly.

She ignored him. 'I don't care if you have had coffee – though you've barely touched it anyway and now it's cold. I've been to your supervisors' garden party before now, remember: I know why you came home on the bus. And I have no intention of letting you drive now. Especially two hours up the A1 or what-ever it was.'

She was absolutely right, of course. His racing mind, his burning purpose – it was only alcohol's false clarity. That he'd temporarily forgotten the link between wine and driving showed just how drunk he was. Damn it. What about trains? How soon would he be able to get a cab, to take him to Waterbeach station? Or perhaps Martin might run him there.

'No. I'll have to drive.'

His brain flickered. Had she just said . . .

206

'We'll take the girls to Martin and Jeremy's, and then I'll drive.'

He had no idea she even had a licence (he *hoped* she had a licence) – and how did she remember their names when she had only met them once? She always referred to Allmendinger on Planning Theory as 'that Humdinger bloke'.

'Where is it we're going, anyway?' She reached to flick the score-sheet from his fingers. '43, Gladstone Road, Intake S12 2LG. That'll be Sheffield, then? Great.'

The wine was most certainly having its effect, because he couldn't fathom the reason for her enthusiasm. Until she enlightened him.

'Sheffield! I know all about it – from that article in *Urban Studies*, you remember. It's not one of my three cities, of course, and I've never actually been there, but – well, you know.'

Peter closed his eyes. Trish, shooting from the hip with her flawed, undentable logic; Mina, missing a daughter, anxious, vulnerable and proud. The combination was one he had some difficulty in imagining, but he must be well over the legal limit and he'd just promised Mina he would be at her door by half past eight. There seemed to be nothing else for it.

'OK, come on then.'

'OK?'

'Yes. I agree. You can come.'

Now that he had capitulated, he was frustrated by her hesitancy. They needed to get going.

'I'll get Cassie and Kim, and grab a coat and maybe an extra jumper. You could probably do with one, too.' He eyed her cotton hoodie. 'It's chilly out and the heating in the Land Rover is a bit dodgy. And it might be a long night. I'll bring the fish fingers – I'd defrosted them already. Jeremy can cook them for them.' Though he suspected Martin might have more experience with that branch of cuisine.

He was halfway to the door when she said, 'Hadn't you better phone them first? To check they can have them?'

207

'Oh, no. They'll be fine. Jeremy might grumble sometimes but he's a trouper – he won't let me down.'

The less so if his hand was forced by the appearance on his doorstep of two hungry twins needing food and shelter.

'But what if they're out?'

'They won't be.' They couldn't be. He moved for the stairs.

The twins weren't even pretending to read, but both taking a rare nap, each on her own bed. Ten minutes later they were laden in the back of the car, cocooned in fleeces and blinking like bush-babies. Ollie, watching from the threshold with a tail that slowly semaphored the vestiges of optimism, was transformed to joy by his summoning word, and jumped up to stow herself tidily between the twins.

'I'm cold,' grumbled Cassie, voice abrasive from her interrupted nap. 'And hungry. What about supper?'

He brandished the packet of Captain Bird's Eye. 'Jeremy and Martin will feed you. And I expect you'll be staying over.'

Cassie's curmudgeonliness obliged her sister to take the contrary part, chattering excitedly from the right-hand seat. 'A sleepover at Jeremy's! Will it be his house, not Martin's? I like his spare room better, it's all full of books and drawings and things to look at, and Martin doesn't have books, at least only ones for adults and they're boring. Will Jeremy make us hot chocolate with supper? Last time he made us hot chocolate and he did this whippy thing on the top with his special frother.'

'It's a cappuccino maker, stupid.'

'Don't call me stupid, stupid.'

Peter's lungs gave his heart a tiny squeeze. Normal bickering. The first time in months, it felt like. 'Don't call each other names, please. And I don't know whose house it'll be, do I, until we get there? And if I find out you've *asked* for hot chocolate, either of you, you know what will happen when you get home.'

The moment seemed to have passed. Cassie's eyes were stubbornly shut again, and Kim was linking the drops of condensation on the right-hand window until they were fat enough to run. He must get that leaking rear sunroof fixed; the inside of the Land Rover smelt like leaf mulch.

Trish, having adjusted the driver's seat to accommodate her shorter frame, was pressing buttons and flicking indicator arms at random like a toddler on an activity mat. 'Are these the headlights? Where is dip? Blimey, these pedals are heavy. It's like driving a bloody bus.' Thank goodness, at least, she was wearing sensible shoes.

'It's got power steering. You'll be fine. Reverse is right over to the side and then back; you need to—' A sawmill sound; he tried not to picture metal scoring metal.

'Further over than that, then?'

The clutch lurched up under her left toe and they crept backwards towards the garage door, Trish not turning round but hunching to observe their progress in the wing mirror; he wished she didn't do so with that air of mild curiosity, as if she were not the one driving. First was engaged successfully if not smoothly, and they were up the drive, and then out into Flattery Fen and second gear. This she maintained steadfastly all the way to the Dorlinsons' – where Topsy was wisely not in evidence – before slowing to a kangaroo hop as they neared the pair of villas at the lane end. It could take a long time to get to Sheffield.

At least the lights were on, and at Jeremy's side: good signs, both. All three girls, plus the indeterminate dog, stayed in the car at his instruction while he went to knock.

There was a considerable pause, and then it was Martin who came to the door. For all that it was only just past six, he was swathed to the ankles in a black silk robe (you couldn't offer it the indignity of the term 'dressing gown'). It was surely a garment of Jeremy's choosing: Peter had Martin down more as a boxers and T-shirt man.

'Pete.' They both flinched slightly at the misfired gesture of welcome; nobody ever called him anything but Peter. 'What can I do for you, mate?'

'Well, actually, there's a bit of a crisis.'

'Another one?' Martin's forehead wrinkled upwards towards the
distant hairline, while his eyes travelled round behind Peter to the
Land Rover at the kerbside – and, no doubt, the four expectant
faces looking out. The man did have a point. Emergencies, missing
children – he had been making rather a habit of it lately.

'It's all right, it's not the girls. It's not me at all this time, really;
not my crisis, I mean. It's a friend.'

'Who is it?' Jeremy's voice drifted out from beyond the hallway.
'You're letting in a small Siberian weather front.'

'It's Peter,' called Martin without looking round.

'In Sheffield.'

'Pardon?'

'This friend, with the crisis. It's her daughter; she went out to
play at a friend's house and now she's gone missing. They're in
Sheffield.'

At this point, Jeremy, forsaking his fireside to see what the intrusion was, came out into the hall behind Martin, still in shirt and
trousers more appropriate to the hour, but signed off with a pair
of fluffy mule slippers that can only have been his late wife's.

'Did I hear the word "crisis"? Then we must put the kettle on
at once. And what's this – the whole family, come to seek succour
and guidance? Martin, I am quite ashamed of you, to have kept
young children and animals waiting out in the night! Come in:
come one, come all.'

Peter could have hugged him. Especially when he remembered,
with a guilty twinge, Jeremy's feelings on the subject of Olivia. The
unfastidiousness of the canine species did not endear them to Jeremy
in general, and his opinion had been compounded in Ollie's case
when she once mistook the fringe of an antique Turkish carpet in
his sitting room for one of her tasselled chew toys. At least she
wasn't at her muddiest today – and there were no obvious puddles
to get her so between the car and the fanlighted front door, through
which she now bounded with undisguised glee. Peter bundled Cassie

and Kim out from the back seat and up the short gravel path, leaving Trish to follow behind, smiling uncertainly at the equally uncertain Martin.

'You look like Professor Snape,' said Kim conversationally, with a nod at the long black robe as she passed him.

Jeremy showed his visitors into the sitting room, where a bottle and two glasses stood by the fireside, shouting their accusation of a romantic evening shattered. *At six o'clock*, thought Peter with a moment's envy, remembering life without children – before ducking, just in time, to rescue wine and crystal from the sweep of Ollie's lashing tail.

'And bearing fish fingers, too,' said the gentleman of the house, taking the slightly limp box from Peter's grasp. 'You shouldn't have.'

'Look, I'm really sorry about this. I honestly wouldn't bother you if I had any other possible notion of what to do.'

Martin was dispatched to put the fish fingers in the fridge and do the honours with the kettle – though Peter had half an eye on his watch and more than half his mind on Mina and could have done without the polite delay.

'It's this friend of mine up in Sheffield – I was telling Martin.'

'The colleague you did the research project with that time?'

'Er, no. This is another friend.'

Jeremy raised a quizzical brow but ventured no comment.

'Actually, it's her daughter.' A further lift – no doubt at the female possessive adjective. (Recalling his indiscretion in the Drayman's, Peter was glad Martin wasn't in the room.) 'She's only ten – not much older than my two – and she's got lost or gone missing, just this afternoon, and my friend is at her wits' end. Needs some help.'

Why did the story sound more far-fetched every time he told it?

'So you are donning the shining armour. And you'd like us to babysit your daughters. And also, it seems, your babysitter?'

'Oh, no.' Trish's voice came out louder than she had probably intended it. 'I'm going with him.'

'Ah. Sancho Panza.'

211

'I'm going to drive.'

'To guide the trusty Rocinante? Not so much squire as *chauffeuse*?'

Trish was staring at Jeremy in some bewilderment. Peter rescued her.

'I'm drunk,' he explained.

'Ah,' said Jeremy again, rather too much as if that explained everything.

Cassie and Kim had colonised opposite ends of Jeremy's William Morris sofa, clutching a cushion apiece across their laps; Cassie, at least, looked as if she could happily have eaten hers. Kim looked merely sulky. Six thirty-five said the mantel clock: forty minutes since Mina had put down the phone.

'The thing is, I can't possibly take the girls with me. It's almost evening now and they haven't even had their supper yet. Goodness knows how long it might take until . . . even if . . .' His mind shied off from processing the thought. 'We're quite likely to be up all night. So I just wondered whether you could . . .?'

Martin's re-entrance with a tray saved him from needing to complete the sentence. Cassie's eyes inventoried the honey jar and the Denby teapot and mugs.

'Oo, I don't suppose we could have—' she began, and stopped under Peter's warning glare.

'Tea!' Jeremy proclaimed. 'Martin, you are a gift from the gods. Would it be terribly wrong, do you suppose, before we partake of the fish fingers, to toast a few marshmallows for our young visitors? I am never without a small packet of them, somewhere about the house.'

'Like at Guide camp?' squeaked Cassie. 'Sophie Grimwade says they always—'

'Look.' Peter pulled himself together. 'Jeremy, you're extremely kind – and really they should have the marshmallows afterwards – but, either way, we'd better be getting going. If you wouldn't mind having them for the night? All they'd need would be somewhere just to curl up under a blanket or two. I know it's an awful imposition, but I can't think what else to do, and I hope to be back first thing tomorrow morning, or it might even be tonight, as soon as . . .' His brain jibbed again. 'As soon as I can.'

As if to underline the point, the unmentioned and least welcome third of the imposition jumped up on to the strawberry thief upholstery and began to clean her paws. It seemed there might have been a puddle outside after all.

To his eternal credit, Jeremy did not even glance towards the soiled sofa, homing in instead upon the agitation that Peter was doing a poor job of concealing.

'Of course, of course. You are worried about your friend. Very natural. Feasting can wait until you are gone. Martin, could you possibly be an angel and fetch the larger of the Thermos flasks? I think Peter and Patricia would prefer their Earl Grey "to go", as our cousins over the Atlantic like to say.'

For this he received looks of gratitude not only from Peter and Trish but also the departing Martin, who no doubt hoped that the dispatch of even half the invading party meant a swifter return to the interrupted hearthside wine. Then Jeremy turned to Cassie and Kim and clapped his hands together like a grand vizier from one of his own illustrations – if indeed such persons still featured in children's books.

'To the kitchen, *mes enfants*. Let's see what there is in the cupboards with which to transform oblongs of recovered fish protein into a spread fit for two princesses. And then we'll make hot chocolate: you shall toast marshmallows and together we shall toast absent friends – and the success of the valiant rescue mission.'

When Martin had returned and he and Trish between them were decanting tea into the Thermos, Peter followed Jeremy to the kitchen, where he kissed his daughters distractedly with injunctions to be good girls and behave themselves, and chucked his spaniel under the chin. *Dog food*, he remembered belatedly, but decided to let it pass. He didn't imagine Ollie would be averse to fish fingers and toasted marshmallows, for once in a while.

Thus it was almost quarter to seven when they found themselves back in the Land Rover and finally nosing out into the High Street. Peter tried to contain his impatience as he directed a fiercely concentrating Trish along dark, ditch-lined lanes, across flat, open country towards the A14 westbound and thence the A1. Mina's voice filled his head, defiantly brave – *she'll probably turn up any minute now* – the next minute beseeching and raw – *thank you, Peter*. Only when they reached the dual carriageway with its alluring sweep of cat's eyes did Trish tentatively depress her right foot by a few additional centimeters. For the first time, Peter wondered what her opinion was of their mission, and what she made of the reasons for it: whether, like Jeremy, she thought he was tilting at windmills. By the time they were passing Huntingdon her shoulders had lost some of their rigidity and the speedometer was nudging sixty-five.

'This is really good of you, you know,' he suddenly remembered to say. 'Thanks.'

'Forget it.' She shrugged, eyes never deviating from the road ahead. 'But it could be a long night. I told you we should have had caffeinated coffee. You don't suppose there's any in that scented tea muck they gave us, do you?'

In his pocket, Peter's fingers closed round the smooth, hard shape of his mobile phone. Of course he hoped for Mina's sake that it would ring, and ring soon. But if it did, they would have to turn round, and go tamely back home. That is, unless . . . He glanced across at Trish's intent profile. Would it be so very wicked? Whom could it hurt, after all? Drawing out the phone and snapping it open beneath the concealment of his coat, he felt for the top right hand button with his thumb – the one with the little red telephone on it. And pressed and held it down.

Chapter 16

The fourth time she emerged from the end of the gennel and scanned the triangle of grass, Mina still expected to see Sal on the swings. Of course, she knew it was impossible: why would she suddenly be playing on the swings at almost seven o'clock at night when she hadn't been there the first three times? But it was still a surprise when the metal chains hung limp and still, and there was no small, hunched figure, pushing herself idly to and fro with the toe of one trainer. It was impossible – but everything else, all other solutions, seemed more impossible still.

This time round, instead of crossing the small park and cutting back to their own street, she turned off the path and walked over to the swings. Calling it a path, though, was an exaggeration – it was really nothing but a groove of soil scuffed bare of grass by the passage of many feet, seeking the shortest route to the newsagent's and the bus stop. Beneath the swings, in contrast, grass was appearing obstinately where it was not supposed to be, pushing its way up between the cracks and crevices of the rubbery safety surface, three changes of legislation out of date. Mina made her way slowly past the struts of the rusty frame, then turned and retraced her steps, eyes sweeping the ground, scouring the discarded sweet wrappers, scratch cards and cigarette butts for some sign, some clue. Something – anything – to connect her to back to her daughter.

It wasn't there, of course – even if she had any idea what she was looking for. She sat down for a moment on one cold, plastic seat; the chains in her hands were clammy with the falling night. This is the place she used to bring Sal when she was too small to sit upright on the swing seat by herself, and had to be supported with one hand on her chest and one on her back, so that Mina could feel the vibration of her laughter as she accustomed herself, eyes wide, to the gentle motion. And then later, one grey Pennine summer afternoon, they had defied the drizzle and stayed out past teatime, as four-year-old Sal finally absorbed the necessary rhythm to propel the swing herself: lean forward as it goes back, then right back against the chains, legs stretching out in front as it swings forward again. And before that with Jess, sitting on a swing each, teaching her the same thing, exaggerating the lean and stretch for her to mimic. Fourteen, and abandoning her own friends and the lure of the shops to play at mother's little helper.

Mum. She took out her mobile and clicked on 'redial' for what felt like the fiftieth time. It had rung four or five times and she was about to give up when her mother's voice sounded in her ear, disorientatingly normal.

'Hello?'

'Mum. It's Sal.' She had no energy for breaking it slowly. 'I can't find her.'

'What do you mean? Can't find her where?'

'I don't know where. She went out to play and she hasn't come back.'

'On the estate?'

'Yes. She went to Danielle's house – you know, Sue's from the greengrocer's – and they thought she'd come home but she hadn't.'

'When? What time did they say she'd left?'

'About four o'clock.'

'Four o'clock! But that's three hours – she's been missing for three hours, Mina!'

As if she needed reminding. As if it were somehow her fault that Mum was only hearing of it now.

'I have been trying—'

'Where are you now?' Any spurt of defensiveness was swept away by her mother's brisk assumption of control. 'I'll be straight over. I'll see you at home in ten minutes.'

Home. She couldn't remember Mum calling it that in years.

'Right. Yes. Thanks.'

Ten minutes was enough to go back down the gennel one more time, past the row of shops, all closed now except the video store on the corner (where a youth with bad skin had already told her twice that, no, he hadn't seen a curly blonde girl, about so high) and back up the hill the other way, by Danielle's house. That meant the main road, where the evening traffic was picking up speed as it thinned, and she had to focus hard on not imagining the crush of bone beneath wheels.

The picture was still strong in her mind when she reached the house, and she picked up phone and telephone directory before she had even put down her door keys, to make the call to the Northern General that she should have made an hour and a half ago. Her mind was carefully empty while she waited the interminable time for the girl on the switchboard to check through to admissions for any record of a Sally Jane Heppenstall. She could almost sympathise, for once, with why people were rude to her at Autocare. When the news came back that there was no news, she was curious to observe that she felt nothing.

Then she called upstairs to see if Jess was back yet, and when she wasn't, went into the kitchen and made a cup of tea. Standing at the stove top, she picked without appetite at the fish fingers she'd been grilling for Sal's tea at five o'clock – and had removed, eye already anxiously on the clock, at ten past. She bit into one; its orange crust, marbled with grey fat and no longer crunchy, gave way to a salty pap that was wetter than it should have been and made her gag, picturing wads of sodden toilet tissue. With a gulp of sweet tea she sluiced away the texture from her tongue, scalding the roof of her mouth in the process.

Mum's ten minutes had already become twelve. Where could she have got to? Having grasped one nettle by calling the hospital, maybe now she should call the police. She had been on the point of doing so at six o'clock; had even lifted and replaced the receiver more than once. Not 999, certainly, but at least the inquiry number at the local station. But she had no idea, she'd realised, where that was; perhaps the one she passed on the bus sometimes, off the Parkway, near the Hyde Park flats. Or there would be a general inquiry number, maybe even a national one, and if not a bank of flunkies like herself then an automated system for putting callers through to the right local information point. *Missing persons*, she'd heard herself requesting of the faceless operator; *it's my daughter.* But it was unthinkable. And so in the end, when Mum's phone rang and rang to no reply, it had been Peter she had phoned instead.

It had been a relief to hear his voice. More so perhaps even than Mum's, just now, because Peter was external to all this; Peter was in the outside world where life was carrying on and nothing terrible had happened. But it was strange to talk to him when it wasn't a Sunday; and there had been something different about him, at least at the beginning, when he first picked up, something distracted, which made her wonder if one or both of his girls was with him, though he hadn't said, and she'd heard no voices in the background. And then there'd been the flood of gratitude when he'd said he would come, so intense that it had knocked her off balance. It was a crazy offer of his, and she knew she ought to have told him as much, but the impulse to hand over responsibility for decision-making to another adult human being was overwhelming. Mum wasn't there, she wasn't answering the phone – and Peter was so sensible. To her imagination he represented, more than anything, a quality of solidity. Solid like that Land Rover of his which could take the knocks and bumps and come off hardly scathed; solid, with his clever university job, raising alone those motherless twins, the resourceful widower, grieving but unbowed.

Peter was on his way. Peter, who had been through all this himself, had described to her the terror ride. That was part of it, too, of course. Peter's coming was like a talisman, because he had been this way before her – and he had Cassie back with him, didn't he, safe and well?

But first there was Mum. Mina was just putting the kettle back on when she heard the key in the Yale. She knew, if she thought about it, that Mum still had a key; it had been her own house, after all, for twenty-five years. Or it could easily have been Jess, either, coming back all oblivious – absorbed in her own problems, and with reason enough – to stumble into the middle of this mess. But her immediate illogical, unshakable conviction was that it was Sal. Sal who had a key but almost never took it with her; Sal who certainly didn't take it with her this afternoon, when Mina was in waiting for her at home. So when she ran into the hall and bumped into Mum, it was all she could do not to burst into tears. She might well have done so, in fact, if it weren't for Dave, standing awkwardly on the doormat and telling her that everything would be all right while Mum enveloped her in a hug. Or even if the embrace had lasted a little longer, she might have given way: if she'd had time to subside into the familiar softness and breathe in the familiar scent before her mother drew back, taking refuge in being businesslike.

'Right. So, Sue says Sal left their house at four o'clock, did you say? And they thought she was coming straight home?'

She led the way through to what had been her kitchen, and sat down at the table. Mina perched on the edge of a chair, while Dave merely hovered.

'So, where have you tried so far?'

'The shops. Mrs Sharma hadn't seen her. Nor had the boy in Blockbuster. The swings, all round the estate, you know. Nothing.'

'Right. And who have you phoned?'

'The hospital . . .'

Mum nodded, frowning. 'And friends? Sal's other friends? Other places she might have gone?'

'Not yet.'

'Right. Here's what we thought, on the way over. You stay here: that's best, in case she comes back, or the phone rings. Do some calling yourself, perhaps. And Dave and I will start at Sue's house, see what Danielle has to say for herself. She and this other lass – it's been hours, now – they might have more light to shed if I talk to them.' Her eye held the gleam of the inquisitor. 'Then we'll go round in the car, get knocking on doors, find out if anyone has seen a sign of her.'

Mina nodded mutely under her mother's gaze, in which appraisal might have obscured the compassion, if she hadn't added, 'She's got to be somewhere, love.'

Mum rose, rezipping the coat she hadn't taken off, and looked expectantly at Dave, who was fidgeting with his car keys. The eyes he raised to Mina held apology.

'What's she got on, love?' he asked quietly. 'What clothes, I mean?'

Like on *Crimewatch*. Last seen wearing . . .

'Her bomber jacket. Jeans – her old, faded ones, with the embroidered butterflies on the flares. No gloves. I told her to take her blue ones but she brought them downstairs and then forgot them. Left them on the side, by the toaster.'

Involuntarily, she glanced across at them now. *Let her be somewhere her hands aren't cold.*

Back out in the hall, she said, 'Make sure you keep your mobile switched on this time, won't you, Mum? And phone me the second you hear anything at all – the smallest thing.'

'And you, the same.'

They both kissed her swiftly, and then they were gone.

Being on her own once more, she found, was almost a relief, though she couldn't have said quite why. It might have been awkward if Mum and Dave were here when Peter came, a complication too much to face tonight – but that couldn't be the only reason. She made another cup of tea and dug her diary out of her bag. Not the current one; her old one where she had scribbled down the two or three numbers of mothers of Sal's friends, the ones she'd had over to the house or been to tea with, mostly a while back, when she was first in the juniors. It didn't take long to try them all – and come back with nothing but negatives and a medley of curious sympathy. 'Trying everywhere you can think of?' said one mum: too polite, perhaps, to wonder out loud why Mina was calling her, when her daughter hadn't been friends with Sal for years. In the infants, the school used to issue a list to parents, with everyone's contact details. Names and addresses and telephone numbers for the whole class, making life easier for mums fixing play dates or arranging birthday parties. Confidentiality, that was the reason they gave for not doing it any more: your child's safety. Ironic, really, since now it made it twenty times harder to find out if Sal was safe. But she wasn't sorry, not really; she could stomach no more of their intrusive concern.

Sitting down again, her hands reached out by force of habit to take and cradle her untouched tea. Nothing from Mum and Dave. Nothing from Sue, who had also promised to call with any news. Quarter past eight. She fretted with her tongue at the scalded place in her mouth; the newly exposed skin tasted sweet and tender. No point in beginning to wait yet for Peter's arrival; he must be another fifteen minutes away at least, maybe half an hour, even if he had got off promptly. A state of acute anxiety was exhausting to maintain; impossible, in fact, to maintain. The adrenalin of his promised coming, along with the expectation that the telephone would ring with news, had ebbed away during the last hour of phone calls, and she was left flat and drained, staring at the ring marks on the table and seeing only Sal.

It was the putter of the Land Rover, slowing in the road for Peter to check the house numbers, which brought her circling back to reality. Not that she was aware of what she was hearing, beyond a stirring sense of urgency: the same clench of anxiety which had gripped her dully for the past three hours, but also something more, an overlay of something akin to excitement. She became aware that a car engine was idling outside the house. Her professional knowledge of the technical specifications of most vehicles, and the ability to identify at least some popular models by sight, did not equip her to recognise the sound of a Land Rover ticking over. Not many people, it was fair to say, drove Land Rover Discoveries in Sheffield 12; not even K-reg ones. If anything, it made her think dimly of a taxi. Not a minicab like Dave's, of course, but the proper city centre kind, ranks of which she frequently hurried past on her way to catch the number 27. Maybe – sudden, insane hope – somebody had found Sal wandering lost some distance from the estate and had brought her home in a taxi. Or was that how police cars sounded? As soon as she was properly alert, though, she knew it must be him.

He was as diffident, standing with his weight on one foot on the doorstep, as he had been that first time on the telephone.

'Mina Heppenstall?'

She had no idea why he should attach her surname – it was only later that it occurred to her it might have been in case he had the wrong house, and was importuning one of her neighbours on a Saturday evening – and the absurd solemnity of it filled her with a most inappropriate desire to laugh, followed by an even more inappropriate desire to hug him. His voice was simultaneously both lighter and deeper than it sounded on the phone, if that were possible, as though the machine somehow filtered out everything except the middle range. The difference emphasised the liveness and realness of him. He wasn't tall, but neither did he look as old as his date of birth suggested and his eyes were kind, and filled with concern.

'Mina? It is you, is it?'

'Yes, it's me.' Then she added, because she found she wanted to hear herself say his name, 'Peter.'

He didn't move, and his eyes remained fixed on her, the concern now laced with what seemed like consternation. Then he shook his head, smiling. 'Sorry. I'd imagined you with dark hair. Silly, really; just an idea that had taken hold.' He could almost have been laughing, somewhere in the depth of those eyes; until he remembered himself, and apologised again, for the second time in as many moments. 'Look, I'm sorry. Have you heard anything yet? Any news, I mean?'

'N-no.' Where on earth had that wobble in her voice appeared from? Bloody hell – she absolutely mustn't cry now, after managing not to with Mum. What kind of a mess would he think she was? 'Come on in, it's freezing out here and I expect you need a drink, or something.'

'Thanks. I'll just . . .'

He turned half round as he spoke, waving one arm vaguely in the direction of the end of the path, where for the first time she noticed that the Land Rover's headlights were still on. Behind their glare it was difficult to see anything but darkness. The streetlight over near June's house was still out, which didn't help. But then the door opened, so that an internal light came on, and somebody else climbed out. A girl.

He'd had to bring the kids after all, was her first, irrational thought; nobody could babysit. But even while she was wondering whether they'd eaten, and thinking how tired they'd be and whether she might put them to bed in Jess's room, later – though it was damper than ever this winter – and if Jess would mind the settee, she knew it was all nonsense. It was the front door, the *driver's* door. And the girl who was coming up the path pulling faces and rubbing the small of her back was certainly not nine years old. Mid-twenties, more like: Mina's own age or a little younger. And strikingly pretty.

'Good grief, Peter, how do farmers manage, driving those contraptions round the fields all day? Less than two hours in the driving seat and I don't think my spine will ever be the same again.'

If she hadn't been so busy trying to hide her own dismay, Mina could almost have felt sorry for Peter, trying to distribute apologies in two directions at once.

'I think it's the distance to the pedals. Probably made for people with longer legs or something. Mina, I'm sorry, I should have mentioned it on the phone, but we hadn't decided then. I only thought later, when you'd rung off, you see I'd had a couple of glasses of wine.' Giving up the struggle, he ended weakly, 'Mina, this is Trish. Trish, Mina.'

The girl, Trish, gave her a companionable nod. 'Men, is what he means. With the longer legs. Bloody sexist car designers. I'm sorry about your daughter, by the way.'

'Come on in,' Mina managed to say, and led the way through the hall and into the kitchen. As she showed them in she swept up the teapot and her collection of used cups, dumping them in the sink; she also found her attention drawn to the scorched and stained Formica of the work surfaces, lifting here and there at the edges where moisture had found its way in some time since the 1960s when the units were fitted. 'Tea?'

'If you don't mind, I'd rather have coffee, if you've got any,' said Trish, taking a chair and planting her elbows on the table. 'We've had nothing but decaf and Earl sodding Grey all evening, and I'm falling asleep on my feet. Not used to driving in the dark.'

'Of course – no problem. Instant OK for you?' She hoped so; there was Mum's old percolator somewhere about, but she'd got nothing to put in it.

'Instant's great. Much easier.' Peter took the kettle from her and filled it while she dug out more clean cups – the last three from the cupboard. She wished he would sit down; she wanted to see which chair he took, to watch him with Trish. At least she wasn't a named driver on his policy; that much Mina knew. Calling up his details on the computer from time to time wasn't against the rules, and seemed a harmless enough indulgence, though she felt a bit ashamed now at the thought of it.

She spooned in the coffee and Peter poured on the water. 'Am I leaving room for milk?'

'Not for me,' said Trish, though surely he must know that already. 'Mina, is it all right if I use your loo? It's that tea of Jeremy's.'

Mina pointed her upstairs and watched her go, slim-hipped in her black jeans. There was something forthright about her that

reminded Mina of her friend Lyn and might, in other circumstances, have warmed her towards her.

'Trish is my research student,' offered Peter by way of explanation.
'Plus she babysits for me sometimes.'

But not right now, unfortunately. Good-looking, indispensable
and brainy; Mina was not reassured.

He pulled out a chair. 'So tell me what you've done, where you've
tried.'

'Right.' The knot in her stomach re-formed itself, driving out
idle vanities. 'Well, I've been all round the streets, several times.
Mum's been round – she and Dave are out in the car, driving round
and ringing doorbells. Asking the neighbours, you know.'

She watched his face as he nodded.

'Oh, and I've called the hospital, too.'

'And?'

'Nothing.'

'Well, good. That's something, anyway.'

When he said it, it did seem like something. She could almost
rid herself of the images of Sal, unconscious; of Sal, too deep in
shock to tell them her name.

'So now, what about the police? Have you been in touch with
them yet?'

She pressed against the table, seeking support. 'No. You think
it's time I did, then?'

He didn't answer at once, skirting carefully round her reluctance.
'What is there to lose? They can't know anything bad, can they?
You ruled that out with the hospitals.'

How was it he had first learned the news, she wondered, about
his wife?

Then he grinned, and her tautness slackened a notch. 'It's not
as if they're likely to have her in the cells, either. If she'd been
arrested for armed bank robbery I reckon you'd have heard about
it by now.' Serious again, he sought her eye. 'Look, it doesn't have
to turn it into something it's not. It just makes sense to alert them,

so they can be looking out for her, too. That has to be positive, doesn't it?'

Having no counter-argument, she resorted to prevarication. 'I'm not sure where to call, exactly. Or whether I ought to go along in person. Only, what if Sal comes back and I'm not here?'

'I could stay here,' said Trish, who had slid back into the kitchen during the exchange and was leaning against the Formica work top. 'You two go. Take a bus, take a cab. Holding the fort here, I can manage. Just so long as you don't ask me to drive that damned tank again.'

'Let's phone first, anyway,' said Peter, his eyes on Mina. 'If that's OK with you?'

She tried to nod but her neck felt stiff.

'Or would you like me to speak to them? Then I can pass it to you if they want to take all the details.'

It wasn't like her to be so pathetic. And she hated that look of understanding that Trish was directing at her. As if she could understand. But still: 'Would you?'

'So she's Sally, you said? And Heppenstall, the same as you? Two p's and two l's?'

This time the nod came more easily. She handed him the phone, and Trish picked up the directory, which was lying next to Sal's gloves by the toaster, and passed him that as well. He thumbed through the business numbers to P for police.

'See South Yorkshire Constabulary. Ah yes, they've got a full page here. What do you think? Maybe "general inquiries" first?'

She liked his way of taking over without seeming to take over. Perhaps it was a teacher thing; perhaps he was like this with his students. Though that brought her back round, irkingly, to Trish.

'Hello, is that police inquiries? Yes, I wanted to report a missing person. Whom should I speak to, please?'

In spite of talking on the phone for a living, she never seemed to get anywhere making calls herself. Maybe if she said "whom" a bit more it might help? It was odd, though, this coolly efficient manner of his, after how awkward and apologetic he was normally.

'Thank you. Yes, her name is Sally Heppenstall. H-E-P-P . . . yes, that's right.' He cupped a hand over the mouthpiece. 'Does she have a middle name?'

'Jane.'

'Jane,' he said. 'And the address is number 43, Gladstone Road, Intake. Yes, with an e, like the prime minister. Sorry? No, I know he doesn't. I didn't mean the present prime minister, I meant – never mind. Intake, S12 2LG. L for Lima, G for . . . Gladstone.'

Trish smirked, but Mina was too full of tension. What if the computer threw up a match? *Heppenstall, you say? I'm sorry to have to tell you* . . . But even her florid imagination refused to supply any plausible end to the sentence.

He was looking at her again, the receiver muffled once more. 'Date of birth?'

'Eighteenth of June 1997.'

'Mina Heppenstall,' he was telling them. 'Mina with an i. Her daughter, yes.' A pause. 'Right. OK, I see.'

What were they saying to him? Agitated suddenly, she wished she had hold of the telephone herself, wished they were telling it to her. 'What?' she telegraphed at him, but his eyes were now fixed frustratingly downwards, studying the table.

'Yes, of course. I understand.'

What were they saying?

'Well, thank you very much for your help. I'll tell her.' He pressed the button and laid down the phone.

'Well?' It was Trish who spoke, while Mina still tried to locate her voice.

He glanced up at her, and then down. The assured, telephone Peter was gone and the familiar diffidence back again. But more than that: he seemed specifically uncertain. What was it? What didn't he want to tell her?

'Peter?'

'They've taken down the basic details.' She knew that; she'd been listening, hadn't she? 'Logged them on the computer, you know. Got her entered on the database, recorded as missing.'

'Great.' Though it wasn't great at all, it was horribly real, horribly formal. *Missing.* 'At least they're looking for her now. So they'll send someone out, will they? I'll have to find a picture; I've got her school one upstairs, from September.' They always asked for a recent photograph, on the telly. 'When will they be here, did they say?'

Now he was looking at her, but his expression was still uncomfortable. 'It's Saturday night,' was all he said, at first.

'What do you mean?' Of course it was Saturday night. It was getting late, nearly nine o'clock, and Sal could be anywhere, she could be—

'They said it might be a while. Not to worry for an hour at least.' Then, catching sight of her face, 'Oh, God, sorry, Mina, of course I don't mean not to worry, it's just what they said on the phone; not to start looking out for them, I suppose, for at least an hour.'

'An hour!'

She might have been procrastinating herself since half past five – but another *hour*! Any further delay on the part of officialdom, she found, enraged her; she could bear nothing short of immediate action. Sal could be, she could be . . .

'For Christ's sake, what do they think – that kids should only go missing in the daytime, when they're not so busy? Not on Saturday night, when they've got more important things to deal with, like people getting drunk, is that it?'

It almost looked as if he'd got toothache. 'It's horrible having to wait, but I'm sure they'll send someone as soon as they can manage.'

As soon as they can manage? This time she lacked the capacity even to parrot him out loud.

He said what he always seemed to say, making her remember that it wasn't his fault. 'I'm sorry.'

It was the inactivity, that's what it was. Maybe she should wash the cups; even that would be better than just sitting here. But inertia rose up and swamped her.

'Is there anywhere else – anywhere at all you can think of – that she might sometimes go and hide away?' asked Peter. 'Some bolt hole, perhaps, somewhere to get away and be by herself?'

Here, her bedroom; this was her bolt hole. *Here with me.*

'I was just thinking, maybe if she fell out with these friends she was playing with or something, and wanted to hide out for a bit?'

'She'd just come home.' Surely she would. 'Wouldn't she?'

'Maybe not.' This was Trish, still leaning on the work top; Mina had forgotten she was there. 'I might know a place. The sort of place, anyway.'

They both turned to look at her; Peter's face was cast in unreadable cloud.

'I was reading about it in this article. You know, Peter, the one in the journal. It said Sheffield had done well out of the new MRA calculations.'

Mina was completely baffled. She was pretty sure she saw Peter wince; certainly, he had closed his eyes, so Trish now turned to her with her eager, incomprehensible explanation.

'Major Repairs Allowance, it stands for. It's a new way they calculate what the local authorities can have to spend on renovating their housing stock, you see. Anyway, the article said they were doing a lot of major renewal here, and it made me notice, when we were coming in just now. That row we passed at the top of the hill, there.'

A glimmer. She meant the empty maisonettes. Maybe this was going to make sense, after all.

'The whole lot were boarded up; I guess they're waiting to be done up, are they? Anyway, I just thought, you know what kids are like. Anywhere they're not allowed to go. We used to climb over the fence into the building site at the end of our road, at home, when they were putting in the drainage for the new estate. Not for any reason, really, except to sit in the empty concrete pipes. You couldn't even roll them along, they were too heavy.'

'The council are gutting them and putting in central heating and new windows, to sort out the condensation. And new wiring and plumbing, too, I gather, better insulation, the works. Those ones are divided into maisonettes, and they use them for the elderly, at least the ground floor ones, so that's why they're doing them and not ours. That's what my friend Lyn told me. But our houses here are really supposed to be demolished, anyway.'

She was talking, but her mind wasn't on the words. Instead, she was thinking: Sal wouldn't. She knows it's not allowed; she knows it's dangerous. Sal's a good girl.

Peter was eyeing her cautiously. 'Might it be worth trying? What do you think?'

The excitement in his voice, not quite successfully contained, decided her. An hour before the police would get here; she'd had enough of sitting waiting. Waste of energy it might well be, but where was the harm, if she didn't raise her hopes?

'Let's go and see.'

This time, Trish didn't offer to stay at home in case Sal came back, and Mina hadn't the heart to suggest excluding her from a quest of her own devising. She would even, it seemed, have overcome her reluctance to get back in the Land Rover's driving seat, but the maisonettes were only five minutes' walk away, and walking, and cold air, were what Mina wanted. Leading the way left, in the opposite direction from the swings, and then right, up the hill behind the gardens of Gladstone Road, she set a brisk pace, so that Peter on one side of her had to lengthen his stride and Trish, on the other, skipped a step or two to keep up.

'Why were you coming in this way, and not up from the main road?' it occurred to her to wonder.

'Don't ask,' groaned Trish. 'Hasn't Peter explained to you about geographers and maps?'

It called for a smile, but Mina couldn't raise one.

'It's just a bit further up. Next street but one.'

Here it was. The streetlights finished, or at least those that it was worth anyone's while to bother to keep lit, and it took a moment of adjustment before the hunched shape of the row of houses emerged from the darkness to the left and in front of them. It was just a single row; across the road from the houses was another small open space, thinly grassed, but lacking the attraction of the swings down the hill. Sal, Mina was almost certain, never came up here. The street itself was not blocked off and nor had proper fencing been erected, but the houses were boarded up, and a strand of striped plastic tape hung damply between wire uprights wedged into the cracks of the pavement, like that used by the police to warn gawpers away from the sites of accidents and worse. The place held an air of foreboding now, at night, which she'd never noticed in the daylight.

Now that they stood in front of the row, the purpose she had felt when walking rather deserted her. Even Trish stood on one foot, showing none of her earlier zeal. It was Peter who took a step forward.

'Come on. Let's take a closer look.'

These buildings were longer and lower than the ones in Gladstone Road and the streets close round it, pebbledashed where those houses were plain, unrendered brick. The windows were a different shape, too: more upright, though still with the same thin, aluminium frames, and there were twice as many doors, leading into the subdivided units. Mina wondered vaguely whether these places were older or newer than hers; she had little idea about inter-war or post-war architecture. Peter and Trish would both know, no doubt – which was odd, when she was the one who had lived here all her life.

Trish went to peer more closely at the first house, but Peter set off along the row. Mina fell in at his side, close enough for their coat sleeves to brush together, almost but not quite; the sound of their footfalls was exaggerated by the breezeless darkness, here where the Saturday night city noises seemed to fall away. She wondered if she should shout, call out Sal's name, but the silence intimidated

her and she let it keep its hold. Her eyes, like Peter's, were trained
on the houses, though she had again the feeling of not knowing
what it was she expected to see. Sheets of plywood secured with
planks were nailed across the doors and downstairs windows, daubed
here and there with graffiti or marked with cryptic lines and
numbers: workmen's runes, presumably, from some earlier use. The
budget hadn't stretched to covering the upstairs windows and here
and there a pane was broken, the evidence of sport by local teenagers
with bricks. The whole place was not only deserted but preter-
naturally so, leaving her to fight the impression that the whole
thing was no more than a stage set, a line of house frontages with
nothing but shadows behind. One abandoned wheelie bin, turned
on its side to show the roughly daubed house number and with
faded cartons and wrappings still spilling out, only added to the
effect.

There were few more than a dozen houses in the row, and it
was when they had almost reached the end and she was thinking
of turning back that Peter stopped still with his head atilt, eyes
screwed up against the stinging black. A second later she saw what
he saw: the front door of the last house was unboarded. One heavy
plank, still bristling with exposed nails, lay propped where the
crusted pebbledashing was cracking away at the base of the wall.
They stood together facing the door, which proclaimed them to
have arrived at number 14A.

'Trish,' called Peter, glancing back over his shoulder.

'Sal,' called Mina, and pushed at the door.

It gave way easily, and she saw that the Yale had been broken,
the catch wedged so that it no longer met its slot. The hall was
darker even than the street outside, if that were possible. Why on
earth hadn't she thought to bring a torch? But then Peter was
behind her flicking open his mobile phone, which cast a dim
greenish light, throwing into view a cramped square of bare floorboards and, directly in front of them, the stairs. 14A: of course,
it would be one of the upstairs units. The steps, like the hallway,

were bare of covering and as they climbed their feet clumped noisily on wood that was too damp for dust. At the top were two doors, and a frame where a third should have hung, through which was visible a room that would once have been a kitchen, before being stripped of anything with a scrap value. On the narrow landing at their feet were signs of recent occupation, but it wouldn't have been Sal, or even Carly and Danielle, surely: not spent matches and the butts of something clearly hand-rolled. Oh, God, if they had been here, please don't let them have touched anything. She shuddered, and was grateful there were no syringes.

Trish had joined them now, and they stood awkwardly close together, the three of them in the small space, uncertain what to do next.

'Sal.' Mina didn't call it out; she only spoke her daughter's name, like a lesson learned or a part in a play. Still, it sounded out louder than she'd expected in the stale, unmoving air, and she felt the start of surprise in the others, too. Peter hardly had to shift his feet to reach and push at the two closed doors, swinging them open. He angled his phone towards the rooms beyond, and even in the receding gloom there was no doubting it. Both empty.

'Anyway, even if she had come here, why would she be here now?' Mina realised she was speaking her calculations aloud, though in little more than a whisper. 'It makes no sense, does it? Once she'd ducked out of the way of Danielle and Carly – if that's what she was doing – once they'd gone, she'd have come back home.'

Unless . . . Peter must have had the same thought at the same time, because he moved forward into the small kitchen, with its doorless units, hinges dangling, and shadowed gaps, shorn of linoleum, where once would have stood cooker and fridge. In the far corner was a three-quarter-height opening, to the side of a descending boiler flue, splintered where it had been disconnnected. At one time, probably, before refrigeration, it would have served as a larder. Across the opening hung a curtain, personal remnant of some former tenant, its once floral pattern blurred by a fogging of grime. And behind it, when he pulled aside the drape, a latched cupboard door.

Her hand might be shaking, but Mina was smiling already as he stepped aside to allow her to lift the latch and open the door. Even then, for a split second she thought she was wrong, because there was no sound of stirring from within. But when he flashed his mobile into the depths she saw that the cupboard stretched further than she had thought – and there in the back corner, coiled as tight as a nest of mice and wide-eyed in the green half-light, was Sal.

Chapter 17

Peter was curious, on their return, to find Mina's kitchen clock telling him it was only half past nine. Maybe it was drinking in the afternoon and slowly sobering up that made him feel it was later than it was; maybe it was the reminder of Cassie's disappearance, when he had been up for the best part of the night.

It was certainly the memory of when Cassie came back that had made him turn away while Mina crawled on hands and knees into the empty kitchen cupboard to take her daughter in her arms. He and Trish had withdrawn to the landing, from where his eyes lingered on the curtain which fell back across the low doorway. The pattern was familiar where it was visible beneath the grey, repeated columns of sprigged yellow roses alternating with stripes of gold, and after a moment he placed it; it was the same fabric which had covered his grandmother's sewing box when he was a boy.

What had passed between them in the cupboard he didn't know, but few words were spoken on the short walk home to Gladstone Road. Sal was quiet: still dull with sleep, perhaps, or subdued by her ordeal or the fear of retribution to come. He hadn't liked to speak at all for fear of saying the wrong thing, and Trish – unusually for her – must have felt the same.

Back inside the house, the police (yet to arrive) had been called off. The grandmother and her boyfriend had been called off, too; in fact, they had been trying to reach Mina before she rang them. Sal's friends, it seemed, had cracked under interrogation and suggested a search of the maisonettes, just as it was taking place. Mum and Dave had gone straight back home without calling in to see the returned prodigal, because there was a film starting on TV

235

and they had promised themselves an evening in with a Chinese. Peter was guiltily relieved; if Mum had come, that would undoubtedly have been his cue to leave. The mothers of the other miscreants had been rung, too, though the details of Sal's whereabouts, and the consequent inquest, were saved for another occasion.

Maybe, as well, it was Mina's face, drawn and pale under the harsh strip lighting, that made it feel more like midnight than nine thirty p.m. Sal was safely back with her now; shouldn't she have looked less strained? Though he knew from his own experience how the dammed up worry could crash back over you after the event. She'd had more colour earlier, surely – though of course he had no idea what her natural complexion might be, and it made him wish he could see her face free of care; see her laughing casually across at him, as she'd laughed so easily and so often on the phone. Tonight it was difficult to believe that she was only a few years older than Trish. He hesitated, torn between contriving some way of making her smile and saying what he knew he ought to say – that they should go, and let her get Sal to bed. He was well past sober; Trish could doze in the back while he drove home. If they left now it might even be early enough to wake the twins and decant them back to their beds in the cottage. But he didn't want to go, not yet.

'Shall I put the kettle on?' It might be trite, but it was a hedge: an offer of companionship, to which a refusal would be a clear invitation to departure.

Her answer was to draw out a chair and sit down. Sal, who had been circling the edge of the room like a cat, came forward and dropped gratefully on to her lap. She was a year older than his own two and an inch or two taller, but just as skinny; the way her head ducked swiftly to butt under Mina's chin was so like a gesture of Kim's that his hand came up involuntarily to his own neck. Did her hair smell of dusty herbs in the sun, he wondered, the way his girls' did? – though probably that was down to the brand of shampoo. Such amazingly yellow hair, too; how absurd that he had ever imagined her a Saleema or a Saleshni. He wanted to know whether Mina's had been saffron, too, when she was small, before it faded to that pale honey dust, but there were no photos in the kitchen and he hadn't seen inside any other room.

He brought over the coffee – only three because it was caffeinated, but Mina poured an inch of hers into her empty cup from before, topping it up with plenty of milk and stirring in two sugars – and seated himself opposite them, next to Trish. Sal's eyes scanned them warily, feline again. The landing of a semi-derelict council house had not seemed the time or place for formal introductions, but now the moment had passed, so he said nothing, just settling for an undemanding smile.

'It's late for you, love. Drink this, and then you must get to bed.'

There was no remonstrance; Sal was scarcely in a position to put terms. But she clung closer to her mother and Peter saw the expression on her face, as bright as the morning and twice as tenacious.

They sipped their drinks in silence for a while, and peace seemed almost to have descended, when Mina surprised him.

'What were you doing in there?'

She asked the question quietly, neither in anger nor in threat, her mouth in her daughter's hair, but nevertheless it jolted him; he had been so certain she would save the inquisition until she and Sal were alone.

'Why, love? Why on earth would you—?'

There she stopped herself, sighed, and tightened the circle of her arms.

'We were playing sardines.'

'We?'

'Yes. We'd been playing it at Danielle's house, and then outside, round the wheelie bins, but Carly and Dani got bored, they said they knew a better place to play. Somewhere that's good for hiding, and scary too, for murder-in-the-dark.'

'They took you there?'

'Yes. I wouldn't have—'

'I know you wouldn't,' Mina interrupted, her haste betraying relief at the removal of her doubts. 'But then, what happened, if you were there together?'

'I got locked in the cupboard.' For the first time, a pleading note slid into her voice. 'I'm sorry, Mum, I know it's stupid. Lucy says it, doesn't she, in *The Lion, the Witch and the Wardrobe*? That you should never shut the door behind you if you're hiding in a cupboard. But I just forgot and pulled it to, and the catch is broken on the inside.'

'Didn't you yell?' asked Trish. 'Blimey, I'd have screamed blue murder if I'd got stuck somewhere like that.'

Sal stared at her in disbelief. 'I was hiding.'

Dur. Peter smothered an inappropriate grin.

'But then, later?' Trish persisted. 'Afterwards, when they didn't come?'

'Then I shouted a bit, yes. But I think they'd gone by then. They were downstairs; I suppose they thought I was hiding some-where outside. And after that, I had my book with me.'

She pulled it from her jacket. Lemony Snicket, one of the twins' favourites. Her choice had Peter stifling another grin: *A Series of Unfortunate Events.*

'It was too dark to read much, though; after a bit it made my eyes hurt, so I just shut them. Then you came and found me.'

Mina's voice was suddenly grim. 'They told Danielle's mum you'd gone home.'

'That's right.' Sal nodded, twisting round to look at her mother. 'That must be what they thought.'

'But they never mentioned the maisonettes. Not until later, anyway, when Grandma went to talk to them.'

Sal shrugged, eloquent with unsurprise. Not so much solidarity with her friends, Peter suspected, as simple ten-year-old logic when being caught somewhere you weren't supposed to be.

He knew how it was, though; he knew how a parent's dark imaginings were not so easily forgotten, even once proved unfounded. Mina, right now, was not to be persuaded of anybody's blamelessness – and that included Sal's.

'You don't know how dangerous those places can be. There's a reason the council has got them all boarded off. The floors might not be safe, even – the ceilings. It's no kids' joke, a place like that; not just somewhere to play at scaring yourself. This wasn't a game, Sal.'

A game – like running off with a beautiful boy to stow away in a boat.

Her voice was rising, its edges shrill now with all the fear she'd been keeping inside. 'They didn't say where you were, Dani and Carly; not until Grandma went and got it out of them. It was hours. I thought . . . Anything could have . . .'

Sally, tell my mother, repeated the old words in Peter's head. *Never coming back; never coming back.*

Leaving seemed the best he could do for Mina and for Sal, and having determined upon it he wanted it over quickly. They had no things to gather together, no arrangements to make for the next time, nor messages to convey. Strangers after all, said a voice in his head, shaming him from his urge to put his arms round her or at least take hold of her hands when she came to her doorstep to see them off, leaving Sal at the kitchen table. Besides which, Trish was just behind him, threatening to fight him for the driving, so there was no chance of more than a rapid, untouching goodbye. And by the time he was in the driver's seat and had fiddled with his seat belt and found the ignition in the darkness with his key, she had turned indoors and shut the door.

The desire to take the wheel was all bravado on Trish's part; once they were away, she settled back in the passenger seat happily enough, keeping him distracted, as he negotiated the multiple roundabouts of the ring road, with an excursus on how greatly the state of Sheffield's public housing stock had suffered through the Tories' restrictions on spending capital receipts from right-to-buy sales. He couldn't exactly claim to be sorry when, the lecture over and despite the early hour, she fell asleep before they reached the dual carriageway. The damp had lifted and a moon appeared, making the scrubby outskirt villages appear as beautiful as their Pennine backdrop, and he was glad of the emptying roads and the loneliness which gathered in the car: a loneliness which was always more intense, he found, with another, sleeping person present than when you were by yourself. It was different with the girls, though; if they had been curled together on the back seat he wouldn't have felt alone. The thought consumed him momentarily with impatience at the miles of carriageway ahead, and the stretch of enforced time which ran along with it; he burned to be back at Jeremy's door at once, and the intervening effort of concentration required of him seemed too exhausting to bear. That's what you get for drinking in the afternoon, he told himself. He rolled down the driver's window, just far enough to admit a blast of South Yorkshire air like a splash of cold water to the face, without creating sufficient turbulence to risk disturbing Trish.

The more distance that rolled out between him and Intake – A57, A1 – the more he felt his agitated spirits sinking back to calm; he was driving away from the difficult, face-to-face Mina and back towards the familiar telephone one, sparky, warm and confidential. He had a visual image now to attach to her: Mina features at last to replace the lingering vestiges of Meena. He had hair to frame them, not long and oiled and black but pale, washy blonde; he had snatches of skin, a corner of jaw and roughened reddish elbows. But her face, her real Mina face, remained as it had been in the empty house and in her kitchen: shuttered, tired and distant.

It was not far short of midnight by the time he was swinging off the A1, enjoying the rare engagement, on this remote and easy drive, of holding the wheel steady round the heavy curve of the slip road on to the A14 eastbound. Trish was still asleep and not available for consultation, but it made sense to drive her back to college first, before going to Jeremy's to pick up the twins. Cassie and Kim could dream on for another half-hour before being roused and ferried home to their own beds. A college, on the other hand, never truly sleeps. There would be a porter on duty to nod to Trish as she walked in through the arched gateway – and no household to disturb as she let herself into her single study bedroom. So instead of taking the turn-off towards Allington and home he stayed on the road as far as a slumbering Cambridge, and round to the Backs to drop her off.

Trish, as he might have guessed, was the kind of person who was fully alert as soon as her eyes were open; distressingly wide awake and ready for more, in fact, as if she were always up and checking footnotes at this time of night. Perhaps she was.

'Thanks, that was fun,' she said as she clambered out, as if he had just taken her to an interesting dinner party.

Half past twelve. Jeremy's door was on the latch, and he must have gone to bed and left it that way in anticipation of the wanderer's return, because the villa lay in silence. The fire in the sitting room had died down to embers, no light from the Anglepoise showed in the 'drawing room', and the kitchen was deserted and scrubbed clean, but for two rinsed wineglasses upturned on the drainer. Peter removed his shoes, realising as he did so what a relief this was after seventeen hours of tight lacing. The black and white hall tiles registered cold even through his socks, but the carpeted stairs were warm, and he padded up them gratefully. Heading straight for the spare room, the door to which was slightly ajar in deference to Kim's refusal to sleep in a strange room without a crack of light, he was intercepted by his faithless dog, pushing open the door from the master bedroom and slipping out to lick his hand. 'Tart,' he told her in a low whisper; by way of reciprocation she began a sniffed inventory at his ankles of the night's accumulation of foreign smells.

Cassie and Kim had a single eiderdown each, a matching pair of handmade patchwork affairs that Ruby might have sewed, though surely never in the anticipation of their use except, as now, by small overnight guests. Or maybe it was Jeremy's mother who'd made them, a generation before – but equally his friend had never mentioned a sibling. Perhaps a grandmother, or a great-grandmother; his overtired brain spun off into calculations: 1920s, 1890s. A quilt each, but one bed between them, the twins were sleeping closer together than they had for some time. Since the early winter; since the Mahoneys. Cassie lay on her right side, facing her sister but knees bent defensively high; Kim, on the right, lay as always on her left side, but her face was flung away, nose towards the ceiling. She was going to wake with a crick. Perhaps he wouldn't move them after all; perhaps he'd let them sleep in peace. Between Cassie's knees and Kim's crooked arm was a space just wide enough for Peter to crawl into on elbows and knees without disturbing either child. Ollie jumped up at his feet, turned twice on the spot and settled in a ball like a cat.

Shutting his eyes felt almost unnatural, and he had to make a conscious effort to cease staring at the coloured lights that dotted and dashed the inside of his closed lids. Even when he succeeded in looking at nothing, his mind filled the void with images of onrushing headlights. Lying here, back so tangibly in the bosom of his family, he found that the whole evening's escapade began to recede into unreality. Most of a bottle of college wine; four hours of dual carriageway; nothing to eat. (Trish: he hadn't fed Trish.) Local knowledge garnered from *Urban Studies*; Major Repairs Allowance; Sal, curled up with a book in a filthy cupboard. And Mina, dejected and unreachable at her strip-lit kitchen table. It was so unfair; the nagging injustice of it was what ate at him as he finally teetered towards sleep. He'd gone all that way, dropped every-thing including his daughters, and forgone a quiet evening by his own fireside at the end of a long term, in order to help Mina. And he'd succeeded, hadn't he? The lost lamb was lost no longer; she

242

was back in her mother's arms. So why had Mina not looked upon him with gratitude?

Rescue missions always worked a treat in the books – look at Mr Darcy. Why hadn't his own had the desired result?

Chapter 18

Walking along, scarcely noticing where she was going as she piloted through the five o'clock shoppers on automatic, Mina was contemplating the broken catch on a cupboard door.

It was Tuesday after work; Sal was at Mum's for her tea and Mina had taken the chance to nip into town at the end of her shift to pick up a few oddments. A new lunchbox after Sal had sat on hers; squared paper for maths; some tights without holes in them. Since Saturday night things had returned to normal. Dani and Carly had expressed contrition for taking Sal to the maisonettes, and for not telling sooner; both girls had been grounded. In Sal's case there was never any need. Jess hadn't come home that night, nor the two succeeding ones either, but that wasn't unusual these days. And Peter had gone back to his own world.

John Lewis was the best place for tights, and it was in Barker's Pool, just past Mothercare. Just as Mina was about to walk by, a familiar movement pulled her attention away from her own thoughts. A way of hitching a bag higher up a shoulder, weight on one foot. Jess.

She had her back to Mina, and the way the light and shadow fell meant that the window threw back no image of her averted face. Instead, unhindered by reflections, Mina could see clearly through the window to what Jess was looking at. Bright display cards proclaimed an end of winter sale: everything 50 per cent off. Tiny hats and mittens in navy blue lambswool; striped matelot suits, 0–6 months, pure wool, too, and impractically unwashable. Caught in the act – in the circumstances there could be no denial. Now was the moment; Mina had to either look straight ahead, walk on past and go and buy her tights or, if she stopped, confront her sister. She did what her mother would have done. She stopped.

If she couldn't see Jess's reflection, then logically Jess couldn't have seen hers, either. Maybe it was some sixth sense, or more likely just the fact of footsteps halting behind her, which made her sister turn. And in her eyes, Mina saw at once the swift flash of consciousness.

'Jess,' she began.

But Jess wasn't looking at her; she was looking beyond her, over her shoulder. Searching for an escape route, it almost seemed to Mina. But her eyes weren't the eyes of someone trapped, they were simply those of one otherwise absorbed. Now it was Mina who turned round. Behind her stood a girl she didn't know, looking straight at Jess and smiling. Younger than Jess; or maybe it was the contrast between the girlish angles of her face and the heavy round-ness of her belly – the preposterousness of it somehow emphasising her immaturity. It was a cold day, and she wore a man's battered leather jacket, too large about the shoulders but split wide open in front by the swell of her pregnancy. Kiernan's jacket.

Relief was the first thing that flooded over Mina, a rush of heat as physical as you'd get from running. Jess wasn't pregnant. It was just somebody else, somebody who wasn't Jess. And, as so often with relief, it was followed rapidly by a surge of irritation against the cause of all the previous anxiety.

'Friend of yours?' she inquired crisply, not even looking at the girl.

'Lisa.' It wasn't an introduction, nor an explanation; Jess was addressing the newcomer. She inclined her head towards the paved centre of the square, where there was a semicircle of stone benches. Lisa nodded and trailed off in the direction indicated, lopsided and lumpy with her carrier bags.

'So that's what this has all been about? That's where all the stuff has gone, from the attic? *My* stuff. Sal's stuff. And the money, too, no doubt, and all your clothes that have disappeared.'

245

'Helping out a friend? Have you got a problem with that?'

Jess had on that truculent expression she usually saved for Mum. Ignoring the question, Mina pressed on with her recriminations.

'And that's where you've been, when you stay out, is it? "Helping a friend"? I expect she's got herself a council flat, has she, because she's pregnant? And playing house with her is more exciting than being at home?'

Leading your own life, making things happen, giving yourself choices – instead of just waiting to be the next one to get pregnant. More and more, she felt like Mum.

'She doesn't have a place, not really. She's living in this squat, over Norton way. I've been helping her fix it up a bit before the baby comes.'

Not, her indifference indicated, that it was any of Mina's business. Twice already her eyes had drifted across to the pregnant girl on the bench. Then casually, not even looking at her sister, she added, 'I'm probably moving in there for a bit, actually. She's due any time, and she'll need the help.'

From somewhere rose up a wave of frustration that breached all Mina's careful banks of patience.

'Need help? She looks like she needs more than your help – she looks like she needs Social bloody Services. How old is she – sixteen? Fifteen? Where are her parents? Let alone the baby's dad – I bet he's only a kid, too.'

Being a parent: did they all think it was just a children's game? (*This wasn't a game.* she'd said the same thing to Sal.) Hands raised to hips, she gazed helplessly at Jess.

'When are you going to bloody well grow up?'

Shit. Why had she let herself be drawn? Why had she said it? It was so stupidly pointless – after all the times she'd bitten words back for the sake of keeping the lines open, keeping things possible.

Jess didn't even bother to tell her to piss off. She just swung round without a word and crossed over to join the girl. Taking a

Mothercare bag each and without a backward glance, they walked away across the square.

The lull that followed Sunday lunch was very much the same with Jess absent as it had been with her lurking somewhere upstairs. *Skulking* upstairs; that was the word Mum would have used. The main difference was that there was no risk of a confrontation, and that Mum had been more readily persuaded to come to Mina's rather than do the lunch herself. Roast chicken in deference to Dave's cholesterol, but her mind had been elsewhere and she had let the potatoes burn, so that they were all crunchy outsides and, mysteriously, nothing left in the middle. 'Like hot crisps,' Dave had said kindly, and it meant more because Mina knew Mum didn't let him have them any more, though he used to love his salt and vinegar.

Mina had determined to speak to Mum about Sal, as well as about Jess, but it was already quarter past three and they were talking instead about Mrs Warburton.

'That cold weather last week was really getting to her, she says. January wasn't the best time to have her hip done, with the bulk of the winter coming up, because there's nothing worse than the cold, she reckons, to make her feel the ache. It gets into the muscles, you know, where they're mending round the joint.'

Dave, shy of surgical details, shifted a little at her side and focused more intently on the Sunday game show.

'But didn't she complain last time, too, when she had it done in June and then there was that heatwave?' Mina had a clear recollection of being taken along to visit Mrs W in an airless ward, and being told how impossible it was to get comfortable.

'Well, I suppose anyone's entitled to complain a bit, when they've got lumps of metal in both hips. But it does mean she can't get down to the boxes on the low shelves in the stock room. Always sends me in for the inhalers and the medi-jectors. Bending is the worst, apparently.'

There seemed no seamless way to effect a change of subject, and Mina was conscious of advancing time: already the competitors on screen had moved across to join their host for the head-to-head. Sal had wandered upstairs to fetch a book, so she plunged straight in.

'Mum, do you think Sal has enough friends?'

'Sorry, dear?'

'Sal. I'm worried that she doesn't have enough friends.' Although actually, the number wasn't the problem. Even one proper friend would have put her mind at rest.

'Why, she gets on all right with the other girls, doesn't she? She's never mentioned them being nasty to her.'

It was almost exactly the same thing she had said herself to Mrs Edwards on the floor cushions, but now . . . Rather too quickly, she said, 'No, of course not. I'm not saying she's being bullied or anything like that. Just that she doesn't seem to have many friends, that's all. I mean, I know she always has been a bit of a loner, enjoying her own company, but lately I've started to worry she might be really . . .' what was the word the teacher had used? 'isolated.'

'Isolated?'

'At school, yes. She never suggests inviting anyone over to play, let alone going out with the other kids, to parties or discos, or even just to hang out at the shops or the park.' Mina saw them on Saturdays at the big park on the other side of the main road, leaning in fours and fives against the skateboard ramp, heads bent together, squabbling and laughing. Passing round a pilfered cigarette, too, sometimes – but that was a problem she would almost have preferred.

'What about last Saturday – when she got into her scrape? She was out with some friends then, wasn't she? And look where that got her, mind you. Maybe she's better without so many friends if they get her into that kind of trouble.'

Mina's stomach tightened like a fist. Last Saturday. The broken latch on the inside of the cupboard door, which could so easily have been snapped off on purpose; the door which could even have been closed from the outside; the calls which could have been ignored. *We thought she'd gone home . . .*

Not ready to give them the solidity of a voice, she glanced away from her fears. 'That wasn't her idea; I made her go. The thing is, she hardly so much as mentions another child's name herself, when she's telling me about school.'

And in fact, how much did she even do that any more, beyond a shrug and the assertion that all was 'fine'?

'Well, some kids can be private about their social lives. Not that you were: you always came home full of who had fallen out with so-and-so, and who was new best friends with such-and-such. I could never keep track of it all. But it's how girls are, isn't it? You're in one minute and out the next, sworn enemies and then friends for life. It can be painful when you're the one on the receiving end; it all seems so important at the time. But it always blows over soon enough.'

It wasn't like that, though. That was just the thing: none of it seemed to be important to Sal at all. Even Saturday.

'I dare say it'll be some girls' tiff,' her mother continued. 'Maybe that's why she doesn't want to talk about it. Give it time.'

The final game-show contender was looking fraught, evidently lost for an answer as, behind her, giant gilded clock hands ticked round towards zero.

'She's had time,' snapped Mina, and Dave as well as Mum looked over at her in surprise. 'I don't mean just now, just recently. I'm talking about the way she's been for ages. The way she's maybe always been, except when she was little and it didn't seem to matter. Lots of little kids are dreamy or off in their own worlds, and people just put it down to having lots of imagination or something.'

'She does have a lot of imagination,' said Mum.

'I know she does. But she's almost eleven. She'll be going to the comprehensive in September. The kids there might not be so tolerant. What if she can't manage to fit in? What if she's unhappy?'

She planted her gaze straight ahead, where the beleaguered contestant had just guessed wildly and lost. However, it didn't mean she wasn't aware of her mother's eyes, surveying her keenly. 'What's brought this on, then?'

Mina puffed out her cheeks and released a deflating jet of air. It had always been difficult trying to hide anything from Mum. Nevertheless, she sidestepped.

'Parents' evening.'

'What, the other week, do you mean? You never mentioned anything.'

'I'm mentioning it now.' But then she unwound a fraction, lying back in her armchair and meeting her mother's glance. 'Mrs Edwards was asking about it. About Sal's friendships, or lack of them. Wondering if she looked forward to going to school in the mornings.'

'Well, plenty of kids don't exactly look forward to school. That doesn't mean—'

'She said she thought Sal might not be happy.'

The closing credits were scrolling upwards on the television screen; behind them the grinning host was embracing the losing final competitor, who had pasted a brave smile over the cracks of her disappointment.

'There's another thing, Mum. She comes into my bed at nights.'

'She – *what?*'

'In the middle of the night. She often comes into my room and wants to cuddle up. Says she can't sleep; says she's had a nightmare; says anything, really.'

'But, Mina, she's ten! You should have put a stop to that nonsense years ago, when she was a toddler. I never let you or your sister come in with me, not once you were out of your cots and sleeping in a bed. If you had a bad dream – which you did quite a bit at one time, when you were seven or eight – then you'd call me and I'd come in to you. Sit with the reading light on a while, maybe have a bit of Winnie the Pooh. But then it was lights out again and back to sleep. I never let you come in bed with me, either of you. Once you start letting—'

'I know.' She was scarcely in need of the lecture. 'But that's not the point. That's not what I'm talking about, not exactly. It's just . . .' The bed thing was a sign of something else, that was the fear. Unimportant in itself – to her own if not to her mother's more traditional philosophy – but a symptom, or perhaps a warning. *The broken catch.* 'She seems happy enough in the daytime, certainly when she's at home. She often seems more on top of things than I do, to be quite honest. But at night, when she comes to my room, it's different. It's like it's a different Sal. I can't explain it.'

Mentioning the nocturnal visits, in any case something of a diversion, had also proved a mistake. Mum was barely listening any more; her lips were pursed, her eyes back on the television. 'It's always a hard habit to break, and at her age, well, it's gone quite beyond what's reasonable—' She broke off, though it was clear there could have been more; much more. Instead, she merely repeated, 'She's *ten.*'

All productive avenues of communication thus effectively barred, Mina lapsed into silence, and tried to summon an interest in the next programme, just beginning. A soap she didn't even watch.

'I think she's a grand kid.' Unexpectedly, it was Dave who spoke. Mina glanced at him uncertainly; her mother's eyes never deviated from the screen.

He tried again, tossing the remark at Mum. 'We're all different.'

No response; in a TV-studio public house, the landlord was pulling a pint, while the two customers at the bar exchanged passing volleys in some long-running, unspecified antagonism.

Dave turned, finally, to Mina. 'She always seems content enough to me, sweetheart. She's a clever lass; I think she'd tell you if she was unhappy.'

She gave him a grateful smile, and tried to believe him.

'*Ten,*' muttered Mum.

The television drinkers moved to a corner table to continue their disconnected sniping and the door opened and in came the subject of analysis, clutching a book and yawning.

'Is there any tea, Mum? Shall I make some for everyone?'

'Oh, that would be lovely. Thank you, love,' said Mina, while Dave turned and beamed his thanks and Mum merely humphed. But a minute later her grandmotherly conscience evidently smote her and she gathered herself up off the settee, stretching to ease the kink from the backs of her knees.

'I'll just go and help Sal with the tray.'

Whatever the substance of their thoughts, Dave and Mina watched the moving images on screen in companionable silence until the arrival of the tea.

When they were all settled again with their cups, it occurred to Mina that once the tea was drunk Mum and Dave would be making a move, and there was the subject of Jess yet to be embarked on. Five days had passed since the face-off with her sister in Barker's Pool. Jess hadn't come back, and there didn't seem much prospect of it now, not after the way they'd parted. She'd been right. Everything she'd said had been right. The pregnant kid needed something else, not Jess. And Jess needed to sort her own life out. But Jess was never going to see it that way, not in a thousand years. Jess would just see her as interfering, siding with Mum in the perennial fight.

'I'm worried about Jess, too.'

This time her mother's reaction was both more immediate and more predictable: the shutters snapped down before she'd fairly begun.

'Well, whatever she's got to put up with, she's brought it on herself. Her choice. I don't know what she imagines she's doing, going chasing off after some poor kid in trouble, probably making things ten times worse by sticking her oar in, encouraging the poor creature not to go home. Actually going and living in a squat, for goodness' sake! She's a silly, obstinate girl.'

Obstinate, yes: Jess could certainly manage that. She hadn't been answering her mobile all week. Mina couldn't contact her to say sorry – even if she wanted to, even if she could have made Jess listen – because she had no idea where this squat was, except that it was 'over Norton way'. Jess hadn't even been round while Mina was at work to fetch her remaining clothes – or the final load of her washing from last weekend, now sitting laundered and folded in a black bin liner by the front door, a mute peace offering. But Mina knew how the argument would go, if they'd had the chance to have it. *Back off. You're not my mum.*

'Haven't you given her a home?' her mother was saying. 'Cooked and washed and cleaned and provided? Bailed her out a hundred times, when she doesn't deserve it?'

'That's one of the things, Mum. I'm sure she's spending all her benefit on baby things. What will she be doing without us to lend her something to tide her over? I mean, of course she's got no rent to pay in that squat, if that's still where she is, but she has to eat.'

She couldn't somehow see the girl, Lisa, cooking casseroles for them to share. Could you cook properly in a squat, anyway? Would there be electricity?

'She'll be getting another cheque from the social this week, won't she?' said Dave before Mum could respond. Daring the blaze of disapproval from beside him on the settee, he added, 'I'm certain if she was really desperate she'd come to us for help.'

For the second time that afternoon, Mina found herself hoping he was right.

'After all, we are her family,' he said.

Mum expelled air through her nose the way she used to do when Mina was late back from a teenage party, or had on some un-approved garment. 'Not that you'd guess. She takes you for granted, that one, Mina; she always has done. Best left to get on with it for a while, if you ask my opinion. Let her stand on her own two feet for a change. See how she gets on without you about to put meals on the table and a roof over her head.'

Sal looked up from her book. Durrell again; she must be working through them. This time it was *Birds, Beasts and Relatives*.

'I thought she'd found herself a roof, Grandma. That squat place.'

'A respectable roof is what I meant. And besides, she won't survive there five minutes.'

Won't survive ... The picture vivid in Mina's mind was of the empty maisonette: bare boards and doorless kitchen units.

'She'll run out of money, or food, or clean washing, and she'll come running back here just like she always has, expecting everything on a plate, everything laid on. Anyway –' she patted Dave's knee without looking at him – 'we ought to get along. This won't get the old woman a new hat, as your nana used to say.'

In the hallway, while the soap's cast continued to argue unheeded behind the sitting-room door, Dave gave Mina his usual sheepish kiss and Sal wound herself round her grandma in a tangle of bony arms. Then they swapped round. Her mother's embrace was warm and generous and smelt of home, and as Mina relaxed into it she tried not to let her mind drift to the roasting tin, blackened and gummy where she had dumped it in the sink after scraping free the overroasted potatoes. Mum was unfailing; Mum was a rock. It was surely the basest disloyalty even to be thinking it, wasn't it?

Thinking that it wasn't the first time she'd left her with more than just the washing up.

Skateboarding. Christmas tree. High heels. Suet pudding. Tuesday. None of these suggested themselves to Peter as being remotely 'neat'.

'I know,' said Cassie. 'Worms.'

They were playing Apples to Apples, a favourite game with the girls and one which Peter never felt he'd fully understood, but in which Jeremy took an extravagant and somewhat inexplicable enjoyment. The aim was to convince a judge – in this case Jeremy – that one of the things on your own five cards most matched a designated key word.

'Why, then?' Kim's face pantomimed scepticism. 'What's so neat about worms?'

'Becau-se,' said Cassie, in the sing-song voice of the better informed, 'Leonie Sivell's big sister's got Worms 08 on her mobile, and it's really neat.'

The judge let out a yelp of delight most unsuitable to the dignity of his office.

'It doesn't mean that sort of worms, stupid.'

'Dad, she called me stupid. Tell her not to call me—'

'It means the wriggly kind, not some stupid computer game.'

'It's not a stupid game, it's brilliant. Leonie says her sister's got on to level three and there are sea monsters and—'

'All right.' Jeremy checked his laughter and held up a judicial hand. 'Worms are neat, Cassie. What else is neat? Martin?'

The trouble was, what else to play. Neither Jeremy nor Martin was a fan of Bananahead, and they lacked Trish's penchant for gambling; the point of Pictionary tended to be defeated by playing it with a professional artist, and charades – well, charades, as they knew, could be a danger to other road users.

Martin, who shared Peter's bemusement at the arcane mysteries of Apples to Apples, thumbed back and forth through his cards. 'How about "teaspoon", then? Jeremy likes the cutlery kept neat in the drawer.'

'Ah, but do you have it in the singular or the plural?' quibbled the organiser of spoons. 'Teaspoon, not teaspoons. Can a single teaspoon be neat?'

'It can be in the wrong place. You're always telling me. So I don't see why it can't just as well be neat, if it's put away right.'

The judge nodded sagely and turned towards Peter, who mustered his resources. 'OK. "High heels". If teaspoons are neat, then so are high heels, because women like to have them laid out in a tidy row in the bottom of the wardrobe.' Not that Bev's ever were: her natural carelessness of domestic regimentation compounded by her daughters' periodical forays into the bedroom to 'try on Mummy's shoes'.

'Just women, you think?' Jeremy's eyebrows were hammily eloquent.

'Have you still got Aunty Ruby's shoes?' Cassie asked; Jeremy laughed and Martin grinned while Peter winced. 'Only, Dad threw away all Mummy's shoes last summer. We took them to the Oxfam shop. Even the silver pointy ones with all the straps; they were so cool.'

'You couldn't even walk in them. Looked like a giraffe on stilts.'

'Did not.'

'Did so.'

'Could we come over some time and try on Aunty Ruby's shoes? *Please?*'

'Well . . .' Jeremy eyed her benignly. 'You know, Ruby had a lot of very sensible shoes.'

'Old lady shoes?' The disappointment was undisguised.

'*Cassie!*'

'What?'

The consummate diplomat, Jeremy turned serenely to Kim. 'How about you, my dear? What can you provide me with that's neat?'

'Dunno.' She wasn't even looking at her cards. Cassie had the air of a bantam cock swelling its chest to crow.

'Have a go,' coaxed Peter. 'Whatever you've got, it can't be as feeble as high heels.'

'Oh yeah? You should see – my cards are all rubbish.'

'*You're* rubbish, you mean.'

'Well, let's say Kim can pass on this round, then, shall we?' said Jeremy, inventing procedure on the hoof. 'Everyone gets two passes, and Kim's used one of them.'

'So who's won, then?' demanded Cassie. 'Whose thing was the neatest?'

The adjudicator surveyed the three cards which had been laid before him. 'Well, your worms did have the virtue of sheer inventive originality, but I think I'm going to have to come down for

Martin's teaspoons.' His air of assumed innocence made it sound vaguely suggestive.

'Didn't mean that sort of worms, anyway,' muttered Kim.

Sunday lunch at the cottage had been a thank you for the previous Saturday night and Jeremy and Martin had shown every sign of enjoying their remuneration – were indeed apparently still doing so, in spite of the crackle of sibling crossfire. Ollie had abandoned her place of duty at Peter's feet and was lying wedged between the two guests on the sofa, flat on her back with her ambivalent genitalia on general display, snoring complacently. Martin's fingers tangled proprietorially with one of her ears. Well, supposed Peter, she had now after all shared his bed. So when Jeremy handed on the judge's mantle to Martin as victor and dealt another round of Apples, he didn't demur and suggest a cup of tea but let things ride.

As the next round came to a close, a sudden urge for fresh air, in spite of the drizzly dusk beyond the sitting-room window, prompted Peter to suggest that he and the twins walk their guests home.

'Get your anoraks, girls,' he told them, a prompt for Ollie to begin to turn excited circles.

'It's only up the lane, Dad.'

'We won't be cold.'

'It's raining. Get your anoraks.'

The rain was scarcely that; more like a denser and slightly wetter version of the fen fog that often rose up to meet the fall of the light at this time of year, wreathing the hedges and haloing the streetlamps as they buzzed into life. Not that there were any lamp posts along the lane; they had to make do with the last glimmers from the sky to avoid the ruts and puddles, and Olivia wasn't tempted to cock her leg, even if she'd known how.

'A glorious repast,' said Jeremy as they reached the doors of the villas, though Peter knew his pork-and-leek hotpot never did Bev's recipe justice. As they retraced their steps, he thought of the evening ahead. Sunday evening meant talking to Mina again.

Last week it had been her turn, and she hadn't rung, but that was because they'd been together the day before. It made sense for her not to phone. She had enough on her plate with Sal to sort out. But now it had been eight days, and he'd found himself wondering with increasing frequency, as the week progressed, how things had worked out. What the friends had said; whether they'd really believed that Sal had gone home; whether the strain was gone from Mina's soft grey eyes. They were left with a problem, though. Technically, this should have been his Sunday to call her, but as she'd missed last week, maybe the onus was on her? He wasn't sure why it mattered, but for some reason it seemed important: he didn't want to jump in and ring if it was still her turn. Perhaps the thing to do was to leave it a little later than usual, and see what happened; if the phone hadn't rung by, say, half past nine, then he could safely call her. Three hours: it seemed a long time to wait. But there was tea to cook – not that they'd any of them be wanting much after that lunch – and the washing up afterwards, and the other Sunday evening jobs, like getting the girls' PE kits out of the dryer and folded and back in their sports bags for the morning, and the weekly polish of their black school shoes. And he could always get ahead with thinking about Wednesday's lecture. As they reached the cottage door and entered the kitchen, he was distracted by the wink of the red light on the answerphone. He went over to the machine while Cassie, Kim and Ollie disappeared in the direction of the sitting room. He had two messages, the electronic voice informed him. His mind was still half on what to cook for tea, as he pressed the 'play' button.

The voice that followed the beep was Mina's. Not her usual, live telephone voice, vivid and intimate, close against his ear; nor her real, flesh-and-blood voice, bleak and unhappy. This was a third version, clipped and diminished by the tape, and more remote from him than either of the others.

Hello, Peter? It's me, Mina. Look, I'm just phoning to say don't ring me tonight. If you were going to, I mean. I'm going to be . . . well, just don't ring, OK?

A whirr and a click, the second beep, and it was Mina again.

Sorry, I forgot, Peter. I never properly thanked you. For last weekend, coming all that way, and doing what you did. I don't think I ever really said it. So, thank you.

Then there was a gap. No more, perhaps than a slight hesitation, but he was certain it was there: a short stretch of empty running tape before she hung up.

Chapter 19

'Here you are. I've put some brandy in it.'

This time it was Dave who had the cold, and Mina who was administering the hot drinks and sympathy.

'It should be whisky, really, but I never have the stuff. To be honest, I think even the brandy is left over from when Mum last cooked Christmas dinner here.' She watched as he lowered an inflamed nose into the steam from the mug of lemon and honey. 'Does brandy keep all right? I mean, I know fancy cognac gets left in barrels for yonks, but I've no idea about Morrisons cooking brandy. And the lemon is only Jif.'

'It smells lovely, sweetheart. Thanks.' Though, actually, 'sweed-hard' was closer to what he called her. Did other people sound like Brooklyn street vendors when they had catarrh, or was it only Dave?

'Are you shivery? Shall I fetch you a blanket down?' If there were any in the airing cupboard that Jess hadn't taken. Or maybe he could have Jess's duvet – it's not as if she was using it.

'No, thanks, Mina love.'

For once Mum and Sal had forsaken what had become their regular Saturday afternoon outing to town: Mum spending a rare idle half-hour in the library for Sal, Sal carrying the shopping home for Mum. Instead, Sal was upstairs re-reading one of last week's selection, and Mum was at Dave's house spring-cleaning the kitchen.

'She wants me to decorate.' Dave took a noisy suck at his drink; but drinking was hard, she reminded herself, when you couldn't breathe properly. 'Hasn't been done since I moved in, that kitchen; it's the one room I've not touched. Twelve years this summer, it'll be.' Another slurp. 'So that's why she's cleaning. More just tidying, really. Having a good sort out so that I can get in there to do the painting.'

'I know what it's like. There must be years and years' worth of clutter stacked up in my kitchen drawers. I could do with going through it, too, and throwing half of it away.' Except that, below the top few inches, most of the stuff was Mum's – just as most of what Mum was no doubt going through and consigning to bin liners was probably Dave's. She wondered if he minded; but he gave no appearance of it, having settled very contentedly into the sanctuary of her settee after he'd finished his lunchtime airport run. Dave, basically, was hiding.

'Your mum's looking at new cooking hobs, too.'

A few moments of silence was all the consideration this statement received from either of them. Since they were, at best, turning a blind eye to her presence here, Mina could hardly ask the council to replace the ancient electric stove in the kitchen, even though one ring had blown shortly after Mum left – and she could imagine how little Dave was interested in hobs.

'And how are things with you, love, anyway?'

'Oh, you know. Pretty much as usual.'

Even with a head full of cold, Dave could spot when he was being fobbed off. To deflect the query she saw forming in his eyes, she said, 'Things have been a bit hectic at work. Nupoor's off on maternity leave, having her third; there's meant to be cover but the temps are unreliable, most of them stick it a day or two and go, and there's always a gap before they find us another. And Debbie's been ill this week, too. Properly ill, Fran says, not just having one of her bits of unofficial shopping leave.' Mina had heard Debbie's calling-in-sick voice; it made Dave's present diction sound like Rex Harrison in *My Fair Lady*.

'So you're a bit snowed under, then?'

'You could say that.' There were times yesterday when the 'call waiting' light was besieging her with six or seven insistently repeating flashes, and Mrs Gordon was patrolling the aisles, wafting clouds of stress as aggressive as her perfume. Coffee break was shaved down to fifteen minutes; if Lyn were still there she'd have been on to the union rep.

She glanced up. Dave's nose had risen from his mug; she didn't like the look he was giving her.

'I mean, of course with being so short-staffed, everyone's under a lot more pressure than usual. There's hardly been time to turn round. It makes everyone snappy, too.'

He was still looking at her. 'You look tired.'

It was always a thing that could go either way. Sometimes, from some people, it could be merely irritating, making her feel older than her years, dowdy, worn down – or firing her to resentful denial. But from Dave, spoken the way he spoke it, the words had her fighting tears.

'Well, as I say, it's been exhausting –'

Still the look.

' – and of course, worrying about Jess. She hasn't been in touch. It's four weeks now. It's – well, it's weird without her.' No crumbs on the kitchen work top, no listening for the sound of a key in the door as she watched late night TV.

He took another glugging dip into his lemon and honey, but it was clear that her answer still hadn't satisfied him. A pause, and the scrutiny again.

'You ought to get out more.' She hoped he wasn't going to add, 'You're young,' because there was nothing so calculated to make her feel the slippage of years.

'Has there been someone special lately?'

Dave had always asked her this, routinely, teasingly, since he first started going out with Mum. *Is there someone special at the moment?* She didn't mind it from him, she found – even though her mother knew never, never to ask; she was amused by it, even when she so often had to admit that, no, there was nobody at present. But now, in the past tense, and in that tone again, she found her voice thickening like his.

'Maybe.' She wished she had a steamy cup to bury herself behind, too.

Even then, if he'd asked, she probably wouldn't have said anything; but he didn't, he just breathed his evaporating brandy fumes and waited.

'It was all nothing. He'd never said anything. It was . . . a friendship. But I suppose I'd come to rely on it.' Sunday evenings. Now they were going to be the hardest part of the week. She found herself contriving for Sal to stay up late, even though it was school in the morning; found herself turning in early. Not that it helped: she'd have been better downstairs with the television for company than upstairs alone, willing on sleep. 'He had a nice laugh.'

'Someone from the call centre, was it?'

The shot was so far wide of the mark that it made her laugh before she had time for caution. Dave looked up in surprise, and pulled an apologetic face. 'No. But, in fact, I suppose you could say I met him there. Anyway, it's finished – before it had ever started.' Despite the gloomy finality of her words, an unanticipated smile still tugged at her lips. It was something about Peter, and the idea of him in the call centre: the incongruity of it. 'Probably all for the best.'

'Well, I'm sorry, anyway, sweetheart.'

She was still trying to snuff the smile – and maybe it was the smile that encouraged him? – when he said, 'Actually, about Jess.'

Then he seemed to lose courage, because what had sounded like the beginning of something turned into a full stop. He laid down his cup, rummaged for a large, old-fashioned cotton handkerchief (Mum had always produced these from some secret stash when anyone had a cold) and blew his nose stertorously. Then he stared at the carpet, until Mina decided she had disappeared entirely from his thoughts. When at last he spoke she was taken by surprise by his voice, even before the words made any sense.

'I've been to see her.'

'Sorry?'

'Jess. I've been to see her. She answered her mobile, finally; we spoke, and I went round to that place she's living in. With some money' – he caught her eye – 'don't tell your mum.'

There were too many questions to know quite where to begin; instead the key thing asserted itself. 'Is she OK?'

He nodded, not with much enthusiasm. 'Bloody awful place.'

Which was her cue to nod, too. It felt like something shared, almost like a shameful secret, although neither of them had cause for guilt. Except . . . *don't tell your mum.* She was pretty sure it wasn't only the money he was talking about.

'And the girl?'

'Still pregnant. Due any time, I gather.' He bent with the stiffness of aching joints to retrieve his cup from the floor.

'And is Jess still' – she felt her own anger rising at the unfairness of it – 'annoyed with me?'

'Oh, she'll come round,' said Dave. Like her, though, was he remembering the stubbornly long time that had passed since Jess had spoken – really properly spoken – to Mum?

There was a sound on the stairs and then at the door, and Sal appeared, with her dressing gown over her jeans and jumper, like an English gentleman breakfasting late in a 1930s film. Except pinker and fluffier. Those sleeves were halfway up her wrists; she'd be needing a new one soon.

'Hello, love. Come down for a cup of tea?'

Sal shook her head. 'I've got to the sad part, so I've just stopped reading for a bit.'

Mina held up an arm. Responding to the invitation, Sal clambered into the armchair with her to a creaking of springs.

'Curly dies. It's the end of chapter two, and the other dogs kill her. And she was the nicest one.'

She spoke matter-of-factly, but Mina's arm tightened round her shoulder. What was she doing reading books where the nicest dog died in chapter two?

'This is as far as I got last time, but this time I'm going to finish it, I've decided. It's all right, because Buck doesn't die at the end, I asked Mrs Edwards. He just ends up left on his own, that's all. In the wild.'

Oh yes, that was it, *The Call of the Wild*. She remembered the picture on the front: a dog with sad eyes alone in a snowy land-scape. Why couldn't Sal have carried on reading *Puppies in the Pantry* just a little bit longer?

'So you fancied some company for a while? I don't blame you. Sure you don't want a drink?'

'No, I'm OK, Mum.' She eyed Dave hopefully. 'I'd rather have a game of Battleships.'

'Sweetheart, Dave isn't feeling very—'

'Yes, I'll play.' He'd had a set when he was a boy, he'd once told them, and could never resist a bout with Sal. 'On condition that your mum makes me another cup of this hot lemon stuff. It's a real pick-me-up.'

Sal ran upstairs to get the box and Mina smiled her thanks as she picked up Dave's empty cup and headed for the kitchen.

There wasn't much honey left in the jar, now, only scrapings. She ran the teaspoon round the base and sides as she waited for the kettle to boil, and up under the rim, but it amounted to less than a spoonful. Would the jar crack if she put the lemon and brandy in there and poured on the boiling water? It would be the best way to loosen the honey. Then she'd put it on her shopping list. Jess loved honey.

But Jess was still not speaking to her. Jess wasn't coming home. Let her buy her own honey, in that dive she'd chosen. But hadn't they also driven her there? First Mum, and now her, they'd driven her away. Out of touch; out of reach.

Except, astonishingly, Dave: quiescent, untalkative Dave. However unlikely it may seem, there was that lifeline to hold on to. At least she was talking to Dave.

* * *

265

'We've started gymnastics in PE now instead of hockey –'

'It's way better. Hockey was horrible, the ball's too hard, they should have a softer ball for when it hits you –'

'Gymnastics is brilliant, we were doing handstands today. Like in the playground except Mrs Moore showed us how to point our toes –'

'– and you have to do this funny, special walk beforehand; you step up to it, walking with your toes pointed, too –'

'– and Mrs Moore looks so funny when she's doing the walk.'

They weren't in the Land Rover today. It was Peter's Easter vacation, though the girls were still at school, and his slightly greater leisure combined with the mild spring weather made walking them home from Afterschool Club something to be relished. As did the resumption of something approaching the familiar stereo broadcast, battering him from two directions as they walked along the lane. At this point in the dialogue they broke off, letting go of his hands to peel away at either side towards the twin swathes of new nettles and cow parsley which hemmed their path, demonstrating the Special Gymnastics Walk – with Kim turning an unscheduled cartwheel for extra emphasis.

'You have to do this thing with your arms, she says. That's all part of it –'

'– like a ballet dancer –'

'– or a circus person on a tightrope.'

They were back holding his hands now, Cassie on the left and Kim on the right, but their free arms were tracing graceful arcs in the air, fingertips extended, and their knees kicked exaggeratedly high as they stepped clear of the drying ruts like something out of the Spanish Riding School.

'Abby Fox hurt her back –'

'She's always hurting herself, Leonie says it's just so she can go and see Eve, and get out of lessons –'

'– coming down from handstand into a crab, and she sort of twisted it; she actually cried.'

'– but why would anyone want to get out of gymnastics?'

'Why indeed?' he agreed, with a serious face and a capering heart. *Normality*, he thought, or at least close to it. He wished he could have stored it up to share with Mina on Sunday. Funny how things seemed somehow to count less without someone to tell them to – as it had been with Bev, and as it had come to be briefly this winter with Mina. But she'd made things pretty clear: not calling, not wishing to be called. It left a space much bigger than he'd have predicted, and took the edge off the pleasure – even this, even his girls – because he wouldn't be laughing over it with her.

'Jason Scrivener brought in a coin he'd found with his dad –'

'They've got a metal detector –'

'– and he said it was Roman, and Mrs Moore said it could be, but it was all too worn down to see –'

'– but it wouldn't be Roman, would it, Dad, not in Allington?'

'And Shannon says they had another one of those notes last night.'

It was Kim who spoke last, and there was very little outward change of tone in her voice, but Peter felt her hand in his tighten a little. Kim was looking straight ahead, and her right arm was still thrown up in the Gymnastics Walk; Cassie's hand tightened, too, and her left arm came waveringly down. It was Cassie to whom Peter turned.

'What's this?'

The high-stepping had stopped; she scuffed through the furrows of caked mud and said nothing.

'Horrible letters.' Kim again. 'Someone's been leaving them on the step of their trailer, under a brick. Or stuffed in the side of the door. Saying nasty, horrible things. Once they left some dog poo as well, with the note all scrumpled up round it.' Her eyes were wide in relish of the shock of it. 'Shannon said so, didn't she, Cassie?'

He watched as Cassie nodded slowly, gaze fixed on the lane ahead.

'Why didn't you tell me?'

Cassie was saved from trying to answer his question by the sudden appearance of Ollie, who could always sense their homecoming, whether diesel-engined or on foot, before it was realistically possible for her to have heard their approach. Did she smell them, Peter sometimes wondered, with that famous sense of smell a thousand times more powerful than the human nose, according to the children's encyclopaedia? And if so, what was it like, the aroma that she caught? What cocktail, exactly, of classroom dust and packed lunch crumbs and ink and sweat and pheromones brought her galloping towards them in a frenzy of sycophantic joy?

They broke their line to huddle round the spaniel, and take their turn to greet and be greeted, so that Kim was facing both of them when she said, 'Paula Mahoney came in and told Mrs Moore the first time they got one of the notes; she went in and saw her before lessons while we were all lining up. But it's kept on happening. Cassie won't tell you, so I am.'

Cassie was concentrating hard on rumpling Ollie's ears. Playing for time, Peter asked, 'What did Mrs Moore say?'

'She talked to the class about it, told them how horrible it was. That things like that aren't a funny joke, they're like bullying but worse. Simon Pullis was laughing and she went mental and hauled him straight off to Miss Cripps.'

'You're not supposed to say "mental",' said Cassie, still to the dog's fur, but not with any acrimony.

'What else? What about since? If you say it's happened again?'

'Lots of times, Shannon says. Mrs Moore says it's not a kid doing it. Not anyone in the class or someone's big brother or anything. She says it's grown-ups, or at least teenagers.'

Cassie, kneeling with both hands buried in Ollie's abundant chest hair, finally looked up, squinting against the light. 'Why would grown-ups do that, Dad?'

Having no answer to give her, he just squatted down beside her and snaked his own hands into the spaniel's ruff to tangle with hers, until he felt fingers curling round his own. Kim joined them in the dirt, and for a second he thought they might both sit down and howl, here in the lane, as they had more than once done in public places when they were small. As it was, they must have made a strange sight had anyone been there to witness it: the small triangle, hands gripped tightly together over the confused but gratified dog.

'Come on, let's get home. Tell you what, I'll do pancakes for tea and you can both help scrape them off the floor when they all go wrong.'

'Can we have Nutella with them, if we have a cheese one first?'

'And golden syrup?'

'And mashed banana, and strawberry jam?'

Straightening, he pulled them up with him, their hands still three-way linked. 'Absolutely. You can have the whole lot together if you really insist.'

He only hoped there was an egg.

Later that evening after the frying pan was scoured and they were safely in bed, he did what he never, ever did, and left them on their own. Only for the time it took him to drive to the end of the lane and send Jeremy or Martin back to mind the ship, but he still experienced a pang of guilt. An unaccountable one, really, because every night he went out almost as far with Ollie to gauge the next day's weather and watch her tracing busy zigzags along the path ahead, showing up pale in either torch beam or moonlight. But that was routine, and the girls knew where he would be. This was different; he even winced slightly as the Land Rover engine roared into life, hoping they wouldn't wake and wonder.

Jeremy had a deadline and was elbow deep in paintbrushes and bottles of coloured Indian ink; Martin agreed readily enough to relocate his planned evening with Bruce Willis to Peter's sofa and Peter's DVD.

'Is Ollie at home?' is all he asked.

269

It was some time since he'd been here, Peter realised, as he swung off the road and down into the cinder yard a few minutes later. He hadn't picked Cassie up either this week or last, nor dropped Shannon back. In fact it must be, what, three weeks since they'd played after school? Since the last occasion one of the generator lights seemed to have failed, miring the nearest corner of the site in blackness. Perversely, he chose that spot to pull up and park; or perhaps it merely chimed with what felt like the clandestine nature of his visit. He was startled, climbing down from the driver's seat, by the sound of heavy feet shifting, the noise amplified in the darkness as his ears compensated for the lack of visual stimulus. Then a soft, rhythmic blowing. The ponies. For some reason, though, tonight, the usual posse of dogs was not in evidence, their absence adding to the feeling of desertion that hung about the yard, even though lights showed at half a dozen trailer windows – including Paula Mahoney's.

For some reason – perhaps because so often she was expecting them, heard the vehicle and greeted them at the door – he felt conspicuously like a trespasser when he climbed the metal steps, alone and uninvited, and knocked on the glass. It was silly, he told himself. He wouldn't feel that way stepping up the front path of any of his neighbours' houses; but maybe privacy took on a more vital complexion when there was so little of it to guard.

It was Gabriel, in fact, who pulled aside the woollen check curtain, slid back the bolt and opened the door.

'Yes?'

'Oh, hello. Sorry, I know you weren't—'

'You're the lass's father. Cassie's da.' He stepped backwards into the bright space beyond the curtain, so that his features sprang into visibility. He was smiling. 'Come on in and welcome.'

'Ah, Peter, hello.' Paula appeared at his shoulder, and between them they led the way through into the small living room, where a gas fire blazed.

'Will I make you a cup of tea?' she asked, and when he demurred, added, with a tilt of the head towards the door at the far end of the trailer, 'Shannon's in bed already. Diarmuid's round at a friend's. Computer games, it'll be.'

Her look held expectancy, so he reciprocated with his own explanation. 'My two are both in bed, too. I've got a friend over, keeping an eye on them, you know.' But of course that explained nothing: not why he had come here, in the evening and on his own. He wished he'd asked for the cup of tea, after all. That would have provided an excuse for preliminary small talk; he could have followed Paula back into the kitchen and they could have fussed over cups and milk and hardly needed to say anything at all for at least five minutes. Or they could have exchanged playground nothings – the fun they'd had last week with the clay penguins; the new classroom smartboard – which seemed too difficult in here, sitting formally on the foldaway sofa. He could hardly entertain Gabriel with the Gymnastics Walk.

Paula tried to help. 'Shannon says your two have been walking to school these days.'

'Yes. The light mornings, and the nicer weather, you know.'

'Shannon's been going in on her bike.'

He almost said something about making sure they get fresh air, before he realised how absurdly inappropriate it was, in Shannon's case, living here. The embarrassment, even in imagination, made him rush on with what he'd come to say.

'I only just heard, and I thought I'd call by and say how sorry I am. About what's been happening here.'

Gabriel, who had been staring into the Calor gas flames, looked up, his expression a blank.

'The letters, I mean.'

Paula regarded him levelly. 'I don't know why you should be sorry.'

She was right: sorry was the wrong word. Not because it wasn't his fault, but because it was too glib, too ordinary.

'It's terrible. I can't imagine . . .' Of course he couldn't. But how was telling them that obvious fact supposed to help, at all? He determined to get a grip. 'Have you no idea at all who might be doing it?'

That didn't seem to help, either. Paula shrugged ruefully, and Gabriel went back to his contemplation of the fire.

'Someone in the village, anyway? Have any of the other families here had—'

'Just us.' This was Gabriel, his gaze unmoving from the grate. No point in even asking whether they'd called the police. Already the man's demeanour made Peter recall the way Paula's eyes had flicked towards her husband, the last time he'd asked them that question.

'Is there anyone you know of with a grudge? Anyone who's said anything to you? Made unpleasant remarks?'

At this she laughed, though not without kindness. 'Plenty, I'd be thinking, wouldn't you?'

He accepted the gentle reprimand, noting the complete absence of self-pity with which she delivered it. And wondered whether he was the only one or whether, in fact, there had been a succession of other callers – interfering; do-gooding; self-righteous – to add to their burden.

Although he knew he was beginning to sound like an investigating officer himself, he could think of no other tack – unless he were just to repeat his apologies and leave. 'When did it start?'

This time, though, his question met only silence from both of them. Even Paula's face had darkened inscrutably.

'When was the first time it happened, I mean? The notes and . . . things being left.'

Gabriel's look wasn't hostile, exactly, so much as appraising; Paula's had now resolved itself into simple disbelief. It was her husband she turned to.

'He doesn't know.'

A shrug.

'The kids haven't said anything,' continued Paula. 'And quite right of them. I wouldn't have wanted little Cassie upsetting.'

Cassie . . . What was this? What hadn't the kids said? Maddeningly, the two of them continued to talk as if he weren't in the room.

'We should tell him now, though.' It was Paula who made the pronouncement, and Gabriel signalled his assent with one concessionary open palm. 'Then he can decide himself what he says to his little one.'

What he says . . . Cassie . . . *Just tell me!*

It was Gabriel who turned to him, his face neutral, while Paula stood up and moved over to the cupboard beside the fireplace. 'The first one was in February. Left on the steps on a Monday night, late. Monday the fourth.'

February the 4th. He felt as though the date ought to mean something to him. Surely it did, by the way Gabriel was saying it, the way he was looking at him. Monday the 4th; Sunday the 3rd, Saturday the 2nd, Friday the 1st. Wasn't that the night . . . His brain made the connection just as Paula straightened from the cupboard and handed him a sheet of paper. It was torn from a spiral notebook, the kind he kept by the telephone at home and used for his shopping lists, the top edge roughly scalloped where the wire loops had ripped through. The words were written in blue biro, not scrawled but inscribed in laborious capitals, everything correctly spelled.

'This one came last week,' said Paula.

There was even a comma, and four emphatic, tidy full stops.

GET OUT, YOU FILTHY FUCKING PIKEYS. KID-NAPPERS. PAEDOS. KEEP YOUR FILTHY HANDS OFF OUR KIDS.

Ice hit his stomach. *Our kids.* It meant his kid, didn't it?

After the pause, it was Gabriel who spoke. 'There'll be some of our neighbours hereabouts, it seems, can't tell a sick child molester from a young lad playing foolish games in the night.'

'But that's . . .' Ludicrous. Appalling. So much hatred, and vented in the name of protecting his daughter – from a boy who'd been her friend. From a childish escapade.

'But it was just two kids messing about.' Why was he telling them what they already knew? 'If I'd known, I could have . . .'

But what could he have done? Set the record straight? How? With whom?

'Look, now.' Paula sat down on the arm of her husband's chair. 'Whoever it is, they're just plain idiots. Scum. Not worth the waste of our breath, speaking of them. They don't trouble themselves about the truth of things. So there's really no need to be going agitating about it. If it hadn't been this business with our Diarmuid and your Cassie, you can be sure it would have been something else, some other piece of nonsense.'

Was he being humoured? He looked from one to the other of his hosts, impotent for words, and met two perfectly similar expressions, calm and even just a little embarrassed. But he was still at a loss.

'How did they— How could they have found out?'

Paula waved a hand vaguely. 'Ach, villages, you know.'

But Gabriel was looking darker. 'It's always the way of it, once the police are involved.'

'I don't understand—'

Peter stopped, and Paula surveyed him, not without kindness.

'There's maybe a lot of things you don't understand,' she said softly.

It wasn't intended as a dismissal, he felt quite certain, but he nevertheless chose to take it as such. They didn't need his outrage, any more than they needed the drama of his running round here in the night, asking foolish questions.

'I'm sorry,' was all he could think to say, as he had said before, and Paula smiled at him and shifted her shoulders in the suggestion of a shrug.

Chapter 20

It was May when the thing of which Peter had so many times despaired finally came to pass. Trish submitted her thesis.

Trish being Trish, the event did not go by without a certain amount of last-minute pother and perturbation on her part, and patient pushing on Peter's. It was now the next morning, and he had been hoping to get down to marking some revision essays submitted by his undergraduates, whose exams were looming large, but Trish was back in his office, and still fretting. If anything, in fact, her anxiety levels had risen since the day before.

'I've found a typo.'

Drawing a very deep breath, he smiled the smile he normally reserved for nitpicking colleagues and obtuse sales assistants.

'Of course you'll find typos if you start going over and over it. Everything ever printed contains typos. My last book had at least five, and that was the University Press.'

'No, I know, but this is different. This is awful.' She swallowed. 'It's in the bloody title.'

Laughter – his first instinct – seemed the incorrect response.

'I've got it right on the actual cover, and on the spine, but it's the title page inside. I've missed out an i. I put "marginalsation" instead of "marginalisation". *On the Edge: Urban Poverty and Marginalsation in the UK.*'

She was priceless. He resisted urges either to go over and hug her or to make a joke about 'alsation' dogs. 'I shouldn't worry. Chances are the examiners won't even notice.'

'Really? You think so?' The eager hope in her eyes reminded him of Ollie when there were sausages on the go. 'Only, it did occur

275

to me, the regulations specify that the table of contents isn't included in the word limit. So that must be true of the title page, too, mustn't it? So the words there don't really count. They're not part of the actual thesis, so they can't mark me down for making a mistake there, can they?'

'Trish, I don't honestly think the fact that there's a spelling mistake on the title page is going to—'

'Only, I did wonder about writing them a note – the examiners, I mean. Maybe not a note, as such, but just a sort of erratum slip, and giving it to the secretary person at the Board of Graduate Studies, the one I handed it in to, and asking her to tuck it inside the thesis. What do you think?'

It was probably best not to let her know exactly what he thought, so he confined himself to solemn reassurance. 'I really don't think that's necessary.'

She subsided somewhat into his armchair at that, but only for a second.

'Well, but then there's that section on housing benefit that I added in chapter four. I woke up in the night and couldn't remember if I'd made sure the data were for the latest available year. Do you think if I went to the OPCS website it would tell me which is the latest year they've published figures for? I meant to do it before I handed it in, I'd even made myself a note, but then I put it in a file and forgot about it. Or I could go to the official publications room and check in the paper sources? I mean, I think I may have done it already, when I wrote the section, but I just can't remember for certain.'

'Look, don't worry. These are tiny things. Insignificant. They're not going to fail you because you use slightly less than up-to-date figures in one footnote. At worst, they'll require a correction, but there are very often minor corrections. You've handed it in. It's done. The best thing is to try to forget all about it until we hear about a date for your *viva*. Get on with that research you're doing for me.'

Not that he needed the survey data she was collating with any particular urgency, but it would keep her mind off things, and go towards this final term's cafeteria and bar bills. He'd miss her when she'd gone, there was no denying it – but his bank balance would enjoy a small surge.

'Oh yes, the *viva*. That's another thing. How long do you think it's likely to be? Am I supposed to keep up with reading, in case they ask me about subsequent developments, do you think? Because what if I've left and got a job in Bromsgrove or somewhere, where there's no research library for miles, and I can't afford broadband or subscriptions to the online databases?'

Mad schemes entered his head, of dispatching all his photocopying by courier to the West Midlands and back.

'And do you think I'll have been *viva*'d before the next round of Research Fellowship applications? And teaching posts. I can't work in a café for the rest of my life, it's hardly exercising my finely honed skills of empirical analysis, is it?'

From missing i's, they seemed to have moved on with unnerving rapidity to the question of Trish's career prospects and future life in general, and Peter felt unprepared for the leap.

'You can't – of course you can't. Be a waitress for ever, that is. But one thing at a time. Get the PhD, and then you can think about the next stage.' Of course she was clever, and she could write. But Trish lecturing? Trish responsible for forming the study habits of a new generation of students? It was an alarming prospect. 'If the examiners like your work, they may well be useful as referees when it comes to applying for post-doc positions.'

'As well as you, you mean.'

'As well as me, naturally.'

She smiled, then, and relaxed just a fraction. 'So you're going to support me, then? If I apply for Fellowships here?'

'Listen, Trish—'

Luckily, perhaps, for both of them, she was never required to listen to what he had to say next, nor he to determine upon it, because that was when the telephone rang. He jumped across to his desk with what he hoped did not appear like too much eagerness.

'Peter Kendrick.'

There was a fuzzy pause at the other end, and the sound of voices off. A distracted undergraduate on a mobile in the Geography coffee bar? Or someone with dead batteries calling from a payphone? Then a female voice, too brisk for a student, told him, 'I've got a call for you from Martin Bryce.'

Some more muffled voices and then Martin's, sounding strange.

'Peter? It's me. Look, sorry. Can't use mobiles in here. The equipment or something. Interferes with it.'

Aircraft? Radio observatory? *Hospital.*

'Martin. What is it, what's happened? Are you OK?'

He sensed Trish, behind him, snap to alert.

'I'm fine.' His voice sounded even stranger. 'It's Jeremy.'

Oh, God. 'It's Jeremy,' he told Trish, hand over the mouthpiece. Then to Martin, again, 'What's happened?'

'Heart attack, they reckon.'

'Shit.' That didn't mean . . .? 'Is he OK?'

'Hard to say yet. They've got him all wired up, and he's still unconscious.'

'Shit.' He wasn't being much help.

'Look, I know you're at work. But we came out without anything. Just in the ambulance. He'll need things – pyjamas, razor – if he . . .'

'Of course. Yes, when he wakes up. His toothbrush and so on.'

'Only, I don't want to go back home, not at the moment.'

'No, of course not. I can go. I'll come straight over and get the key from you, shall I? Are you in Addenbrooke's?'

'Yes – still in emergency at the moment.'

'OK, I'll be right with you. Wait there.'

Why did he always say such stupid things in a crisis, he asked himself, as he rang off? But maybe everybody did.

He turfed Trish unceremoniously from his office as he was putting on his jacket. She was genuinely chastened by the news about Jeremy; in fact, he was relieved that she didn't suggest coming with him, because he was certain it was in her mind to do so. The last time had not exactly been an auspicious precedent, grateful though he remained for her assistance. Anyway, this time he was sober.

He strode through the cloisters at the back of Old Court towards the new accommodation block and the car park, breaking into a trot as soon as he was clear of the public eye. Running, and then accelerating with uncharacteristic aggression to fill the smallest gap which opened in the mid-morning traffic, satisfied a tension in him by creating the illusion that he was doing something. Then there was nowhere to park; having taken a ticket from the machine he drove up and down packed rows of vehicles, wondering whether the electronic 'car park full' sign was broken, before eventually squeezing the Land Rover's considerable bulk, on the angle, into a corner which was almost certainly not meant to be a space at all.

When he reached A&E and was directed towards a side room down at the end, he found Martin standing outside the glazed double doors, looking very much as if he and not Jeremy were the cardiac patient. His high forehead was rinsed of colour, so that his face was the same putty grey as his hair; his cheekbones, always lean, appeared positively cadaverous. And he was doing what men traditionally do in hospital corridors: he was pacing.

He acknowledged Peter's arrival with a nod and the confession, 'Christ, I wish they'd let you smoke in here.'

Peter wondered whether he ought to put an arm round him or at least a hand on his shoulder, but it wasn't the kind of thing they did, and would probably only create awkwardness. In any case, Martin's 'Thanks for coming, mate' told him that it wasn't necessary.

'How is he?'

'Still unconscious. They've dosed him on some intravenous drugs

— some clot-busting stuff, I think. And now they're running tests. Everything's wired up and beeping in there.'

Peter peered through the cross-hatched safety glass. Several people in white coats, who could be doctors or technicians, were bustling about and frowning at monitors. The floor was as strewn with cables as an amateur radio station. What fragments he could see of the body in the bed he found hard to connect with Jeremy.

Martin had shifted round to stand beside him. 'I felt a bit in the way in there.'

Peter nodded, but didn't turn his head.

'Not that they told me to leave, or anything. They've been really good. There wasn't even the usual crap — about being next of kin and all that.'

'They are good, here.' They'd been good when he'd come in the police car after Bev's accident. The young doctor who took him in to see her called her 'your wife' — as if she still weren't dead. They'd had the twins for him that night, the three of them, while he came here: Jeremy and Ruby and Martin.

Swinging away suddenly on his heel, Martin said, 'I need coffee. Let's go and find some.'

There was a vending machine Peter had passed in the A&E reception area, but Martin marched past it and outside, turning left towards the main hospital entrance and the shopping concourse. When he said coffee, evidently he meant coffee, not a warm brown liquid in a limp plastic cup.

Every time Peter came to Addenbrooke's it appeared to him less like a hospital and more like a small, independent city state. In addition to the usual array of newsagent's, florist's and gift shops, and the range of North American-style coffee shops with Italian-sounding names, he noticed today a new building society branch, a shoe shop and a travel agent. Fancifully, he imagined visitors booking a week at a European mountain health spa for their recuperating loved ones. Martin led the way to the nearest counter behind which puffed and hissed an industrial-scale espresso machine.

'I'll have a double,' he told the girl behind the bar, as if he were ordering Scotch. 'Peter?'

'Americano. I'll get them.'

As they waited for the machine to get up its head of steam, Martin disappeared with a muttered apology, and when he returned was sliding the cellophane from a packet of twenty Silk Cut.

'Mind if we go outside?'

For some fresh air. Wasn't that the second half of the smokers' joke? But Peter said nothing, merely followed his friend out towards the foyer with its row of automatic doors, and then through them and over towards a small bench, set into the square bulk of a concrete planter. A mulch of fag ends and squashed, empty packets littered the soil beneath the shrubs.

'Not bloody fair, is it?' Martin closed his eyes and drew hard on his cigarette, the sucked in cheeks making his head appear more skull-like than ever. Then he blew out slowly. 'I'm the one pumping my system with caffeine, and lapsing back to these things whenever I get a whiff of stress. Eating fast-food shit on the hoof at lunchtime and whenever I'm working late. He hardly even drinks – just a glass or two – and barely touches all those puddings he makes.'

'It'll help, won't it?' tried Peter tentatively. 'With the recovery. The fact that he's got a healthy lifestyle has got to stand him in good stead.'

'Dunno. Just means he's got nothing to give up, doesn't it? Nothing to do to make a difference.' Martin stared straight ahead through the mantle of his cigarette smoke. His eyes were glistening. 'It's not fair. It ought to have been me.'

Two cigarettes later, their coffee drunk, they walked back together to Jeremy's emergency room. Nothing had changed; the white coats still busied themselves round the trestle bed, boxed in by machinery.

'Why don't I go and fetch the things he needs, then? There's not a lot I can do here.'

'You and me both.' Martin managed a painful grin as he handed over the house keys. And towards Peter's departing figure, he called, 'Bring books.'

The lift of relief Peter felt to be back out in the May sunshine, on his own and heading for his car, brought with it a salting of guilt, but he shrugged it off. There really was nothing he could do back there – and it always felt good to get away from a hospital. The feeling merged and blended with the illicit pleasure of playing hooky: out of college, out of the Faculty, at not quite lunchtime on a term-time weekday. Not that he had any more classes today, only a Gardens Committee meeting, for which he could call in his apologies later. As he reached the fringes of the city and the road opened up, along with the broad fen sky on either side, the sense of freedom was even greater. What kind of friend was he? Jeremy in the hospital, unconscious; Jeremy's coronary arteries struggling to let through a trickle of blood. But Jeremy would understand; there was nothing like a vicarious brush with death to make the fact of breathing seem miraculous. He opened wide his window and breathed.

It was odd to be stopping at the top of the lane rather than carrying on down to the cottage. The twin villas looked more empty than they had any right to, simply because he knew that they were. As he slotted the key into Jeremy's front door he also felt the discomfort of intrusion, more strongly than made sense. He had never been inside Jeremy's bedroom, and bridled against the necessity of hunting round and opening drawers, locating carryall, clean pyjamas, hairbrush and bedside novel. He found himself looking for signs of the morning's drama, a rushed exit as the ambulance arrived, but found none: only the ordinary, intimate, mingled commonplaces of two men's lives. As he was leaving the room, he paused, went back and opened the window just an inch, the way he did when he got up at home, to let in a wedge of sun-warmed air. In the bathroom he hesitated over the two toothbrushes, not knowing whose was whose. But it made sense to put both in the bag; Martin wouldn't be going anywhere any time soon, and even if he couldn't shower and change he'd be glad to freshen his mouth from the coffee and nicotine.

Back out at the adjoining pair of iron gates, Peter turned his nose briefly towards home, drawn by the idea of a word with his dog, and a slice of bread from his own crock instead of a pre-packed hospital sandwich. As he did so, he caught the unexpected sound of a vehicle engine approaching from that direction. Actually, from down the lane. It wasn't Tuesday and, besides, the dustbin lorry had always come and gone long before this time. Nor was it a tractor: the noise was wrong. He was right, it was neither of these. Round the corner a white Transit van bounced and jolted towards him; he took in an Irish licence plate and, blowing from the left window as he watched it approach, a snap of Paula Mahoney's long, red hair.

She pulled up beside him and leaned down, but didn't get out.

'Hello, there. I was just at your house. Didn't think you'd be around in the daytime.'

'No, I'm not usually. I was just— No, I'm not.'

'Right, so, I was just leaving you a note. And dropping off a couple of trinkets of your Cassie's, that she lent to Shannon one time. A necklace and some other bits.'

'That's very kind of you.' It didn't make a lot of sense, so he sought refuge in good manners.

'We're leaving tomorrow.'

She spoke easily; she was even smiling.

'Leaving? Leaving the site, leaving Allington, you mean?'

It was the anonymous messages, the dog shit on the step, it had to be. It was because of his ignorant, hate-filled neighbours.

'Are you going for good?'

Her raised shoulder was testament to the fatalism of generations. 'Who knows what's for good? We're off back to Ireland.'

'Well, Cassie will miss you all, I know that. Shannon's been a good friend to her. But, Paula, I really hope this isn't because . . . *Because of us.* 'Because of what happened.'

The green eyes surveyed him dispassionately. 'We're just moving on, that's all. Gabriel and Michael have got themselves a contract for the summer, laying floors for some new housing over west, near Galway. It's good work and good money. So don't be thinking the world revolves round you and your daughter, now.'

But the chiding was kindly, and amusement lit her eyes. Extending her arm through the open van window, she laid a hand briefly on his shoulder. 'We're moving on,' she repeated. 'It's what we do. Will you tell your girls goodbye?'

Then her hand went back to the wheel, the engine revved, she slipped the clutch and was gone.

Jeremy, when Peter arrived back at the hospital, was awake and milking it. Not that he found him straight away. By the time he had succumbed to the temptation to nip home, cut a cheese sandwich to split with Ollie and read Paula's unsentimental note, it was gone two o'clock; after that, thickening post-lunch traffic meant he didn't make it back to A&E until closer to three, only to be informed that 'Mr Fisher has been moved to cardiology'. There being no ward formally bearing that name, it took a number of conversations with persons with insider knowledge to reveal that the place he wanted was D4. There, in an open ward, still wired up to a portable electrocardiograph but otherwise looking absolutely as normal, Jeremy was holding court to Martin, two nurses and a tea lady.

His audience dispersed as Peter appeared, hailed by an imperious Jeremy – whose voice, he noticed, for all the bravado sounded raspy and weak.

'Ah, Peter, good to see you, my friend. They have moved me in here because I have been declared officially "stabilised". No more for me the emergency room, hotbed of volatility, where dwell the dangerously unstable. I have ceased to pitch and roll; my ship is back on an even keel and I have been brought up here to harbour.'

It was impossible to hear him and restrain a grin. 'It's good to see you, too. I've brought you some things you might need, from home. I dare say it's all the wrong stuff, but you'll just have to lump it.'

He dropped the holdall on the side of the bed, but Jeremy made no move to look inside. One arm was lying loosely on top of the covers, a tube attached with clear tape just below the elbow; his other hand was held fast in Martin's.

'Thanks,' they both said together.

'So, what have they told you?' he asked. 'Anything?'

'Not a lot, yet.' Martin answered for Jeremy. 'Beyond the fact that it was definitely a heart attack. They're keeping him in for tests. Probably about a week, the houseman said. But the consultant does rounds in the morning, so we might know a bit more then.'

'A week, he says.' Jeremy rolled his eyes heavenward, a difficult feat when lying horizontal. 'A week, as if it's nothing. Nothing, perhaps, for those who are able to go home and sleep in their own beds, and read the morning newspaper sitting at their own kitchen table at a civilised hour with a pot of decent Earl Grey, instead of being woken by the clanking of institutional teacups while the larks are still sleeping off the indiscretions of the night before. I'm officially stable: why can't a man be allowed to go and be stable at home?'

'You know why.' Peter saw Martin's fingers twitch and tighten. 'They've got to do these tests, they said. Find out what's going on in there and why it happened. Find out if you're going to need surgery.'

'Oh, Lord preserve me,' grumbled Jeremy, the undoubted irony buried deep. 'Days of waiting around, just for some overworked and uncommunicative individual to come and wire me up again, or stick things in me, or wheel me off to be scanned like a supermarket sausage.'

An orderly walked by with a stainless steel tray. Jeremy watched him go. 'And why is it only the girls who get the nice uniforms in here?' Then he sighed – only partly a stage sigh. 'Hospitals are all well and good when they're making you better. Actually giving you helpful treatment. Excellent – very grateful. But it's quite another matter having to lie here while they devise ingenious ways of making you worse.'

Martin addressed Peter, but his knuckles, where his hand covered Jeremy's, flexed white. 'Terrified of being cut open. Silly old sod.'

Keyhole surgery; radical improvements in technique; matter of routine these days. Peter knew all the things to say, but knew that Jeremy knew them, too. Instead he merely grinned ghoulishly. 'Hard luck.'

'Hey, mate.' Martin was grinning, too, and looking at his watch. 'Do you mind sticking around here while I nip off for a minute? Too much coffee.'

That, and a sudden lack of nicotine, Peter suspected.

'Of course. Provided Jeremy doesn't mind having someone else to hold his hand?' Best to get the line in before Jeremy did.

Alone with his sick friend, Peter felt cheery bonhomie fail him; self-consciousness invaded in its place. He felt impelled to talk about something else – as if he believed in the implausible notion of 'taking his mind off it'.

'Trish finally submitted her PhD thesis,' he began, and then stopped.

Jeremy wasn't listening, anyway; his gaze was fixed on the double swing doors at the end of the ward through which Martin had just disappeared.

'What would he do?' Conscious, no doubt, of a limited opportunity, Jeremy was suddenly completely serious. All the fooling had stopped, and as the effort subsided, his face reshaped itself into the haggard lineaments of pain. 'Without me. What would Martin do?'

'Don't say that.' The words came out sounding more pleading than bracing; Jeremy ignored them, an irrelevant hindrance.

'How would be cope? What would it do to him? First to lose Ruby, and then me.'

Peter stared at him. His eyes, bloodshot and filmy, still rested on the double doors. It was the first time Peter had heard the acknowledgement from him – heard it from either of them – and in such an intimate way, as well: the acknowledgement that Ruby's death had been Martin's bereavement, too. Jeremy might have clowningly referred to Peter and himself on occasion as 'the merry widows'; Martin and himself, never. Moved beyond words, Peter sat down in the chair, which still held traces of Martin's warmth, and took hold of Jeremy's hand.

You're not going to die. That was what he most wanted to say, but as well as sounding like a bad line from every hospital drama he'd ever seen, it was also self-evidently untrue. Instead he thought about Martin, and, doing so, succeeded in recapturing a smile.

'He'll be OK. He might not be quite as macho as he makes out, but he's still a pretty tough old bugger.'

Jeremy couldn't smile, but his eyes registered gratitude and he gripped a little tighter on Peter's fingers.

'Stay a while, will you, if you can? I think it helps him to have you here as well.'

Helps you, you mean? 'Sure.'

By the time Martin returned, they were laughing about Trish's spelling mistakes, and Martin never saw Jeremy discreetly releasing Peter's hand. Time was ticking on, though, and Afterschool Club finished at five today. Having given his word, Peter was determined to stay as long as they seemed to want him.

'I'm just going to call Trish,' he told them.

'No mobiles in here, still.' Martin nodded at the machine by the bed. 'There's a payphone in the corridor.'

'Right. I thought she could come and get the keys, take the Land Rover and go and pick up Cassie and Kim. She needs something to keep her occupied now she's no longer got a PhD to write. And I'm sure even she can't burn the cottage down cooking beans on toast.'

Actually, he was sure of no such thing, but he rang her anyway, and she came straight over on the bus, eager to be of use, bringing flowers, which Jeremy much appreciated and Peter knew she couldn't really afford.

'It's in the main car park, the part marked for visitors and out-patients. At the end, under some trees. Next to a red Volvo – or at least it was when I left it.' Though the Volvo owner could well have had corneal laser treatment – or given a sperm sample or been catheterised – and left again by now.

Martin moved to sit on the side of the bed and Jeremy began absently stroking the inside of his wrist, so Peter decided it was the moment to go and ask about a vase for Trish's freesias. Once out of the ward, he wondered, too, about Earl Grey: whether any of the coffee shops in the concourse might supply such a thing, and if it would be permitted to a patient who had suffered a major coronary thrombosis that day. It seemed worth testing the odds on both counts.

He met with success at the third place he tried. After paying and waiting for some minutes at a high, round table at the end of the counter he was served with a vast plastic cup, sleeved in corrugated cardboard – a wholly redundant protection against the lukewarm water inside. A tea bag, weakly leaching clouds of red into the water, was attached by a thread of cotton to a paper fob that proclaimed it to be, indeed, Earl Grey tea. Honey was too much to expect, so he stirred in two spoons of sugar from the bowl provided and clicked on the plastic lid.

The vase was trickier; he should have sorted it out first. By the time he had followed directions to a small kitchen-cum-storeroom, and been through the entire miscellaneous contents of four cupboards before he found a chipped, olive green vase, the tea was almost completely cold. Jeremy was visibly touched by the gesture, and even though he made very little serious attempt to drink, Peter was able to feel pleased with his mission. It was a shock, though, to see how the effort of shuffling himself sufficiently upright to be able to sip the tea left Jeremy exhausted, and Peter determined not to stay much longer. His presence might protect them both from whatever would follow the exertion of cheerfulness, but it was also keeping Jeremy from sleep.

He was looking at his watch for the second time when the nurse appeared to call him to the phone.

'Hi, it's me.'

Trish.

'Are the kids OK? How was school? Did they want to say hello?'

'In a minute, maybe. But, um, actually I've got a bit of a confession, first.'

She'd remembered some other fatal flaw in her thesis? Or maybe it was a beans-on-toast fire, after all? He should never have joked about it.

'I'm really sorry. I don't know how it happened. I was chatting to Cassie and Kim, of course, but I really thought I was concentrating. But you know how high the back windscreen is, and when you're reversing the visibility isn't great, is it? I mean, of course I ought to have known what other cars were there, looked before we got in, or before I started to back up. Or even if I'd checked the wing mirror at that side, I'd probably have been OK. I'm sorry, I really don't know what to say . . .'

'The Land Rover?'

'Oh, Peter, I feel awful about it, I really do. You should never have asked me to drive it. But, yes, I'm afraid I've pranged your car.'

Chapter 21

'Autocare Direct Motor Insurance. My name is Mina, how may I help you?'

'Oh, hello. I think my car's been stolen.'

You think *it's been stolen?* On mornings as uneventful as this one, it would sometimes be nice to say what she thought for a change rather than sticking to the script.

'And what's your policy number, please?'

'Um, let's have a look. Is this it? JDN/0040-6943H.'

The clue would be where it says 'policy number'.

'Thank you. Now, please could you confirm your name and address for me?'

The caller managed to do this without any difficulty, except that he told her he was Jep Hoskins when the file said James. He also knew the make, model and registration of his vehicle – an elderly Opel Corsa.

'Thanks. And when was the vehicle stolen, sir?'

A pause. 'I'm not exactly sure, to be honest.'

'Well, when did you discover it was missing?' Maybe he'd been away. Car thieves liked it when you went away on holiday.

'Today, I guess. Cath came round and I asked her if she'd had it this week and she said she hadn't, so then I got worried.'

'Ah. Cath's your girlfriend, is she?' Though there were no other named drivers on the policy, she saw.

'No, just a friend. Well, more a friend of Tom's, really. He's my flatmate. But Cath quite often borrows the car because she's doing Education, and they have teaching practice, and sometimes the schools are miles away, the other side of Manchester.'

Light filtered in: students. But in the space on the form for 'occupation', it stated 'bar manager'.

'You manage a pub, Mr Hoskins, is that correct?'

'Well, sort of. I work in the uni bar.'

'And that's a full-time job, is it?'

'Not exactly. Just a couple of nights a week at the moment, and Saturday lunchtimes.'

'And in between, you're studying?'

'Y-yes.' He was beginning to sound so unhappy that she hardly liked to go on with this. But it was the infuriating irresponsibility of it. Kids his age could be so blind.

'A full-time course?'

'Yes.'

'But on your form you've written your occupation down as "bar manager".'

'Yes. Look, am I going to get in huge trouble for this? I just thought – well, actually Tom's brother told me, because he worked in the cash and carry right through uni, and he said that if you put that down and not that you're a student, then the premiums are lower.'

So stupidly blind. Like Jess.

'I mean, it's not actually untrue, is it? I am a part-time bar manager. I haven't given any false information. Just not quite the whole truth, I guess. What – what will happen to me?'

There was genuine alarm in the boy's voice; Mina softened. He was young, she reminded herself. He was allowed to be stupid now and again.

'I'm going to alter your occupation to "student" on the form, and then run it through as a change of circumstances. There may be an adjustment to the premium.'

Though not a very major one, she suspected – and very nearly said aloud. There was an unworldliness to his sharp practice: the idea that a bar manager would be a low risk for car insurance was almost touchingly naïve.

'And that's all? I won't be prosecuted or anything? And my insurance will still be valid?'

'I should think so, yes. I'll sort it out, don't worry. Now, about
the theft. When was the last time you drove the vehicle?'

'God, I can't remember. Ages ago. Maybe about February?'

That was three months. 'I'm sorry, sir, did you say February?'

'Round about then, yes. It's hard to recall exactly. I don't often
use it at all. Mum and Dad have taxed it for me and they had it
serviced in the summer, but petrol's so expensive, and really it could
do with a new clutch. Reverse is sticking, and you can only get
third gear on the way up. If you're slowing down in fourth you
have to go into second and then back up again.'

Is the vehicle roadworthy? Luckily, she was only required to ask that
question in the case of accident claims, not thefts. They could worry
about it if the car turned up – which in Manchester was pretty unlikely,
except smoking gently on waste ground somewhere in Moss Side.

'Cath seems to get on with it OK, though. And they get an
allowance for travel when they do their teaching placements, so
she can afford to fill it up. Anyway, I thought I'd seen it near the
White Hart last Monday when we went for a pint, but the other
day it wasn't there, but then Cath couldn't remember where she'd
parked it, but anyway she hadn't driven it this week, and she said
maybe Phil had had it.'

'Phil?' Mina's hands, which habitually sat poised over the
keyboard, drifted up distractedly to her temples and embedded
themselves in the roots of her hair.

'Yes. He's on the B.Ed with Cath, and she got him a key cut.
It's OK,' he added, perhaps noticing her lengthening silence, 'I
told her it was all right. It is, isn't it? Third party, fire and theft
– any driver with my permission, provided they've got a full
licence and are over eighteen.' Then, less confidently, 'I think
Phil's got a full licence.'

Shutting her mind to this new morass of potential illegality,
Mina asked, 'So, this Phil. Have you asked him about it?'

'Yes. Or rather, Cath has, and he's positive he hasn't used the car for over a week.'

'Right. So it was outside the White Hart on Monday – that would be the twelfth? Is the pub in your own street?' She scrolled back up the form. 'Dillwyn Street?'

'Oh no, it's a long way away, the other side of the Stockport Road. There's a residents' parking scheme round us, and you have to pay if you want a permit. But it's unrestricted in the streets near the Hart. We always leave it over there.'

Jess wasn't ever having a car, she decided, not if she had anything to do with it. Not that she was likely to have anything to do with it, she remembered with a jolt.

Cutting her losses on the precise timing and location of the theft, she asked her final question.

'Was the vehicle alarmed at the time it was stolen, sir?'

'Not exactly.'

She waited, not with much hope.

'I mean, it's got an alarm fitted, but I don't suppose it was switched on. I never do, and Cath knows not to, if she's the one who had it last. The thing is, one of the rear windows won't close properly, so there's a little gap, and when it's wet and windy it seems to blow in and set the alarm off. And then, you know, people get annoyed.'

You could bet they did. Not his own neighbours, mind you, but the poor benighted residents in the vicinity of the White Hart. Which was probably rowdy at chucking-out time, too. Sal was never having a car, either. And when she was a student – as none of the rest of them had ever been, or were ever likely to be – she could get the bus like any normal person.

Coffee break couldn't come soon enough. Things weren't quite so stretched this week, and they were back up to twenty minutes. Nupoor's temporary replacement, Sîan, used to work at Direct Line and had hit the ground running. Mary and Gwen were busy on their mobiles, and Debbie was cracking open a Diet Coke. For once, Mina decided to join her, and defy the bubbles that would rise later.

'I had a right one just now,' she began, but then felt her mobile, in the pocket of her jeans, begin to buzz. Her first thought, as it had been with every call for two months and more, was Jess. But the screen showed her mother's number – or, rather, Dave's.

'Hello?'

'Hello, love, it's me.'

'Mum.'

'I've got the time right, haven't I? Only I know I mustn't call at work, except for in your break.'

Mum never called at work, break or no break.

'What is it? What's the matter? Has Mrs Warburton had a fall?'

'No, nothing like that. I'd taken my half-day today, anyway.'

'Dave, then?' The cholesterol. His heart.

'Everything's fine. Really, there's nothing to worry about.'

Which was always the signal to start worrying, wasn't it?

'Actually, it's good news.' There was something decided about her voice, a certain grim determination, which didn't seem quite to fit with the words.

'What, then? Tell me.'

'Jess has come home.'

'Really? Mum, that's fantastic! How is she – is she OK—' *for money*, she'd been about to add, before thinking better of it. She covered up with a joke. 'She hasn't caught pneumonia in that squat of hers, has she? Come home for a bit of my tender nursing care?'

'She's fine.' The words might be clipped, but Mina heard an edge of relief – and affection. 'Mind you, it was nothing to do with me. I'd have left her there to come to her senses in her own time. It's been Dave's doing. Soft bastard.'

Mina smiled; Mum only ever swore in moments of high emotion.

'Anyway, I've said to him, she'd better sort herself out this time, if she's staying. She can't expect us to give her a roof over her head and all her meals for ever. A job, I've said to her: she needs to get out and find herself some proper work, or else find out about college courses, pick up a prospectus. I thought, computers, there's a skill that's always useful . . .'

There was no real need to listen. Mina had heard the litany many times, and it wasn't one which required responses. 'So how did you know she'd come back? Did she call you? Have you seen her – have you been over to the house? I haven't aired her bed, and you know how damp that room is. And I'd better pick up an extra chop on the way home, and another loaf of bread, she's sure to have eaten most of the one that was left from this morning.'

Jess back. Jess leaving the margarine out. Jess coming in at midnight and making the window frames rattle. It felt wonderful.

Down the line, though, her mother had gone unusually quiet. You'd think she'd have had some words to say about the state of Jess's return: her clothes, her pennilessness, her lack of contrition. Instead, she simply said, 'No.'

No, what?

'No, you've got it wrong. Didn't I say? She's come home. Not your house – home. She's come back to live with me – with me and Dave.'

'Autocare Direct Motor Insurance. My name is Mina, how may I help you?'

Caller number sixty-seven, according to the log.

'Oh, thank God for that. Finally! I thought I was going to be here all day. I did ask whether I could be put through to you, but the woman told me, no, they can't put callers through to a particular person. I don't see why not, myself; you wouldn't think it would be that technical, would you? But she was quite adamant about it – got rather shirty with me, in fact.'

A woman – and a faintly familiar voice.

'Anyway, it meant all I could do is keep phoning and then ringing straight off when it wasn't you. This is about the thirtieth call, I reckon, at least. How many of you are there, for goodness' sake? My phone bill's going to be a disaster.'

To say nothing of Mrs Gordon's call throughput statistics.

'But I'm so glad I've got you at last. I want to report an accident.'

With recognition came both a lurch and also a foolish leap, quickly repressed. It was the girl. The clever, pretty, Cambridge girl; the one who was going to be a doctor like him.

'It's Peter's car. The Land Rover, you know.'

Mina had his file up already. Still no second named driver on there; but she hadn't been wrong about the girl, had she? Not if she was making calls to his insurers for him.

His details were up on screen – as if she didn't know it all by heart, anyway – but still she stuck to the script, listening in pain to the familiarity with which Trish recited his full name and address, trying to force herself into having some sense. (*Flattery will get you nowhere*, she remembered with a stab.)

'Date of birth?'

'How should I know? Don't you have it on the computer?'

That did seem odd. Mother's maiden name, fair enough – she hadn't even asked her that one – but date of birth? It could almost give her hope. Surely he'd recently had a fortieth birthday? How did she not know the date?

'Anyway, I've managed to crash his Land Rover. I went and backed it into a parked car at the village hall, picking up the twins from Afterschool Club. I can't believe I did it – so stupid.'

Mina forgot birthdays and dragged herself back to the task in hand.

'Do you have the details of the other vehicle involved, please?'

'Yes, here, I wrote it all down. It was one of the mums, a Mrs Phillipson. Volkswagen Polo, registration X962HBJ. Metallic grey, she said, though I'd have called it silver. She was ever so nice about it, when I told her Peter was at the hospital.'

'In hospital?' She heard the squawk of alarm in her voice. 'Was he in the car? I thought it was just a minor bump?' It didn't seem to make sense.

'Oh, no, sorry, you don't understand. He's not *in* hospital, he was just up at the hospital yesterday visiting someone. This friend of his, Jeremy; he's had a heart attack. But he looks like he's going to be OK.'

Breathing again, Mina tried to focus. 'Right, now please could you tell me exactly how the collision occurred? Where were you – where was Mrs Phillipson's car? I'll get down a written description, and then you'll have to draw a sketch for us, later, when I send out the claim for you to verify and sign. Or, rather, for Peter to sign.'

She wished she could have called him Dr Kendrick without sounding rude, because even saying his name was painfully distracting.

'Well, I was parked facing the wall of the hall, and her car was over the other side, under some trees. All I did was stick it in reverse and back up to turn round; it's quite a narrow car park and Land Rovers are huge, and I suppose I can't have looked properly. Once you get near something, especially a little, low car like that, it disappears below the level of the back window, you see. There was this crunch, so I stopped. Cassie shouted, "You've hit Daisy's mum's car" – it was more over at her side. And we got out to look, and I had.'

'So you accept responsibility for the accident?' They were always formally required to ask.

'Yes, I guess so. But they're like bloody tanks, you know, those things. Ought to have a lookout turret on the top.'

'Thank you. Now, I'm sorry, but I do have to warn you – that is, maybe if you could tell him? – that there may be an impact on his no claims bonus. He's got it protected, but with this being the third accident within twelve months, there might be a recalculation for next year's premium.'

'Oh, shit. All this hassle I've made for him, and now it's going to cost him, too.'

'I'm afraid so.' Best not even to mention the £250 excess.

'Shit,' she said again. 'I ought to offer to pay the difference, really, didn't I? But I'm totally skint, to be honest. Maybe one day, when I'm the Regius Professor.' An attempt at a laugh. 'Will he mind? What do you think?'

Mina refrained from replying. Five minutes later, her list of questions had all been asked, and answered with at least passable coherence.

'Thanks very much, then, madam. Trish, rather – sorry, it's just force of habit. I'll put a copy of the claim in the post.'

'Thanks. Listen – before you go . . .'

She had almost forgotten to wonder why the girl had been so keen to speak to her personally, on the basis of the acquaintance of one strange evening. One she was trying hard to forget, but still found herself treasuring up to remember.

'Yes?'

'Look, you can shoot me down if I've got this all wrong. I'm always getting the wrong end of the stick, so I shouldn't be surprised. I wouldn't say anything, because it's none of my business. But I saw . . . well, I thought I saw, that night . . . and he's been different since then. He thinks no one notices, but he has, he's been sort of flatter. And I know you think, or, at least, I think I know you think . . .'

The rambling was exasperating, but that surely didn't explain why Mina could feel her own pulse, muzzy and distorted inside her head. 'What? You think you know I think what?'

Trish stopped; Mina heard her draw in breath.

'It's just, we're not together, if that's what you thought. I'm not his girlfriend.'

The line went dead. Mina clicked through to the log. Call ended: 12.08.

Chapter 22

There were always day coach tours to Cambridge advertised at half term. 'See King's College chapel and the other historic sites of this world-famous university town.' And this time, she was determined, she would skip the shops and actually visit some of the colleges. One of them in particular.

It hadn't proved as difficult as she'd feared to find out which one. He'd never mentioned the name of the place, but when she Googled him on the computer at the library, while Sal was immersed in the teen and young adult section, there he was, listed as Official Fellow, Tutor and Director of Studies in Geography. And when she clicked again, she'd come face to face with a photo of him, sitting formally in front of a wall of books and smiling a slightly embarrassed smile, the way she'd always imagined it – the way he hadn't smiled much at all when he was in her kitchen. He looked younger in the photo than he had that night, too – scarcely a credible forty. Which was surprising, considering he was so obviously trying to look donnish: trying and failing. It was a good thing she had no PC at home, because she feared she might have been calling up the photo at regular intervals – or even printing it off, which of course she couldn't possibly do in a public library.

Sal had been looking forward to the trip with eager anticipation, for different reasons.

'Mrs Edwards says the library at the university in Cambridge is a copyright library. That means they have every single book that's published in the whole country. Magazines, too. Even *Girl Talk* and the *Beano*. Everything.'

'You do know you might not be allowed in to see, don't you, love?'

But just to be in proximity to so many books together in one place seemed to be enough for Sal.

Mina had even asked Jess if she wanted to come along. 'I'll pay for your ticket. Go on, it might be fun.'

Jess, though – remarkably – had been busy. 'I've got a job interview that day.' Her eyes had rolled in weary resignation. 'Some stupid thing Mum's lined up for me.'

Sal had read her school book all the way down on the coach, so that by the time they were passing the first green signs to Cambridge on the dual carriageway Mina had had more than enough time to think. She still wasn't sure, though, why she hadn't just called him, after the conversation with Trish. The coach slowed and pulled over into the left-hand lane, joining a single line of cars, all showing their brake lights as they funnelled down from the sweeping slip road, flanked by its dashes of white, into the pavemented, suburban street. The road was still broad here, though, and lined with mature trees, which screened out all but a few discreet glimpses of the stately, individual houses on either side. Professors' houses, perhaps. Trying to analyse it, she discovered that she hadn't wanted to speak to the comfortable, telephone Peter. Maybe she didn't want to spoil what they'd had – or else instinctively knew that they couldn't go back there, to where they'd been. Or maybe she needed to see him in the flesh again, if only to banish the other real-life Peter, tired and concerned, whose kindness she had shrugged off in Sheffield.

Girton College: Entrance proclaimed a sign to the left beyond her window, and behind it she made out a three-storey archway, turreted and crenellated like the gatehouse of some red-brick fairy-tale castle. *Ivory towers*, she thought to herself – wasn't that the phrase? Another world: Peter's world. It had never been just the girl, Trish, that had been the obstacle, had it? Maybe this trip, this whole idea, was a bad mistake. But it was too late for cold feet now.

The road narrowed again; the houses crowded closer, tall townhouses with iron railings in front, all spickly painted, windows winking in the early summer sunshine as the coach slipped past. Then they turned down a hill and round a series of right-angled bends, before straightening out, after a small roundabout, to glide along a road that Mina remembered from before with Mum, when she was a teenager, and from every tourist-brochure photograph. The road with the water meadows and the river and the pale stone backs of all the colleges. How could anybody really work here, surrounded by such intimidating beauty?

She had a city centre map, supplied by the coach tour company. It marked the various colleges as a series of ink-and-wash sketches, too big for the maze of streets they straddled, making finding them on the ground unnecessarily confusing. Peter's college wasn't in the line with the others along the river, but set apart, separated from the rest by the width of the tiny city centre, with its pretty market place and its ugly 1960s shopping precinct. This time she walked straight past the Virgin megastore – except it now seemed to be HMV. Maybe she had just forgotten.

At the college entrance she almost turned away. A signboard on a metal base stood sentry in the middle of the arched doorway. *We regret that the college is closed to visitors during the examination period.* For a minute she and Sal stood silently and stared at it, and as they did so a gaggle of students came up behind them, laughing and talking, walked past them and straight past the sign as well, and disappeared into the cloistered courtyard beyond. Not in a million years, thought Mina, could I pass for a student here, even though there must be mature students, postgraduates like Trish. It wasn't that she was dressed wrong – they all wore jeans and T-shirts much like her own – she just felt wrong inside. Even if she hadn't had a ten-year-old girl with her instead of a rucksack full of files. She was turning to leave when Sal put a hand on her arm. A man in a fluorescent bib had appeared beside them, carrying an armful of parcels and fat, padded envelopes; rather than continuing straight ahead past the notice and into the courtyard, he turned right, up two stone steps and through a glass door marked *Porter's Lodge.*

301

Before she could stop her, Sal had followed him. Inside, there was a smell of beeswax polish and brown paper and bicycle oil, a smell like stepping back in time, but the man in the crested tie who took the parcels from the courier was greeting him with a joke in an accent that could not be from further south than Chesterfield or further east than Worksop. It was a connection, however flimsy. It was enough to embolden Mina into stepping forward when their turn came.

'I've come to see Dr Kendrick,' she said.

Do you have an appointment? She was certain he would ask it, and if he did she'd decided to walk away and never come back. But instead his face divided into a wide grin.

'Do I hear the sound of my home town, there? Sheffield, is it?'

She nodded, grinning too. 'Intake. You?'

'Carbrook.'

'Really? My friend Debbie lives there.'

'All the best people do. So, Dr Kendrick, was it? He's in the Erasmus Building, room G4. You just go across the court here and under that archway in the far corner. Then across the small garden and G staircase is on your left.'

The archway was deep and shady and vaulted, and the garden into which they emerged was dazzling, like a picture from a glossy magazine. Or not a magazine – more like a painting in a gallery. There was a high border overflowing with flowers; pristine green grass and a stone bench beneath a canopy of roses; a small, circular pond with a statue in the middle, a fish or a dolphin, glistening green under the bubble of a low fountain. And ducks.

'Look, Mum, there are ducklings!' cried Sal, stepping forward towards the pond, and Mina glanced round and resisted the urge to shush.

They counted eleven of them, scooting round their mother on the mirrored surface of the water: nine speckled brown and two perfect egg-yolk yellow, the same shade exactly as Sal's hair.

'Can I stay here, Mum? I'll be quiet. I'll just sit on the bench and read and watch the ducklings. It's perfect here. Like a garden in a book. Can I – please?'

In some ways it made things easier – but at the same time, possibly much harder. She hesitated.

'Yes. All right.'

She was on her own, therefore, when she knocked at the heavy wooden door, with the name *Dr Kendrick* painted above it on the gloss white of the frame. She almost giggled at the improbability of it. Did colleges in the twenty-first century really employ a man with a brown coat and a pot of black paint, to inscribe names over doors in a fine copperplate hand?

He didn't call 'come in' as she'd expected, and she was even deciding that he might not be there after all – or thinking that it might be just the outer section of one of those funny double doors that she'd seen on old re-runs of *Inspector Morse*, and he hadn't heard her knock – when suddenly the door opened and there he was. Closer than she'd ever seen him, barely a foot away from her, so that she could see the lines that hadn't showed up in his website photograph. But she wasn't noticing the lines, she was watching his eyes as they registered first the shock of recognition, and then a kind of amazement. And something else, too; she hoped it was something else she saw.

'Mina. What on earth—? How—?' Then he smiled, the way he'd been smiling in the photo, just a little bit shyly. 'It's all right, I don't care how or why; I don't care at all. I'm just very happy to see you.' He stepped back, awkward in the peculiar formality of the moment. 'Come in.'

And here was the office, or study or whatever it was they called them, with the wall of books from the photograph, and an enormous desk covered in stacks of papers, and two smaller tables buried in papers, too, and lots of ordinary things, like a kettle and unwashed coffee mugs, and a pinboard with lists and Post-its and a snapshot of the twins.

She leaned towards it. 'Is this Cassie and Kim?'

He leaned with her, so that the hair above his forehead almost brushed hers; but he was wholly absorbed in his daughters' faces and it was her turn to feel self-conscious.

'Last summer, at the beach. I'd let them stay out all day and they'd both caught the sun. Kim always burns quicker than Cassie, it's funny. You can see here, her nose is redder. Of course she thinks it's terribly unfair.'

Maybe awareness struck him, too, at that point, because he shifted away slightly, and his hands strayed to the back of his desk chair. He wasn't looking quite at her as he said, 'Trish spoke to me. She told me you'd talked. I wanted to ring you straight away, but it seemed . . .'

Whatever it had seemed, did those reasons now appear as crazy and inexplicable to him as not ringing him now seemed to her?

'Sal,' he said instead. 'Is she OK? No harm done? After . . . what happened?'

So she told him that Sal was fine – Sal would be just fine – and he told her how glad he was, and she could see he really meant it. By then the embarrassment was all dispelled and the Peter in front of her shaded back into her old Peter, the telephone Peter, and it felt very easy to be sitting in one of his armchairs with him in the other, and talking the way they used to talk on Sunday nights.

'Is she at school today, then?'

'No, it's half-term. She's with me, but I left her in the garden down there, the one with the pond. She's doing some reading for school. They've started on some Shakespeare.'

He nodded. 'My two have been doing *Romeo and Juliet*.'

'They're only doing it in *Stories From Shakespeare*, but she had this notion of reading the original.' He was someone she could tell and feel nothing but pride. But then it occurred to her to wonder, 'Will it be OK, do you think? Leaving her down there, I mean? I know it said the college was supposed to be closed because of the exams.'

'Reading?' His grin, she decided, was even nicer than his smile.

'I wish the undergraduates would do a bit more of that, some-times. Yesterday a bunch of them were playing spacehopper polo down there, when they're meant to be revising. I was terrified they were going to squash a duckling. Goodness knows where they got the spacehoppers from. And before that it was Frisbee, but then one of them got hold of a plastic missile thing that you toss about instead, made a noise like a buzz bomb, and it went straight through the Bursar's window. So, Sal reading Shakespeare in the college gardens? I hardly think the Founders will turn in their graves, do you?'

'She wanted to see the University Library.'

'I'll have to take her round it some time. She might enjoy some of the old, hand-illustrated materials in the rare-books room. The map room is astonishing, too – and I speak as a geographer who can scarcely read one. And you can look at the morning news-papers for the day you were born, or war was declared, or England won the World Cup. Though Cassie and Kim like the tea room best.'

She laughed. Saturday trips to the library were evidently rather different here. Then her eye fell on another photograph, in a small frame half hidden behind the clutter on his desk. A woman with dark hair, and dark eyes full of life and laughter.

'Is that Bev?' she asked.

'Yes, that one's Bev.'

There was a short silence, but not an uncomfortable one. Then she asked, 'Are your two at school, then?'

'No, it's half-term here as well.' He stood up. 'They're here, actu-ally. Let's go and get them.'

'Here?' She was confused.

'In the television room.'

He made it sound like a hotel. But she supposed that all teenagers – even Cambridge students – watched TV.

They went back down the staircase into the sunshine, where they picked up Sal from her bench, and then crossed to an ivy-covered building at the other side of the garden. The signwriter had been at work here, too. *Edward Warrener Room*, she read above the door to which they'd come. Not exactly informative: perhaps television was not publicly mentionable. Inside, the wood-panelled dignity of the room was offset by the presence of three long, airport-lounge settees in a startling shade of mauve; at either end of the nearest one sprawled the girls like a pair of untidy bookends, watching an estate agent showing a couple round what appeared to be an aircraft hangar. Did they really spend their holidays watching daytime TV?

As if reading her thoughts, one twin announced proudly, 'Cassie was sick.'

Peter grimaced. 'The Holiday Club has pretty strict rules. No return for twenty-four hours after any episode of vomiting.'

'Cassie really hurled,' said the one who must be Kim. 'So we're having a day off.'

Did the rule apply to siblings, too, wondered Mina – or only twins?

'Only it's silly,' said the one who must be Cassie, 'because it's not catching. It's not a bug or anything. I just ate too much chocolate.' She sounded unrepentant, bordering on smug. 'We were playing the chocolate game. And nobody rolled a six after me for ages and ages, so I got to eat loads.'

'It was our birthday.'

'We're ten.'

'My Sal, here, is nearly eleven.' Mina almost regretted saying it, as two pairs of disturbingly identical eyes turned in Sal's direction.

'Hi,' she said.

'It wasn't really a proper party.' Kim wasn't grumbling; she was addressing Sal, and she sounded apologetic, if anything, reminding Mina all at once of her father. 'Just Leonie Sivell and Sophie Grimwade from school. And Trish, of course; and Jeremy and Martin, only they couldn't stay long and Jeremy can't eat chocolate.'

'He had a heart attack.' Clearly, in Cassie's view, something even cooler than vomiting.

'And Trish crashed Dad's car.'

'I heard,' said Sal. She was edging closer to the settee.

'Are you right-handed or left-handed?' Kim nodded towards Sal's left hand, which still clutched her Shakespeare. 'I'm left-handed, and Cassie's right-handed.'

'Well, I'm ambidextrous, actually.' Sal sounded a bit abashed; she hated anyone to think she was boasting.

'Is that like Ollie?' Cassie turned to Peter, looking puzzled, and Mina wondered why he was laughing, until she remembered the dog, and giggled, too.

'It means you can do things just as easily with either hand,' she explained.

'Wow.'

'Brilliant.'

'Shall we show you the ducklings? There are eleven of them, and that's nearly the most there've ever been –'

'Usually it's more like eight or nine –'

'– except one year there were thirteen, but half of them got eaten, so it doesn't really count.'

The three girls ran outside, and Peter and Mina followed. But he hung back in the shade of the building out of which they'd come, and she lingered with him, watching the children at the pond: Peter's two chattering like a pair of starlings and Sal nodding carefully.

'It's just a day trip, then, is it?'

She wasn't sure how to answer this, so she nodded mutely, looking down at her trainers.

'Do you need to go back today? Are you working tomorrow, I mean?'

He was trying to get her to look at him, she knew, but she didn't quite dare.

'Come back home with us; stay over. I can easily book you a coach or a train in the morning.'

Someone else asking her back for the night on a second meeting, it might have been presumptuous, or even creepy. But Peter was just Peter. It was ages since they'd spoken, and she knew that, like her, he wanted to talk and talk and talk. She did glance up, then, and saw that his eyes were merry as much as pleading.

'I don't want to let you disappear again.'

It was a moment when he might have taken her hand, but it didn't happen, and then he was busy with practicalities.

'I can drive you to the station in the morning on the way to work, after I've dropped off the kids – assuming they manage not to be sick again. The cottage isn't very big, only three bedrooms, so either the twins can bunk up or else you'll have to share the futon downstairs with Sal, if that's OK?'

Laughter was bubbling up inside. 'Oh, I think we can share, all right. I don't imagine Sal will mind, somehow.'

'I'm not sure what I've got in to eat, either. Not for five of us. It might have to be frozen pizzas or something.'

'We love pizza.'

'And also, I hope that downstairs room will be OK. Shouldn't be too bad at this time of year; it's been warm and sunny lately. But there's terrible damp in there. I used to use it as a study but the books went spotty and the paper all wilted. I ought to get someone in to take a look, but I always put it off.' He pulled a face. 'These old places are a bit of a nightmare.'

The laughter, mysterious and unbidden, had reached the surface now and was clamouring for release. But she couldn't possibly laugh about his maintenance worries; instead she smiled at him and said, 'We have damp at home, too. Especially in Jess's old room.'

They gathered the girls together and he led the way to a gravelled car park, and the slightly dented Land Rover. He opened the door for her, and then let the kids into the back: Cassie on the left, Kim on the right, and Sal between them in the middle.

'Are you strapped in, Sal?' Mina asked, swivelling round to check. Then she turned to the front again and fastened her own seat belt – smiling, because she'd seen Sal's book, closed now and abandoned beside her on the seat. She knew it was silly; she knew it was nonsense. She knew that this wasn't an ending at all, but just another chance at a proper beginning. But she couldn't help it: this time she had to let the laughter burst out aloud.

It was the title of the play that tipped her over. *All's Well That Ends Well.*